Wild Boy

Jill Dawson

Wild Boy

SCEPTRE

Copyright © 2003 Jill Dawson

First published in Great Britain in 2003 by Hodder and Stoughton
A division of Hodder Headline

The right of Jill Dawson to be identified as the Author
of the Work has been asserted by her in accordance with the
Copyright, Designs and Patents Act 1988.

A Sceptre Book

1 3 5 7 9 10 8 6 4 2

A CIP catalogue record for this title is
available from the British Library

ISBN 0 340 82296 1

Typeset in Sabon by Palimpsest Book Production Limited,
Polmont, Stirlingshire
Printed and bound in Great Britain by
Clays Ltd, St Ives plc

Hodder and Stoughton
A division of Hodder Headline
338 Euston Road
London NW1 3BH

for Lewis and Felix

Stories about the boy were spread through the entire Republic. As usual, the most extraordinary details were added. Some said he was hairy as a bear; others that he swam and dived like a duck; others that he could leap from tree to tree like a squirrel, and so on.

Many papers ran the story. All Paris was buzzing with word of the Savage of Aveyron. But the central administration for the district has still received no official report on the subject.

Pierre-Joseph Bonnaterre, naturalist
France, January 1800

Man is only what he is made to be.

Jean-Marc-Gaspard Itard, 1801

Part One

Thermidor 16
Year Eight in our Glorious Republic

This morning the most extraordinary opportunity has walked out of the forest and into my life. It was just before midday when the Abbé Sicard apprehended me in the courtyard of the Institute. We paused by the giant elm and the abbé asked if I had heard news of a wild child who, having escaped the capture of huntsmen a couple of years previously, had now wandered out of the forests of Lacaune into a house in the village of St Sernin in search of food and been recaptured. I replied that all of Paris had heard of him and it would be curious, would it not, if the news had not reached us, even in an institute for the deaf ... He ignored my shabby joke and seized my arm, marching me through a doorway and out the other side. We emerged into the vegetable gardens; a part of the grounds hitherto unknown to me, but I was scarce able to register my surprise as the abbé was speaking excitedly, at the same time pointing his scrupulously manicured finger at something. The only words to penetrate my thoughts did so by dint of being uncharacteristic of the abbé. *I am defeated.* As I pondered over what could vanquish the indomitable abbé, he who had survived the guillotine by a hair's breadth and a matter of seconds, my glance followed the line of his outstretched arm.

I shaded my eyes against the sunlight and made out a dark shape: a dog, black and gangling and unnaturally still, tethered to a tree with some rope. As we approached I remember thinking that it was a strange way to tie a dog – why tie the rope to its middle, why not to the animal's neck? And then suddenly the abbé stopped, some cautious distance away, and said breathlessly: there he is!

His words had the miraculous effect of adjusting my perception and, as I looked, the dog transformed himself. In front of my eyes emerged a crouching, dark, filthy creature, but a human creature none the less. I was looking at a boy I judged to be around eleven or twelve years old, squatting in the position of a monkey, or a dog sitting on its haunches, with his face obscured, his shaggy black head drooping towards the ground. Dressed only in the shreds of a blackened shirt, tied at the waist with a belt, which was then roped to the tree, it was hard to distinguish his clothes from his filthy, also blackened, pock-marked skin.

This was my first glimpse of the remarkable creature I read about seven days ago in the *Gazette de France*. As I stared at him, hungering to see him with my own eyes, wanting to judge for myself the differing descriptions I had read, my heart battered my ribcage. I had to steady myself, leaning against the outer wall of the Institute grounds for a moment. I took a breath, straightened up, swallowed and tried to summon a casual word that would not betray the turmoil inside me. The abbé was regarding me closely.

This then is the child they call the Wild Boy of Aveyron, I said calmly.

I had an inclination to step forward but the abbé's hand shot out.

Be careful, Itard: he is not called the wild boy for nothing!

The abbé's voice was loud enough but the boy gave no sign that he had heard him. I could now identify a low, guttural murmuring and realised that it came from the boy. He had not lifted his head: I longed to see his face.

He has a severe aversion to surprises and is apt to spring at strangers . . . The abbé's tone was rather gleeful.

Was it my imagination, or was the abbé enjoying my frustration, knowing well what this child might mean, could mean, for me? He held a snowy handkerchief over his nose, and scrutinised me over the top of this. A foul smell surrounded the child, as we stood there in the heat of the sun. He had opened his bowels exactly where he was tethered and evidently no attempt had been made by him or anyone else to clean it up. Worse, he had stepped in this mess, now dried and firmly encrusted around his bare feet.

Has no one offered the poor child a bath? How long has he been here?

I realise now that my tone was one of affront and that it was probably not judicious to begin with implied criticisms of Abbé Sicard. After all, it could only be Sicard's reputation, his authority, his status as Father of the Deaf Mutes, which has brought the boy to my feet, as it were. Despite the man's brush with death, or perhaps because of it, Sicard has an irksome quality that never fails to provoke me. I often think of the story, I cannot remember now how I first heard it, of Sicard's arrest by the Revolutionary Commune, it must have been 92, two years before I arrived in Paris. Of course he has never mentioned it himself. But rather than the glory of his release, within minutes – inches! – of the scaffold, with a clamouring mass deciding that since there are more deaf born poor than rich, he belongs first and foremost to them – rather than that, I can never picture his capture without my mind turning to the most foolish of trivialities. How did he survive his prison experience, his scrape against the stinking poor of Paris, he who is so fastidious? Surely to be deprived of powder for his hair, lavender water and amber to scent his cheeks, a stone to polish his nails, would cost him more dearly than that other privation, loss of liberty? How is it that his experiences – to be rescued by a Paris mob, who saw him as one of them, in spite of his refusal to sign the oath of allegiance to their Republic – how is it that this has been the opposite of humbling to him? He now seems to believe in his own indomitable nature, that he can never be proved wrong.

Naturally, I endeavour to crush my irritation, whenever I am in his company. However, here I am not remedying events with the benefit of hindsight. At that moment I was not behaving as a scientist or a philosopher or a young man thinking of his career; not even as a doctor: I believe I was responding simply as one human being to another. I have of course seen a fair number of filthy street urchins before now, but I do not recall ever seeing one of them tied up like an animal. I have certainly never seen a child as cowed and unnaturally still as this one.

He has been offered many baths, Sicard said wearily, in answer to my question. Offered! At this he gave a sarcastic grunt: you can take it, Doctor Itard, that he has been bathed indeed and that it took no small effort and resulted in many small injuries to the bather. The boy prefers to wallow in filth.

How many days . . . he has been held here since . . . ?

I could not discover a means to ask the question without implying further insult.

Four days . . . a week. Perhaps longer. Yes, that's it. A fortnight. Your visits to us have been infrequent of late, Doctor Itard. The boys have sadly missed your ministerings and so, I am sure, have their ears!

One has to admire his skill. He now had the advantage and I was forced to mumble my excuses. My work, my duties at the Val-de-Grâce . . . Perhaps Sicard recalled my telling him that, despite my appointment there as surgeon second-class, I had not completed my medical studies? He nodded, smiling, and I was shamed, immediately regretting my irritation of a few moments earlier, yielding to the foolish sensation that he had been able to read my thoughts.

We continued to speak at a normal level and there were other sounds too: the squawk of a bird flying overhead; the voice of a governess scolding children somewhere on the other side of the courtyard; the clatter of hooves outside the walls and the shout of a coachman on the Rue St Jacques; but still the boy did not lift his head. Nor did his neck cease its slight bobbing; the way a bough jerks gently in a breeze, weighted by heavy fruit at the tip.

The child is indeed deaf then? This has been established?

Again, this question trembled under the weight of my doubts and in retrospect it might have been wiser to have held my tongue. (Could I have had a hint of what was to come, the great honour and opportunity about to be bestowed on me, perhaps patience would have helped me keep my counsel.)

Ah, well this is where you come in, Itard. The boy's deafness is *not* well established. There are reports, we have a report from Citoyen Bonnaterre . . .

It was the first time I had heard the abbé using the word *citoyen* without struggle and I was temporarily so struck by this unlikely sign of progress that I did not catch who Bonnaterre was and had to interrupt him to clarify it.

Bonnaterre? After his capture, the boy was taken to Rodez in the region of Aveyron. The local priest and naturalist there – Citoyen Bonnaterre – has furnished us with a report which I will of course let you see. He notes several discrepancies, contradictions in observations by others. As you see, most times the child responds not at all, is most certainly an idiot. But watch this.

Here the abbé reached into the pockets of his cloak, producing a chestnut and pliers. He held the chestnut in one hand, while with the other, he opened the silver pliers. At the instant the tool met with the chestnut and at the first crack of the shell splintering, the child, so still and apathetic, tensed up, ceased his subtle swaying and guttural moaning, became alert, almost, one might say, to prick up his ears, the way a dog does. It was a tiny change, not a substantial one, almost imperceptible. But we had both seen it.

The abbé looked at me with those famed kindly eyes. I stared back.

Did you see that? Is it our imagination or could it be possible that a child deaf to all around him, to the sound of gun shot – we've tried it, Itard, believe me! Deaf to human voices, that such a child is able to hear a chestnut shell cracking at a hundred paces?

In reply to his own question the abbé laughed. I had never seen him laugh before and it took a moment for me to appreciate that this was what it was. The noise he made was like the delicate sniffing of small rodents; a rabbit for example. Perhaps I appeared startled? I hastened to adopt the right expression.

Astonishing! He did, it's true – I would have said – yes, he did *seem* – well, who knows . . .

The abbé then nodded towards the Institute, indicating that we should now walk back.

You must read Citoyen Bonnaterre's report. You will find it fascinating, I'm sure.

Nothing could be more fascinating than the child himself, I spluttered.

Once again, an unwise remark. After all, the abbé would be only too aware of my avowed preference for observation and the value of empirical evidence over received opinion. Being of the same generation as Pinel he could not fail to consider my many protestations on the subject to amount to over-enthusiastic boyish nonsense. But fortunately the abbé – his handkerchief held like a mask to his face, his eyes watering – appeared not to have heard me, and was keen to walk back. Despite the stench, foul as it was, I could not bear to leave. I kept an iron grip on my impulse to spring forward and touch him. Could it really be true that he had lived entirely alone in the savage woods of Aveyron since early childhood? How had he ended up there? Why had no one claimed him, and why had he not found

– or sought – shelter in one of the many villages of the region?

Perhaps I could spend a moment alone with him, Abbé? I wish to observe him –

The white-haired figure of the abbé was already striding back towards the doorway leading to the courtyard. He scarcely paused to call back: don't touch him, Itard. He bites like a rat.

More than anything, I wanted to see the child's face. I nodded disingenuously.

It has been decided – if you agree, Itard – that he should be your charge. That you should teach him. We have observed – the Society is sensible of – your particular interest in the affliction of deaf mutes and your assiduous attentions, when time allows, of course, towards our boys. We would like to employ you as the Institute doctor, that is, if you are willing, with the savage as your especial – *task*. Pinel, as you know, has pronounced the boy an idiot. As for me . . .

I am defeated. He did not say it a second time, but everything about his demeanour conveyed it. I could hardly believe that he should feel so pessimistic on little more than a week's flimsy evidence and have to conclude that, like Pinel, he had seen an indelible stamp of idiocy on the boy's forehead the instant he had set eyes on him.

The abbé walked away from me, from the child, without a backward glance, seemingly unaware of how casually he had altered the course of my life. His step was spry. He walked like a man escaping.

Alone with the child, my heart began battering the cage of my ribs again. I gulped at the clean air behind me before turning to face him. Thrusting my hand into my jacket I jingled some coins: no response. I took out a pocket watch and dangled it some distance from him, crouching down to better approach his face. Again, no interest. I glanced around the courtyard for something to tempt him with and then

9

remembered the abbé's trick with the chestnut. The scattered shell and nut were behind me on the cobbled stone, where they had been abandoned. I picked them up and put them into my hand, conscious as I did so of holding my palm out flat, the way I had been taught as a child was the best way to feed a horse, if you wished not to be bitten.

I edged towards the boy with my palm outstretched.

My reward was this: he lifted his head. He sniffed the air, jerked his head forward, and I felt his warm mouth glance my palm like a little kiss, and then the chestnut, broken shell and all, disappeared. He did not instantly resume his position and I had time to note his sloe-black eyes, fringed with long eyelashes like those of a girl, and a scar, raised and thickened like the abandoned skin of a snake, across his throat. I remembered reading of that scar: of its terrible implications. In the warm sunlight of the Institute gardens, with the sound of birds twittering, with a white butterfly fluttering like a torn corner of paper from one flower urn to the next, I found the child's story, such as it has been told to me, impossible to imagine. Wicked, implausible. His story belongs to another time, to other people, to another country. His emergence from that place mirrors the task of the Republic itself: to shake off its ignorant, violent past and now emerge fully into the light.

I watched the wild boy crunch noisily at his gift and for the merest second, his eyes held mine. He was looking at me. My legs trembled as if the gaze was red-hot, but he was the first to drop his eyes. I had the sensation – a deeply disappointing sensation – that he had immediately lost interest in me. Instead his eyes raked the ground for more food.

A door clanged in the Institute. I knew without turning to look that behind me a long line of strange, gesticulating deaf children were filing out into the courtyard like marion-ettes, their limbs waving and shaking silently, to begin their lunch-time drill. My instinct was to untie the savage then and there, knowing that if they marched past him they would torment him. I paused, but I did not untie him. Something had profoundly unsettled me. Something in that fleeting intelligent glance. Even in the calm of my cramped study, scribbling by the light of my carcel lamps, conjuring up again my first sensations on catching his eyes, I found that my attempts to capture it in my journal were worthless. Words eluded me. I had the most powerful impression of having been glimpsed, assessed and dismissed. Worse, the sensation was familiar to me; it provoked a memory too peculiar to write down. I shuddered; I had the queer sense that we had met before.

A gauntlet had been thrown. The abbé had promised me my chance. Whatever his motives, and for the record I believe these to be laziness and a wish to wash his hands of the case, without the need for personal embarrassment or admission of failure, Abbé Sicard has offered me nothing less than the opportunity to change for all history the sum of our knowledge of our own human nature.

The beautiful savage has kissed my hand. He has measured me with his dark gaze, with eyes as fringed and shady as the forest itself. Our destinies are now to be linked.

I've seen the doctor around before of course, him with his cane with the carved duck's head for a handle and his high-necked shirt and black coat that's all the fashion now and his nose like a giant beak peeking out beneath that great shelf of a brow. Maybe some would call him handsome but not me. And I heard about the boy – how could I not when I'm living here at the Institute? He's been hanging round like a poor forgotten wretch for many a day now and every day visitors saying look at him, saying the noble savage, all the secrets of man's inner being held in that sorry soul; but for myself I don't see much more than a sad boy left for dead by a wicked being. A boy who has lived like a beast for far too long. Maybe it was wolves who suckled him, maybe it was his own mother or father who tried to slay him: all I know is nature here is upside down and however much people marvel that he survived those five years – some say seven – it is clear to anyone with half a brain or half a heart that the boy has not survived in one piece; part of him is missing.

The first time I tiptoed up to the child it was Sunday. I mean to say, of course, not Sunday but Decadi, the new day of rest but it still feels like a Sunday whatever they might choose to call it, except Sunday without the worship. Anyway I was not working. Well, that's not true either for I'm always working but that is to say I did not have teaching duties and so I tiptoed up to him. It was early evening, the hens were strutting around the yard showing more life than he did, it was the time the bell next door used to peal, that was in the days when it was struck at a certain hour. Which I can't seem to get out of my head now, even though the bell is long stolen and the Virgin has her legs hacked off at the knees and the ringing doesn't happen any more. It still happens on the hour in my head.

So I approached him. It made a poor body flinch to think what he had been through, how *bored* – that's what I kept thinking, how bored he must have been, all alone. With no real work to keep him busy. Then I thought that's foolish, because he had the work of living, of eating and scavenging and hiding from hunters and making a shelter and gathering berries and keeping out of trouble and fending off sadness and any amount of other emotions and God knows that's surely work enough for any human being. You might think boredom is a trifling affliction, the least amongst those greater ones. Each to his own, I say. For myself, I cannot bear idleness, so that's the one would wring me the worst.

I stared at him for a good long time and he did not lift his head. The evening sun peeked at us, a glowing pink eye behind the flopping fringe of the weeping willow. I stood by the pond staring at him too, but the child might have been sleeping for all the attention he paid to me. Something in his look made you nervous, nervous and attracted both at the same time, the way a woman falls for a man she knows is a drinker and liable to take his fist to her and still she has no power to prevent herself.

He was rocking back and forth, nodding, rocking. I am not sure what you might call it only that he did it and did it all the time too. It gave me the idea that he was awake and thinking about me, that he was staring down at his feet but really hiding his true thoughts from me. And any minute now he was going to look up and stretch open his mouth wide, so wide his head would swallow me up; show me his yellow fangs and how he could sink them right into me. He knew all about me. Terrible things, things I wouldn't tell another soul.

Well thinking this, naturally enough I jumped back, made a little jump. My keys jangled in my pocket and when the keys jangled – what do you know – he looked up. He had black-brown eyes, very pretty, with lashes as long as a deer's and he didn't open his mouth to show me his fangs, but I've no doubt that he could if he wanted; no doubt that he kept his jaw clamped shut just to trick me. And I said hello there boy and I felt foolish for speaking, but again, had no strength to prevent myself. He made you want to talk to him. I could not have said why but it might have something to do with his prettiness. It is his eyes and his eyes tell you he's not stupid either, there's no doubting it: that young doctor is right and the savage is no idiot. The so-called great Doctor Pinel is quite wrong about that. Even Henri said it when he saw the child – he said the boy was 'in there'. But that doesn't mean the savage is normal either. He might not be an idiot and he is taking everything in, and he knows, I think, what we're saying and what we're thinking. (Henri says that last part is nonsense and your superstitious nature Marie-France getting the better of you again.)

He has a smell like nothing you ever smelled in your life and no one can dispute that. He smells like dirt and rotting tree roots and the smell of fear the chickens have when the fox has sniffed at the coop. And the smell you have just under your nose when you wake up from a nightmare, a nightmare in which you were loyal, more than loyal, God knows, you were devoted; although no one could have found you wanting, one of your neighbours has turned them against you and here, here you are: now it is your turn. There are footsteps outside and the thud of a gun banging against the door; here is the salad-basket rattling down the street, the cage on wheels you saw so many times, with others tossed about inside it, and here it is now, coming for you. You are shaking and sweating, on your way now, bumping along the road, towards what some used to call the Louisette, but that was in the old days, the days before this nightmare, days when we still thought it was a blessing, a clever, humane invention. And in the dream you are silent, trembling, you have your children clutching at your knees, you cannot call out *Not me, not me, was I not loyal, was I not true*, and still the journey continues, delivering you right up to the feet of Mount Unwilling, of Mount Against-the-Grain Abbey, the Scythe, the Louisette. Madame Guillotine. And then you wake up and there is that stench so powerful, so salty and freakish: you have no idea if it is sweat, if it is your own body or if it is something else. What fear smells like.

Like I say, the boy smells like that.

The boy crouches in the kitchen, in the home of Madame Guérin. In his filthy rags, on swept red hexagonal tiles, is the boy who smells like fear. His skin so finely stretched, hunger visible as the bones beneath and yet everything she offers him, he refuses. He does this with a gesture of the head, a jerk, which makes her leap back, as if he might bite her. Once, he sniffs, lifts his chin. The scar raised and shiny, or a line drawn, an indicator: as if someone might have pencilled there just exactly the place to slice head from neck, as so many, in these years past, have had heads neatly scythed from necks.

The boy rocks, sways his head back and forth. Occasionally, his fingers trace the scar, as if he might find it comforting to do so, or compelling, as if his fingers might have memory. But mostly, the boy sleeps. He sleeps crouching and he sleeps standing; he can, it appears, sleep in any position at all. He sleeps the slumber of a victim or predator, of one who must be always on guard. It is only one tissue-fine layer beneath being awake. If necessary, he can stir in an instant.

There are new, nameless smells and unpredictable figures; there is the woman who moves around him always in a flash of white, and with that animal heat and hands which ring and hiss, clang and clatter, flap and shake at him without warning. The warm dark place is nowhere and all the smells are with it. The scratch, the roughness, the silky mud. Leaves to dig his feet beneath. He cannot find the sound of the birds, the babble of the stream. He rocks and he rocks, he lifts his chin upwards, he points his face to the square of night sky, he allows the strange heat of the woman to ebb and flow at him, her hands to loom in front of him with sounds, with hisses, with water. He does all of this, but no bats swoop down to stroke his face.

Thermidor 17
Year Eight in our Glorious Republic

My new charge is causing a furore throughout the Republic. I have heard the most brilliant but unreasonable expectations voiced by the people of Paris. Citizens who are not particularly renowned for their intellect, as well as some who are, have approached me, asking if the boy has beheld with astonishment the fine sights of the capital. I have expressed bewilderment. Why should he find the capital 'fine'? I ask. Is he not as likely to find a chestnut 'fine'? Facts, facts and above all facts – these are what matters. Scientific observation, keeping conjecture to a minimum. Remembering that a child so long in the wilderness, so long deprived of human society, may be a long time in returning to it.

The Abbé Sicard tells me that so far one family have come forward to claim the wild boy, but that they took one look at him and the mother fell to weeping, said it was not her baby, a child snatched from her by Republican soldiers during a raid on a church in which she and the boy were hiding; she had maintained for a good many years the hope that her child had been set free in the woods nearby after one of the soldiers had failed to slay him, and been nurtured there by a wolf-mother, but on seeing this savage boy she screamed and declared it a terrible mistake. I am sure she will not be the last to come forward.

I am surprised that more information does not seem to be available about the child's origins, nor how he came to be abandoned in the forest, despite Bonnaterre's interrogation of the local community. The scar beneath his throat seems incontrovertible evidence that someone tried to murder him – it is too big and too clean to correlate to any kind of animal-bite. Whether it was a parent, wishing to be rid of an idiot child, as Pinel proposes, remains unproven. How he recovered from such a brutal attack is another mystery. And having recovered, all alone, how he then survived in the wilderness – the greatest mystery of all. I have been reading the reports the abbé gave me, written by those who first witnessed him in Aveyron after his capture, this man Bonnaterre and others. They are often contradictory. It does seem though, that over a period of seven years there were repeated sightings by peasants and others, of a boy, living wild in the rugged terrain of the Tarn valley and elsewhere in

Aveyron. Even allowing for exaggeration, there are too many confirmed accounts for it not to be true. If, as I judge, based on height, limbs and supposition, he is now twelve years of age, the most astonishing conclusion cannot be avoided. The boy must have lived alone since he was a child of five.

After my first meeting with the wild boy yesterday morning and the news that he was to be my charge and that this had been agreed by the Society of the Observers of Man, who were even now drawing up a contract of employment for me at the Institute, I hurried to find someone to help me untie him. I reasoned that it would be a risk to do this alone. I found a stout woman, Madame Guérin, a governess at the Deaf Institute. She was on her way to the kitchen, where she doubles as a cook at lunch-time. I have seen her before now, working with the gardener, whom I assume to be her husband, a great giant of a man, gaunt and stooping, usually seen wheeling his barrow in the courtyard, or bent double as a folded knife, coughing, hidden behind the rows of beans. I infer from this that the man is an invalid, at pains to hide his condition in order to retain his post. The woman, Madame Guérin, is therefore the one who carries the greater burden of work, which says much for her being of sound body and robust health.

It is apparent that she is unafraid to dirty her hands. I also inferred, as I stood in front of her, explaining my strange request, that it was she who had taken the wild boy his plate of food, since she nodded vigorously, remarking more than once on the 'poor wretched child' that the others seemed to have forgotten. As she said this, I was astonished to see tears spring to her eyes. Inwardly I complimented myself on my choice; she has compassion and good sense, and fine fat arms which can lift a great basket of fruit as if it were full of feathers.

We hurried together towards the boy and I warned her to bring her handkerchief, which she held obediently over her nose. 'Joseph', as she referred to him, was just as I had left him, his head drooping sadly on his neck like a tulip.

There was a moment when I was afraid to approach him.

But for some reason that I cannot explain, I did not want Madame Guérin to see this. I tried holding out my hand to show him that I had brought further gifts of chestnuts. Again, he sniffed the air before pouncing hungrily, and in that manner, whilst continually reassuring him that we meant him no harm, I distracted him sufficiently to enable Madame Guérin to untie him. Without disgust, putting the handkerchief into the pocket of her apron, she took hold of one of his skinny, filthy arms. He did not resist. Using further chestnuts as incitements, we persuaded him to come with us towards a side entrance to the Institute. (We wanted to avoid the gaze of the other pupils.)

The governness acquitted herself calmly throughout. She did not hold her handkerchief up to her nose as I did. Of course, being a woman, and working in such a place, she would be in the habit of emptying pots and accustomed to the smell of human excrement. I discovered as we walked together, with the lolloping boy between us, his face in my hand, sniffling at my palm like a dog, that she lived in some quarters on the fourth floor of the Institute. This seemed the obvious place to take the child.

More than anything, I wanted a chance to observe the boy properly, to allow me to write a full description of him, to transcribe to my journal later. Since his mood was quiet and I had the reliable Madame Guérin beside me, heating up water on the stove for his bath, this was the perfect occasion. My hostess offered me a cup of chocolate, which we also waved under the child's nose and, although I accepted, the wild boy did not.

Her kitchen was cosy, one of those female environments where not a single surface, a spoon handle nor a dish-cloth, is denied its decoration. Everywhere I looked there was a painted tricolore flag, or an embroidered one. The wall opposite the giant stove was lined with shelves full of plates painted with the usual figures in black hats, orange jackets and blue trousers, the swords and opened cages of freed birds, the Revolutionary slogans. *Vive la Liberté, Abandon de tous les privilèges. Liberté, égalité, sûreté.*

Pride of place on the dresser was a large white jug painted with the words: *Vivre libre ou mourir.*

Again, I was reassured by my choice in Madame Guérin. It is possible to wonder whether women of her type would not harbour some closet allegiance to the old order and I could not have felt great confidence in leaving the boy in her care had I suspected that this was the case. Uncle warned me for all those years that there would be many in our Republic who would be swift to shower scorn on the gains we now see before us and that we should be on our guard against such fellows. A virtuous individual such as Uncle, who wished nothing worse than freedom, truth and fairness of opportunity upon his fellow-man, should not do so in hope of being rewarded by their love and regard. To illustrate, Uncle would use the fate of Jean-Jacques himself. He would tell me how Jean-Jacques, despite the marvellous generosity of his *Social Contract* and other writings, was hounded, cast out by the French, towards the end of his life. Uncle's eyes filled with tears as he read to me from Rousseau's *Reveries*, which to a young man's ears sounded more like an old man's fantasies of persecution than the indictment against an unjust world that Uncle believed them to be.

While fond memories of Uncle faded, I tore myself back to the present moment. I took some snuff and made myself as comfortable as is possible on those woven chair seats, the kind that are beginning to fray, and perilously close to collapsing in the middle. I watched as Madame Guérin heaved the water from the stove to a tin bath. She also placed a chamber-pot beside the boy on her clean and polished red tiles. I believe we would both have been very surprised if he had made use of it.

Then with great gentleness, she undressed him. His clothes had to be peeled from him. The skin beneath was dirty but pale in places, and hairless. Again, he did not resist. As long as a nut or a piece of apple accompanied each gesture, as long as her movements were steady and not designed to startle, the boy acquiesced.

His skin bore recent pock-marks, signs of his brush with small-pox since being in human company. Sicard tells me that the child contracted it – although not a severe case – on his long journey between Aveyron and Paris. He was forced to rest at an inn with Bonnaterre, the naturalist who was accompanying him to Paris, for several days until well enough to travel.

> Some observations: His body is patterned with scars, big, small; both silvery and red; that is ancient and new. None as significant as the large scar already discussed. His genitals appear to be normal, if small for a boy of twelve. As mentioned, he has no body hair, nor signs of impending manhood.

His bath was drawn. Madame Guérin had placed cloths on the floor around it. Now she needed my help to lift him in. We were both tense, but picking up the child was surprisingly easy. He was light as a bird's nest. His thin limbs dangled above the water – pleasantly hot – and holding a leg and an arm each, we dunked him. I fully expected a rebellion: I held my breath. But the wild boy sank like a piece of cloth, soaking up liquid, and soon was happily immersed in the bath, his knees up to his chin, his arms huddled beside him.

He likes to see me prepare the water, Madame Guérin said, suddenly. She has an accent which I cannot recognise, although I can tell it is not Parisien. Somewhere south perhaps? Her remark was made firmly, as if to challenge something that I had not said. I did not know how to reply.

Last time, he would not allow it. I think it will be better if he sees me heat the water: if he knows what's coming.

Last time? Have you attempted to bathe him before?

She nodded, turning to the stove to get a cup. With this, she trickled water over the child's back, at the same time caressing him with her other hand, rubbing at the dirt-encrusted skin. The bones of his shoulders protruded like folded wings. The water turned black.

It was you who helped the Abbé Sicard to bathe him?

Helped him? She snorted. I did not understand her meaning. But she nodded, continuing to scoop the water with the cup, trickling it over the child's bony back. The soap she took from a plate on the floor beside her was cracked and veined with black. I noticed with satisfaction how she showed the savage, by holding the soap in front of her, what she was going to do; how she warned him before trickling water on his hair by lifting her hand up and pretending to do it first; how she made each movement flow into the next, taking great care, as she had said, never to startle him. In this manner she washed the whole of his body, including his hair. She then fetched a comb and attempted to bring some order to the unruly mess but at this the child baulked and flapped at her hand with his own, screaming in sharp cries: she soon gave up.

She sat back on her heels with a look of satisfaction.

There, that's a lovely boy, isn't it? She spoke as a mother to a very young child.

The child's eyes did not fix on her when she spoke to him. He did not, as one might expect him to do, follow her eyes. Instead he followed the progress of her hand, or the soap, or the comb, or fixed his gaze on one of the black-hatted peasants on her decorative plates; in short, his gaze remained fleeting and as bewitching as it was when I had first stared into his face.

> The somewhat frightened gaze of the young Aveyronnais does not fix on anything apart from his nourishment or the objects he seeks to avoid or take; in these cases a confident glance, a fast look, suffices, for he seems to have sharp vision.

With the wild boy's toilette finished, we attempted to lift him out. First Madame Guérin showed him the towel – the way a matador will flick his cloak at a bull – so that he might know what our intentions were. He did indeed seem to understand us and began to shout: the sharp, high-pitched cries of an angry bird when its nest is threatened. So we leaned over together – one, two, three, and attempted to heave him out, taking a slippery wet arm and leg each and labouring to place him on the waiting towel. The child was so light and yet at the first touch of our hands on his skin, he began a frenzied kicking and splashing and such a commotion that my first instinct was to drop him back into the water. Madame Guérin was more robust and held on to her part of the catch; rather to her misfortune since he then gave a blood-curdling scream, turned his head towards her hand and plunged his teeth into her forearm.

Now it was the governess's turn to scream.

I saw at once that he had drawn blood and scolded him in an angry tone.

First you wallow in dirt, next you refuse to leave your bath! You are both naughty and illogical, I told him. He stared just past my shoulder with wet black eyes, his body beginning again his rocking movement, but he did not seem concerned by the anger in my voice.

Madame Guérin stood in a puddle beside the bath, stemming the blood flow with her apron.

I don't have all the time in the world! she said, addressing her remark to the boy, but intending it, I think, for me.

I suppose we had better try again.

This time I was resolute. I leaned forward, taking a firmer grip of the child's arm. As before, he instantly began his noisy cries, his wild flailing. Within moments we were both drenched in water. It was astonishing to note the strength of one undersized twelve-year-old boy, set against two strong adults, but I will say that it was not easy to lift him from that bath. It was made more difficult by the memory of the bite Madame Guérin had just received; I was careful to keep my forearms or any other vulnerable flesh away from the child's teeth. He tossed his head at great speed, making it tricky to judge at any given moment where those teeth might be. By the end of this debacle I felt foolish in the extreme. A man of twenty-five in his formal work clothes is no match for a stout woman, with the experience of a mother, where rebellious children are concerned. In fact, such were the strengths of Madame Guérin in this difficult situation that I immediately hatched a perfect plan.

At the back of my mind, ever since the abbé's earlier astonishing announcement of my new post (astonishing in its casualness, as well as its portents), I had been wondering how I could address the practical problems of the boy's upbringing. Where would he live, who would take care of him on a daily basis? Who would dress him, prepare his meals, put him to bed at night, see that he is not abandoned again in the grounds of the Institute? If I am to bring him back to civilisation through treatment and moral and mental education, then I need an assistant to do the unskilled work, to take care of him as a mother would. Who better than this calm, strong woman, with her lack of fear and her good thick arms, which would be able to withstand the worst his teeth could offer?

I did not put the question to her right then. I took some more snuff and pondered. She was on her knees, mopping the floor around the bath, and I judged that I should not proceed without the abbé's blessing and a substantial sum of money to offer her.

Meanwhile, the boy, having been roughly dried by Madame Guérin, was standing, wrapped in a towel, by the window. Neither of us had seen him move over towards it, but now, as if alerted suddenly to the dangers it presented – dangers of escape or of violence – I and the governess both turned our gaze towards where the boy stood. Sunlight streamed over him, making his already pale skin waxy rather than luminous. For a second his skin reminded me of mushrooms, of things damp and faintly mouldy, things which grow in forests where the dense trees only permit the finest slivers of light. But as I looked at him, at the child wrapped in his white towel like a baby, I saw something else. Something new, clean. A blank slate. A pure white envelope, unsealed, holding a letter written in invisible ink, in a language that no one else can read. *A language that I alone will come to understand.*

I resolved to consult Madame Guérin immediately about my plan. She would have the night to put it to the husband, although of course these simple people could only be pleased and astonished at the honour bestowed on them, and the husband's approval a matter of formality.

I couldn't scrub the smell long after the doctor had left and after I'd burned the boy's clothes and dressed him in a clean shirt of Henri's, a shirt I washed myself just yesterday so I know it would normally smell of the river and the hot sun, of lavender and rosemary-vinegar. What I'm saying is it should smell the same as the rest of my laundry but not on this boy. He could make a rose smell foul.

I wasn't afraid to touch him – no not at all, not one whit – I was not put off by his countenance nor his smell; I'm not faint-hearted, not me. I picked up each pitiful limb and he's light and feels just like the bleached chewed-clean bones at the end of a meal. Oh I'm fearless me, when the doctor is there, when the sun is bright. But now the moon is up I'm sitting here knitting by the grey pool of light pouring through our window on the fourth floor and I'm knitting and thinking (that's the way I like to do it knitting and thinking together I mean, in a rhythm, soothing, I find it) and there he is. Only a whistle away from us in Julie's old room, sleeping.

Henri's last words before he fell asleep were if he terrifies you so much why on God's earth did you say yes?

With that said, the great lump rolled over and fell to snoring. Fine for him, I thought and how could I tell him that it's the money and nothing else dragging me along like a fish with a hook in its mouth? Money like we haven't ever seen, more money than I could earn here if I worked every minute of every hour. More than I'd make if I taught a hundred deaf children, if I cooked a thousand suppers. Money for bills, for doctor's bills for Henri, but if I tell him that he will fathom out how ill he is and I can't have that. So I'm lying beside Henri with that terrible rattle in his throat as he breathes out and naughty Georges, the naughtiest deaf boy, running along the corridor upstairs where he's out of bed again, the little devil, and then listening to that low murmuring coming from the savage's room and thinking: God almighty I might just as well be sleeping in the wolf's den myself. Trapped between the lot of them with their pounding feet and their wickedness and their hacking and snuffling and soft growling.

There was a wind up despite the sultry heat and a branch banging here and now at the bedroom window and other fretful noises. Tappings and bumpings and such-like from the room next door: a genie caught in a bottle smarting to get out. When you lie in bed and just picture things it's always worse I've found, it's better to get up and do something, because there's no point in letting your mind dwell on things that can't be mended or prevented.

It's true that lying in bed made the boy next door seem

bigger than he is, like a great swooping dark crow banging against the walls. And more shadowy. His yellow fangs longer, his evil smell more evil, his shaggy hair wilder and crawling with lice, his ink-black eyes bigger than they are and prettier, more bewitching; full of more evil magic, more mesmerising. By the time I'd finished lying here listening and imagining him I was ready to leap up with the axe and finish him off myself. And maybe you think a woman wouldn't be capable of such a thing, but there you are forgetting Renée Bordereau who killed twenty-one of our Blues in one day and the last one broke her sword with his head. All to avenge the deaths of her brothers. Well she might be a Royalist and fighting on the wrong side but my point is this, she is a woman with a heart as staunch as any man's when it comes to what she believes has to be done. None can disagree with that.

What I'm saying is if you lie there wide awake with your eyes tight you might just as well *invite* evil thoughts to slide in, so best leave your bed and take up your knitting.

So finally, with my heart knocking louder than Georges's pounding feet on the floor above us, I jumped from my bed and roused myself to go next door, to satisfy myself that the boy has not been sent from the Devil or somewhere worse to punish me, that he is just a child. A poor forsaken child. That I should find it in my heart to pity him. It's not as if I didn't try to tell the doctor earlier today. Poor wretched boy, I kept saying with such feeling you would have felt sure the doctor might have noticed it. It's bad enough the witless abbé has made me take him in once already, never seemed to notice my huffing and puffing and cursing under my breath when the water splashed from one end of my kitchen to the other. Henri said – think the likes of the abbé or the good doctor worries over the opinion of a mere cook and mop and dogsbody like yourself? Dogsbody I might be I says but I'm one of the few round here who can mop shit from the floor *and* spell it, and it'd be better for them to remember that. I felt unkind after saying that, after all it's not Henri's fault that he can't read his letters. He wasn't an orphan like me and so he didn't have the great good fortune as the nuns were always telling me to be taken away by *such* a grand lady to live in *such* a grand house and the lot of them seem to forget she was nothing more than wife to a glove-maker and though it's true she did teach me my letters it was no real kindness on her part, only practicality, since then she could lie there with her eyes closed and have me read to her until long past midnight. But it's best not to remind Henri of those days and, as I say, it is not his fault if he did not have the same twist of fortune in *his* life, which took a mother in child-bed and a father soon after. We each have our stories, some with more beginnings and endings than others.

So now I was all up and roused to go next door. I didn't trouble to wake Henri, knowing from experience that I'm the one most likely to be able to fend off violent attack from any quarter. Should the boy leap at me and sink his jaws into my throat I'd be better off defending myself than waiting for Henri to do it, in which case I might just as well wait until the Widow Capet rises from the dead, sews her own head back on her neck, and saves me herself.

I wrapped my fichu around my shoulders, for no good reason since the night was hot and sultry, but that's what I did and I felt better once I had done it. I bent to the dying embers of the fire, lit the candle and took that and the axe down the corridor and stood hesitating outside the child's door, having had the good sense earlier to lock it.

I had to move the key in order to spy through the keyhole and naturally enough the child heard this and his clamour, the thumping sounds, stopped. He must have thought I had come to release him. I put my eye to the keyhole, but of course I couldn't see, since my head blocked the light from the candle. But I could smell him well enough. The smell of the Devil.

Who sent you? Who are you?

I can't tell you why I asked him that. Why I spoke at all. My own voice surprised me, rising from the darkness, a shivering voice, dangling those fabulous questions.

The thought came to me then and you can understand why. To open the door. To let him out, release him, pretend it was an accident and no one would know any better. I rubbed at the place in my arm, remembering his teeth sinking there. My little Joseph used to bite me sometimes. That's how I knew.

I touched the key to the lock again. As I did it, there was a movement, a noise behind me. I dropped the candle and screamed.

Marie-France –

Henri!

Come to your bed, Marie-France. The wretch will be fine. That is, if we are not all burned in our beds.

He knelt to pick up the candle, scraping the soft wax off the floor with his thumb-nail.

I didn't think to help him: my thoughts were elsewhere. I was looking down at his hands in the semi-dark, the shape of them. I was thinking of the gloves I used to make, the palms of my hands near rubbed away by all that smoothing and stretching of the leather, all that stitching and stabbing. I always used to dream of gloves. As a child I mean, at the glove-maker's. You would think that after a day stretching those flattened leather hands over their white wooden stands I would be glad to think of something else come bedtime, but no, not one whit. Sleep was filled with gloves, with leather that flopped like pastry, with metal cutters digging out the flat-hand shapes. Empty hands, every colour under the sun, skipping, dancing on my bench. And in later years the gloves dripped blood from the wrists, were not gloves at all, but cut-off hands, scolding, beckoning. In the worst dreams of all, the limbless hands crept over my face, like great spiders, flattened themselves over my mouth. Those nights, I woke up struggling for breath. You'll agree, I am a woman truly afflicted by dreams.

Henri said as we climbed back into our bed that he should be chained up, the wild boy, like the other idiot children in Bicêtre, but he didn't mean it. He has a habit of saying cruel things to hide his sweetness; whereas with me it's the other way around. My cruelty is what I know, I know it all too well. It is always my sweetness that can surprise me.

Fructidor 1
Year Eight in our Glorious Republic

I was frustrated at not being able to visit the wild boy this morning. I received my official summons from the Society of the Observers of Man and the formal letter confirming my new post as his guardian. The original letter from Lucien Bonaparte, the Minister of the Interior, was included. I drew in my breath sharply as I read it, reminded anew of the importance of the child now in my charge.

> I learn from the newspapers that a young man has been found in the woods of your department who only knows how to utter indistinct cries and who does not speak any language. If this is the case, and if you have no hope of discovering the parents of the unfortunate boy, I claim him and request that you send him to me forthwith.

He only utters indistinct cries. *He does not speak any language.* I shivered as I considered the voice of this wild sliver of pure nature and how it might sound. For how long have philosophers longed to have an infant, a child shielded from human influence, living so many crucial years in isolation that he forgets the sound of a human voice, forgets what little he had learned of human behaviour, so that they might more clearly determine which of the characteristics we consider to be human are truly so; which are merely products of education and custom? What wretched, *wretched* idiocy that the fools who first caught him in the woods of Aveyron did not think to maintain his isolation this past few weeks, so that by the time the savage reached my dominion I might truly be able to judge that very question. My only solace is that the boy seems little affected by the last few weeks and behaves in much the same bestial way described by those who found him.

> The most brilliant but unreasonable expectations were formed by the people of Paris respecting the Savage of Aveyron before he arrived. Many curious people anticipated great pleasure in beholding his astonishment at the sight of all the fine things in the capital. On the other hand, many persons eminent for their superior understanding, forgetting that our organs are less flexible and imitation more difficult the further man travels from society and from his infancy, thought that the education of this individual would be the business of only a few months, and that they should soon hear him make the most striking observations concerning his past manner of life.

I hurried to my first official attendance at a meeting of the Society of the Observers of Man, which took place in a sweltering, box-shaped ante-room of the Collège de France in the Latin Quarter. I was not a little flattered to note that I am its newest and youngest member. The astronomist Lalande presided over matters, his white hair smoothed to perfection, his eyebrows forever raised, arched and cool, as if residing permanently in the heavens, above the lowly discourse of grants, appointments and disbursements. He has just returned, he informed us, from the latest expedition seeking the passage of Venus and would be delighted to update us on its progress, as soon as the 'business' – he could not hide his distaste – of the morning was completed.

Cuvier, the anatomist, smoked sulkily on a pipe throughout the meeting and gives me the impression he was piqued by my new appointment, but I believe he had been voted down by the others. I have of course attended many of Cuvier's lectures at the Lycée des Arts and a few years ago, as a younger man, was probably – I will admit – impressed by his flounces; the rapid freehand drawings on the blackboard, the oratory skills. (He is rumoured to have taken lessons from the actor Talma. Now that I am a little older, I find this ridiculous.)

Pinel repeated his view that the boy was an incurable idiot, victim of a failed murder attempt, afterwards abandoned perhaps by wicked parents owing to his lack of speech. He made this statement quietly, without undue aggression, fixing his eyes on me with his customary expression of pinched concern, an expression which reminds me of Uncle and never fails to provoke anxiety. I could never imagine him wearing a wig, as Sicard does. For some reason this thought only added to my misery. With a genial smile, Pinel claimed that 'nothing should please him more' than that his marvellous young pupil should prove him wrong. He passed his report across the table.

Virey spoke next. As a fellow surgeon at the military hospital of the Val-de-Grâce he had, he said, long observed my extraordinary affinity with the deaf mutes, my dedication and devotion to the cause of medicine and had noted, not without a trace of envy (here the others laughed lightly), the speed and tender age at which I had been promoted to surgeon second-class. He was glad to support my new appointment and did not share Pinel's entirely pessimistic diagnosis, although he had some other reservations of his own. He did not go into these. My task, he opined, would not be an easy one.

There was some confusion and more laughter when I spoke for the first time, mentioning my intention to employ the services of Citoyenne Guérin. Cuvier said something I could not understand about the pleasures of being bathed by

73733

her and when the others laughed, I replied in bewilderment that I found her to be a 'motherly' kind of woman and as such, ideal.

Scarcely old enough to be mother to a newborn, sneered Cuvier again, and there was another burst of laughter.

Finally, the misunderstanding was made clear by the Abbé Sicard, who informed me that the Citoyenne Guérin (of course we are careful on these occasions to use the proper forms of address) the others were thinking of was a lively brunette called Julie who must, he suggested, be the daughter of *my* Citoyenne Guérin. This Julie Guérin works as a nurse at the Val-de-Grâce.

Surely you noticed her there, Itard? drawled Cuvier in mock astonishment. I shook my head. I was thinking a rather subversive thought that I would not have wanted to share with the others: that this incident points out the usefulness of the old terms. Naturally, this is a *Mademoiselle* Guérin we are speaking of, and as such, she would never have been confused with her mother. It's no wonder that in common speech most of us revert to old habits.

Sicard then spoke at length of his regard for me, the accident of our meeting in the street when one of the boys from his school fell ill some twelve months ago and the marvellous cure I procured for the boy. He continued to speak softly, his voice slippery in the heat of that sun-soaked room, so that I was almost lulled to sleep by his words; his praise of my passionate interest in the afflictions of the deaf, my extraordinary gifts as physician to these sad, lonely boys; how honoured, how fortunate our young savage was to have been entrusted to me.

I longed for a glass of icy water, but not to drink. At last, after three and a half hours, the meeting came to a close.

As soon as I was able (I had also to collect my things from the Val-de-Grâce and give a hasty notice of resignation) I made my way to the quarters of Madame Guérin so that I could see for myself how the child passed the night. It was four in the afternoon by the time of my arrival and the day's lessons were over. I imagined that Madame Guérin would have been forced to tie the child up whilst she attended to her lessons and was therefore surprised to discover that she had in fact remained at home with the child all day, having obtained a dispensation from the abbé to do so. (I imagine Sicard feels some guilt for the way the child was treated in his care.)

I cannot get him to use the chamber-pot, was the first thing Madame Guérin said to me, almost before I was in the door. A lingering smell, although faint and overlaid with soap, was proof enough of her complaint.

I was startled to turn around and see the child sitting at the kitchen table. He wore a clean white shirt and breeches. He was rocking and murmuring, and he sawed back and forth at his teeth with a little piece of straw, but for all that, I would have said he appeared happy in his new home.

I'm glad you did not see the need to tie him up –

Now, see, Doctor Itard –

You will be pleased to know that the Society have sanctioned my request, and agreed a larger sum!

A larger sum?

Is something wrong, Madame Guérin? You are not ill?

No, I –

My thought was to take the child out. For a walk. On his lead of course. What was it you wanted to say to me, or can it wait?

It can wait.

At my mention of a walk, Madame Guérin fetched some shoes she said belonged to another boy at the Institute.

Not that Joseph – not that the child will wear them.

Joseph? The savage has a name?

It was a slip. I don't call him Joseph. It does not suit him.

I heard you call him Joseph just then, and yesterday. Is that not his name?

It does not suit him.

Madame Guérin was not looking at me when she said this but struggling under the table with trying to get the shoes on the child's feet. Her voice sounded rather strangled, almost as if she were sobbing. I was relieved to see her emerge from under the table quite tearless. The child had been kicking and protesting at the arrival of the shoes: presumably it was this which gave her voice a breathless quality.

He does not like to wear shoes? I asked.

It was not a question requiring an answer. None was forthcoming.

Madame Guérin stood puffing loudly, wiping her hands on her apron and tucking strands of her dark hair back into the bonnet on her head. I noticed a scab forming on her arm – it had the appearance of a dark leech – in the place where the child had bitten her yesterday and found myself quickly glancing over her to see if there were any other signs of a skirmish.

Has he attacked you again?

No, Doctor, but –

She paused, looking over at the child as if she were wondering how much he understood.

I am often quite afraid of him. My daughter is not allowed to live with us here at the school but when my Julie visits –

Ah, Julie. So you do have a daughter! Does she work at the Val-de-Grâce?

She seemed pleased at this. One might even say she simpered a little.

You've seen my Julie? She's a looker, isn't she – you're not the first young man to comment on it to me.

I wasn't aware that I had.

Pardon?

Commented on her looks. In fact, I have never seen her.

34

I thought . . .

Perhaps we should be going. Whilst he is in this calm mood. Do you have the lead from yesterday?

Glad to cut short this awkward conversation and glad too that her appointment was now firmly accepted by her, I waved my hat and cane in the child's direction so that he could see I intended to take a walk. After some gesturing at the window and some marching around the room, swinging my arms to and fro, feeling rather foolish, I approached the boy and managed to slip the rope around the belt at his waist and tie it. It took no further persuasion, once Madame Guérin had opened the front door, to convince him to leap towards it. Much of his instinct so far is towards escape. The sight of the world outside, the great blue sheet of sky and the grand elm tree in the courtyard, produces a visible excitement, which he expresses in hopping from foot to foot, slapping his hands against his thighs, banging on the door with a flat hand, or tugging at the fabric of my trousers, thus showing me by all the means he has available that he desires to go out. I am delighted to see that the apathy of my first encounter with the child has disappeared and was no doubt a product of his confinement.

I hardly needed to lead him to the door; the child fair dragged me there.

He set off at a lumbering trot, soon kicking off the shoes, which were much too big for him. I picked them up and placed them hastily by the stairs before following him into the garden. Some boys from the school spied us and began running beside us, three blue-uniformed figures, accompanying us with their eerie, wordless cries. One, Georges, bolder than the others, picked up a stone and threw it – a crack shot – right at the savage's neck. Although it hit him, grazing the place where his scar snakes, I was interested to note that the savage appeared completely unconcerned and maintained his half-run, tugging me excitedly. It was the proper direction for the gate in the Institute wall, but I cannot believe he knew this. Over my shoulder, I brandished my cane at the boys. The beak on the duck-head wagged like a finger.

Our destination was the Jardin du Luxembourg. Of course, it is only natural that passers-by should stare at us. Many of them, one presumes, had gathered at the savage's cage in those first few days, when he was displayed in Paris, before arriving at the Institute. By the time we had entered the gates of the gardens, a small group being entertained on the grass by Les Marionettes du Théâtre du Luxembourg switched allegiance and decided that the puppets were not as entertaining as the spectacle we provided. We soon had a straggle of hangers-on, but again, the wild boy seemed not to notice. Such was his enthusiasm for our walk that the rope strained and tugged like the twitch of an animal's tail.

I noticed something remarkable. Outside the house, sur- rounded by vegetation, walking between the rows of chestnut trees or cedars, listening to the crows and squirrels squawking territorially as we passed them, or pausing at the fountain to watch the white finger jet explode like a firework, something happened. The boy's agitation left him like a spell lifting. In its place came a calm, thoughtful demeanour. A look of rapture. Watching him, I felt a curious mixture of sadness and envy. Impossible not to see plainly the strength of the child's attachment to Nature, his longing for the open skies of his former home. How swiftly he cast aside his experiences of the last few days and slipped into the present, how simple were his pleasures: water from the fountain. His eyes fixed on the light-filled darts. He grew quiet. His limbs seemed at last to belong to him, ceasing their convulsive motions.

We carried on. Although his pace did not slow when he saw something that caught his eye, he now allowed me to pause occasionally, so that he might sniff every twig, acorn or pine cone and listen with an alert expression to the rustlings of birds or rabbits in the shrubs. Our admirers stood behind us laughing and mimicking him, but none approached us. I was able to pause at La Fontaine Medicis and admire the restoration work of the architect Chalgrin for a few minutes. (He has finished three niches, which cry out for a little Venus or something similar, to fill their empty cavities.) The child stared towards the ducks and tugged at the rope. He managed to stretch it to the point where he could dip his head into the water. After lapping at it with his tongue, he shook back his newly shorn hair, spattering me with drops. Then I heard something so queer that it took me a moment to work out what it was. The boy was laughing.

Until this point, I had not believed that he could make such a sound. Of course, mention is made of it in Bonnaterre's report from Aveyron. *When the wind of the Midi blows, his bursts of laughter can be heard during the night . . .*

One might describe it as a giggle: his laugh is natural, light, childish. It is also deeply unsettling. I glanced around quickly to see what others – the onlookers – made of it. Two boys were laughing too, giving a passable imitation of the sound. But I was not surprised that they could only approximate it. Of course, none other than myself could know that this was the first time I had heard it. At first an answering giggle – a crazed giggle, the sort favoured by the inmates of Bicêtre – rose in my own throat, but by the time it reached my mouth it had twisted so giddily that it had transformed into a sob, escaping with a rude explosion, the way that wind escapes the gut. The boy laughed again. At the same time an old woman carrying a yapping dog, bedecked with ribbons, made a step towards us, shouting: is he the savage from Aveyron? In an impulse, an impulse to protect him and to escape from her, I flung my arms around him in a sudden embrace. He did not resist, although his body remained stiff and unresponsive. Beneath the soft white linen of his shirt I felt the bones of his shoulders; inhaled the soil and the woods in his rough hair. I knew that my tender outburst might frighten him, so drew away. Pulling at the rope, I quickened my step. I wanted to shout at the onlookers to leave us alone but when I turned towards them their number had increased and the words froze in my mouth.

He had given me a sign. I had heard his voice. That, for now, was enough.

We strode back towards the Institute with me holding the rope, very differently now: lightly, using only my fingertips. I felt ashamed of it and vowed to do without it in future. Onlookers pursued us, a dark persistent shadow, a hive of bees. From their calls and whistles I reasoned that some had heard of the boy, some were simply convinced that a crowd signifies importance and that they were obliged to swell its ranks. I hastened my steps. The savage is disconcerted by people in any number and I could feel by his tugs on the rope that he was becoming anxious. At one point the buzzing hive pressed on us to such a degree that the savage began flapping his arms, making little squeaks and showing with every sign of his body and face that he was afraid. The calm demeanour of a few moments before had completely deserted him. I sought a way to push through the throng.

An old man was shouting to me and after a moment I was able to hear his voice above the others. It took me a while to notice Citoyen Lemeri, the gardener at the Jardin du Luxembourg, especially as he is so short, his back bent from his hours working in the sun, like the warping of wood by a fire.

Doctor Itard! Here!

He motioned us into his building, little more than an ivy-covered hut. Entering it, the heat and sunshine of the day were sapped, instantly, as if a cloud had passed over the sun. The old man stretched out his arm to embrace the child, to usher him away from the crowd, so that we could close the door. When Lemeri saw, by the flicker of a gesture, that the frightened boy was about to resist him, he produced a pitcher and a glass of milk from a shelf in one corner and managed to coax the savage to drink. I knew he had drunk milk before. Bonnaterre says in his report that after an initial capture of the boy which failed, he continued living in the woods but wandered once or twice into villages, allowing the citizens there to feed him potatoes and milk, before disappearing again. Milk, Bonnaterre notes, was a favourite.

Unfortunately Lemeri was rewarded for his troubles by the child spraying the rough boards of his floor, marking his territory the way a beast does. The old man shook his head at the spreading stain in a gesture that might have meant *never mind*, or might have meant *the bastard!* Lemeri is a man of few words and limited facial expressions.

Citoyen, I must apologise, the boy is not *propre* – I said.

The old man shook his head, fetching some newspapers, which he used to mop the floor. This time the sweeping of his hand and his expression seemed clearly to indicate tolerance, and when he brought a handful of freshly picked mushrooms, and held them in his outstretched palm towards the child, I knew that my guess was right. The boy sniffed in his customary way and Lemeri laughed his old man's chuckle, nodding and patting the child's head as he ate.

We could still hear voices outside the hut and knew that the small crowd had not yet dispersed.

I have no difficulty in understanding his horror of crowds, I told Lemeri.

The old man regarded me shrewdly.

We've all seen *citoyens* doing things we could never have believed a human being was capable of, had we not seen it with our own eyes.

He spoke with pointedness. I felt in some way included in his damning of Revolutionary crowds and thus had an illogical but compelling desire to defend those citoyens he referred to so witheringly.

Desperation, hunger, *fear* will make a man behave like an animal, it's true –

And blood-lust, and the heat from a crowd, countered Lemeri, without waiting for the end of my sentence.

I saw at once that I had been wrong in my assessment of him, over all these years, as a man of few words. He is a man of very many words, few of them conciliatory ones. His only lack is a listener. I thought again of Uncle's warnings about those persons who so hastily dismiss the benefits of the Revolution. I thought I should summon a sharp response of great wit and political acuity, the sort of response that Uncle himself would have delivered. Instead I found myself stuttering and only mumbled that my fear of crowds originated long before – before recent events. Worse, I went on to say that from earliest childhood I remembered trembling behind my mother's skirts on every sort of social occasion, and once spent an entire evening under the table when my father had business associates to supper!

Lemeri's manner, the way he stroked at the side of his nose with one filthy earth-stained finger, was not encouraging.

To make amends I added a hearty laugh to show that I am well recovered now from my childish fears. Facing a mass of people – *pff!* Nothing to me. But as I spoke, I remembered that in agreeing to take up the position at the Deaf Mute Institute, I was committed to delivering an important paper to the Society of the Observers of Man, which would mean a large audience, made up of its sixty or so members in addition to guests. I was thinking of this and not of our present situation, but as I spoke I wandered over to the door and peered out through a makeshift window, little more than a moss-lined rectangle, the size of a brick, just below eye-level. I was glad to note that the onlookers were losing interest and had mostly moved on.

Lemeri busied himself pouring the boy a second drink of

40

milk. He watched the child drink, tipping back his head to drain the cup.

It is true then that his parents slit his throat and left him in the woods to die?

Lemeri's question was interesting to me as it revealed what the public has heard so far about the child and what their assumptions are about his origins. I gave a non-committal answer, presuming that Lemeri had noticed the white scar on the boy's neck.

We managed our escape eventually but not before I had endured quite a few more of Lemeri's opinions. I was relieved to discover that he is not entirely against the new Republic and is – thank God – not a Royalist either (he came out with a sobriquet for the Widow Capet more obscene than any I have yet heard) but instead a deeply religious man who finds it difficult to adjust to the details and not the essence; to the new day of rest for example and the looting of the churches. Although not unintelligent, he is not an educated man, but I was truly surprised when I mentioned a quote by Jean-Jacques Rousseau in passing, only to discover that he did not recognise it.

And you, a man of Nature, at one here with your garden! I exclaimed.

Lemeri gave me a quick look; a searching one, which I could not understand. Then he laughed shortly and went to fetch his brandy. He brought the bottle back to the table (it seems this is how he occupies himself when it rains, or in the twilight before the park closes, or rather, in the interests of accuracy, for most of the time) – and poured us both a tiny glass.

The boy was resting on his haunches on the floor between us as we spoke, preferring his position there to the chair Lemeri had offered him. Back and forth he rocked impatiently, the dirty floorboards accompanying him with a squeak, their rhythmic music attesting to the power of his desire to be outside again. He did not seem interested in us, except to sniff Lemeri once, then all his pots and shelves, his spades and other garden tools, the blades of grass sticking to the wheelbarrow, the brandy glass, the pitcher, the bottle. Lemeri offered him two cherries, pulled from a jar of brandy on a window ledge: the child sniffed them too and then leapt as if on fire, thumping his chest a few times, before crumpling to the floor to take up his crouching position again.

Lemeri and I surveyed him for a moment.

When you regard such a barbarous creature, Doctor, you can see exactly what the church means by original sin . . . If ever evidence were required that man needs the word of God to civilise him, then – boff! that boy is it, Lemeri announced, jerking his glass towards the child.

There is nothing worse than a discussion where one is assumed to agree with the exact opposite of what one believes. I never understand how it happens, and yet it does. There have been many occasions in my life when I've found myself firmly entrenched in a particular position with no memory of how I arrived there. For instance, only a few hours ago, did not Madame Guérin hint in that repulsive feminine way that I had expressed an interest in her wretched daughter, a girl I have never met!

In vain I tried explaining to Lemeri Rousseau's premise of the child born not in original sin but in innocence; a child whose instincts are towards freedom and the natural pursuit of his own needs, exactly like our boy here. One who has no consideration for the conventions of society, no embarrassment about being naked and no concern whatsoever for what others might think of him. My annoyance at Lemeri's assumptions may well have had the upper hand, or else a general anxiety about being misunderstood on this point. In any case, my words lurched and tripped, with much stuttering and stumbling. Lemeri was not persuaded.

The child in the corner chose that moment to expel the

gas in his stomach as loudly as possible. Here Lemeri nodded sagely.

And it's your job, Doctor, is it, to learn him? The ways of the world, how to sit at a table and fart on the pot, that kind of thing, eh?

Again, I felt cornered into a statement I did not make. Such are the tricks of discourse, of language. Lemeri has one of those confusing faces. His grey beard curls distractingly around his mouth and chin, often blurring or disguising his expression. I found myself most of the time watching the creases at the corners of his eyes, with a strong suspicion that he was laughing at me.

Well, although of course our customs must be explained to the boy, my main concern is not just those matters –

Not just farting then?

No, matters of far greater –

I was forced to shout, since the child's impatient rocking and the accompanying squeaking were becoming insistent. With a sigh I gave up my point and instead downed my brandy in one gulp and picked up my hat and cane. And then something happened for which I was quite unprepared. At the sight of my movement towards the hat, the boy leapt up in great excitement, his hand reaching for the locked door.

Lemeri chuckled.

Doesn't like to be indoors, does he now?

But is it not remarkable? He knew that my hat and cane signified an intention to leave . . .

Well, that's not so impressive, Doctor, if you don't mind me saying. My dog knows as much. When I fetch my coat, his tail wags like a fishwife's tongue.

Now the gardener was becoming irritating. This is my first sign that the child has intelligence, that he is thinking, remembering, *predicting*. I wanted a moment to savour it. After all, it is only a matter of months since the wild boy first came across these strange objects: hats and canes. Seen

43

like that, it is extraordinary that he should so soon ascribe to them their relevance to our comings and goings. I decided not to explain this to Lemeri. This wonderful new Republic of ours might well be unique in bringing a gardener and a doctor together in discourse but, given the novelty of the scenario, one should not be surprised if things do not progress smoothly. That men are born equal is naturally a given; but that their education and learning are *not* equal, an unavoidable fact too.

I really cannot be blamed if I find trying to talk to a gardener not an altogether comfortable experience.

I emerged from Lemeri's hut with the boy, his rope held lightly in my hand, the brandy making my head swivel. Noticing the child's exaggerated sniffing I was aware for the first time of how pungent is the scent of the giant sequoia that we stood beneath. Also the piles of horse manure, which the child so delighted in dipping his head to inhale. This time, if we had determined followers, I was not conscious of them. All I could feel was the trot of the child beside me, the difference in his gait, the way he led with his nose thrust forward, his chin jutting. My usual ponderous walk was transformed into a ridiculous gallop, but for all that, it was enjoyable. I cannot remember the last time I *ran* in Paris, or trotted as I did just then, with relish, swinging my arms and laughing. The late afternoon sky hung over the Jardin du Luxembourg as if a billowing cloth; a warm rain threatened. A couple of drunks sat on a bench and held out palms and tongues to welcome the drops; a pair of lovers with arms entwined held the man's black overcoat in a tent above them, nestling together. A dog with an injured leg ran crookedly beside us, yelping as we flew past, but we outran that and the worst of the summer rain, arriving at Madame Guérin's in perfect time for supper.

Here's the wild boy at Madame Guérin's kitchen table, groomed, clean, surrounded by a throng of visitors. The dark shapes chatter and fling their words at him, strike instruments across his head like tuning forks. They open his mouth as if he were a horse. They jump back when he sprays the floor, scold him when he lashes out.

He sees only noise. A great murmur envelops him, a cloud. He can't escape it. Stiff white linen scratches at his throat, his cuffs. Smells assail him, his tongue throbs with the new stinging tastes. She presses him, she screams at him. There are no spots of light to lose himself in, no green, no soft warm mud to cover his eyes. He puts his hands over his eyes and the visitors, the dark hats, peel them away again.

Not the wretched gloves, that night I dreamt I'm perched high in the branches of a tree, something I'm sure it's true to say that I have not indulged in since I was a girl, and holding a gun. Down beneath me is a giant white anthill. Someone gives an order to shoot and now pouring out from the holes in the anthill two wolves are running, running fast and scattering. Then a third wolf emerges from the biggest hole and this wolf, she is ferocious, yellow teeth dripping with saliva, you know: the kind of detail that some dreams are full of, details that almost force you from your bed, so vivid they are. She makes sure I understand (the way a body does understand in dreams) that she is the mother. She is tense, ready to spring. Protecting her cubs inside.

But then from nowhere, two arrows pierce her flank. She falls silently and with no trace of blood. I hold onto my gun but I make no attempt to fire it. Even now I am awake I can remember the feeling of my hands around the barrel, cold and heartless as a Royalist's prick.

The men upturn the anthill using their guns and spears to turf out the mound and unearthing the monkey-ball of cubs inside and now villagers are gathering, murmuring in terror, saying that monsters live in the anthill. I creep down from the tree and join the crowd to stare at the cubs.

45

Someone has a smart idea, to throw a blanket over the ball to separate them. Then what they are becomes plain for all to see: two girl children. Giant heads of matted hair atop skinny bare little bodies, bodies scarred all over with pock-marks and scars, signs of vicious fighting. Their bodies look just like the body of the savage. Even in my sleep I know it. The girls snarl like wolves. They crouch on all fours, they snap and hiss when anyone approaches. Everyone is afraid of them.

We've killed their mother! one of the villagers shouts.

How will they survive now? Their tender bodies, their blunt little breasts – forever scarred by the forest, all alone in a strange world without a mother? We've killed their mother.

Then I woke up and, as I did, a picture of Joseph floated in front of my eyes. My little Joseph at a few hours old. His tiny white monkey face, his matted fair hair, everything about him still tightly wound like a rose-bud that hasn't opened out yet. *How will he survive so tiny and so helpless?* His little arms flailing, his little legs kicking, all alone without a mother to hold him, to nurse him at her breast with her own precious milk? *How will he survive?*

I was awake by then but not my Henri. He sleeps like one without a conscience, or maybe I should say, someone without a memory. You might think this would make me lonely but how would it help for both of us to suffer?

I knew what I had to do. The child is all alone. He has a scar at his throat from a hand the doctor said was not practised. Those were his words, and I have taken them to heart, I find some comfort in them. Not practised. Not practised is not the same of course as not intentional, but there is comfort there just the same.

I rose up at the first cries of the rooster in the Institute gardens, as I do every morning, but this morning I could smell hot dank animal before I had even opened my eyes. My

46

waking thought was so stirred in with dreams that I believed at first that a fox had leapt in through our windows in the night and was sleeping right there on my bolster beside me. Then I spoke severely to myself, saying Marie-France, you are letting fancy have the upper hand with you. This did the trick.

There was no sound from his room so to shore myself up with courage I set to making up a good fire from a pile of wood and put a pan on to boil and when I'd set the wood to crackling and snapping and the smoky sweet smell of burning cedar filled my kitchen, only after all of that did I feel recovered enough from last night's fears to venture to look in the savage's room.

I made a little start as I peeped through the keyhole. The boy was wide awake and sat in the position he seems to favour most; the one he was adopting when I first acquainted myself with him, rocking back and forth on his heels in the posture of a crouching monkey. He had picked up a piece of straw and was passing it through his teeth first one way then another with great slowness and his big dark eyes were dreamy and downcast.

Well, raised by wolves or no, the boy must be hungry and I touched my key to the lock. I was still startled when he sprang up and could not prevent myself from uttering a little cry of *oh, Dieu!* Which seemed to have the same effect on the savage as his springing up had produced in me and the door, which by now I had unlocked, swung open and the two of us surveyed each other. It would have been hard to say whose fear was the greatest. The wretched little devil chose that moment to piss all over my clean floor. That was enough to break the spell between us. I ran at him, shouting and pointing out the chamber-pot and making a great undignified pantomime to show him what I meant by it. He acted like the most ignorant heathen giving me not the least sign that he understood me until I yanked him up by his flimsy little wrist and marched him into the kitchen, bundling his sodden bedcovers under my arm and cursing freely. (The doctor says the boy can hear perfectly well and it's true that the tiniest chink of a key will make him twitch but when it comes to language he gives so little indication of understanding that I feel at liberty to act as if his ears are full of grass.)

You must be hungry, boy, and here you will find that if you behave yourself as befits a child of your age and make yourself useful you will be well provided for, I told him, in my firmest voice.

Later, Henri was sitting by the fire in the kitchen enjoying his sweet rolls and a plate of eggs, when the boy rushed past him in a great whirlwind, snatching the bread from his plate before sniffing it, and flinging it on the fire. Well of course Henri jumped up and grabbed the nearest weapon – a wooden spoon – brandishing it with a great show of menace. This seemed to concern the boy not one whit. He stood with his back to the fire, calmly sniffing his fingers, with an expression of disgust. Henri's face was a delight. I hid my mouth behind my hand, to prevent him from seeing my expression.

We can't live with this beast! I had not a wink of sleep . . . began Henri.

You slept like a log, I corrected him.

I was pouring the child a cup of milk, which I've noticed he has a great craving for. I held out the bowl and the boy crept forward and took it, then moved back to his position in front of the fire.

Henri tried another tactic. He is too much extra labour for you, he said, indicating the sodden bedcovers, piled on the floor.

My duties have been greatly reduced. I'm to cook lunches and aid Doctor Itard, who plans to teach the boy right here in our home. The exact sum has only been hinted at.

How much?

Enough. It frees me to take better care of you.

Henri replaced the spoon on its rack above the stove. He began coughing and, although his back was turned to me, I could imagine well enough the expression on his face. He took his hat and unlatched the door without a further word, as was his custom at this hour, but as he opened the front door, the boy – moments ago as still as any wax doll – sprang to life as if a flame had shot through him and pushed past Henri and onto the stairs.

I was after him in a shot but a woman of forty is no match for a boy of twelve who has lived these last years like a deer in the wilderness. I had lost sight of him by the time I was down to the bottom flight of stairs, my only consolation being that the walls of the Institute, provided the gate was firmly locked, would certainly provide him with a challenge. Panting, holding my ribs and with the other hand attempting to clasp my fichu more firmly over my bosom, I ran towards the vegetable gardens and the pond, knowing by some instinct that this might be his first choice. I spied him at once, sitting by the water. No other child was yet up from his room and the Institute was quiet. My breathlessness made it impossible to approach quietly, but in any case the child gave no sign of noticing me. He sat on the side opposite the willow and bent his head towards the water just exactly like that tree did. His eyes were fixed on the pond. He sat by an urn, his shirt flapping around his skinny thighs, his small hand tapping the surface of the water, watching the ripples fan out.

Come now, boy, the doctor will arrive soon. I spoke gently. My cajoling voice again. Come, boy. We need to go back.

I took two steps towards him, and I assure you they were careful steps; measured, cautious, not hurried in the least. Designed not to startle him, nor increase his fear of me. All that notwithstanding, the moment I was within grasping distance of him, with an odd little twitch of his head he tugged himself away from me and dived headfirst into the water, with the speed of a kingfisher spearing a fish. Seconds later he burst out, throwing back his head, splattering the air around him with his great shock of dark hair. That little bastard laughed like a child possessed.

Water is what the boy misses. Here, water only happens when she brings it to him, in the bucket or bowl, in the big tub or in a small one, to drink. He stands by the window, holding the glass and sipping slowly, his eyes raised above it to stare outside. That way he can see the green, the leaves, trees reflected in the water in his hand. He can lift the trees up, tip them down his throat, drink them.

It does not move much, this water. It doesn't bubble or sing. There are circles of silver in his glass and the moon around the edges, on days when it does not have the trees. The best part is that no one disturbs him when he drinks his water. He is allowed to hold it and watch the circles, the green and yellow and the silver shake and blur, break up and join again. He is allowed to sip as slowly as he likes.

Fructidor 14
Year Eight

This week I intend to start work with the boy in earnest. He is rather more settled in his new home and new routine with his kindly governess and I believe he is ready for his first instruction. I have been refreshing my memory for Condillac's work and have identified five priorities.

Firstly, to make his new life more pleasant to him. He has a strong attachment to the wilderness, and his only passions so far are to eat and to sleep. His only pastime is to sit on his haunches, rocking or staring into space. I will instruct Madame Guérin to do all in her power to make his life physically comfortable, with a warm bed and his favourite foods, a vigorous walk (or rather, run) twice a day, many warm baths. (She was surprised that I should favour warm baths over cold but I told her it was a new experiment of mine, entreating her to have patience with it.)

Secondly, to awaken his senses. I have already observed that smell is his most powerful sense. He sniffs everything and everyone, the way a dog does. He sniffs his food and refuses meat and bread, and most cooked items. He cannot abide wine and on one occasion, when he was impatient and in great haste, he took a huge swig by mistake, then ran about screaming and spitting.

He seems strangely insensitive to pain – the scalding heat of a potato straight from the pan of boiling water, for instance, or the burning sensation from a pinch of snuff. Twice now I have pushed the snuff into his nostrils only to discover that he does not even sneeze, nor appear in the slightest disturbed! We must see what we can do to refine his sense of touch. This will be most effective if I first excite his emotions. So far I have observed extremes of joy and anger, but little of the subtle and infinite range of emotions of which human beings are capable.

His hearing, as has already been noted in the example of the chestnut cracking, is inconsistent. One might even say that he chooses what he wants to hear – ignoring requests to put his shoes on or come to the dinner table, but pricking up his ears at the sound of the ladle touching the pitcher of milk, or the key in the lock. He has an unnatural – that is, passionate – interest in keys. He spends many hours sniffing and exploring any key that he is given. We are currently observing this interest and I am puzzling over ways to make use of it in my work.

The limits of his vision – looking not quite at you, but slightly past you – this I have yet to fully explore.

As for his sense of taste, we have tried to tempt him with any number of sweet treats that a child his age would normally desire, only to be disappointed. One is tempted to conclude that a child whose palate has been shaped by the wild from such a formative time might always prefer a simple glass of water, or the sharpness of berries and the mouldy taste of mushrooms, grasses and nuts to the more natural delights of sugar, honey, alcohol and cured sweetmeats.

My third objective is to expand his world by giving him new desires. A child of this age (twelve, I have decided, more through a wish to be decisive than through conclusive evidence) should be floating his boat on the pond in the Institute gardens or knocking down nine-pins, or chasing his ball or hoop. I intend to introduce him to all the wonderful toys and distractions that the civilised world can offer and to teach him new ways to occupy his time rather than his present choices: idle contemplation of nature, filling his belly, emptying his bowels and bladder, running madly about, laughing, shouting, sniffing, or sleeping.

My fourth intention is of course to teach him to speak.

My fifth and last goal is to teach him the use of tools.

I intend to present to the Institute in a year's time a boy perfectly unrecognisable from the filthy, wild, God-forsaken creature they first observed. I also intend to prove that *idiot* is wholly the wrong diagnosis for the child; that it is environment and its effect on the individual which have the greatest impact on a person and that we are each and every one of us the result not of an accident of inheritance, but an accident of circumstance.

On my way to Madame Guérin's quarters this morning, striding through the gateway of the Institute grounds, I collided with Doctor Pinel. He was preoccupied as usual; his countenance wore a harried expression, his brows knitted together. On seeing me he stopped short and ventured a smile, slowing his step. He seems at great pains to show me he bears me no malice for my public disagreement with him, the stance I have taken. Naturally, instead of stemming my guilt, his kindness only increases it.

Bonjour, Doctor! Our greetings clashed, sounding more like an attempt to out-shout one another. How is your wild boy this morning, Jean-Marc? he asked me, and the use of my first name unnerved me still further, so that I could only mumble: he is sleeping . . . I do not know . . . I have yet to meet him . . . which, the instant I uttered it, struck me as foolish, since it sounded as if I have not met him yet, which is not what I meant at all.

Then to compound matters, a blood-curdling shriek was heard from Madame Guérin's apartment and I was compelled to hurry in that direction, without offering explanation. As I rushed away from Pinel I had two impressions simultaneously. One was of the great doctor leaning against the giant elm tree, watching me as he opened his leather wallet of snuff and pressed two huge pinches into his nose. The second impression was a memory, one to which I have given so little thought that I was startled by my ability to recapture it in such detail. I was picturing my father, with his huge hat, leaning against a tree and watching me leave, after he had delivered me into the instruction of my uncle at Riez. Racing away from Pinel, I remembered an impulse I had felt at eight years old to wave to my father. Naturally I stifled my childish desire, instead plunging my hands deep into my pockets, composing my face in an attitude towards Uncle that would betray nothing. Escaping the solitary figure of Pinel, knowing him to be watching me, but not looking back, I felt eight years old again, with something terrifying hovering in front of me, beating great wings in front of my face.

I considered this memory to better understand its appearance at that precise moment. My conclusion did not reflect well on myself. Is it that I was seeking approval from Pinel – a wave of his hand – permission perhaps, for something?

Why should this be, when I am confident of my predictions about the child and confident of the erroneous nature of Pinel's prognosis? Time did not permit me to reflect on this. Arriving at Madame Guérin's, I was immediately immersed in domestic drama.

An astounding sight met me on entering the kitchen. The gardener and daughter – I assumed it to be the daughter, a young woman of slight build with a mass of undressed dark hair obscuring her face – were holding the wild boy firmly in his chair, whilst his governess bent over him, holding a pair of scissors. The floor was covered by a great mound of thick dark circles of hair. It looked as if some strange beast had been killed in that kitchen and scattered feathers or fur everywhere. Indeed, there was much truth in that perception, for the boy I could now see in the midst of that huddle was quite a different creature from the one I saw yesterday. All four were in such deep concentration that they did not hear me knock and enter. The screams, I gathered, were from the daughter, who was quick to shriek whenever the child bared his teeth at her. He seemed to understand this – or even to enjoy its effects – for he used the threat often. Monsieur Guérin, a great giant of a man, but with a gentle disposition, as far as I can tell, did not shirk from his task, keeping the boy firmly fixed in the chair.

Good day, Madame Guérin! I called out, as loudly as I could. I felt like an intruder. Something about the scene immediately advertised itself to me as intimate, a scene a family endures in private. It has been so long since I was part of any family that I believe I am unduly sensitive to this. I wished I had knocked and waited before entering.

Madame Guérin was unperturbed. She did not turn around but continued with her snipping and her commands to the child to sit still and be patient. She did not welcome the 'uninvited guests' that the boy's hair was teeming with and she certainly did not want them running wild in her kitchen.

Only the girl seemed conscious of my arrival. She turned to me with a courteous nod of the head and I saw at once that she *was* familiar to me. Cuvier was right; I had occasionally seen her at the military hospital, amongst the nuns, in the uniform of a nurse.

Doctor Itard, she said politely. We are – Maman is – she gave a wave of her hand. Her point was obvious. The boy needs a haircut.

The three of them moved away from the child, releasing him. He shot from the chair and towards the front door, which I had not closed properly on my arrival. Monsieur Guérin was quickest to see the danger and in a flash had kicked it shut. He then reached to the very top of the door, closing an enormous shiny bolt (clearly a new addition). At the sound of this bolt sliding across the boy fell on the floor and set up a great howling.

To my surprise the daughter crumpled like a doll, falling on the floor beside him. She moved so quickly, with so little self-consciousness, that one might mistake her for a child of the same age, not a young woman. She gathered her dark curls up in one hand, so that she could put her face close to his.

Come now, don't be sad, it's not so bad here. Look, little boy, Maman will prepare you a drink, and we can find you your favourite keys to play with . . .

A cup of milk was produced. The boy sat up eagerly to drink it, abandoning his howling so quickly that it was difficult not to assume he had been play-acting. He sniffed the girl – even I could smell the hospital carbolic, overlaid with a cloying smell of sweet violets – then allowed himself to be petted on the head by her. He looked quite different, newly shorn. His small white face, the pointy chin, the big eyes and beautifully curved eyebrows, all were more open, more discernible. I could finally see his face properly. He now appeared younger. Old scars, the white tattoos of some ancient battle, were now visible near the hairline. Again his eyes roamed quickly over and around me, barely brushing me and then focused just beyond me, over my shoulder.

Do you feel as if he *sees* you?

The Guérin daughter did not seem startled by my question or the lack of introduction between us. Her reply was confident and quick.

Oh, yes. He looks very, very quickly, takes in everything he needs to and then looks away again. It is as if it hurts him to meet our eyes.

The gardener slumped into a chair, breathing heavily. Madame Guérin was sweeping the great loops of brown hair into a pan. She paused on her knees to say to the daughter: offer the doctor a drink, will you, Julie? And then to me she said gruffly: I have spent the best part of the morning trying to dress him. He has the strongest aversion to clothes.

If the boy will not wear clothes, let him freeze, was my suggestion.

I put it to Madame Guérin that when the colder weather arrives we should leave him in his room without a fire and with his clothes clearly visible and within reach. In time he would learn that in order not to feel the cold, he should dress himself. She seemed doubtful of my plan but in her usual taciturn way did not express this. A mere sigh and *oh, Dieu* was the sum of Madame Guérin's comments.

The daughter had none of the mother's reticence.

Is it true he survived the bitter winter of 94 in the mountains? He must be hardened to the cold . . .

I admitted that this was true.

And is it true – I heard a story, so sad it was –

Yes, it is likely that someone slit his throat. Attempted to kill him. Left him for dead in the forest, where he survived for, we believe, between five and seven years –

Oh, it is evil, *evil*! Heartless, cruel – what wicked devil could do such a thing? They deserve – I would – pah! The guillotine is too good for them.

I found this young woman's language immoderate, her ideas sentimental. She did not seem to see any illogic in her violent expression of hatred for persons whose motivations or circumstances she had no knowledge of and I told her so. I did not add – although I believe it to be true – that it was exactly this type of improvident remark and heated sentiment which fanned the flames of anger and mistrust between strangers and neighbours in the years we have just endured.

I do not care to understand the motivations of such persons! It is *unthinkable*, a little boy of five years old, to *imagine* –

But imagination is sometimes all we have! I told her. I was surprised to experience a quickening of my heartbeat as I spoke, a feeling close to anger.

Nothing is unimaginable. We must never refuse to imagine . . . I said, with more control.

Julie appeared not to have heard this statement, for she did not reply. She was fiddling with a cheap locket she wore on a piece of violet ribbon around her throat, but for the longest moment, she refused to lower her eyes. Then, with one of her sudden movements, she switched her attention entirely to the newly shorn boy, coaxing him to the table with the help of a plate of lentils. There appears to be no end to his appetite and in the days that I have observed him, he has already grown visibly plumper, although he is still painfully thin. I sat down opposite him at Madame Guérin's invitation and accepted my cup of chocolate and the brioche she presented me with. The boy sat opposite me, a few shreds of cropped hair on his neck and throat, cramming his mouth with the food, splattering lentils onto the table in his haste to squash the greatest number into his mouth in the briefest possible time.

He has not breakfasted? I asked.

Oh, he has eaten aplenty! He takes anything he pleases –

It was then that I noticed. Whenever Madame Guérin said her customary *Oh* in that accent she has, the child responded. If she was behind him, he turned around. If she was near him, his eyes flickered and his head jerked – only a little, but enough. It seemed only to be the word *oh* which produced this response. I decided to experiment.

Is it possible to bring me some water, please, Madame Guérin? *Oh*, thank you. *Oh!* That's delicious.

Madame Guérin eyed me suspiciously. I was watching the child for his response. She is a quick thinker and soon understood what I was doing. *Oh!* Would you like some more, Doctor? she offered. Or, *Oh!* perhaps you would like some, Julie? The latter she directed at her daughter, who held out her glass and accepted with an *Oh*, thank you of her own.

Yes! He does hear it. He moved, didn't he? This achievement, slight though it was, was declared with a sense of great excitement.

We agreed that it was true, the child seemed to respond whenever the sound *Oh* was uttered. Julie sat down at the table and began a test of her own: *Oh*, what a clever child you are! *Oh*, you do hear us after all, but perhaps you only hear some of the words, not others?

And so it was that I made the most useful discovery of the child's ability to distinguish some words, or rather vowel sounds, from others. Naturally, having been so little exposed to language during his developing years it is not surprising that he is slow to discern one sound from another within the noisy babble which must be human language to him. Doubts about his hearing must be revised. He hears what he needs to. In the forest, his ability to hear a pine cone or twig cracking would alert him to danger; his ability now to hear keys turning in locks alerts him to the possibility of escape. Other sounds he may reject, deciding that they are of little use to him. I once believed it natural for children to develop their hearing in a fixed pattern, without giving due regard to the context in which they learn these sounds. I must revise this too and state that even in this area, culture, it appears, plays its part. This discovery bodes very well for the savage's future ability to learn to speak. I have high hopes of it.

It is also through this discovery that I have decided on a name for the boy. I made the choice of Victor. When it is spoken in a loud voice, he never fails to turn his head. It contains the 'oh' sound that he seems to recognise most easily and has proved a great success.

Little other work was done. Our spirits were high and all that was managed was a quick walk with 'Victor' around the grounds. The triumph we felt at discovering the child could isolate and identify a single vowel might be difficult for an outsider to appreciate. I say 'we' rather than 'I'; so convinced am I of Madame Guérin's extraordinary commitment and suitability to her new role. It is good to feel that there is another human being who cares as much as I about the progress of this lonely child.

Once home I could not sleep and paced my room until past midnight, when Madame Richard banged on the ceiling of the room below mine with her cane, to point my attention to the hour. Her evil little pug, Fanfan, echoed her by barking in sharp raps. Monsieur Itard, my poor little Fanfan, she cried. Would I keep the poor darling awake all night? For answer I stamped my feet on the floor in return. I soon regretted my fit of temper and instead lit a fresh candle from the dying embers of the fire so that I might still myself, sit quietly at my desk and write up the day's events.

The child has a name, I wrote, and with it has surely entered human society. No one has need of a name in the forest. No one has need of a name when he is utterly alone, especially if he has no concept of himself. A name, something to be called by – it announces our arrival in the world.

As for Julie Guérin, I believe she too will be useful in my work. Her passionate outburst and violent language must in some degree be attributed to her youth, her lack of a proper education. It has only strengthened my belief in the value of an education which teaches us how to question our prejudices, hold our hearts up to the light, to be scrutinised, measured. She has a certain manner with the boy – not warm and motherly like his governess – more the playful feminine approach of a sister. As I never had a sister of my own, perhaps I romanticise the relationship; however, a boy of his age can benefit much from feminine caresses. In fact, I left Madame Guérin with instruction to increase the child's baths to three a day, and to supplement them with rigorous massage over his entire body to awaken his senses. I am sure this will have a stimulating and remedial effect on him. I will eagerly note his progress.

He likes her, I can tell, our Julie. You would not say his eyes are fixed on her but then he would never be so plain as that, so *evident*. Naturally he disagreed with every word she said but that's as you would expect too, when a learned doctor meets a girl not quite sixteen whose only schooling was done by her mother and is apt to speak her mind before she has measured it. It is as if he lights up, he changes, when she's in the room. She plays to it, of course. Swishing her skirts, flouncing more than usual. It made me smile, noticing it and having to act as if I never did. Well it is no surprise really. It is a rare male who can resist our Julie.

The doctor stayed for supper. Henri joined us at the table, although he is no better and had to leave twice when the coughing was so bad that he was in danger of blowing the bread right off the plates. The moment never arrived to ask the doctor about Henri's health, about whether he would be willing to bleed him, or donate to us some other medications, or just the benefit of his expensive professional advice. All talk was about the savage. It was not a restful supper. The boy ate like the worst kind of beast, food spraying everywhere. Anything he saw he seized, no matter whose plate it might be on and if it did not please him he spat it out. Twice he stood up, farted loudly, and sat back down again to grab another plate full of beans. Julie laughed but the rest of us acted like it was our regular custom.

Then we were interrupted by visitors, three men in black coats and stiff collars and fancy hats wanting to 'discuss' the boy with the doctor, but really it seems to me wanting to fill my kitchen with their snuff and their foreign talk and their sour smell of chalk and ink and too many old classrooms, then to prowl around and around the child, taking out their strange objects, measuring his head and peeking under his shirt, until the wretched child is worse behaved than ever. When finally they left, the cassoulet was in need of reheating on the pot hook and the boy was wound tight as a clock and bounced from the table to the floor with repeated movements, in between grabbing a piece of bread from someone's plate or a hot potato from the trivet and after this shrieking as if someone had attacked him, although he never had the sense to throw it back.

Amidst all of this the doctor asked questions, constant questions and politeness forced me to answer them, although most times my back was to him, wiping a spilled drink from the floor or turning an upset plate the right way up. Did I come to Paris a long time ago, he wanted to know, and where did I grow up and he was 'intrigued' (his word) that I grew up in a village in Aveyron and I knew the village where the boy was eventually captured. Then a long conversation about Millau, the glove capital of the world he said, and a great long description of some 'exquisite kid gloves in finest grey leather' that he possessed, he thought they came from there, and all I could think throughout all that talk of fine stitching and 'butter-smooth leather' was the toughness of the material, how it bites at the needle, how sometimes you felt as if you were stitching your own skin. One time (but I did not tell the doctor this) that is exactly what I did: I was so tired and the candle was down to a flat saucer of wax and then Henri startled me, he must have been fifteen or so and already courting we were, that great boyish lump, knocking on the window and I leapt up, and what had I done but sewn a finger of the glove to the skin of my own thumb.

Yes, said Doctor Itard to my offer of more wine and more bread, munching his way through another plate of bulots. (Funny how these were of no interest to the child, although I know we had them back home when I was a girl.)

Did you ever hear of the boy? he asked me, which made no sense, as I told him (in between yelling at the child for snatching the last bean from Henri's plate), since I left some years ago. But oh yes, we did hear of other such boys, wolf children, children who grew fur in strong moonlight and long nails and roamed the woods, looking for human babies to eat. Yes, we knew of them. And would you like a pear, Doctor, it's from the garden here, Henri picked them this morning? There were many such children.

Then he turned his questions to Julie and I was glad of the pause to allow me to wrestle with the boy over a plate he was insisting on banging on the table, one of my good ones from Sèvres – if he smashed that one I told him under my breath I would break his neck. The child laughed in that sudden way he has and held on all the tighter. (And if you are wondering how a woman like me comes to possess a piece of such value I say it is better you don't ask, but would add in my defence that you will travel far in Paris these days before you will find a woman who would *refuse* such a plate, if it fell into her hands.)

It was impossible not to believe that Victor knew exactly which one mattered most to me and was enjoying my anger. But just as suddenly the smile slid off his face and he handed it back. I understood at last, God knows why I could not fathom it, that he wanted me to fill it with more beans – now why did you not say so, boy? – so I turned to the trivet and filled his plate to the top, only to discover when my back was turned that he had swiped the half-finished plate from under the doctor's nose and was now tucking into that instead.

Julie laughed and made the comment that the boy had been hungry for a long time – many a long year, she said with that terrible dramatic sympathy she is fond of conjuring up for every last waif and stray – and it was all I could do, I had to bite my tongue not to say, well weren't we all, hungry, I mean? But then you, my girl, are too young to remember.

Julie and the doctor were discussing the theatre, well not discussing since the doctor said that he never goes and made it clear with a little sniff and a stiffening of his neck, fiddling with that linen cravat so tightly wound there that it's more a bandage than a collar, that he does not approve of the theatre. Well, of course, Julie has never been, but she reads the *Gazette* and it pleases her to act as if she has, so she asked him about that play, this one by Pixérécourt called *Victor, the Forest's Child*? Why not take Victor to the theatre, given that the play is all about him and Doctor Itard said: the theatre, the theatre, take Victor to the theatre? He repeated it just like that, pushing his chair back from the table and wiping his mouth with his serviette and I could not tell, though I could guess, what he might mean by a long-eared question like that.

Henri's head nodded against his chest. He was breathing with a rattle as if a snake lived there; the savage was on the floor searching for stray beans, and farting gaily. I dared not open a window, as he would surely climb through it.

Julie, I can tell, was piqued that no one was taking her suggestion seriously and she was keen to show the doctor the range of her knowledge on the subject. She fiddled with the ribbon on her bonnet, a purple and white striped silk ribbon, that I happen to know cost her more than I spend a week on bread, and she was asking more and more questions about the great Doctor Pinel and was it true it was he who had called for the inmates of the Bicêtre to be unchained, and had such a great man, a champion of imbeciles throughout the world, already examined the child and declared him an idiot, because she read that in the *Gazette* too and it also said that Pinel was firmly of the belief that the child will never speak, nor learn to read and is, in fact, less intelligent than most animals, his imbecility having probably been the result of a fright during his mother's confinement, or else the after-effects of teething troubles . . .

It was unfortunate for her that the name Pinel seemed to have a queer effect on Doctor Itard. He stiffened further, like a man who has just sat on his own cane and replied carefully: we did not get to the point we are at in this great moment of our history *Citoyenne* Julie (now I notice he did not use the term earlier in the evening, when things were more cordial) by accepting as a given everything our elders and *betters* dish out to us . . .

Sadly, I did not hear the rest as out of the corner of my eye I caught sight of the child getting ready to stand up and I knew full well what he was about. He has the oddest, most disgusting and backward habits; squatting down to piss and standing up to shit. In an instant, I leapt from the table and excused myself as best I could, leading the boy roughly by the arm to his room, tugged at his breeches with great haste, and forced him down onto the pot. It all happened so speedily that he was too surprised to offer resistance. He stared at me and then past me with his big black eyes, his long lashes touching his brows, lifted his chin defiantly. He has no shame at all. I dropped my own eyes, turned away, told him that it's not right to look at a person's face during such a private act and that he should learn to take care of his own needs because he won't catch me playing this game for much longer. Of course,

I've no idea whether he understood me. But we returned to the kitchen table with our hands washed and dignity intact.

Now they had moved on to politics, God help them. Henri was flushed with the wine and telling the good doctor what a fine Goddess of Reason I made in 93, although according to Henri I drove all thoughts of reason from a fellow's mind. Here matters were in danger of taking a saucy turn, so I did my best to interrupt, asking Henri to help me out and roast the coffee. He took his turn, winding the handle of the grilloir a few times, until the boy looked up from his place under the table to sniff at the sharp smell of roasting beans filling my kitchen. He jumped up and ran to the grilloir, sniffing at the drum which was hot no doubt and then jumped away again when Henri stopped winding and offered him the handle. Of course he would neither take a turn nor settle down: I fancied the sound of rattling beans troubled him. He only sat down again once the coffee was poured and in the cups and Henri was back in his seat beside the fire and finally nodding to sleep.

Julie had to remind me that the hour had come for her to return to the hospital; and I scarce had a chance to ask what would I do on my own with these two great dolts. She said, seeing my look, that she wasn't the one who made the rules. She knew this remark would make the doctor curious and sure enough he asked her, so she explained patiently that the abbé is very strict and she is never allowed to stay with us, no matter how sick her father might be. The doctor seemed unaware of this, being newly in his position here. Julie then went further to tell him how hazardous it was considered for a young woman like her to live in a school for boys and the doctor said of course, why yes, of course. He did not realise at all that she was teasing him. It is amusing to see a man of some authority – a man I judge to be well past twenty years of age – blush like a schoolboy.

Only the child shows no sign at all of being tired. That

boy had more wildness in him than usual. I despaired of ever making him sleep. Earlier today Henri added a second bolt to the door of the boy's room and I decided that the only solution was to take him there, lock him in and let him bounce around the walls until sleep wins him over. But Henri with his soft heart seemed to hear this suggestion, even though I believed him asleep, and roused himself instantly to arrive at a better solution. Instead he opened the front door, knowing the child would tear out and down the stairs, and sure enough he did. The doctor gave a small shout, following at a run, but Henri called: let him be, let him run around, the boy will soon tire and then we'll bring him in again.

There was a low full moon on the wane, slipping behind the Institute walls, shaped like a great red egg and fire enough to see by. The boy gave a whoop of delight fit to wake the dead, fit to wake the children who sleep here, deaf as they are, and sprang into the garden from the lowest stair. An owl burst from behind the great elm we call Sully's tree shouting *who! who!* at us, as well it might.

I followed him out there, folding my arms and pulling my fichu around me. Fine indeed for them, I said to myself. It will be me, tired as I am, who has to sit here all night. The doctor and Julie will leave, Henri will fall asleep and it's me who will be rounding the child up like a horse, long after the others are warm and snug and safe in their beds.

I must have fallen asleep. I woke with my back to the pear tree, sitting on the cold ground, cool darkness tickling me, a pear clasped in one hand. The little devil was still racing up and down with unearthly strength of purpose but without the red moon he was no more than a shadow and the sound of breath. I tried to rise, to call him in, but my legs were like melted sugar and I thought for an instant that perhaps I was still asleep, that the hard bark pressing through my fichu behind me and the dark figure skipping in front of me were

66

not real at all but one of my dreams. And then a moon rose, a fine white thumbnail of a moon and I thought how strange that a great red moon should shift to a fleck of one and then the boy's panting became louder and I felt his breath on my face and his voice, his little voice, soft as feathers, whispering to me. Well you know that child cannot speak, so dreaming it must be. I closed my weary eyes and the moon took its place again in the darkness behind my lids.

A fine white thread of a moon hangs between the trees, where a man walks with a child lolloping beside him. The boy, five years old, is barefoot; his feet crackle on sharp twigs and crunch the tough, petal-shaped segments of pine cones. After each noise he makes a little cry, his voice hitting the same note as a jay. The forest prickles with these noises; animals pause, crouch in their dens, shivering beneath wings or under stones; talons, whiskers, claws, twitching; poised, as they listen, sniff the air, suspend themselves. The child smacks noisily through all of this wariness, even occasionally breaking into a tuneless song, a cross between a hum and a growl; a racket, in any case. The father and son carry with them the smell of the village; the smell of fire and smoke and leather and roasting fat; of women and wet linen, of rye-bread and squalling damp babies. The forest sets itself against them, waiting for the smells, the sounds and the intruders to pass, so that it can resume itself, return to its business.

The father's jaw is set, teeth clamped together. He holds in one gloved hand his lit torch of woven sticks, scattering sparks on the wet, pine-steeped ground; in the other he carries his axe. His shoulders are raised up towards his ears, his hat pulled down towards his eyes. He can hardly see in front of him, keeps his eyes on the ground, trying to make out the blue-iced twigs, the moon-licked stones, the rise and fall of the earth beneath his feet. The child will follow, with no need of words, nor of a hand to hold. The child will not hesitate, not even when they begin to hear the first soft-muffled howl of a distant wolf, far into the deepest forest, where the white speck of moon, the red glints of flame can't penetrate. The boy is fearless or simple, or both. Only the father shudders at the voice of the wolf, draws his coat more closely around himself.

It has always troubled him, his son's fearlessness. Earlier today, when he'd said, with a cough, we're taking a trip, yes, a trip to the woods, there was a fleeting moment when he thought the boy knew. He even, for an instant, entertained the idea that the stones the child was gathering, filling his pockets with, were for the same purpose as the pebbles in the story, the purpose of finding his way back. But then he shook himself awake, he knew it was guilt talking. The boy doesn't think ahead like that. He gathered stones today for the same reason he has done every day and that is for no reason at all, or for devilry.

The child has only his terrible present and that's what makes him so unnatural. Caught in the glass hour like a genie in a bottle. A man without a past or future, without the ability to picture or mind about his future: is that a man at all, in any case?

The boy is like a slab of marble, nothing can dent him. He learns no lessons from experience. When the father beat him, only two days ago, for helping himself to the last dish of beans, with no thought for his father or step-mother, the belt might just have easily been hitting stone. Two days later – this very morning – he was caught in the larder again, drinking a pitcher of goat's milk that Félicité had been saving. This is what leaves him no option, this is why a simple beating can never be enough. This and his promise to the girl, to Félicité. The Simpleton, she calls him. She is only seventeen years old, no children of her own, a heart that has not been unfastened by the cry of a baby calling for her in darkness, the feel of a small heartbeat, steady beneath her own. Her body is smooth and dark and closed as the lake in summer; but when he dives into her she parts for him, like butter for a knife.

Deeper, deeper into the forest, a slide into darkness, into a route so twisted, so tangled and deep and shrouded, even to the creatures living there, that the boy could never, never in his wildest dreams, find his way back. The father is sweating. He smells himself – salt, heat – and knows that the animals must smell it too. It is the thought of her, the sound of her voice, murmuring close to his neck, her hand on the small of his back, low down, on his buttocks, pressing. Driving him, the way a farmer drives the steer; a pat on the backside, a hefty whack, if need be. He likes to think of it like this. Isn't this always the way? Driving, driving with her bad nature. How she bewitches him, how she squeezes out the boy. *What do you want to keep a simple boy for anyway? There's scarcely food for yourself, let alone another.* These are hard times. In every village there are families who take drastic measures to reduce the numbers of mouths to feed.

But the boy is not simple; he knows that. If only it were that easy. It is worse than that. The boy is in there somewhere, he has glimpsed him. Once – maybe twice, in five years, the way he has glimpsed the huge silver-backed wolf – only three times in as many years, but he knows it is there just the same. Dominique used to say he was like her uncle, a changeling baby: the fairies had the real one. She'd said this cheerfully, with love: she had no fear of him. But that was in a different time when there was still God and you could still pray: maybe she'd believed he would change. Her uncle, the changeling one, was a priest, too stubborn or guileless to sign the oath the Convention clamoured for, and when they burned down the little wooden church, they made sure he was in it. He was glad, glad to his soul, that Dominique was not alive to see that. So many things in the last four years that she with her gentle nature would have found impossible to believe. In some ways, he prefers it. Félicité, that is. She has grown up during a Revolution, wearing a blood-red ribbon round her throat, for fashion and remembrance. He knows from her cavorting, from her suggestions, that there is nothing too terrible for *her* to imagine. Her imagination, like all things about her, seems boundless.

She wants him to start all over. With her. He's thirty years old, a widow this past four years and no one has made him feel wanted like this. Not the boy. Especially not the boy. Thankless, his care of the boy. As he thinks this, as the word *thankless* forms, he is picturing the boy when his mother was still alive; a tiny, brown, mop-haired child on hands and knees, watching a spot on the floor in mysterious, self-absorbing delight. And when Dominique came to stand beside him and watch him, he makes no effort to call to her attention the mysterious object of his pleasure; the light speck dancing on the floor, a reflection through the window of a great cross that hangs from Dominique's neck, scattering patterns on the wooden floor.

It's for the best. Félicité is right when she says he makes no sign that he cares for us; why should we care for him? And that other time, that night when she wrapped her legs around him, the way a rider grips a horse, dripping her long red hair all over his chest and face, laughing at the sound of the child rocking himself in his crib beside them and whispered: saucy little devil: he's not human. He's not one of us, never was. That time, he knew, he knew he would do it.

That was the night that she came to him, long after he was spent, after he was exhausted, she came to him again, slipping barefoot through the sleeping houses to get there, bringing a candle. And lying in bed beside him, her sharp young breasts pushing through a muslin nightdress and her teeth bared, slowly pulling up the flimsy dress and saying: *You want it, do you? you can have it, forever more, Jacques Colombe, if you'll make me your wife* ... and then she turned on her stomach and raised herself up to show him what she meant, and he saw the pink glinting there like a mouth inside a beard, something no woman had shown him before, so boldly: and he rose high, high as a spire above the rooftops, so that although he was tired and spent he could not help it, he was all over her, he gave in to her, he knew he would do whatever she asked of him, now and forever.

Howls from the wolves weave between the tree trunks like wafts of smoke, but only the father shivers, raises his head to listen. He holds his torch a little higher. The animals are still far, but not so far. Father and son press on.

Part Two

Vendémiaire 14
Year Eight

The wild boy, Victor, has been with us for a number of weeks now. He is progressing well. Madame Guérin performs her duties with warmth and motherly devotion: I could not have made a better choice of guardian. He has a snug room to sleep in, we are increasing the amounts and varieties of food that he will eat; Madame Guérin and her daughter spend time tickling and massaging him and he rewards them with laughter. Against Rousseau's advice for cold baths, I advised hot ones – a hunch, no more, that they would not be debilitating and might sensitise him to temperature changes and enhance his comforts. Rousseau's aim, after all, was to produce a child of nature, impossible to manipulate; mine is the exact opposite. So far, his governess has not reported ill effects from the hot water, but the tickling and massage – for reasons I should perhaps have foreseen – have had to cease.

The abbé has made the library available for teaching duties. Either I collect him from the Guérins', or he is brought by his governess in the morning and I await him with the props I need for our work.

My heart was light, *light*, this morning, as I took the wide marble steps to the library two at a time. I paused, leaning on a banister, to recover my breath and for some reason I glanced up, possibly for the first time. I found myself bedazzled by a low and creamy autumnal light, and when my eyes had adjusted, I was able to marvel at the intricate spiral of the balustrade, as it wound towards the sky, creating a whorl of black and white, coiled like the delicate chambers of an ear. I had the most curious feeling as I climbed those stairs. All the ears I have gazed into, searching for their secrets, and now at last, it is as if I have laid down my instruments and stepped right in, to the vortex itself.

A fancy, of course. I did not share it with Madame Guérin.

When I work with Victor I request that she remains with us, to assist me. If Victor succeeds in his lessons, she pours him a glass of water from a pitcher, which he drinks with exaggerated slowness, usually standing by the window. This little reward could not please him more.

My greatest hurdle is to induce him to sit still and pay attention. He prefers to leap up, scamper around the room, tug on Madame Guérin's arm to beg her to take him for a walk, or scatter the books to the floor, or try the key in the lock. (He is not adept at this, but now, for security, we remove the key and place it on its hook out of his reach.) Once Victor seized my cane and hat, and thrusting them at me, pushed me towards the locked door. Madame Guérin tried to veil her smile behind her hand. I scolded her, reminding her of the importance of our united efforts; she sulkily replied that she thought I was searching for signs of his intelligence and there could be no doubt about Victor's meaning, muteness or no. I had to concede that this was true.

Finally, when the doughty governess and I have succeeded in making him sit still, progress can be made. I am teaching him his alphabet. We use metal letters and I fit them into slots on a wooden board I made myself.

Last week I arrived to find Madame Guérin and Victor already in the library. The governess leapt up on my arrival to tell me with excitement that the child had put all the letters in the correct order, holding out the crude board as proof. My delight vied with disbelief. I demanded, of course, that Victor repeat himself. I handed him the letters. I should have paid more attention to the way in which he grasped them, holding them as if they were a deck of cards. He did indeed carefully place them on the board, starting with the last letter, fitting it into the last slot and working backwards. At the same moment, Madame Guérin and I were both undeceived. He had simply reversed the order of letters given to him. He did not recognise the distinct shapes of the metal letters. A hasty shuffle of them – which now Victor was hopeless to place in corresponding slots on the board – proved our hypothesis. I was disheartened, but Madame Guérin pointed out that Victor's method was ingenious. She called him a 'clever monkey' which, of course, contradicts my scientific methods. The boy is lazy and endeavours to find the quickest solution to any problem without engaging his intellect. I told his governess to refrain from praising Victor, unless taking her cue from me.

A man without my persistence, my strength of character might by now be feeling somewhat disappointed by the slow pace of Victor's progress. To me, it is only further proof of the indelible imprint of Victor's experiences in the wilderness. For seven long years the child lived without the civilising influence of other human beings, without observing human behaviour, without a maman to fondle him with tender caresses, a papa to lead him by example. To expect him to cast off those barbarous habits in a matter of weeks is foolhardy. I have stated as much to anyone who cared to ask me, but the temptation to look for signs of progress where few exist is powerful, as the following example shows.

His walks – his runs – in the Jardin du Luxembourg remain his chief amusement. I have grown accustomed to the straggle of onlookers who besiege us and am better able to ignore them, although not to calm the beating of my heart. Now, as a habit more than a refuge, we regularly call on Citoyen Lemeri. I endure the man's prolixity for Victor's sake. The child anticipates a visit to Lemeri's hut with glee; but the source of this glee is no mystery. Lemeri never fails to provide

Victor with a large cup of creamy milk (and myself with a shot of brandy, which compensates me for the trouble of listening to him).

Yesterday Victor accidentally dropped the cup and the brown earthenware shattered. The milk was finished – that is, the cup was empty – but still Victor was upset, shrieking and falling to the floor to try to put the pieces back together. Lemeri assured him that it was no matter (unlike Madame Guérin who scolds him bitterly, as women are wont to do, if he breaks anything of hers) but Victor was not reassured. His agitation and squeaking increased and it was all I could do to calm his mood before we left to return to his quarters.

This morning, after our session at the library, Victor would not leave Madame Guérin's without first I allowed him to fetch something from the kitchen. He made this apparent to me, by tugging on my arm and using my hand, which he grabbed hold of, to help him reach the desired object. Victor often uses this gesture. Madame Guérin complains of it, grumbling that she is little more than a 'hand' to the boy, disliking the intensity of his grip and having some irrational dislike of hands, it seems. For myself, it fascinates me to see such a clear expression of his desires. Some weeks ago he grabbed Julie's hand, demanding that she ruffle his hair. I felt a pang of envy that the boy should seek her hand and not mine, but now I have no reason to feel bereft. Victor regularly clasps my hand, or the cuff of my jacket, and tugs me towards his goal. Bonnaterre had noticed in his original report that 'When someone stops tickling him, he grasps their hand to get them to continue' but I had not observed this for myself until that evening at supper with the Guérins.)

We ignored Madame Guérin's under-her-breath complaining and left the house in a great hurry, with Victor's booty. La Fontaine Medici in the Jardin du Luxembourg this morning held no charms. (Usually, I enjoy some snuff, watching the stone-smith at work, carving a little Venus – as I predicted

– in the central niche, while Victor prances in transports of delight, sinking his face into the water, or chasing a squirrel, or sniffing at the tree stump where it disappeared. The stone-smith makes a great show of not noticing us.) Today Victor was in no mood to linger. He tugged on my sleeve; we hurried to Lemeri's paltry hut.

The old man was waiting for us in the doorway, having heard the cackling of a few old women, laughing at my 'little dog' running beside me, wanting, they said, to pull his tail. Lemeri had the grace not to comment on my raised colour and the peals of laughter that pursued us. Like Madame Guérin, Lemeri sometimes seems under the impression that I am an adolescent boy and not an esteemed doctor. I was thankful for his tact, at least on this occasion.

Once inside Victor tugged again at my sleeve, demanding that I produce the cup. He snatched it from me and thrust it at Lemeri. It was gratifying to note Lemeri's surprise.

The savage has replaced my cup!

However, Victor was not searching for approval and we were soon divested of our assumptions. He continued with his noisy squeaks and thrust the cup again at Lemeri, with some aggression. He did this twice more, until Lemeri understood. He was asking for a drink of milk. No more, no less. He had secured a cup from Madame Guérin's in great anxiety, in case the absence of one in Citoyen Lemeri's hut forced us to deny him his treat.

He did not care to replace a broken piece of property. He had no more awareness of social niceties than the birds in the trees. I realised then how fervently I had wanted to attribute to Victor motivations that his behaviour did not merit. My desire – longing – to believe more of Victor than he is yet capable of threatens a truthful interpretation of events. I must renew my vigilance at conquering my feelings. They are the enemy of reason, of science, of proper empirical evidence. The enemy of truth itself.

79

Naturally Lemeri, the ignorant gardener, was oblivious to the mental anguish I suffered. He chuckled and pinched Victor's cheek and called him a 'clever lad'. (It is the first time he has not referred to him as a 'savage'.) He poured the boy the longed-for drink of milk, smiling as Victor supped greedily. For me Lemeri poured the customary brandy and did not seem to notice when I downed my glass in an instant and stared meaningfully at the bottle. Our conversation was then conducted – with difficulty – whilst Victor flung himself from wall to wall between us, like a bat. Lemeri shouted that he had seen the Minister of the Police, Fouché, walking in the gardens yesterday. Did I remember the Revolutionary Marriages that Fouché had invented, during the years of Terror, Lemeri smirked, and I told him (then repeated, to be heard above Victor's crashing) that I had not been in Paris back then, omitting that I was only seventeen, since I dreaded Lemeri making much of this. Still, I was not spared Lemeri's questioning: why did I give up my father's desired profession for me, had I not mentioned in some other conversation that I was destined to be a banker? Then he proceeded to answer his own question, saying with a chuckle that, of course, what happened was the Revolution. Bankers were hardly the most popular of citizens. There was a pause in which I prepared to change the subject but soon he was ruminating on how it was that I stumbled into medicine, since the two professions were so very different?

I knew of no reply that would satisfy Lemeri. I hardly know the answer myself.

My uncle found me a place, I said, in a military hospital. I was a pupil of the great physician, Larrey. He had heard of him perhaps?

No, Lemeri said.

Or Professor – Citoyen Pinel, the father of mental medicine? No.

Well, it was discovered that I had a – gift for medicine.

Far beyond any I had ever shown towards banking.

I did not add: a gift and a *passion*, for I felt such a word would betray me.

Your father was a doctor then? Lemeri asked.

My father was a carpenter.

A carpenter?

Well, yes, a master carpenter. I suppose it might be more accurate to say he was a merchant . . .

My cursed fidelity to the truth! Why could I not simply have allowed Lemeri to believe Father a simple carpenter and be done with it? Now the man was staring intently and I felt myself forced to continue.

Father had – ambitions for me. The eldest son. I mean the only – remaining – son. He sent me to my uncle to be tutored since he – my parents believed I had some talent.

Speaking of myself had caused my colour to rise again and my stutter to resurface. Thankfully Victor rescued me from Lemeri's interrogation by suddenly squealing with pleasure as he discovered a nut on the floor of the hut. Lemeri fetched a bowl of chestnuts and laid them at Victor's feet. He then leaned his back against the little window of the hut (I could not but notice how he barred the light with this gesture; I felt somehow that it was deliberate) and returned to gossip about Fouché, the Minister of Police.

The Revolutionary Marriage. I did not remember it? It was the trick Fouché invented of throwing a man and woman tied together into the Seine, the better to observe them attack one another, struggling all the while for breath and usually going under. Lemeri recalled that the women 'fought like hell-cats' and, despite their size disadvantage, were by no means always the first to drown. He had seen one bite through her rope, gasping and spluttering, and make it to the banks of the Seine, only to have her 'Revolutionary Divorce' (here Lemeri laughed a great deal at his own joke) annulled by the touch of Fouché's boot.

81

Lemeri is one of those men who delight in being outraged at the extremes of wicked behaviour in others. His hut is piled high with pamphlets and newspapers of the lowliest sort, which feed and inflame his outrage further. A quick glance at the illustration on the cover of the magazine at the top of the pile – Madame Veto in a compromising position with a hog, the animal depicted with the face of her own son – gives ample clue to their contents.

To prevent another lengthy anecdote I told him of signs of Victor's progress, at last succeeding in engaging his interest.

We wondered if Victor understands representation, I said. That is: one thing being represented by another. I asked Monsieur Guérin to add extra hooks to Victor's room and from these we fixed a key, a pair of scissors, a hammer and a pen. I drew pictures above each hook of the objects in question. Then I gave Victor the key, the pen, the hammer, and he put each in its correct place. Beneath its correct picture. He did this many times.

I did not add, although the phrase ran through my head: now tell me your dog could do as much!

Next I tried writing the word for the object beneath the hook, I said. He could do that, too.

By remembering the order, as he did with the letters, suggested Lemeri, infuriatingly.

Perhaps. But even so, he is learning that objects have a word, have a name. One cannot underestimate the importance of this idea for a child who has lived without language for so long.

Lemeri's silence was discouraging. We now sat opposite one another on rustic wooden chairs and Victor finished his brief repast and leapt up again, refreshed, and began bouncing at the door, rattling the key ineffectually, eager to leave. Not for the first time, I wondered what it was that compelled me to take into my confidence this ignorant old fool. Is it that I lack trust in my colleagues, my intellectual equals? Whatever the answer, I decided not to seek Lemeri's opinion again. Something in the man's face, the way his mouth hides inside his curly grey beard, or perhaps the lines fanning out from the corners of his eyes, gives him an uncertain expression. I think I have written here before that I have a sense in his presence of being laughed at. Contrary though it sounds, I fear it is exactly my dread of such a thing that draws me here. This is not a good reason to seek a man's company.

These thoughts weighed, I stood up to unlock the door and to release Victor. The boy bolted towards the fountains; an agreeable diversion, since I had to chase after him, leaving no time to bid the gardener good-bye.

It was dusk as I made my way along the Rue St Jacques alone, having returned Victor to his home. Glimpsing the cosy world of the Guérins – the steaming quenelles de brochet on the stove; Monsieur Guérin bringing a great new stack of wood, piling it beside the fire and pouring himself a generous glass of wine; Victor ensconced at the table and applying himself keenly to the task of shelling peas – I was reluctant to return to my rooms above the cordonnier. This was not eased by the arrival on my stairs of a distraught Madame Richard, weeping about the disappearance of her little Fanfan and hinting heavily that I had something to do with it. I scarcely troubled to reply, turning my back to her and holding my breath against the smell of stale linen, wet dog fur and cooking onions which never fails to greet me as I open my door. Wearily I let myself in.

One thing is certain: I can congratulate myself on my choice for Victor of a home and a family. Simple comforts; the homely smells of bouillon and fish, the crackle and spit of a good fire, the rhythm and routine of having a task, a place, a purpose within a family – in all these areas Victor is now rich, richer than he's ever been, richer than many other children. Or indeed adults. These ruminations, though, failed to improve my mood.

I stood at the window and watched the street below. By craning my neck, I spied the clock-tower of the Deaf Mute Institute. I am only a short walk from where Victor sleeps. I considered venturing to one of the guinguettes on the Rue des Feuillantines for a simple meal, but my appetite had deserted me. I pulled back the cold sheets of my bed and lay flat on my back. I did not trouble to undress, or pull a blanket over myself.

The bedsprings briefly groaned. I must have fallen asleep instantly, like one being felled by a tree. My dreams were of Victor. He was kneeling by a lake, and this lake I knew was not in Lacaune where he was found, but instead somewhere in my childhood, in Oraison. The boy was naked, his hair grown wild again; lying on his stomach, lapping at the water with his little pink tongue. But then I saw that it wasn't water he drank at all: the entire lake was a great white bowl of milk. The creamy liquid dribbled down his throat; with drops of it clinging like wet pearls to his sun-baked skin. Sitting back on his heels the child scattered white drops from his hair. I felt the warm splash on my own skin and discovered I was naked too, with creamy white beads spotting my stomach. Then Victor gave a sudden hysterical giggle. I kissed him once on the top of his head. He tasted of milk and of marzipan studded with raisins; the délices de la mère de famille, soaked in rum and milk chocolate, that I have not eaten since I was a boy, a boy much smaller than Victor. I lay down beside him, the grass scratching my stomach; tentatively stretching my hand, and then my tongue, towards the milky lake. But as I did so the lake disappeared. In its place was a strange flat land, at first green and then wooden: a polished floor. And there were shoes and people; the loud heels of men in the garb of priests, others with stiff white collars and long black coats; the noise was deafening and everywhere I looked I was taunted by children waving canes and stamping their black boots. Victor and the lake of milk had disappeared.

Now the child has a name, Victor, and he is not Joseph, no matter how often my tongue tricks me into calling him that. His smell creeps into the corners of our home, and all the same Henri, even when he is well, does not complain of it, which is a great puzzle in a man not usually shy of complaining. The doctor, when I asked him, agreed to bleed Henri and the fee, he says, can be forgotten in view of the care I'm taking of the child. So this dark little monster has brought me already the thing I wanted most, the treatment for Henri. Why am I not more grateful?

We had more visitors this evening. Every night since the boy came here we have had visitors, I am heartily sick of them, only this time it was my own daughter and her friends when I opened the door. So I did my best to sweeten up my face and called Henri from the bedroom, where he was lying on the bed wheezing, cutting short his day's work and told him to build up the fire and offer the girls some wine.

You would not believe the dresses they were wearing, those girls. Dresses that would barely serve the task of a handkerchief, and none of them considers the trouble it causes to me when they show the shadows of their legs like that, giving Henri plans he has no strength to carry through, nor has he been able for a good many years.

One of the girls, a plump one, with a face flattened as if someone took an iron to her and pressed all the features out, held her nose as she entered my kitchen. One glance from me put a stop to that. She and her friend gasped when they saw Victor, who was crouching in his favourite place, beneath the key hooks, sitting on his heels, dandling a great bunch of keys in his hands.

I do not know what those girls found to gasp about – he was quiet and calm and neat in his shirt and breeches: nothing like he was a few hours ago, when his restless mood was upon him and he wanted to go out into the garden. Henri had been sleeping and I was busy clearing up his mess from earlier, so I kept the door firmly locked, which provoked a terrible rage. Victor began to thump his chest and scream and then kicked at the door over and over, with such force that Henri woke up and ran in here. I was crouching in a corner, reaching for the hot poker, never meaning to use it, of course, but only to defend myself if need be. A noise like that, the sight of a person so wild and angry, his eyes blacker than two spots of coal in the fire: it can melt the resolve of the steeliest of women.

I was afraid to approach him. Nothing we said, no matter how sweet our tone, would calm him. His next great kick brought one of my good plates crashing from the shelf but my little shriek did nothing to deter him. Eventually he was shouting so hard that blood began to pour from his nose. By this time, Henri and I were holding each other, feeling our hearts knock against each other in terror, having given up all thoughts of defeating him. But the nose-bleed was a blessing. The sight of the dark blood trickling down his cheek, the taste of it, seemed to frighten the boy. I have told you my Henri has more patience, more sweetness than any man I've known, a nature gentler than Sainte Thérèse herself. He could soothe a raging beast with that gentle tone but what he lacks is courage. I had to nudge him forward. I have the resolve but less patience. Together I suppose you could say we make a soldier.

Come now, boy.

Henri spoke soft and low to him, holding out his hand with an offering of a fat pod of peas.

Victor sniffed at the air, tasted the blood on his tongue. His eyes were wild, nearly rolling in his head. Anyone can tell that he doesn't see you during these rages. It's not directed at *you*, Henri says, the poor wretch is angry at the world. But that's exactly what terrifies me. You feel he could kick you into a thousand pieces; red white and blue, just like one of your plates. Not through cruelty, or not quite. Cruelty is never the word which springs to mind, when I think of Victor. Cruel would mean he cared. He is no more cruel than the wind blowing across the Tarn valley, but of course there are times when people call it so.

Victor dipped forward and snatched the pea-pod from Henri's palm. While he was occupied in shelling it, a skill in him so swift that a blink would miss it, he allowed us to offer him more, and usher him into his room. Once in there, we locked the door behind him.

Staring through the keyhole a few minutes later, we saw that he had fallen asleep, squatting as he sometimes does, his fists balled into his eyes. When he woke up an hour later I gave him a whole plate of peas to shell, and his mood was calm as a cat in the sun. Truly, aside from the wreck of my plate now swept up and wrapped in newspaper, it was as if nothing at all had happened. These rages sometimes leave him drained and exhausted, but more often than not it is only Henri and me who feel that way and the boy himself is rested, like today: light as a feather, in a mood you might describe as happy if you were speaking of anyone else. He has not one jot of care for the mayhem caused and no more concern for the extra labour he's made for me.

So here he was sitting like a prince or a jailer, jangling a bunch of keys from one hand to the other, for Julie and her friends to admire him.

And is he truly wild? said the one with the flat-iron face: I hear he was suckled by wolves and has nails as long as claws . . .

See his nails for yourself, I said, and the girl took a peek. She drew back, disappointed.

Shall we feed him?

He bites! said Julie, enjoying the little shriek that this

remark produced. She had brought him some sugar, wrapped in a pocket of lavender velvet and tied with a black ribbon. She refuses to give up her efforts to tease him with sweetmeats and fancies but I could have told her the result. Of course he refused it.

Look at the scars on his hands, his feet, the other girl, a freckle-faced, bonny one, whispered.

You've no need to whisper, I told them. He is not like the rest of us. He has no care on earth for what you say of him.

The girl ignored me, as girls her age are wont to do, and addressed her remarks to her friends.

He must have been in fights with wild beasts – imagine! A boy of his age, surviving alone, and from so young an age. Do you find it hard to believe?

Julie opened her mouth to answer but I was there first.

Not me. Not one whit. Now I know him better. He is not stupid and he has a speed – such speed! And strength – you'd be astonished. And cunning! He can grab hold of a plate of lentils from under your nose before you've blinked. And determination. *Mon Dieu!* Is that child determined, I've never met a will like it.

But wolves, wild-cats, bears perhaps – a five-year-old boy?

I put my hands on my hips and turned to her.

Doctor Itard states – the well-known doctor who has been appointed the boy's tutor, I'm sure you know of him – Doctor Itard, no?

Oh yes, of course. We all know him, he was a doctor at the military hospital –

Here Julie and her friends smiled at one another in a smile which was not meant to include myself or Henri, but which I caught the tail-end of none the less.

Well, my girl, Doctor Itard is certain that all evidence shows that the Wild Boy of Aveyron is not a fake and did indeed live alone in the forest for at least five years, but more likely seven –

Does no one know how he came to be there? Why no one came for him? Who was his family, what was his name? Why did someone want to kill him?

The savants of Paris are not interested in that. I have never heard it mentioned. No, all they speak of is – well, a lot of nonsense if you ask me. Man in a state of Nature. The marvellous questions the boy holds the key to. They measure his head, they dress and undress him, they sit at my kitchen table with their notebooks and their furrowed brows – they'd examine the water in his pot if I let them!

But what *are* these marvellous questions? What does he hold the key to? asked the flat-iron girl, who was not easy to shake off.

Don't ask me. The most Pressing Question of our Time. That's all I know.

It was gratifying when she nodded sadly and turned her attention back to Victor.

And what was Victor doing during all this? He had dropped his keys and was cleaning his teeth with a piece of straw, running it back and forth like a saw. His big black eyes did not land on the girls, but were fixed straight ahead. And he delivered a grand fart, just like a stopper exploding from a bottle, scattering all three girls as surely as if a cannon had just fired.

When they had recovered and stopped giggling, the bolder one, Mademoiselle Flat-Iron, told Victor she had brought him a present. I told her not to trouble herself, since we are already bursting at the seams with gifts and Victor shows not a twitch of interest in them. I showed them the knife with its ivory handle, the piece of stone wall – supposedly a piece of the Bastille – the pocket watch with the porcelain face and the words *Vivre libre ou mourir* engraved on the back, the silk bag full of sugar plums, the doll in the uniform of the sans-culottes ... Henri piped up that the boy must be a Royalist, since he scorns their Republican gifts. At this Flat-Iron broke in excitedly, not gathering that it was a joke, and squealed: oh well, wait until you see what I have for him – it belonged to the Widow Capet herself!

From a bag she produced a little mirror and Julie and the other bonny girl crowded round it. I was not surprised when our cynical Julie soon broke ranks and said in a disappointed tone: you can buy any number of such mirrors on the quai for twenty-five sous.

Let me have a look, I said and it was handed over to me. It was true, the mirror was gaudy, with a red frame and Chinese figures painted on each side, the sort of thing that would only impress a silly girl.

But Flat-Iron snatched it back and said in some pique: it was lent to Marie-Antoinette on her very last days by the maid who served her in prison, Rosalie Lamorlière. She was a friend of my mother's.

For a moment, squabbling over the mirror, it was true to say that we had forgotten Victor. Now in snatching it back, Flat-Iron had made the low sunlight pouring in through the window bounce from the mirror to the wall opposite. And Victor was captivated.

Look how he watches it! said Julie, and we all turned our attention to Victor. The owner of the red mirror offered it shyly to him and he seized it quickly, afraid she would change her mind.

After that Victor 'woke up' – that's the best I can do to describe it. The boy was in different spirits entirely. He giggled like a maniac every time light from the mirror bounced over his skin, or the walls; and all his attention, every ounce of his concentration was now given up to flipping this light around and laughing at the results. The only other time I have seen Victor so concentrated is when we are outside and he stares with reverie into the pond or at the blue sky and Sully's tree above him.

With much teasing and noise the girls then established that Victor is clever indeed because when a walnut was held behind his head and he was looking in the mirror, after a very few attempts to grab it, he worked out that it was behind him and turned around to gain his reward.

There! Maman – don't forget to tell the doctor that he did that! remarked Julie with satisfaction, Victor's mouth snapping shut over the meat of the nut in her hand.

Doctor Itard is looking for signs of the boy's intelligence, she told her friends. I smiled to hear how she spoke as if she and the doctor were the firmest of friends.

Then they fell to discussing the doctor in all his glorious detail. Henri and I might just as well have been invisible: they held nothing back. His hawk-like nose, his high forehead (terribly common in savants, Julie said; the others laughed like madwomen); his serious expression, his deliberation in choosing exactly the right word, which at times made him pause so long or stutter so painfully that one longed to break in and help him. Does he ever laugh? asked Flat-Iron. No one knew the answer. They went on: his curly hair, his great black fashionable coat – a subtle dandy, Julie suggested, which sent them into fits of laughter again. Julie told the others exactly where he lives, declaring it quite nearby on the Rue St Jacques, in the lodgings of a Madame Richard. Then Flat-Iron wondered out loud why he was never seen with a lady-friend, for is he not twenty at least, if not older, and as such surely in search of a wife?

Now I listened to all of this with my arms folded across my bosom and my tongue held silent. It is not so far in the distant past that I cannot remember what it is like to be a girl of nearly sixteen but Henri as the proud and jealous father had more trouble and was soon spluttering and coughing as men are wont to do in these situations, when their tongue cannot keep pace with their outrage.

It was as Julie uttered innocently that the field was then *wide open* that finally Henri leapt from his seat and said with a pained expression: a daughter of mine, a daughter of mine! Which of course did not mean anything much to the girls and only had the effect of shaking more giggling from them. By now they were seated beside Victor and freely caressing and tickling him and the atmosphere and noise level in our kitchen were about to go through the roof. So Henri said: enough! Shoo! Leave a man in peace, and began coughing so badly that the girls (nurses, remember) were chastened finally and decided it was time to leave.

Well, he might be handsome but I don't believe he is to be captured in the usual way, Julie murmured, after she had kissed us – she surely ate a lunch of sugared violets – and headed for the door.

He might race up a tree for cover – we would need a great net! The parting shot of Flat-Iron. Another explosion of giggles. I was glad to close the door on them. Victor spied his chance of escape, but for once, distracted by his mirror, he was not quick enough and the lock was turned before he had reached the door.

So he took again his position with his back to the wall, while I prepared his bath. I had feared I would have the devil of a job to calm him after the girls took their leave, but instead he seemed happy with his new toy – the first he has ever shown an interest in – and remained fixed on it, tilting and tipping it to catch the last rays of the sinking sun and seeming not to notice that his admirers had left. What he did notice eventually was that the sun had slipped in the sky and was no longer willing to play with him. He flung the mirror on the floor in disgust. I snapped my tongue at him: it was a miracle it did not smash. But then seeing the direction the evening needed to go in, I changed my mind and used my tender voice on him, tickling him the way the girls had done, to coax him towards the bath.

Come, let me take your shirt off, Victor.

Keeping up the tickling with one hand, I signalled with a nod to Henri, to kneel on the floor beside us, so that when I needed both hands to strip Victor's shirt, Henri could replace my tickling hand with his own. This Henri did, knowing the routine. I don't know what I would have done these last few weeks if it weren't for Henri. His has been the kind of help you would never dream of in a husband; more like the help of a daughter, although God knows my own daughter is too flighty and too busy with her own reckless thoughts to give her maman and her new troubles the time she deserves.

Releasing Victor, I now turned my attention to the pan of water on the stove and to making the bath the right temperature. Victor hopped from foot to foot, making excited squeaking sounds and slapping his arms against his body. I don't mind telling you what a fancy I think it is, Doctor Itard's idea of warm baths. A child who has spent so many years bathing in the freezing river Tarn – and now that I have seen him so often plunge into the pond here I know he must have swum freely – such a boy will hardly shed a tear if his bath is too cold. But out of duty and a proper pride in doing my job I always do as promised and add two great pans full of hot water to the cold in the tub. This night, the girls' visit had made the evening late, so instead of putting the water back on to boil, I topped the bath up with some cold water and told Victor to get in. He dipped no more than a toe into the wooden tub but then snatched it back as if something had bitten him.

I slapped the surface of the bath water with my hand, saying: come on now, Victor, in you get.

The boy's skinny little body shivered but that rascal did not budge.

Henri tried to help by holding Victor by the shoulder and leading him – a kind of shove-push-pull – to the edge of the bath, splashing at the water with his hand and telling the boy to cease his dawdling and climb in. The odd splash flicked onto Victor's bare stomach and he flinched, springing back.

Your bath, Victor! I told him, loudly. (The voice I use with the naughtiest deaf children. If they cannot hear it, they can at least see my face.)

Henri said to give the child a good kick; that should do the trick. Of course he didn't mean it: I've told you how he is full of bluster. But we could see that Victor had not the smallest intention of getting into that bath. The little devil leapt from foot to foot, flapped his arms across his chest and shook his head from side to side, squawking just like one of those wretched parrots in the painted cages at the quayside. Finally, I lost patience and went to lift him in. As I did, the boy leapt away from me and then in a movement so swift and surprising, seized my hand and plunged it into the water. I couldn't help but shriek. The kettle of hot water had scarcely skimmed the chill off: the water was icy.

Henri was on his feet, ready to scold him. I think he was surprised to see me laughing.

Did he hurt you?

No!

I looked for a cloth to dry my sleeve.

He was trying to tell me something . . .

The poor child stood by his bath, naked and shivering. I had not closed the shutters for the night and so the pink light was creeping through the kitchen window, painting Victor all rosy and peach, like one of those little angels that used to play their trumpets in Our Lady's ear. It would take a heart of marble – and Henri's, as I have said, is made of something much softer than that – not to feel a great sadness then, looking at Victor, naked and trembling and trying to tell me, with all the powers he possessed, that his bath water was too cold.

The child who has bathed in streams in the coldest winter in living memory has decided the bath isn't warm enough for him, grumbled Henri. But there he was, already stirring up the fire, adding another log.

I found nothing to say. Instead I wrapped Victor in a blanket and for the first time, he allowed himself to be cuddled on my knee. He is a great gangly thing with legs that go up to his ears, but snug and bound as he was, he gave no protest. Henri glanced at us and then looked away; busying himself with the pan, scooping it into the cold bath water to refill it.

It took some time for the water to heat and it pressed us all to sleepiness, sitting there with the fire built up, heat flushing our skin and darkness falling and neither one of us in a great hurry to light the lamp. When Henri declared himself sure the bath must be warm enough for any child – *Mon Dieu*, for a *dauphin*! – I unwrapped Victor again and this time his countenance was peaceful and he clambered into his bath by himself, with a small splash and no need of coaxing.

Then Henri and I bathed him together, in a soapy silence. The moon obliged us by rising as full and bright as a shiny coin and casting enough light to bathe him by. His skin had the look of the glove-maker's best silver, polished hard enough to make your wrists burn, but your spirits soar. I said to myself, looking at him, that his own naked body with nought but the moon to robe it would likely be the most familiar sight in the world to our Victor.

We sat either side of the tub, me and Henri, and we lifted each limb one at a time, stroking and soaping it. We tipped water over his hair, making him laugh when it ran into his mouth; and when that was done, we fell to splashing and playing with him, as if he were a small baby. While I warmed his towel, holding it up to the fire, Henri took a wooden sail-boat from the window-sill, one that he himself had carved, and bending his cramped old shape over the side of the bath, he floated the sail-boat on the water. I watched him like that for a long time. I need not tell you that it is a few years since I have seen Henri play with that sail-boat. Not that Victor knew that, nor cared. He took no heed of us, of our silence. He didn't grab at the toy as another boy his age would surely have done. His love is for the water, for the sounds it makes. Or for the light he can catch in his little mirror. He can take a cup and pour it out, fill it up and pour it out, over and over. He would do it from dawn to dusk, I am sure of it, if no one made to stop him. Which for the longest time, no one did.

Finally, I said to the pair of them: enough! Time to sleep now.

I could not look at Henri as I reached for Victor with the towel. Henri kept his head bowed and stared for a long time at that little sail-boat, then he shook the water from the torn silk sail and dried the hull on his own shirt, with such tenderness as made my heart twist. After that, he pulled his shirt up again and buried his face in it, while Victor, all this while dripping on the floor beside him, seemed finally to notice him and to look with curiosity at the top of Henri's head. It was only a glance, the most slant-eyed and fleeting of glances, you might say that it signified nothing at all, and that I suppose is true, I can't rightly say what it *did* signify, I can only tell you this: that I saw it.

The ghost of our baby was in that moonlit room with us.

Here's the child called Victor then, back in his own bedroom, with the shutters now closed and latched, a fire in the grate, filling the room with its sweet-smoky smell of cedar, snapping at him and spitting occasional fierce red flecks at the floor. Victor crouches in front of it, and when it spits at him, he spits back. Beside him on a faded woollen rug are the toys the Guérins have left with him: the sans-culottes doll, the bag of sugar plums, the piece of Bastille wall, the Chinese mirror. A wooden hoop that had belonged to their own child, a sail-boat with a square of torn silk for a sail.

He sits there for a long time, while the rest of the Institute takes itself to bed. Sounds of children shouting, feet running along corridors and up and down steps, doors clanging are replaced by the rolling snores of Henri Guérin, the call of an owl. The sheets on his bed are folded down, the bolster pushed against the wall, but he makes no move to sleep in it.

When the fire dies down Victor builds it up again, using the wood he's been left and then, when that is done, he looks around for something else to burn. The hoop breaks easily and burns with intermittent sharp crackling, like the splinter of twigs underfoot in a forest. The sail-boat is a slower burn. Crouching in front of it, he warms his hands on its snapping heat, shifting his weight from foot to foot. The damp silk sail curls, stiffens and retreats to a tiny ball of black. Finally Victor's head begins to bob gently on his neck as if a wind were blowing through the room. He slips into a light, watchful sleep.

Vendémiaire 21
Year Eight

I have decided that Victor would benefit from a wider experience of the outside world. With this in mind, I took him with me today to a restaurant. I had two purposes: firstly, to introduce him to new tastes and secondly to show him, by example, how a boy of his age should behave in polite society. It is my aim to make this a regular excursion.

Our first little hindrance was how to get to the restaurant, given that Victor runs at a pace that makes it impossible for me to keep up. After some hesitation, I assured myself that we should take a carriage. Of course, I had the devil of a job getting Victor to enter it. Monsieur Guérin had to accompany me to the Rue St Jacques for this express purpose.

Guérin said gloomily that he'd never ridden in a berline himself, nor one of the new cabriolets, and preferred the heavier carriages of the old regime, which he was persuaded had more dignity. I did not find his remarks consoling.

The Lord knows I can understand the boy's reluctance, Guérin muttered.

Victor was naturally terrified of the contraption. The coachman sat impatiently glaring down at us from his wide-fringed cushion, while Guérin and myself tried to persuade the child to enter. We succeeded with a combination of stealth and force: we placed a chestnut on the floor of the carriage, Victor sniffed it out and Guérin pushed him in, whilst I, planted inside, shot my arm out and dragged him in beside me. I held tightly to Victor's arm, yanked him onto the seat and yelled to the driver to set off. Guérin gave a little wave of triumph, or surprise, at our sudden departure.

Once we were splashing through the muddy streets, Victor seemed to enjoy the motion and the noisy rhythm of the wheels and was quite content to sit down. He was, after all, brought to Paris from Aveyron in a carriage and I do not remember reading reports of rebellion. After a while he was brave enough – at my behest – to peep out of the window. These new carriages are swifter, lighter and with more windows than of old and, for myself, I find all three things a great improvement.

I could tell from the constant twitching of his nostrils that Victor was taking in the excitements of Paris through that particular sensory organ. His eyes widened when we passed the fish markets at Les Halles; he was able to tell by the stench of foul water when we were crossing the Seine; he flared his nostrils excitedly as we rumbled over the stinking cobble-stones and, poking his head through the window, sniffed at the rain, enjoying the sensation of drizzle on his face. Yet he paid no attention at all to the grisettes with their dark spots of rouge and their stink of strong perfume, even when one stuck her head into our carriage and promised him delights such as he'd only dreamed of. Glorious release, she said, for a matter of sous. I waved her away with my hand and urged the driver to continue.

Victor sniffed at the perfume but showed no other sign of disturbance and did not even look with curiosity at the girl. I would have liked to call after her: what he dreams of! Neither you nor I could hope to know! I said nothing of the sort, of course.

However, after all the trouble of this journey, I suddenly decided that the restaurant I had chosen was a poor choice, being too confined a space. The moment I pictured Victor in close proximity to other diners (more importantly, to other diners' plates of food) I knew that calamity threatened. So I instructed the driver – a surly type with an unlikely little dog sharing the cushion on the seat beside him – to take us back across the river into the heart of the Faubourg St Germain. I remembered that the Hôtel Caraman in the Rue Dominique, although grand, has a southern aspect looking into a fine open garden, should we need to make use of it. (Before my post as Victor's guardian I would of course have shunned the debauched finery of the Hôtel Caraman, even had I been able to afford to eat there; but the child's highly specific needs forced me to put aside my principles on this occasion.)

We reached the restaurant at an early hour, chosen to minimise public interest in our arrival. Even so, there was a hubbub as I entered, gripping Victor's arm, and the waiter took some moments to approach and offer us a table, choosing instead to stare at us, open-mouthed.

It's the boy from Aveyron, isn't it! The savage? he whispered.

I sighed. A young man in formal dress, gripping the arm

of a noisy, gesticulating boy with his shock of black hair. There was not a soul in Paris who had not heard of us. There would be no escape from scrutiny.

I'd like a large carafe of wine and a table further from the door, I said loudly and without stuttering.

Victor was sniffing at some drapes by the window, and I had some trouble entreating him to come with me to another table. Shown the chair and a glass of water, with much pantomime effort, he did however oblige me by sitting down. My wretched skin was betraying me again, I could feel my colour rising – the very thing I dreaded. I tried to think of something else, spoke firmly to myself: *Jean-Marc, you are not important and no one is interested in you* – honest advice Uncle used to give me, on a regular basis – and, in time, the reprimand worked and my skin felt cooler. Soon enough there were new reasons for embarrassment: Victor exploring the linen and every dish as it arrived with his nose and then tongue, Victor slurping noisily at his water then tipping his glass up on the table in annoyance once it was empty; Victor grabbing at my glass of wine by mistake, taking a great slug of it and then running shrieking round the restaurant, squealing like a pig, as his tastebuds registered their error.

Ladies smiled at us and fell silent.

Victor was persuaded back to his seat and I resumed mine, nodding to some of the other diners, signalling to them that the drama was over; that they could now continue their conversations and look elsewhere for entertainment. (A vain hope.) And so the meal progressed. Determined to at least demonstrate to Victor what civilised dining was about, even if I could not persuade him to participate in it, I enjoyed a delicious fish soup, followed by a good terrine de la maison, a plate of pheasant stuffed with oysters and chestnuts, and for dessert a most unusual yellow fruit, its flesh both sharp and sweet, which came sliced into circles, the edges still decorated in its prickly skin. (I cannot remember the name.) Victor, of course, would not touch it. He accepted a mouthful of the stuffing from my pheasant, but spat it on the floor with much show and noise, once he had discovered the oysters. The yellow fruit provoked howls of protest. He drank several glasses of water, slowly and with much savour, as he does, and I fed him a tiny piece of white bread. After that, I gave up.

What amazes me is that the child must be hungry and yet is steadfast in refusing foods which are not familiar to him. One would think that after the years of deprivation and starvation, he would be only too glad to try some tender rabbit stew, or a honeyed chicken basted in bacon-fat. What is strangest of all about the limited diet he had when living in the wilderness is that it seems from his behaviour to date not to have been limited by availability, but by choice. Surely the child must have had occasion – and skill enough – to catch a rabbit, a squirrel, a mouse? Yet despite Bonnaterre's report that he saw Victor tear a canary apart and eat it raw, stripping it with his bare hands, he now shuns all meat and has not yet been coaxed into trying it, either cooked or raw. The boy is inexplicably rigid. It seems to me that his *will* – and not, as Rousseau insists, his *need* – is dictating his behaviour. Then again, it is curious to write of 'will' in a child who in so many ways seems unformed, passive, as impressionable as warm wax.

This problem of will, of intransigence, reminds me of battles I had with Uncle as a child on the very same issue. He would complain that my passions were too strong and while under their sway nothing could equal my impetuosity. By nature measured, extremely timid, and so much a slave to fears and shames that I long to vanish from mortal sight; when roused by anger, or a sense of injustice, I am amenable to no restraint, respect, fear or decorum. Except for whatever seizes me, the universe is for me, at that moment, non-existent. Naturally, Uncle worked hard on this unruly, passionate side to my nature. We would spend hours in his study, for example, attempting to conquer my stutter, which had begun shortly after my arrival from Oraison. At times when I was tired and could make no progress, required to recite one of La Fontaine's fables, I would flatly refuse, even going so far as to fling the books on the floor. Uncle was ever patient, ever kind. I remember a glass case resting on a shelf in his study, which contained a fox and a crow, two woeful creatures: very poor examples of the art of taxidermy. The crow's feet were attached to a dusty branch; it had only one eye and carried a greying round of cheese in its beak. It was an illustration of La Fontaine's famous story, the one it is claimed he wrote here, beneath Sully's tree, of the fox who charms the cheese from the bird, flattering it mercilessly about its beautiful voice, until the foolish creature is persuaded to sing, opening its beak and relinquishing the cheese to the waiting fox. Uncle would point at these two creatures and insist that I recite the fable faultlessly. After I had stammered through it, he would always tell me: beware of vanity, Jean-Marc. That and your wilfulness are your greatest weaknesses. I knew it was true but I could only think that if I had a fine, eloquent voice like the bird, I too would sacrifice all I possessed to sing, just that once.

There is always a child who will take the wrong lesson from any teaching.

As Victor and I left the restaurant, a young lady ran to the door (which I was attempting to open, whilst keeping a firm grip on Victor, who was sniffing the air outside, crazed with the scent of freedom) and said: you are Citoyen Yzard, the doctor, isn't that it?

Yes, was all I could mutter, as Victor dragged me outside. My unprepossessing speech did not embarrass me as I too was occupied with pondering the identity of the young lady. It was – it must have been – Madame Récamier. I had had a sensation that she was a personal acquaintance but then realised it was because I have so often seen her portrait, whether in the *Gazette de France* or hung in a gallery, with those dark curls, so artfully arranged around her face. For a moment this unexpected brush with 'the most beautiful woman in Paris' froze me. I waited for some command, as if she were Napoleon Bonaparte himself.

Thankfully, once on the other side of the door, distracted by Victor's running trot and the diners crowding at the window to watch us leave, I soon shook off this foolishness. After all, it is merely the opinion of others that gives her this title, not some intrinsic quality, measurable in any objective way. One might just as easily describe Julie Guérin as the most beautiful young woman in Paris, taking into account an assessment of natural attributes, such as length of nose, height of cheek-bones, quality of curl in the hair, depth of the eyes; liveliness and flexibility in the mouth . . . In short, I decided that, flattering though it was that this society lady knew my name, I was not in any way persuaded that she was someone of importance. I was suddenly glad that I had scarcely acknowledged her; despite it being an accident.

I returned Victor to the Guérins' home after his second exciting carriage ride of the evening. This time I was confident that he would not try to escape, so I took the risk of hiring a cabriolet, so that I might drive it myself. In the past I have been afraid of doing this, fearful that the horse might prove impossible to control. (I am not generally confident with beasts.) My successes with the wild boy, that is, Victor, has enhanced my evaluation of myself and my abilities with animals: I felt a new certainty that such a task would not prove beyond me. Fortified with wine and in high spirits, we sped clattering over the wet paving stones; the horse behaved as horses do in my dreams, rain fell on my hands and face; and light from the sinister lanternes – they will always be sinister now – cast a feeble yellow pool over the roads, in between shadows from the giant signboards.

To my surprise, once we stopped, I discovered that amidst the swaying Victor had managed to fall asleep. I tethered the horse to a lanterne, then reached inside to pick Victor up. His head fell against my shoulder, and his breath brushed my neck as I lifted him through the gates of the Institute and towards his home. Warmth seeped into my shoulder from his mouth, his head nestling in the crook of my neck. I have never carried a sleeping child before. I had not realised how much warmth one body transfers to another, nor how tender it is possible to feel when one carries another human being, one so utterly abandoned. I tried at first to adjust my gait so as not to disturb him, but soon realised from the regularity of his breathing that there was no need. Striding through the moonlight in the Institute grounds, listening to the soft muffled calls of an owl, with the child's breath against my neck, I thought of what bedtime might have been like for Victor for all those years in the forest. My heart shuddered with loneliness, as if it was *I* who slept alone, small and afraid.

An infant of five years, what does he know, what does he remember? I remember Mother sitting at the little desk of Brazilian rosewood, which I now have with me here in Paris, and I remember playing in the folds of her skirts as she sat, and running my childish fingers over the smooth surface of the desk, gathering up a little ball of dust. The sound of her faint quavering singing and the taste of the crystallised green walnuts she used to feed me, the smell sticky on her hands, clinging to her hair, her skirts, her lap, as I climbed into it. How impossible to imagine the sensations of the child who has no mother's lap to climb into, who sleeps huddled in a cave, fearful of every twitch of grass, every falling pine cone, aware that danger lurks in every shadow. Wondering whether he will ever see a human being again, let alone his own dear parents. Perhaps forgetting altogether what a human being is, what human comfort can be.

I shook the image from my mind and addressed myself to

knocking gently on the door of the Guérins' home. I was admitted by Madame Guérin, who helped me carry Victor to his room. She had been waiting up for us. She leant over me, holding a candle, while I laid the sleeping child on his newly made-up bed. A great wash of emotion swelled in me at the sight of that bed, the blankets folded back, the sheets worn and patched, the bolster awaiting the imprint of the child's head. Perhaps it was the wine I had drunk but I remember thinking that there is no sight in the world as tender as a child's bed, prepared by a loving mother, waiting to be slept in.

The boy looks younger when he is asleep, with his small mouth firmly pursed, dreams flickering over his eyelids. I mentioned this to Madame Guérin but she did not reply. More than this, she actually turned away from me and for the first time I had a strong sensation of – what was it? Hostility? Anger? I wanted at once to explain myself, but my stutter prevented me. We both turned from his bedroom in silence and Madame Guérin offered me neither coffee nor brandy. She did walk with me to the door and as she opened it she turned her face to mine and said: he bewitches you. He climbs into your dreams. You have to resist him.

I shook my head against this superstitious nonsense and left without replying.

After returning the cabriolet to a driver on the Rue St Jacques I made my way on foot to my lodgings. The rain had ceased but its smell, a smell of damp soot, hung over the streets; mud splashed over my boots. Now that the season is beginning to turn, my thoughts turn again and again to that picture of Victor unprotected in the woods: shivering in some makeshift cave, whilst a downpour soaks all around him. The question returns to me: why for all those years did he not seek shelter in one of the villages? It has been shown that he occasionally found his way to them, but that he ran away if he was approached.

As I walked the short distance of the Rue St Jacques from the Institute to my lodgings, another memory came to me. Myself as a child in Oraison again, before being sent to study with Uncle. An improvised house that I constructed in the garden, from twigs arranged in a hollowed tree trunk felled by the gardener. I remember vividly – reminded by the damp air and the mud on my shoes – the sensation of creeping into that dank world; how I covered my face with grass and twigs and lay on my stomach facing the house, hiding. There can scarcely be a child in the world who has not at some time or another played at making a den, a hiding place. What strikes me about this memory is that there were no other children present and I have no idea what I was hiding from. I can remember the smell of wet leaves and grass and cèpes nestling in the rotting bark, and the sense that I did not want to come out and *was not going to come out* no matter how much Maman might call me. I can remember, or rather I have the sensation of, my will again; a tremendous stubbornness which I recognise in Victor and which makes me feel, occasionally, a greater closeness and respect for him. For what is will in a child is determination, courage, ambition in the adult. What is it, other than *will*, which has made me contradict Pinel's diagnosis, offer an unspoken challenge to him and to the savants of Paris, risk my future, my reputation, my career, all resting upon Victor's fate?

Sometimes, increasingly, it is possible to say, or write: he is like me. The child, the wild child of Aveyron has qualities that I have, that I prize in myself, qualities that have served me well. Have served him well. It is, after all, that same will, that strength of character, to which he owes his survival. Yet in all our efforts to raise children we set about to break that will. When the child will obey us, is pliant to our commands, we consider our task accomplished.

This line of thinking left me muddled and unsatisfied. I flicked in a desultory fashion through Locke's *Thoughts Concerning*

Education and, of course, luck would determine that the page fell open on his exhortation that small children should look on their parents as their lords, their absolute governors.

This seeming so far from achievable with Victor, I threw the book on the bed in disgust and soon flung myself after it.

God took my boy Joseph not once but twice, how God could do that to a good mother I'll never know. It just goes to show you that God is cruel and wicked and no better than his worst subjects here on earth. I'm glad I've long since stopped caring for him, that I don't offer him any of my prayers now or light candles for the Virgin. I wouldn't say this to a soul but sometimes it gladdens my heart that his churches are burned and his prayer-books rendered into fine shreds and fluttered in the Seine like the feathers of a great white bird. Sometimes in my wickedest moments I think to myself that it was no more than he deserved.

Because when my Joseph had lived just two bare summers God sent someone in the night. Someone or something, some fairies or evil spirits, or just some wicked person. I don't know who. Somebody who leaned over the crib where my little blond angel was sleeping on his back with his arms flung out and his cheeks flushed bright because he was a hot child, you know one of those infants who kick off the covers. Always flushed, always too hot. While we were dreaming in bed right next to him this wicked person leaned right into the crib and scooped him out like a bird stealing a fish and in his place he slipped another infant child who looked just like him. The same little nest of blond curls at the back, the same wide eyes and faint eyebrows rising right up into his fringe in fine curved arches. But not the same boy, no nothing like him and only a mother, a loving mother like me, could tell.

The very next morning I peered into the crib. I went to pick my Joseph up, I was ready to nurse him and my milk was good and full but when I looked at him the milk turned to ice in my breasts. His eyes were wide open, but instead of smiling at me like he usually did, he was staring right past me as if there was a great glass pane between us, like the windows of the church. Me on one side and him on another. For one terrible minute I thought he was dead and a scream rose in my throat but then the child who wasn't Joseph but looked like Joseph turned his head and blinked and my heart ticked into life again and the scream stoppered itself in my mouth. Well, my soul was gladdened and I picked him up and showered him with kisses, pressing them all over him as if he were a cherry cake. Milk rose in me the same way milk tips at the rim of a pan when it's boiling and the day seemed fine after all. I thought no more of it.

But that was just the beginning and if you are wondering now what might befit a mother to work in a place like this with all these God-forsaken children mouthing and uttering their strange cries, waving their arms like banshees or bats, then I suppose the only answer is that when you have had a changeling child of your own you learn to forgive what others find strange. You learn to accustom to what others find evil.

It wasn't that my boy was sick in his body. A stronger constitution you could travel the length and breadth of this land and never find, but this new Joseph had a sickness of sorts, it was a sickness of the heart perhaps, or the soul, for how else to describe it? The new boy did not meet my eyes in the same way the old one did, nor did he hold out his fat little arms to be picked up, nor did he seek comfort from me – his own mother – when he fell and bumped his head. As days went by the handful of words he'd spoken were abandoned, so that I no longer heard the chime of his 'eau', 'eau', or the sweet trill of Maman or Papa! Now the only sound I heard was an angry wail if I crossed him, if I didn't bring him his ball or his drink the instant he held out his hand for them. He would scream at me and beat his small fists on the floor in a fury, the like of which you've never seen. No scolding nor beating would deter him. Even Henri at last was roused one day, seeing him face down on the mat in front of the fire, tearing at the floorboards with his bare fingers, to wonder out loud if his only son was not possessed by an evil spirit.

I was losing all heart in knowing how to put things right.

And it is a long long time since I have surrendered myself up to thinking of this and wondering what it was that I did to make my own child hate me so. Something tonight in the presence of Victor has done it, has tricked me into remembrance. He has brought back Joseph in a fashion no other child at the Institute ever has.

It was the choosing of the smoothest blanket tonight that hurt me so, after Doctor Itard had brought the boy back all sleepy and warm and damp from the rain and the man, with his tongue no doubt loosened by wine, making those foolish remarks about the boy and his dreams. After I had sent him away, I took the candle and went back to Victor's room to lock the door and that's when I saw him. Crouching with his back to the fire, his bed untouched, fists balled into his eyes. I know now he is asleep when he squats like that, and have learned not to trouble to wake him. It is his preferred method of sleeping. It must come from nights in the forest when he had to be on his guard. Still, as I say, it hurt me.

The boy squatting in the corner of the room with his dark caves for eyes and no love there at all for me, no gratitude, and my heart bobbed in my chest like that wooden boat on the water. Joseph, my heart said all over again. I cannot tell you why.

It's morning, a new day, and here is Victor, his dark head craning forward, searching for something, sniffing the air. He is crouching by the pond, the keyhole shaped ornamental pond in the gardens of the Deaf Mute Institute, staring into the water. He leans forward to tap his hand on the surface, watches ripples fan out and dissolve into the reeds at the edges. He can smell the constant movement of the water, smell the leaves, smell even the speckle of stars on the surface: the sunlight.

A feather floats on the pond, above him a swift dips and lifts. Marat, the black great dane, dozes on the high Institute wall. A door bursts open, spilling the children in their blue caps, blue uniforms; a burst pocket of blue beads, pouring into corners, knocking up against one another, before being rolled into straight lines, and guided back inside through another door. Victor gives no sign of having seen or heard them. Nor does he raise his head at the familiar voice of Doctor Itard.

He only protests when the doctor tries to lead him back towards the library. He touches the water again, touches a twig, watches the lines on the water wobbling, shaking, moving, living: their pattern is trying to reach him. He can see circles, infinite circles, his eyes rest happily on these, but only if he stares and taps, stares and taps, he must not be interrupted, he will *not* be interrupted, he needs the circles, they are trembling and fading, always coming towards him but never reaching. He too trembles and fades just like the circles of water. He trembles and dissolves and reappears again, over and over. He could stay here all day and do this, shaking like endless wrinkles in a huge sheet of silky fabric. When Itard touches his arm, Victor screams. He thrashes and he bites. The doctor is tearing him from himself, from the ripples.

The doctor jumps back. Two other masters come running and help to usher him into the building, still screaming, kicking, lashing out with fists and feet.

He trembles and dissolves and disappears again, he fans out in ripples, hits the edge of something, breaks up and starts again. All the while they shout at him, call him back.

Brumaire 1
Year Eight

Gladdened by the success of my trip to the restaurant with Victor, I went further today with a more ambitious trip. The outcome was extraordinary; a breakthrough of the highest order.

My plan was to take Victor to Versailles. Although immodest to say so, it was an *inspired* idea. It was partly occasioned by a desire in my own breast to see for myself the scene of such momentous events, now that a decent period of time has elapsed. Being Victor's official tutor and guardian has some unexpected rewards. Certain doors are now opened to me. Official requests and invitations have poured my way since knowledge of my work with Victor has grown.

Early in the morning I told Madame Guérin of my plan, asking if she might accompany me. She rather slyly produced a better suggestion: why shouldn't her daughter, Julie, be my companion for the day, since it was her day that month without work duties? I could fetch her from the Val-de-Grâce on my way out of Paris and she would be a great help with the child, since he was so fond of her. (It has not been my observation that Victor favours Mademoiselle Julie more than anyone else; more than myself, for example. But I kept silent.) Since Madame Guérin's duties at the Institute must keep her at home, I had no choice – such a trip could not be ventured alone with the boy. When Julie unexpectedly turned up, with a gift of marrons glacés for her father, and some plain chestnuts for Victor (who shuns the candied kind) the matter was decided.

The road to Versailles is about twelve miles over a good pavement. This time we took a berline, as I did not wish to drive all that way. It was a fine autumnal day, crisp leaves occasionally blowing in through the open window of our carriage. We allowed Victor to sit near the window. This had the unfortunate result that I was occasionally thrown against Julie, despite all efforts to maintain the proper distance between us. On one such occasion she nudged my elbow, laughing and pointing at Victor, who had his arm across the basket of provisions. Once he had seen Madame Guérin prepare it, he guarded that basket with his life.

Several times we had to stop urgently when Victor needed to relieve himself and would happily have done so then and there, had I not prevented him by prompt action. Each time I hastened to the woods at the side of the road with him, as far from the berline as was decent in the available time. Keeping a firm grip on Victor's arm, helping him with his loathed breeches, I knew from the agitation in his behaviour and the intensity in his eyes that escape is never far from his mind, even now. We have not yet succeeded in making his new life so agreeable to him that it can compensate him for the loss of his freedom.

We returned to the berline from each of these impromptu excursions with our boots much muddied, our hair decorated with leaves. We resumed our journey. We arrived at Versailles at midday, entering the gardens of the Grand Château from a back door of the auberge. Seated on the grass, we opened our modest picnic, admiring the straight walks between thick plantations leading from one large lake to another. Whilst occupied with his food, Victor was not in danger of escape.

Thus we enjoyed the simple rustic food Madame Guérin had prepared for us, washing it down with plenty of wine and talking amiably of the gods, goddesses and other illustrious personages placed in various attitudes in the lakes beside us to serve as water-fountains. Victor was unable to resist capering towards these fountains. Choosing the most voluptuous of them all, he buried his head in her breasts and began drinking. It was an awkward moment. Julie laughed easily but I confess to finding the sight disturbing. Of course Victor also succeeded in soaking himself and then scampered back to our company, where I fully expected him to shake himself over us like a dog. Thankfully, he did not. Food was still laid out; his appetite this happy day overwhelmed all other urges. His diet consisted of water, rye-bread, beans and walnuts, but of these he ate copious amounts.

We stood up, and were greeted by a waiter from the auberge who indicated his wish to act as our guide to the Petit Trianon. This very pretty place, which a few years back was the seat of the most perfidious luxury, is now occupied by an ale-house keeper who lets out rooms in summer for the accommodation of parties. The impertinent man offered us the same, glancing slyly from Julie to myself. Being assured that we did not want accommodation, he demanded twenty sous and a further ten for allowing us to bring 'the idiot boy' inside his establishment. At this Julie was moved to retort tartly: citoyen, do you not recognise the famous Savage of Aveyron?

For once I was glad of her boldness, as the ignorant waiter indeed seemed impressed and, after accepting our fee, allowed us to wander unaccompanied around the rest of the gardens.

Many of the buildings are now hastening towards decay. Presently we entered a kind of grotto and instantly recognised the cottage where Marie Antoinette used to wear her famous muslin dresses and play at being poor. Here we had a brief disagreement: Julie called her the 'unhappy queen' and wondered if she had sighed by this same bubbling brook, weeping for a happiness that being royal could not give and waiting for her little Dauphin to visit her in his ploughboy dress for further scenes of 'innocent enjoyment'.

I cannot remember what I said in reply but I know it was rather sharp.

I must remind myself that Julie Guérin is very young.

Having had no sisters myself, I am conscious that perhaps my manner with the gentle sex borders on the brusque. After all, many Parisiens are currently at great pains to rewrite the past and Julie Guérin is not alone in her perspective. Lemeri mentioned only last week that on the anniversary of the King's death last January, he found a black flag near the church of the Madeleine with the inscription *Victimes de la Révolution, venez déposer ici vos vengeances*. Maybe it was a trick to catch a few Royalists? I naively suggested. Lemeri spat at the ground, making a gesture which left me in no doubt as to what he did with the black flag.

There was scant time for a debate with Julie however, since Victor demanded our full attention. His trotting progressed to running and his running was swift and skilful. One or the other of us ran alongside him, laughing and panting, and when he outran us, the other, resting on the grass, would sprint ahead. Julie soon flung off her fichu and pulled the ribbons from her shoes, running in stockinged feet. (Seeing her, one is forced to conclude that Rousseau is quite wrong in his statement that women are not made to run.) This way we preserved our strength, taking it in turns to run in circles alongside him. It was I, not Julie, who eventually could not keep up with him.

It made an agreeable sight to see the two of them together, bounding over the grass, Julie being no more hampered by her long skirts than Victor was now by his boots. From my position seated on the grass, I watched them. Nothing about Victor in this scene was unusual. Although some reports tell us that he ran on all fours, I have never seen it. His rocking, his humming, his unusual gait, all were smoothed out by this activity at which he so excelled.

This thought, being rare, pleased me. Victor as perfectly ordinary. It struck me for the first time that Victor might even have had a sister, might well have run like this beside her in his mysterious other life; mysterious that is to me, but not to him. Watching him, I felt a rush of pride. That child would win any race with another boy of his age – no wonder it took two huntsmen as many days to track and capture him!

Finally even Victor tired of running and Julie replaced her shoes, feigning dismay over the green stains now covering her white stockinged feet. We made a steadier promenade to the Grand Trianon, stepping under colonnades of the finest marble and making our way at last to the château.

As we approached the doors an official appeared, examined my letter of invitation and insisted on another ten sous to take us inside. A large part of the palace has now been converted into a barracks for a corps of invalids and this man presides over that, but for a price, he will take visitors around.

We were somewhat silenced once through those heavy portals. Victor, walking between us, flared his nostrils suspiciously at the smell of decay and sickening bodies. Julie wanted to see some of the old splendour and so we wandered from room to room, Victor with his nose in the air, sniffing the cool musty smell of neglect, the great deposit of dust layering everything. Although much has been torn down and destroyed, many old paintings and superb statues remain, which struck me not as 'sad', as they did Julie, but as decadent and disgusting.

I carefully explained this to Julie. To my surprise she barely let me finish. I have observed that she has her mother's boldness, without the mother's commendable habit of silence on matters where she can have no hope of being my equal. When I told her this, the young Guérin's eyes widened and her pale face flushed with colour. She clutched at her kerchief and then at her bodice and seemed to struggle to find a way to keep her hands from flying up to her face. In short, she conveyed with every aspect of her demeanour an annoyance or agitation that was quite inexplicable. Finally she contented herself with a loud: *Well!* and marched on ahead, catching up with Victor, who was already through the doors and back into the sunlight. I had almost to run to fall in step with them both. We walked in silence at this unnatural speed through the grounds towards the spot where the driver had tethered the horse.

I have no idea why, but gloom descended on me as we made our way back to the berline. I reassured myself that only a man made of glass would not feel something on leaving Versailles, no matter what his political sentiments. I put the conversation with Julie – and her response – out of my thoughts.

Walking away from the château, I glanced up at a window. A ghostly hand – a flutter of white paper – waved there. Victor made a little squeak. For a moment, one breathless moment, I thought he had seen it, I believed – I must have wanted to believe – that he imagined the same thing I did; that he had an imagination at all, capable of translating everyday objects into meaningful symbols, giving flesh to fancies, fluttering handkerchiefs or gloves where in reality only paper – blank white paper – exists.

But his squeak was for a different reason: he had spotted a nut on the floor of the carriage. He sprang on it with enthusiasm. Our marvellous excursion came to an end.

But the marvellous outcome has not yet been recorded.

It was when we returned Victor home that the day's joys were completed. Madame Guérin greeted us, her husband in his customary position by the fire, a smell of chocolate simmering on the stove and the offer of a delicious gâteau à la broche. For Victor, who made his desires clear by taking a firm hold of his governess's hand and guiding it to the pitcher, a cup of milk was offered. *Lait*, said Madame Guérin as she poured the drink. *Lait*, she said, as she habitually does, as she gave it to him. Victor took one large gulp and drained the glass. And then: *lait*, crowed Victor and the rest of us nearly collapsed with surprise.

There was a silence, in which I heard my own blood pulsing through my brain. Then, again: *lait!* said Victor.

I had not imagined it, then: the wild boy speaks, after all. After a second, we all began talking at once.

Clever Victor, clever boy! Julie cried and in her spontaneous fashion she pounced on him in a passionate clasp, from which he struggled to emerge as if drowning. Madame Guérin, to whom surprise seems a foreign emotion, managed to invest her usual *oh, Dieu* with such feeling, none could doubt her astonishment. She too knelt beside Victor and pulled him to her in an embrace. It is the first time I have seen her do this. Victor did not entirely submit to her caresses but neither did he struggle to escape. I deduce that he enjoyed it, in his fashion.

Her husband laughed and addressed his remarks to me: well, Doctor, there you have it. He said a word. You were right: he's no dumb imbecile after all.

For myself, I wished the others were not there. I would have liked to embrace Victor, to press him to say the marvellous word again and again, but my cursed shyness prevented it. I had to be satisfied by patting Victor on the head and murmuring: well done, child; to which he made his splendid new response: *lait, lait!* he said again. We all laughed.

Another cup of milk was poured. The evening came to an exhausted but exhilarating conclusion. Mademoiselle Guérin seemed to have recovered her equanimity towards me and bade me goodnight with no sign of ill-humour. I walked home alone, my head ringing with Victor's voice.

Even though this was many hours ago now, the sound of that *lait* is as fresh in my mind as if Victor were still in the room with me. As I recorded the event in my journal, dripping ink spots on the page in my haste, scribbling by the light of both carcel lamps – feeling the need for as much illumination as possible! – I could still hear his voice, the exact timbre, the exact note. The voice did not sound the least bit human. It was like no sound I have ever heard. It was more like birdsong: high-pitched, tremulous, clear, true. It did not feel to me as if Victor was asking for milk. Rather, it seemed to come from somewhere else; a note deep inside him, a pure sound, older than the forest itself, purer than the sound of water babbling over a stone, as natural as the whisper of wind in the reeds. As if Nature herself rose up and spoke to me. My whole body shivers now, as I remember it. I long to have the child in the room with me, to ask him again and again to speak, to hear the exquisite fluting sound.

Dear Victor. How fitting that your first word should be *milk*. To name in some peculiar way your own loss. Human milk, human connection, the sustaining love of a mother. Now I believe that in a profound, convoluted fashion, you understand this very well.

Here perhaps my thoughts should be reined in, as they trample undisciplined ahead of me, taking their own heady path, skipping with joy at the infinite possibilities that Victor's new abilities suggest. What else can he learn? What will he tell us, once he speaks? It is only a few weeks until I must give my first paper to the Society of the Observers of Man to summarise my findings thus far. The timing could not be more auspicious. I could not possibly suppress my discovery to Pinel, to any detractors – to the world at large – that the wild boy can indeed be taught to speak.

And that I am right and they, every last one of them, are wrong.

My Julie's first word was milk, just like Victor. Or was it Joseph's? In any case it was the word for drink, for wanting a drink, for enjoying a drink, at least I think it was. More likely meaning: give me a drink, if I know my children! The words at first, the few that an infant has, they have to do a lot of work, they have to serve for everything. I think the doctor, for all he is clever of course and knows such a lot about the ears and throats of poor damaged souls and about this man Locke he is always quoting, and even about this strange ear contraption he showed me once that he is making to help the deaf to hear, for all of that, I think the doctor does not know a great deal about infants. Well hardly surprising, since as far as I can tell he has no nephews or nieces and does not seek out the company of any married ladies with children. Or any ladies at all. Which you might say is not unnatural. Might only be a further sign of his ambition, his dedication here to Victor. Doctor Itard himself would no doubt say that. That he has no care for any other task, that the boy leeches every ounce of him. He would doubtless say he is wedded to his Great Endeavour and think no more of it. If a person should dare to ask him or suggest otherwise, that is. Which none would.

But it means he expects a lot of Victor. That he is not very pleased with advances which the rest of us are ready to spring up and dance over.

I mean, the first time my Joseph said a word I thought that he was the first person in the world to speak, I thought he had invented language, just for me, just to give his maman the pleasure of hearing that particular note, that pure sound. And I felt some of that today too, hearing Victor. His word had the exact same note, it gave me the same feeling of being, well, a word, of course, but also something else, the first sign, the start of something so much bigger. We all of us praised Victor, we flung our arms around him, Julie now, she had tears in her eyes, but the doctor, he just stood there. It looked like it pained him to even pat the boy's head. The man is as stiff as his own cane and wanders around with a head full of books and a nose full of snuff so that when a miracle happens right under it, the most he can do is sneeze.

Well I have said my piece. It is not for me to chastise the doctor, who is a good man at heart, I am sure of it. He can't be blamed if he has no experience of infants, and no more understanding of them than any other man of his age or station. The most that can be said of him is that he tries. That he wants to learn. That's something after all. Rousseau, he says yesterday, tells us that when we say no to a child, we should make it clear that circumstance, not ourselves, does the forbidding. Show him the empty dish, let him know that there are no more sugar plums, not that it is we who deny him. But what does Melancholy Jacques know of infants? He abandoned all five of his own to the foundling hospital. No wonder his ideas are wanting in good common sense. I doubt Jean-Jacques Rousseau walked the floors, night after night, with a screaming babe, nor understood half the little tricks that a mother knows to make a child biddable, without the child feeling duped or cajoled, or any less the master.

Later that night I talked to Julie and discovered that the poor girl is so smitten that she truly believes the man might be falling for her. Of course, a few weeks back I might have hoped for this very thing but listening and watching Itard has taught me better. I tried to warn her but she would not hear a word against him. She didn't tell her mother much but the few hints she gave me, the flush that rose in her neck when she spoke of an argument they'd had at Versailles, a pocketful of little details she gave me, all added up to the same sorry tale. She might just as well have opened a locket and shown me Itard's picture.

I have enough to occupy me without finding a fresh worry in Julie. Still, I did not have a peaceful night. That girl has the looks and figure of a dark angel; her father's sweetness, his terrible gentleness of heart; and the whole lot topped off with my daring, my bold nature. It is a fearful combination you would not wish to visit on any child, least of all your own daughter.

Victor is sitting at the table in Madame Guérin's kitchen, concentrating on his task of shelling beans. In front of him is a cone of sugar on a wooden stand, but he is not tempted to break off a piece. He is focused only on his beans, on his task. Sameness. Preservation of sameness. To his right, an earthenware bowl for the beans, to his left, a basket full of pods, piled up in a tumble. In front of him, a square of muslin for the bad beans.

At his feet are the abandoned pods, shells scraped open with his nail, popping the beans along the seam like buttons from a shirt. Victor sorts with a razor-sharp gaze, he slips the black, the pocked, the mildewed beans to one side. No bad bean escapes him. He works with the speed of a bird spearing fish in a river.

If Madame Guérin interrupts his task he screams angrily. There is a rhythm to this, a rhythm which is calming and occupying; the snip of the pod opening, the scrape of his nail down the spine, the green juice that squeezes under his nails, the beans piling up like pennies on a market table, the odd black one, bad one, bad boy, bad child, bad penny. Turning up, turning out. Turning him out: selecting the wheat from the chaff.

Rejecting. Bad boy: what did you do to be cast out?

His limbs are long, carved and slender as bones. He carries them with all the grace and gracelessness of an ape. Everything concentrates on his task: his heart-shaped face beneath the shorn hair, his eyes unlit, the colour of roasted coffee; the little pointed yellow teeth, the thin lips, the back of his head, his neck, his ears tender as thumbs, tender as the heels of babies.

He works hard at the beans. When one pile is finished, he looks around for more. If Monsieur Guérin enters the kitchen, heaps more pods, the last of the crop, in his basket, Victor is silent and content.

When Madame Guérin asks him to set the table for dinner, all hell breaks loose.

Brumaire 5
Year Eight

My elation at Victor's first word has been blunted by my discovery this past week that he uses his word indiscriminately, not for communication. Neither his governess nor I can persuade Victor to use '*lait*' to request a drink of milk. In vain we hid the milk pitcher in the cupboard, hastened his thirst with salted bread and a day-long denial of water. Despite this, despite clearly longing for a drink, he would not utter the word '*lait*' as a request. Finally his governess could stand his begging no longer. All day he had attempted to direct her to the milk pitcher with the pitiful banging of a spoon on his drinking bowl, and when that failed he pushed her towards the cupboard, thrusting the key in her hand. Victor knew that this was where the milk was hidden. (He seems to have great difficulties in using keys for their purpose, although he has a great fascination with them. I have never seen him succeed in using one to open a door or cabinet.)

I had told Madame Guérin not to give in and she carried out her duties faithfully, although clearly my instructions caused her pain.

Say *lait*, Victor, I implored him, standing close to Madame Guérin, to ensure that she did not weaken under this assault on her emotions.

It was to no avail. Finally I nodded to Madame Guérin. The milk was poured into Victor's bowl and then and only then did we hear him cry *lait!* He uses it as a sign of pleasure, as a meaningless accompaniment to eating and drinking (or sometimes bathing or walking); the equivalent of idle whistling or humming. He does not utter the word to request a drink. The real meaning of spoken language remains mysterious to him.

This is a grave disappointment. On questioning Madame Guérin, my worst fears are realised: he utters his word night and day, regardless of circumstance and has even been heard to murmur it in his sleep, along with another sound, something like a liquid *lli* sound. Madame Guérin claims that he is trying to pronounce 'Julie'. She says that this word *lli* occurs more frequently following visits by Mademoiselle Guérin. I find this supposition unlikely. Further observations will have to be made.

My initial disappointment has since been alleviated by a conversation with Virey, whom I visited this afternoon over in his 'study' (little more than a rented room above a shop in the new Passage du Caire). Virey seemed delighted to see me; I suffered a pang of regret for my preoccupation with Victor of late, my neglect of social engagements. Virey is writing his own report on Victor, based on the early days of Victor's captivity, when he was held at the orphanage at St Affrique.

He talked to me about it as we strolled together along the passage, wandering between the smoky braziers, the stalls of fine linens and the endless tables of goggles for sale, which it seems it is the fashion for every Parisien (including Virey) to sport, regardless of the condition of their eyes. Of course, had I not been secure in my new reputation, I might have suffered the professional envy that used to make my friendship with Virey so vexed. My new status has cured me of that old envy. I was able to listen to Virey's opinions – delivered in his usual excited fashion – with a new equanimity. He reminded me that eighteen months of a careful and assiduous education are usually necessary before a child can lisp a few words: have we then the right to expect that a rude inhabitant of the forest, who has been in society for so few months, several of which he has passed amongst the deaf and dumb, should have already acquired the facility of articulate speech in a matter of only four months?

The real difficulty is the mystery shrouding Victor's first five years of life. If he already possessed the power of speech, and lost it over those seven years of isolation, how long should I allow for him to recover it? But if – as is perfectly feasible – his early infancy was also isolated, or he has been abandoned for longer than is presently suspected, or the effects of isolation are more injurious than even I presumed, what then?

You have revised your opinion of the savage as incurable? I asked Virey, stopping so suddenly that Virey was propelled onto the shoes of the lady coming towards him. She was a young blonde in the usual diaphanous white robe, despite being with a respectable companion. Virey apologised extravagantly to her before replying. Let us say, my friend, that I am willing to be proven wrong! he bellowed, this time hastening across the street to avoid a carriage dog, a great dane, hurtling towards us, threatening to knock us under the wheels of the carriage.

This conversation with Virey and the supper we then enjoyed together in a café in the Rue des Boucheries convinced me that I have one ally in the Society. I feel greatly comforted. The shadow of the paper I must soon give throws itself over my daily work with Victor. Given my dread of public speaking it could hardly be otherwise. Knowing that Virey's mind is no longer closed to my hypothesis has encouraged me enormously. (Although I wonder at my desire for corroboration from an inferior intellect such as Virey's and can only conclude that it stems from lack of self-confidence, which further accomplishments will soon assuage.)

I rushed to my work with Victor with new vigour this morning. I determined not to mind when he uttered his meaningless sounds. I took him on an energetic walk through the Jardin du Luxembourg and wandered as far as the Observatoire, allowing him to pause and enjoy the sight of the men going about their work. I did not reprimand him when he insisted on smelling every last twig and acorn, every pile of stones, every ladder and bucket. I endured the laughter of the labourers and the curiosity of passers-by. One kindly builder tried to show him the telescope they are erecting, some twenty-five feet in length; a magnificent specimen which would beguile any other boy of Victor's age. But the man was soon bewildered when Victor simply fell to the floor and started sniffing his boots. I shrugged my shoulders and muttered something about the forest, Victor having had no need of telescopes there. To which the witty fellow replied: are there not stars in the forest, citoyen? I ceded with a gesture that this was indeed true, and with a jerk on Victor's arm, managed to drag him away from the man's boot. (He was in danger of being kicked off. Workmen, I've discovered, do not appreciate being touched unexpectedly, any more than Victor does.)

I hurried away, dragging Victor with difficulty but managing to give a jaunty wave to the builder, to show how much I had enjoyed our discussion. En route I talked to Victor about his progress, firm in my belief that only constant immersion in language will allow the child to reproduce it.

On our return home occasion arose for Victor to demonstrate his excellent memory. An old crippled man, whose legs were mere stubs, so that he appeared to rise out of the paving stones like a tortured soul, was seated at the corner of the Rue St Jacques, entreating passers-by to place a bet on three cups in front of him, one of which hid a coin. Victor's eyes were attracted by the flash of silver. Not, I am sure, because he attaches value to it, but because he is a magpie, he loves all that shines. (His squirrelling capacity would have been essential to him in the forest: it is not surprising that it is well developed.)

We paused and the old man encouraged us to place a bet. Risk a sous, monsieur, gain a fortune, he mumbled without conviction. His gnarled hands worked at an incongruous speed, swapping the cups with much dexterity, but each time, Victor outwitted him, choosing the right cup. The coin was reluctantly handed to Victor, who bleated *lait lait!* with such excitement that a crowd soon amassed.

Eventually the old cripple protested that we were cheating him and began angrily poking Victor with his stick, demanding the return of his coins. I had trouble prising Victor away but succeeded with some pantomime efforts to indicate that Madame Guérin would have a good dinner ready for us. I felt foolish, standing on the street corner, waving my arms and rubbing my stomach, then making an action to indicate food entering my mouth and wine being drunk, but my efforts were rewarded. Victor understands pantomime language very well. It is the language that he himself uses, albeit in a restricted way.

My lesson of today is that it is more effective to coax the boy than to use force. Force he can well resist, a chestnut he cannot. To give credit to his governess, she made this discovery long before me. She has told me her best weapon is to appeal to his stomach. She has experiences as a mother to draw on. Simple though she is, the lessons life have taught her have many advantages over my training as a banker, then a doctor.

One last matter.

In conversation with Julie a few days ago something she said was disquieting. We were discussing Victor's capture in Aveyron. The exact details of it, the fact that after an early capture and escape in 98, Victor was recaptured when wandering in search of food into the house of a dyer in St Sernin, a man named Vidal.

For the result, do you believe Victor *wanted* to be found? was Julie's question.

I had answered quickly. Oh, no – he put up a good fight. He resisted with all his might. He tried constantly to escape . . .

Julie paused (it was in the carriage, returning from Versailles,

Victor slept between us, his head on her shoulder, and she spoke in a whisper, smoothing down his hair with one hand), opened her mouth to utter something and then closed it again. After a moment she could contain her thoughts no longer.

But he wandered into a garden . . . he had survived for all those years in the mountains on what? Acorns, mushrooms, berries? Why would he at this late point seek out a village, a road, a house? He was supposedly terrified of people and ran from anyone who approached him. Does it not strike you then as significant? Perhaps Victor was tired of his journeying, of his struggle. Perhaps he had tired of being alone.

Victor had murmured in his sleep and Julie had stopped talking, not wanting to wake him. With much vehement head-shaking, I tried to make it clear that I found her theories fanciful. But the suggestion has taken hold of me. Tonight, I stood at my window, the toe of my slipper resting against one rotten, creaking floorboard. Like Victor in one of his reveries, I stared out of the window. Rather than water, I sipped a glass of pastis. The shutters were folded back, the clock-tower of the Institute in my sights. It was not a calm night. The sky was thick with smoke from a hundred chimneys. In the rooms beneath me the wretched Fanfan yapped relentlessly. (Evidently he has been found, unfortunately unharmed by his adventure, his spirit not dampened in the least.) Across the street a child's wails scraped the walls. Coachmen yelled at horses, female voices screeched at them to shut up, slopped water from windows, then slammed them shut. Only a street away, the wild boy slept.

He wanted to be found. He had tired of being alone.

It was Uncle who floated into my reverie. Uncle with his long face, narrowing almost to a point, where it seemed to form seamlessly into the wisp of a beard. As a boy, his face reminded me of nothing as much as a long white feather. And now he is gone, a feather is what he has become. Insubstantial. I can only catch fragments of him, the scraps

127

of his voice, the slightly nasal, rasping breathing that he did when he was concentrating, when he was reading, for example. Never fear being alone, Jean-Marc, he would tell me. It is a position far preferable to a life of false friendships and trifling attachments. You will find few men – and even fewer women – who deserve your full affection. Then he would read, at length, from Jean-Jacques' Sixth Walk and I would make myself comfortable on his leather chair and pull at my own chin, pretending a beard grew there, planning all the marvellous ways I would fulfil Uncle's dreams for me.

I have admired Victor enormously, I suddenly understood. For his endurance, for not having died of solitude, if such a thing were possible. For the fashion in which, even now, he excludes us, he appears to need no one. Least of all me.

Could Julie's words be true, that in fact he really did give up, the day he wandered into Vidal's garden? That he decided to abandon his life in the wilderness, had a gnawing desire to be with others, after all? Later, Julie had said that the idea should please me, make me feel less guilty. Guilty for what? I asked, startled. Her face was briefly lit by the lanterne and I saw her expression, but could not understand it. Not guilty, I mean, responsible, she quickly said. I assured her that I felt neither and that her theory about Victor wanting to be found lacked weight. It was, in short, unlikely.

Julie has, as I have noted, a strong resemblance to her mother. The same brown eyes, the same firm, expressive mouth. She is quicker, less steady in all respects, and more volatile, not given to holding her tongue. But she has the same ability to indicate with just a narrowing of the eyes, a lifting of the shoulders, precisely when she is in disagreement with me. I find it no less infuriating in the daughter than the mother. The subject was closed. Julie helped me to lift Victor from the carriage and we did not mention it again.

Her comments were surely petty, inconsequential. Why should I find myself so disturbed? It has created a picture that I do not care to dwell upon. Victor, his hair long and shaggy, his skin browned and naked; studded with scars, bruises and embedded thorns, lolloping down that street in St Sernin. A scrap of shirt flapping on his back, a great foolish grin on his face. Hoping, missing, longing for something that now it has become my painful duty to find for him, although the Lord knows I cannot find it for myself.

I tried again to talk to our Julie about Doctor Itard but she was having none of it. We were at the banks of the Seine with a great bundle of washing, Victor locked in at home with only Henri to guard him, so I was in a hurry, using the bat with more vigour than normal. Julie assured me in breathless cries that there was *nothing* about *men* that I could tell her that she *did not* already *know* and had I not *remembered* that at her *age* I was already *married* and that every last day of the *week* she spent her time at the military hospital *bathing* and *lifting* and *tending* to soldiers, to men in every state of *injury*, often in the most *vulnerable* of places, so did I not think that by now she might be *familiar* with them? Her words were emphasised each time by a great thwack of the bat against the sheets, so that I could hardly hear her and was given no chance to reply. She then plunged the linen back into the river, stirring up a silty cloud and quite defeating her own purposes.

I said when she fell silent and sat back on her heels that bathing men and tending to their injuries in the most vulnerable of places was not the same as knowing their hearts and that there were still some sides to their natures that she might be ignorant of. Some men who were cooler than others. Some *tastes* she might not have imagined. This was enough to make her leap up, gather up the bundle of wet linen and take off down the banks, her black boots sinking a little into the mud, in her haste to escape me.

I sighed, as any mother would.

There was no time to linger nor continue the lecture, since Henri is no match for Victor in one of his moods and I can never leave them alone together without a pressing fear of what might happen. I scoured the bank for someone I knew amongst the washerwomen and soon spied Angeline, the widow of the baker on the Rue St Jacques. She helped me spread the sheets along the branches of the overhanging trees and together we rued the impetuous nature of daughters, the wickedness of men and the general warp and weave of things, which is all toil and servitude from birth to death.

I felt a good deal better after that.

Brumaire 15
Year Eight

This morning my anxiety was intense. I had a headache, I was crestfallen in an inexplicable way; I did not want to work with Victor and stayed in my room until the bell struck one and I knew it was too late. I sent no message to Madame Guérin; I do not know what she made of this.

At two o'clock I took my place on the podium in front of the Society of the Observers of Man. The smell of the dark oak panelling in the room almost choked me; I might just as well have been imprisoned in my coffin. Pinel sat opposite me, his chin lost in his collar, an inscrutable expression in his eyes. Many extra members of the Society crowded into the room, some I had not seen before. More chairs were brought. Still more men arrived and were forced to stand at the back of the hall. Much shuffling and jostling ensued. Pinel stood up in irritation and insisted that we were now full, as the door opened again and another flurry of gentlemen arrived. A short discussion and they were admitted. Amongst them I thought I glimpsed the white of a bonnet, a purple dress. I was astonished that a woman might be admitted, even more astonished that she might *want* to attend. There was no time to consider this.

My papers were in front of me on the lectern. When the room came finally – at Cuvier's impatient insistence – to a hush, I moved to pick the papers up but they leapt from me and swished themselves away like the angry tail of a horse, fluttering to the floor. Dust motes danced in front of my eyes. My throat constricted. I bent down, retrieved the papers and straightened them; coughed, swallowed, took a sip of water, splashing a great drip over my very first word; opened my lungs and took a breath. The room contracted into a tiny circle. The faces of my interrogators swam in front of me: monstrous reflections, like those on the convex side of a spoon.

You may begin, Doctor Itard, said Pinel, dangling his watch at me like a mesmerist.

An image of Victor slid between the professor's face and my papers. In this picture, Victor too was opening his mouth, straining, straining to make the sounds I demanded of him. I could see his tonsils, the pink of his tongue, a bubble of saliva. I could almost see the word itself, trapped there; a bird in a cage, a spider held tight in a fist.

Citizens! Gentlemen, esteemed members of the Society . . .

I sipped more water. My voice cracked, taking up a note I had never heard before. It sounded like the voice of a girl, of someone else. I felt shame at my betrayal by this high-pitched voice. My legs shook so hard that the lectern rattled. I tried again:

. . . Cast on this earth, naked, weak, devoid of knowledge, the human infant has a long journey before taking his place in Nature, as the highest ranking member of the species. We believe this status to be his natural destiny . . . um . . . But – but – many philosophers throughout the ages have suggested that without the nurture provided by family, society and civilisation, in fact man would be amongst the weakest and least gifted species on the planet. Until now, this truth, although insisted upon, has been impossible to demonstrate. Some have claimed that wandering tribes – the savages of other lands – are evidence of how ignorant and uncivilised man would be in a pure state of Nature. However, I would argue that simply because these people are not civilised in *our* understanding of the word, does not mean they are not civilised at all . . .

I reminded myself to breathe. I tried taking sips of water but the sound of my lips closing, of the liquid slipping down my throat, was absurdly loud; the whole room seemed to swim in water whenever I swallowed. I could no longer see their faces, nor the ink marks on my papers. I wrestled with myself, rebuked myself for childishness. I tried to summon forth a picture of Uncle in his angriest incarnation: his white eyebrows lifting up at the outer corners, ready to fly from his face, his sternest voice, ordering me to stop this stuttering, commanding the words to come. But still the words bumped clumsily over my tongue, footsteps timidly stepping between stones on a river. Rushing torrents between each stone. Long waits whilst I judged the current; whether it was now safe to leap.

Cuvier drew on his pipe, one arm draped along the back of his chair. It was a mistake to glance at him; my place was lost and I struggled to find it.

To determine – ahem – my intention was to determine what would such a young man think, what would he understand, deprived from infancy of all education? And what could this tell us about our own innate nature, of who we might be, without the imprint of society . . .

The coughing and fidgeting in the room had stopped. Even in my nervousness I detected it. A shift of interest, a movement of the minds and bodies of the assembled men towards me. It did not help my voice, which continued to squeak and falter. But it allowed my heartbeat to settle, my palms, which I had been rubbing compulsively against the fabric of my jacket, to calm themselves sufficiently that I might keep them by my side for a while, and let the agitation flow out of them. And I had seen her, near the back of the room: a woman. Julie Guérin.

It occurred to me, as I continued to read out, that my spasmodic movements, my nervous rocking, my compulsive hand rubbing, all had a quality reminiscent of Victor. At that moment I was describing my work with Victor's senses, showing how I drew on Condillac's ideas. I was also wishing that I had been more concise in my report, at the same time noting the contradiction of how quickly the minutes flew past. And at the same time as reading my paper and turning the pages and thinking all of this, underneath it all, bright as the blade of a knife, was another thought. Victor. Is it that you are unbearably anxious, almost all of the time? Is this what you are feeling, when you rock from side to side, when you draw your straw through your teeth, over and over, when compulsive movements, compulsive sounds, grip your body?

Finally, still trembling, but with steadier voice, I came to my conclusions.

It must be said that – despite depictions to the contrary by certain thinkers eager to paint a romantic picture – man is inferior to a great number of animals in a pure state of Nature . . .

I hurried on, hearing a suspicious little intake of breath from Abbé Sicard, hoping to make my final conclusions without interruption. I could now sense a restlessness, and when I finally came to an abrupt halt, swallowing the last words about Victor's puberty as hastily as possible, I raised my eyes from the papers and looked up. It was as I had feared. The room heaved with expectation: all eyes fastened to me. A moth pinned on velvet. Impossible to move, or step down.

A cough from Doctor Pinel. De Gérando crossed and uncrossed his legs and beamed at me.

Thank you, Doctor Itard. Most interesting! Fascinating!

This broke the silence and there was a general hubbub of questioning, while Pinel waved his arms, urging the members to take an orderly turn. He allowed Virey to ask the first question.

Your savage speaks two words after less than six months in your care. *Lait* and this other sound – *lli*. Astonishing . . . you now fully expect him to master language?

I do, citizen.

So you believe that he is not a mute, nor an idiot, but that his silence and his other strange behaviours are wholly the result of his barbarous life, deprived of human company . . .

Yes . . .

There could be no question that the cut to his throat, which you mention, did not sever the muscles of his vocal organs and render him dumb?

I am sure of it. It was a long cut, but not deep. It was united by what we surgeons call the first intention. It healed well.

So in fact any one of our – citizens – assembled here, if left in the same sorry condition, might have developed as this poor wretch did, devoid of human speech, devoid of the knowledge of how to conduct ourselves in human society . . . ?

Yes, yes, I believe so.

Virey was not questioning me, he was giving me a chance to state more clearly, state again, my contentious position. Gratitude made me smile for the first time. There was some disorder amongst the assembled audience, a murmur of protest, which I tried to ignore, nodding instead towards Cuvier in the front row, who was also indicating that he wished to ask a question.

Have you an idea of the meaning of this liquid '*lli*' sound that he pronounces? Is it not astonishing that this sound, which in children in general is one of the most difficult to imitate, should be one of the first he has accurately produced? What do you deduce from that?

There have been suggestions –

I did not fully concentrate, as part of me was observing the movement of white and black and purple as the young woman at the back of the room shuffled her way between assembled persons towards the door, closing it softly behind her.

His governess believes, I continued, that he is attempting to pronounce her daughter's name. Julie. For evidence she cites the fact that he repeats this sound more frequently, sometimes even crying it in his sleep, after her daughter's visits.

And you do not share that opinion?

It is impossible accurately to ascertain the cause.

You mention the boy's puberty and then retreat from the subject. How does it manifest itself? What is this 'suspicion' which is cast on the 'origin of certain affections of the heart which we regard as very natural'?

I did say – I meant – that I wished to wait a while before drawing too hasty a conclusion from this.

Are you referring to love? To the highest sentiment known to man and suggesting that these are not natural feelings but must be taught, as we teach the catechism?

Before I could reply, Cuvier had glanced down at the notes on his knee and was quoting.

You say that you wish to refrain from destroying the 'most consoling illusions of social life' and yet – how can you now draw back, having offered us this most tantalising suggestion about the behaviour, the nature of men? Come, Itard, tell us what you mean!

It was a trap. Cuvier's mouth twitched with mischief. Having discovered in our earlier meeting how easy it was to fluster me, he was now, I saw, at pains to punish me for some perceived judgement on him, on his behaviour. It is true I have heard much about Cuvier and women and that I know he has a mistress and a child, for example. But I had

135

not intended to sit in judgement on him. There was no way to extricate myself from his challenge, especially in such a public situation. With my face blazing, I stuttered out a reply of sorts.

It is only that, as yet, the boy has not demonstrated any sign of that universal emotion which stirs all creatures and so, as I said, I cannot draw any clear conclusions.

Not *all* creatures, Itard, you are confused. It does not stir *all* creatures. For does a dog love the bitch it mates with? We assume surely (here he looked around the room, smiling at those his eyes fell upon) that it is man alone who is transformed by love. And yet you contradict yourself. A moment ago I believe you suggested that man's amorous nature has more in common with a – mountain wolf?

I said nothing of the sort!

The young gentlewomen of Paris must be living in great terror if every man is a wild beast in need of your tutoring. Or perhaps you are suggesting that it is not young *ladies* who should be afraid? That all which we hold to be *natural* is false and that the vilest vice known to man is, in fact, the most natural of all?

Laughter at Cuvier's words drowned my protest. When it died, Cuvier turned to me without a smile.

But if it is true that your savage struggles to pronounce this young woman's name, that he cries out for her in his sleep, could it be that you are quite wrong? His heart is not that of a beast at all?

He cries out for her in his sleep. Cuvier's words made the skin flame anew, my heart thud furiously.

No, no, I am sure I have never said he has the heart of a beast, neither do I believe – what you are suggesting. It is as I said. What Victor means cannot be ascertained, at this early stage –

I would have liked to say more, but my chance was lost when the Abbé Sicard interrupted. It was to ramble on at great length about man's innate sense of a Supreme Being and whether Victor had yet given a sign of possessing this sense. Skilfully phrased, so as to inspire no anger at the religious sentiment, whilst at the same time leaving us in no doubt as to his beliefs. He did not require an answer. When he sat down, De Gérando stood up and, prefacing his remarks with a polite That's as may be, proceeded to ask whether I was now persuaded that language came before thought? Was it possible to think without language? What evidence could I have, if he were not able to tell me, that my wild boy had abstract thoughts, had concepts such as justice or fairness or the ability, for example, to recall memories?

I did not answer him clearly. I could not put aside the exchange with Cuvier and fresh arguments were racing through my mind, arguments which the situation did not permit me to express. *He cries out for her in his sleep.* The phrase grew horrible, as if it were swelling, filling the room. A picture came to me unbidden, of Victor lying on his side on his mattress, naked, his legs bent together, drawn up towards his chest, the pale flesh stretching from his knees, fine as the wings of bats. His hands covered his eyes and in his sleep he murmured it: *lli, lli,* until Julie entered my vision, kneeling beside him, just as I have often seen her do, her dark hair hanging in sheets, as black moss hangs from a tree. My hot skin grew damp. Sickness rose in me. She turned to me, her smile wide as a slice of lemon. Uncle's gentle voice, warning me, was powerless. She was triumphant.

I battled. With a Herculean exertion, I returned my attention to a long and convoluted discussion of Condillac's ideas about perception. The discussion lasted the best part of an hour. Discussion then progressed to the quotidian details of Victor's life. Pinel asked about Madame Guérin's suitability for her post; I assured the Society that she was an excellent choice.

I longed for a glass of brandy and a darkened café. I wiped

137

at my eyes with my handkerchief. At last, Pinel thanked me for my report and announced the Society 'extremely pleased' by my progress and called a halt to the day's proceedings. He did not fail however to let us know that *he* was not convinced that he had been wrong in his diagnosis and that these 'small signs of progress' were no more than he would have expected. I counselled myself to remain silent. Finally, I was released.

I stepped down from the podium and my heart resumed its customary beat.

I struggled alone to carry that great bundle of linen home, dropping one of Henri's shirts in the mud at the Quai St Bernard and I cursed freely, especially my daughter. She was always a wilful child. At two years old I can remember her saying a hundred times a day: Maman, Maman! She knew what it meant, but for a time, when she had no other words, it meant everything. Do this, do that. Come, fetch. Pick me up, put me down. I can remember days when she tugged on my sleeve, just as Victor does, dragging me from room to room, and I was her willing puppet.

Joseph, now he was another kettle of fish. That time he was so wicked, drinking and drinking so much water, he wouldn't stop drinking, I thought he was a giant cloth, a sponge, soaking up water. It was a poor time, before we came to Paris, days we did not have clean water. Eighty-nine, it must have been, if Joseph was a year old.

And then I would go into his room at night and the sheets were wet with that warm sour smell seeping from the bed and I was tired, he was wasteful of our good water, how angry I felt. How I wanted to shake him, to shake the changeling child out of him, to bring my own little boy back. I stood in darkness in our room and I picked him up and he screamed and screamed and I wanted to dash his head against the wall, to crack open his skull like a walnut, and pluck my own dear angel – my real little boy, the loving one, the one who loved me still – from inside it.

You might think that was a wicked thought but I have no need of your judgements. I have more on my conscience than that. And you are forgetting, these were hard times. Bread that was black and crawled with weevils. Queuing in the market square at Millau for an hour and a half just to buy it, and wine as sour as vinegar and half as cheap.

It is Victor, I swear it, that musty dark boy as foul and foreign as the rotting secrets in the deepest part of the woods, it's Victor who keeps bringing back Joseph for me. Little baby Joseph with his fair cluster of curls just at the back of his head, his searching blue whorl eyes. How he looked at you – that baby – like he meant it, like he was wondering about you, and then one day – like that – that look was gone. I can remember one night, trying to wash some plates with the baby on my hip, and he must have been a year then, it was before he changed, and I was showing him a bubble on the end of a wooden spoon and that bubble trembled, and my baby Joseph stared at it, and so did I, and that's how long he was mine for. That's how long God allowed me to keep him, my darling boy, my tiny little son.

See Joseph, see how it holds all the light? All the colours, yes?

All the things I wanted to show him in this world. He was hungry, always hungry. And life was not bubbles and light. There was that time, that other time when I bent to pick up a rotten apple in the market square and the trader put her spiked heel on my hand and Joseph was on my hip crying and I begged her, I begged her, I told her he was thirsty and she had cups strung about her neck and a pitcher in one hand but she told me the price and said: we are all thirsty, madame, we are all hungry.

Joseph with his big eyes saying make the bubble come back and put food on the table and worse things, accusing me, night after night, you can't imagine. How that smell of the forest disturbs me, how it rises at me, rising in cracks between sleep and waking, like the white fleshy mushrooms that live in the cracks between the tree roots, that look like an innocent ball and then, when you pull them, surprise you with the most disgusting of shapes, a film of white sticky slime around their bulbous, their foul heads. My Joseph rises in my dreams more dangerous, more ugly yet.

If my own darling son haunts me how can a wretched woman complain because it is no less than I deserve. But it is more than I can bear. Today, I made Victor a bowl of lentil soup, I offered him the choicest chestnuts, I poured him creamy milk, I emptied his pot, I swept his room, I wept over the toys he'd burned that time, but I refused to scold him, and all the kindness, all the food in the world could not banish that hunger, that hollow nest inside me.

They come to a clearing in the trees. A circle dipped in blue, the moon directly overhead. It is a clearing the father has imagined many times, so many times he has dreamed it, seen it; he is sure the son has not. The little boy stops, dutifully, and squats on the floor beside his father, humming his customary tune. The man is very still. He holds his torch, smouldering red at one end. The dying embers provide barely enough light to see the shadowy boy by. But he holds it aloft, as if he needs a weapon. He looks all around him. His heart drums on the walls of his chest. The trees creak, the boy hums, the wolves moan. The boy's black eyes absorb the light, drawing every trace of moonlight to his own dark face. For once his mood is still, at peace.

This morning, as he left, Jacques had composed a speech. He had words to say, special words, in case God was still watching. Now, come to the centre of this terrible place, he knows that all such notions are false. There surely is no God, no God who could bring a father to this, only an aching belly, aching loins.

He knows his son is not stupid. And yet. The things the child *does*, the things he has driven Jacques to. If he is not stupid then it can only be malice, and that is worse. Three nights ago, returning from the woods with a rabbit dripping blood onto his jacket and a groaning hunger in his belly; dreaming of the good fire and the good food and later, the good feast with Félicité, what does he find? The door is locked, the child on the other side, rocking and humming and jangling the door-key like a jailer. No amount of cajoling, shouting, threatening, could persuade the boy to open the door. Jacques felt sure it wasn't fear that had driven him to lock the door, to keep the door securely locked, but sheer devilishness. His passion for keys, for lining them up, for polishing them, for sitting, dangling them from his hands for hours on end; for rattling them pointlessly in a keyhole without fully turning them, so that they neither locked nor unlocked; for replacing them on their hook or in the door – this had been evident since the child was little more than a baby. Dominique used to remark sadly that he was already too keen to lock her out. And now the obstinate child could not be persuaded to take his key and unlock the door, no matter how much the father – his mouth to the lock, his cheek on the door – entreated, bellowed at him. Finally, more desperate than he had ever been, Jacques had taken his axe and smashed at his own front door, no longer caring if the boy was too close behind it, until the heavy door ceded with a great splinter and on the other side, there was the child, quietly rattling the keys in his hand as if he hadn't a care.

Which, it seems, he hasn't. Now he is drawing in the earth with a stick. It is a pointless gesture, like all his gestures – he can't see what he is doing in the moonlight and has no interest in making shapes. He just makes movement, random movement, with the stick, without knowing if it draws a straight line or curved. A circle or a letter – a clue, a message – or a cross. Or most likely, nothing at all.

Suddenly fury, frustration, long-held-in anger at the boy, is coming to his rescue. He knows it is the right thing. The very fact that the child must know what he is planning – of this he has no doubt – but chooses not to care, incenses him.

You don't even *want* to be here, do you? You never did – you're completely indifferent, it is only me who suffers, me and your mother . . .

He does not invoke the girl, he doesn't say 'me and Félicité'. He is not stupid enough to believe that Félicité suffers; at least, not yet. In his mind, *not suffering* is further justification that the boy is not human, but he does not want to extend this thought to his young wife-to-be. Along with the special words, he'd had plans. How he would make a fire, leave the boy alone to struggle, survive perhaps, leave the glimmer of a possibility that he might make his way back. A kind of lottery that would show up whether the act was right or wrong; if the boy made it back, he would do his penance somehow, give up the girl, return to God . . . something. But now he sees that this option will be impossible. Cruel beyond belief – beyond his belief, anyway – to leave a child alone. Circled by these soft encroaching howls, the smell of earth and damp fur and the flickers of yellow flinty eyes; the approach of the wolves.

No, he must be resolute.

He lays down his axe, abandoning his plan to cut wood, to make a small fire. Instead he reaches deep into the pockets of his coat, finds his knife. The handle shaped like a guard from the Bastille. His *grand canif*, his souvenir knife, the blade smeared with wax, where he'd recently trimmed a candle wick. Sometimes the boy liked to play with the knife, opening and closing the blade. Since he didn't explore possibility, as other children do, there was no danger in allowing him this small pleasure: it would merely be ritual, repetition. The blade opening and sliding back beneath the Grenadier's ivory britches and boots. A rusty squeal, a click.

Come here, boy.

The blade opens its arms in a great arc, like a bird. *Come here.* The forest is silent. He crouches behind his child, one arm fatherly, firm, around his shoulders, the other hand, now gloveless, showing him the blade, the plaything. Now cupping his hand just under the boy's chin. Feeling the light bone of his jawline, his pulse.

God forgive me, he whispers, and plunges.

He makes the cleanest cut he can. It is not the child who cries out, slicing the silent forest in two with a wail. Nor is it the child who staggers, weeping into the trees, dropping his torch, his glove, feeling the warm black blood trickle over fingers. For all time, seared on his memory, the feel of cut flesh, white as the flesh of a mushroom, melting into softness, melting into a place more evil than any he'd yet to travel.

He wants to run, he is crashing noisily in the direction he came in, picking up the torch, the glove, but forgetting the axe, but he forces himself to pause, look back. In a gesture he knows, even as he does it, makes no sense, he takes off his coat and flings it over the child. The small dark shape is slumped forward. He cannot make him out properly; the shaggy head of hair fallen towards his knees. He might be a lump of earth, a stone, a tree stump. He might be a devil or an angel, a beast or a monster, an alien.

What he mustn't be, couldn't be, is a little human boy. Nearly six years old. Jacques-Pierre Colombe. His son.

Part Three

Brumaire 19
Year Eight

Yesterday I received an invitation from the so-called Great Beauty Madame Récamier to bring 'my wild boy' to dinner at her château in Clichy la Garenne. I know why I am invited and it is not on my own account. Unlike Lalande and Cuvier – who, I discovered, will also be at this dinner – I do not have the status of the fashionable savant, except in regard to Victor. This knowledge annoys me, although I would not confess it aloud.

When I arrived at the Guérins to collect Victor for his excursion, Madame Guérin had excelled herself in fitting the boy for the occasion. She was very flushed, wore a torn apron and showed signs of scratch marks on her arms and face. But the boy looked immaculate: his hair so slicked and oiled that it might have been a black painted cap on his head; his shirt spotless, his britches clean and pressed. He was even wearing shoes and silk stockings.

It is the stockings! his governess told me, panting a little, explaining why I found Victor so angered.

I took my hat and placed it firmly on my head, my sign to Victor that we are about to go out, and opened the door with care, holding his arm as I did so. My pockets were full of chestnuts and walnuts, the better to persuade him into the berline, which was waiting at the corner of the Rue St Jacques.

Thus our arrival at the Château de Clichy la Garenne was uneventful and punctual. The house was suitably impressive, situated in a vast park which sloped down to the Seine, the lawn dotted with lamp-posts and approached by stone steps, although I had scarcely time to take any of this in, as I was concentrating on coaxing Victor from the carriage. The nuts were used to good effect and we managed to walk to the door with some dignity, where we were announced as: Monsieur Yzard and L'Enfant Sauvage and were almost immediately herded up the stairs towards our hostess's bedroom.

Naturally I had heard – or read, I suppose – that this was where the 'famed lovely' entertained guests but still I felt like an ingénue; my surprise mingling with disgust that these decadent habits of the old regime are now, from what I have heard, resurfacing all over Paris. I kept a very firm grip on Victor as we slowly ascended the staircase, behind several other gentlemen. The boy watched his shoes and stockings on the lavish Turkish carpet. He lifted each foot as if it were mired in sugar-syrup. He was not in the least dazzled by his opulent surroundings, but he was rather puzzled by his shoes with their shiny silver buckles, and the white stockings on his legs.

We entered the room behind a small crowd of others and it was only through the reflection in the high wall mirrors surrounding her bed that I could see that Madame Récamier – dressed of course in white and gold, in a material more suited to catching butterflies than preserving human decency – was present. Victor, who does not like to be jostled, wriggled his shoulders angrily at the men pressing on him and I took care to keep my hold firm on his arm and to position myself between him and a small gentleman with a gold pince-nez. Victor was eyeing the pince-nez with great interest.

Madame Récamier laughed her tinkling laugh at the remark of someone standing next to her and did not notice us. Her bed – the 'couch of the goddess' in Cuvier's ridiculous phrase, yesterday, when he elbowed me meaningfully and wondered how on earth I had 'weaselled' myself an invitation – was also draped in white and seemed to be resting on some kind of platform, further adding to the delusional lady's sense of her own standing. Tired of waiting in line, I was suddenly appalled at myself, realising that here I was, caught up in precisely the kind of nonsense I have long despised, and wishing that I had found a polite way to decline the invitation. As I looked around me for an opening to steer Victor out of that bedroom, Madame Récamier spied us and it was too late.

Oh, Monsieur Yzard! You have brought me your wonderful boy. Let him through ... here, make room. Come, child ... that's right ...

And she held out her hands, meaning for Victor to step forward.

Naturally, I had to follow him. My hand was on Victor's arm and I nudged him forward, towards the bed. He tripped once, his feet awkward in the hated shoes and I held my breath as an elegant vase on a shelf behind him wobbled and then miraculously righted itself. The group hushed, all eyes on Victor. The back of my neck prickled.

Come and sit by me, said Madame Récamier, patting the bed.

Victor stood in front of me, motionless. Then, in a quick movement, he dipped his head to the bed and sniffed at it, brushing Madame Récamier's dress with his nose.

There was a burst of laughter and applause.

He has an unusual way of greeting his hostess, said Madame Récamier. Victor was now sniffing at the cushions behind her head.

Forgive me, Cit – Madame ... you will appreciate that in his previous life, his nose was his strongest guide.

And now? Has he learned no better guide?

Victor was fingering the violet damask curtain which draped the wall behind the bed. I could hardly blame him for his incredulity at the excesses of Madame Récamier's boudoir – I had the same sentiments.

When he is shy, he resorts to his old habits, I muttered, as do we all.

Fortunately, there was no time to say more, since one of our hostess's servants announced the arrival of Talma, the actor, who was scheduled to perform a scene from *Othello* in the drawing room. Madame Récamier only managed to say: he shall sit next to me at dinner and I can take a closer look at his pretty face. One of her admirers quickly added: and he will be bewitched by yours, madame. The others looked at him in irritation, presumably wishing they had said it first.

I coughed loudly and heartily to stifle a sound I hoped I was the only one to have heard, which Victor squeezed from his gut with his usual insouciance.

Talma performed his piece in the drawing room, man-fully continuing despite the odd interruption by Victor who appeared to appreciate the speech, so much so that he could not prevent himself from bleating *lait!* or *lli!* occasionally, which produced titters and whispers. Then Madame Récamier sang a song by Plantade, accompanying herself on the harp, flanked on both sides by two tiny Negro boys seated on stools, the little Blackamoors recently imported from dark continents that I have seen in the laps of society women in the cafés of Paris. These vain women believe, one presumes, that their snowy necks are thus better displayed, contrasted against this dusky backdrop. Glancing at the smallest of these dark children, a boy of around six years old, who sat as still as a vase beside his mistress with a glazed, sad expression in his eyes, it occurred to me for the first time that to be a pet was perhaps a fate she also intended for Victor. Whilst Juliette Récamier's light voice plucked at the air like the notes of her harp I looked at her afresh, and anger flared. I had taken it for a joke, the remark that her beauty would 'bewitch' the wild boy. Now I saw that these doting idiots surrounding her, that she herself, genuinely believed Victor would be moved by her.

I remembered his glance at me. Our first meeting. To be dismissed like that made me tremble to recall it. How rarely his eyes have brushed mine. So rare that when they have, my heart has leapt towards my mouth, words clamouring there like blood. The vanity of the woman and all her consorts left me breathless. To believe that the Wild Boy of Aveyron would honour her with a gift he had not given *me*, his guardian, his tutor, his companion, in all the months I have known him, despite all the attentions I have lavished upon him.

Victor meanwhile, having initially seemed rather lulled by the music, was in fact only a little stupefied by his new surroundings. He soon recovered himself enough to sniff at the inlaid doors, shrieking periodically with delight, and running his hands over them. I did not think it was the 'artistic workmanship' he was appreciating, despite the helpful whispers of a guest beside me. My breathing quickened and every time Victor yelped, it was all I could do to stifle a nervous cry of my own.

I knew it was the texture, the feel of the brown beading and raised bronze ornamentation, that Victor liked; his hand smoothing over it again and again, and seeming to enjoy very much the feeling it produced. (We have been doing some work lately where I blindfold him and he is given objects, such as acorns or coins, to feel, to see whether he can tell from this sense alone the difference between them. His ability to use his sense of touch to discern things is much improved. But the game makes him very excited and he often squeals and leaps up, flapping his hands, just as he was doing then. I was torn between pleasure at this behaviour, and terror that it might progress to more intimate areas of discovery.)

Dinner was – thankfully – announced shortly afterwards, and we were shown into a dining room with more colossal vases of flowers and giant candelabras with six or eight branches lighting a groaning table. Servants lined the walls, stiff as furniture.

Victor sat down promptly and Madame Récamier again laughed. The wild boy – does he have a name?

Emile perhaps? suggested a wag.

Or Candide, surely? called another.

His name is Victor, I supplied.

Well, Victor, you must sit with me, said Madame Récamier, patting the seat beside her.

Victor appeared not to have heard her but stared hungrily at the tureens of soup in the centre of the table. I quickly stood beside him, pulled out his chair and said firmly: you are to sit *here*, Victor. My hands, I noticed, as I placed them on the back of Victor's chair, were slippery. I did not expect Victor to follow this instruction but, happily, a servant was passing at that moment with a steaming plate of – thank God – beans and, following his nose, Victor leapt up and re-seated himself where I was indicating, presumably believing he would be served more quickly there. He grabbed his plate and held it out, jabbing it at the servant, who pulled her dish away in some surprise.

Victor! You must be patient, I scolded, in a limp voice.

Madame Récamier was much amused. She implored her guests not to stand on ceremony and sat down herself, so that the gentlemen could do the same. And she nodded to the serving girl, saying: let him have his beans before his consommé if he wishes – I expect they do things differently in the forests of Lacaune –

And while everyone smiled at the joke, Victor began his feast.

Your spoon, Victor, I said quietly, pushing the spoon towards him.

He ignored me, so I did as I have seen Madame Guérin do many times and lifted his hand from the bowl, placing the spoon in his grasp, then pushing it into the beans to remind him how to use it. Whilst Victor ate, I relaxed slightly. I poured him a glass of water, knowing that he would drink it very slowly, savouring every drop and with the air of reverie that comes over him whenever he drinks water and that the guests would mistake for refinement. I also knew he would dismiss the many other dishes that were brought out for us – anguilles au vert, foie gras de canard, coquilles St Jacques, tripes à la mode de Caen – either sniffing them once and turning away, or not granting them a second look. It was true: the plates and dishes kept on arriving, while Victor ploughed through serving after serving of beans. After his fourth helping, I piled the beans onto my own plate, then after a quick glance to make sure we were not observed, heaped them onto Victor's. I was anxious that he should not grab the serving girl too often. Fortunately his preoccupation with his favourite food meant that apart from splattering the table with the odd bean from his mouth, he behaved very well.

Conversation was mostly about the state of Paris, the amount of building taking place, how one's horses could scarcely move these days without more construction workers impeding their passage. I was only half listening and was startled when Madame Récamier addressed me.

So Doctor Yzard . . . (I did not know how to correct her, so let it pass.) . . . I have heard from Doctor Cuvier that now your boy speaks, and knows his letters, and sleeps in a bed, rather than a den, or a tree, so is making all round excellent progress. When she spoke, the table fell silent and all eyes were once again on Victor.

I stuttered out a reply of sorts, protesting that 'speak' was an exaggeration, although the child had uttered a word. Beside me, Victor was searching for more beans. When none were forthcoming he picked up his plate, meaning, I knew, to thrust it at the serving girl as she passed. I tried to take the plate from him; we wrestled in silence for a moment; two splashes of oil fell on the snowy tablecloth.

But he does not run on all fours, or swing from tree to tree? asked another lady, a very fat one, with a head so small that it was quite lost in the folds of her vast neck and chin.

He never did, madame, I said, curtly. I then tried to make

this sound polite by adding: there has been a play about Victor, perhaps you saw it, no? And many pamphlets, and all of them I'm afraid are grossly exaggerated . . .

How can you be so sure, Itard? shouted Lalande from further down the table. Belatedly I realised his remark was playful; I had already begun a painstaking and stuttered explanation of why I believed Victor had not swung from tree to tree, nor run on all fours, thinking that he genuinely wanted to know the evidence.

I could hardly be heard over other lively conversations at the table and now, to my further humiliation, Lalande asked me to repeat what I had said. I was also becoming conscious that Victor, sated and no longer interested in food, had turned his attention to his loathed shoes and managed to kick them off. He was now pulling in fury at the silk stockings. His flappings and scufflings beside me were distracting in the extreme; I tried to shout an answer down the table to Lalande at the same time as putting a restraining hand on Victor's shoulder.

His – his knees and hands were not particularly CAL-LOUSED, as they would be if he had RUN ON ALL FOURS – come now, Victor, leave them on –

You truly believe then (this time it was Madame Récamier and, although for myself I do not consider her a great wit, the company at the table fell into attentive silence whenever she raised a question) that man is shaped by his environment, by the circumstances of his life, far more than his inheritance, or the existence of innate ideas? And does this belief extend to women too, by chance – or do you share your views on this with your friend, the young Doctor Virey?

Of course the question was a good one, and deserved an answer. Which at the best of times would have taken me a while. But just at that moment, Victor, shoe-less and stocking-less, had released his britches too, and with a yelp of triumph, pushed his chair back and struggled free. All that

154

remained between him and propriety was a fine linen shirt. That was a challenge he would not long resist.

Victor – excuse me – come – here.

He had spied an open door behind the dining table, opening onto the gardens, and there was nothing I could do, once he had lurched under the table, but follow him. Of course his speed startled me and everyone else; there were gasps from the ladies and piercing screams when he tore off the shirt finally, flinging it behind him, knocking over two chairs as he pushed past a servant and flew through the door. Every head at that enormous table turned as one, an audience in a theatre. And there was just this slim white figure, flying for the open, like a rabbit in a field.

I was no match for Victor and after an initial sprint after him was soon exhausted. Outside, in full view of everyone, I leaned forward, resting my hands on my knees, breathing heavily, a fierce stabbing pain under one rib. A fellow guest, Monsieur de La Harpe, rushed to my side, holding out his coat as if to shield the ladies from a view of the boy and announcing pompously: I'd like to see Jean-Jacques here, with his declamations against the social state!

I could not speak; the pain beneath my ribs grew worse, and I wanted to laugh.

Victor had reached a wall and, cornered, decided to climb the nearest tree. Again it was his speed that gave him the advantage, and he reached the highest branches with ease and then sat there, perched on a branch of preposterous delicacy, whooping a little and throwing down twigs.

I will ask my gardener to fetch a ladder, said Madame Récamier calmly, joining us from the dining room. La Harpe stepped in front of her, his coat aloft.

Ladies! Stay back! he called, his voice a panicky shriek.

This time I succumbed and laughed deliriously. I could not prevent myself; wave after wave of laughter rolled over me and, although I was conscious – dimly – of a number of guests joining us on the grass and staring at me, their bewilderment only made matters funnier still.

I will not go into details here of the next few hours. Suffice to say that it took a very long time and many different gentlemen's efforts (spurred on no doubt by the opportunity this presented to impress Madame Récamier with their bright ideas, persuasiveness or skill at climbing a tree) to coax Victor down from his refuge. There was not a man among them who could reach the branch that Victor had so effortlessly reached. There was not a ladder long enough. Threats, and the release of two large dogs belonging to the gamesman, had no impact at all.

It was the gardener, a man cut from the same cloth as Lemeri, an individual who managed to indicate with every fibre of his taciturn self how much he despised us, with our fancy stiff collars and our endless discussions and theorising, who succeeded in persuading Victor down, with a basket of freshly picked peaches and a silent, entreating hand. In truth, I think that Victor had simply decided it was time to descend: the peaches, when he reached the ground, were rejected after a dismissive sniff.

It was now dusk and we wrapped Victor in a heavy silk blanket offered by our hostess and he, and I, were shepherded by servants to a waiting berline. Victor's shoes and clothes were bundled into my arms as the driver snapped the reins and the horse pulled away. Madame Récamier did not say goodbye.

Victor's feet, sticking out from his opulent blanket, were blackened, his shoulders smudged in mud, his hair entangled with twigs. His head bumped gently against my shoulder. I stretched my own legs beside his, then leaned back in my seat and closed my eyes. The smell of wet grass, rich dark mud, bark, pine cones – a smell almost of the sky and clouds themselves – filled the carriage with me. I breathed deeply, finding the smell profoundly familiar and profoundly soothing, easing away the powerful scent of ladies' perfume that had assaulted me all evening; smoothing and blurring even the image of myself, doubled up on the grass, laughing like a madman. Instead I was back in the den of my childhood, lying in a hollowed tree trunk, ignoring their shouts and pleas to come out, safely invisible – *impenetrable* – to all.

We arrived at Victor's home at a late hour, and after I had dismissed the coachman and knocked with my cane for a good while on the Guérins' door, I soon realised that the family had retired to bed. I was afraid that I would wake the whole Institute with my knocking and shouting and yet, of course, being mostly populated by the deaf, no one stirred. It would be tempting, looking at Victor, to describe him as 'shivering' beside me on the landing in his inadequate blanket, but honesty prevents me from using such a word when, in fact, the child seems as insensitive to the cold as ever. Still, there was a chill in the night air and I myself was cold and impatient. I decided there was nothing for it but to take Victor to my lodgings and try to smuggle him past Madame Richard.

Providence was on my side, since the wretched woman was snoring vigorously as I steered Victor past her door. Fanfan, however, was not fooled and set up a feeble barking, which thankfully Madame Richard ignored. We mounted the stairs and, once in my own room, the dog gave up and settled for a vigil of low growling and, finally, a grudging silence. The dog made Victor anxious. He flared his nostrils and paused at each step whenever he heard it; sniffing fiercely at the banister, the drapes, the candlesticks, the mirrors. Dust flew whenever he breathed out.

Once in my room, I locked the door. I told Victor to sit on the bed, which he did. He showed his usual disdain for decency, and without me to hold it around him, the blanket slipped from his shoulders.

I sat on the bed beside Victor. The wine and plentiful food I'd consumed weighted me, I was sleepy and stupid and laughed again when I recalled the details of the evening. I told Victor that we should never be invited back and that the pair of us had behaved abominably. Then I laughed so hard that tears streamed from my eyes. I put up a hand to wipe them away but, to my astonishment, Victor suddenly took hold of my hand. So surprised was I, that for the longest moment I could barely recognise the feel of skin touching skin. His palm was like a pebble; cool, smooth, dusty.

He held my hand up to his cheek and stroked it. Then he placed my hand on his own shoulders and clumsily tried to stroke them too. I was sitting too close to him for this to be achieved easily but was so spellbound that I dared not even shift position on the bed, lest the moment was lost and he should drop my hand. At the touch of his warm, naked shoulders, the feel under my palm of his many tiny scars, of the little round pock-marks; at the touch of these tears drummed in me again. I could do nothing to stem them. And thus we sat like that, for how long, I have no idea. Victor, using my hand in his firm, cool grip, stroked and smoothed at his own shoulders, neck, face, arms, torso and then to his thighs, to his knees, all the time uttering his little squeaks.

I sat as stiff as a chair-back beside him, tears sliding down my face.

I fell silent. I could not think of any means to withdraw my hand. The feel of Victor's skin, his warm, living body beneath my palm, the knowledge that he was *asking* me to do this, that he *wanted* these caresses, mesmerised me. We might have sat like this all night long had it not been for a disturbance in the street outside, which set Fanfan to barking again. At the sound of the dog in the room beneath ours, Victor tensed, dropped my hand, his eyes narrowing suspiciously.

It is nothing, Victor, don't be afraid! My voice was almost a sob.

I sat completely frozen. My hand lay on the bed at my side, like a discarded glove. He did not reach for it again.

After many minutes of holding my breath, of waiting, I saw that Victor was no longer fully present with me; his attention, no, not just his attention, something less tangible but more important, something I am tempted to call his *self*, had slipped away again. His head nodded drowsily towards his chest, then in an abrupt gesture, he flung himself backwards onto the bed, throwing his head to the bolster and closing his eyes. It was the position of someone in a deep sleep.

Madame Guérin has always assured me that Victor's preferred position for sleeping is crouching, watchfully, often with his hands over his eyes. And so a most curious thought presented itself to me: that Victor was pretending. The notion is both farcical and unfeasible, given all we know of Victor's guileless nature. And yet I could not shift it. I stared at him for a moment, even leaning forward to gaze closely at his shut eyelids. Then I sighed noisily – perhaps a little theatrically – and extinguished the lamp. Removing only my boots, I lay down beside him. I pulled the fancy Récamier blanket over us but the feel of it, after Victor's skin, was cold and leaden.

I smiled in the darkness to think that Victor might be playing some kind of trick on me. The idea tickled me, kept me awake. I wriggled and fidgeted beside him.

Yet I could no more have ventured to return my hand to his skin than fly through the window. We slept side by side with barely an inch between us, but it might have been the distance to the stars, for all it could be bridged.

Henri is sick, so sick that his coughing shakes his body until his eyes are fit to pop from his head. He came in from the garden just after Victor and the doctor had left for their fine party at the château and simply collapsed inside the doorway. I turned on hearing the great basket of wood that he was carrying smash to the floor and there he was: my Henri sliding down the wall as if someone had put a bullet in his shoulder. The shock it gave me was worse through being so sudden and the memory, the remembrance it caused in me of a man, a sans-culotte, I once saw sliding just like that, in a crowd, a man melting to the ground as if whatever held him up had turned to string, and in his case it was a soldier's knife in his back that did it. I cursed God and our Julie for never being here when I need them and ran to Henri's side, my heart swooping down quicker than a diving bird, but I recovered myself, as best I could, I was telling myself that this kind of thing will not help Henri, and that if Doctor Itard can describe me (as he did three days ago to his friend that other doctor, the fat one with the flaxen hair) as 'stout-hearted' then stout-hearted I must be, for never did Henri need me more.

I had to heave and drag with all my might to get my poor Henri to his bed. I had more strength than most women would with a husband of Henri's size, but a terrible realisation only added to my misery, and that was how light, how paper-fine and light he is now. He opened his eyes and stared up at me, muttering something, but he was not able to help me in my efforts and so his feet in his muddy boots dragged black marks across the red-tiled floor. I wish I had not seen these marks and I wish even more that I did not care about them but I cannot in honesty tell you that either of these facts was true. And so here I was dragging Henri, my arms crossed under his chest, he coughing weakly against my bosom, his face twisted in pain and here was I, through some strange quirk of my own wicked nature, cursing my ruined kitchen floor.

A short while later, lying back against his own pillows, drinking a few spoonfuls of my bouillon, Henri opened his eyes again and after another bout of coughing – blood staining the sheets in a splash of brown – he took hold of my hand and gripped it hard, shaking his head against further mouthfuls.

You must eat, I began, meaning to give him a long lecture. I had made a good snail and milk paste – which Julie says is a fine cure no matter what the doctor says and what does he know about tuberculosis, in any case, he has not lived with it for fifteen years as I have – and a pitcher of lemonade to ease Henri's lungs. It would have soothed me more than him for true if he had taken some but he only increased the tightness of his grip and shook his head more urgently. He reminded me just then, for the first and only time, of Victor. The struggle Victor has to make himself understood without words. Most of the time, if truth be told, I understand perfectly well what Victor means and only pretend otherwise when it suits me. It is so much like the insistence of a babe before he has language to match his budding will, it would make you laugh if it didn't wear you out so. When I do not want to take Victor out for another walk, for example, and he is pushing my fichu and bonnet at me, then pressing the key into my palm, then shoving me towards the door and practically pushing me through the wood in his efforts. It is easy – easier day by day – to know exactly what Victor intends and Victor wants. But a man like Henri, a man with so much to say – scarce a day has gone by when Henri has not said more than I would have wished him to – I cannot bear to see him speechless. It does not suit him: it is not natural.

A great spasm of coughing took hold of him again and I struggled to free my hand so that I could hold a muslin cloth beneath his mouth, but his grip was an iron shackle, my hand squeezed limp beneath it.

Shall I run and fetch back the doctor? They've only just left, I might be able to reach him . . .

He shook his head, finally released my wrist and let his head fall back on the pillow. I say 'fall' for that is just what it did, as if his head was no more attatched to his neck than a child's ball would be. And at the thought of that, my staunch resolve left me, and I took to blubbering.

Oh, Henri, I am sorry, take no notice of me, your silly Marie-France, here, take some more bouillon . . .

Where have they gone – where is – Victor?

A party, I sniffled. At some fine lady's château. He has invitations now all the time and talks to me, can you believe it, he asks my advice – of how such 'fripperies' disgust him. But still he goes –

I was prattling. Seeing Henri's eyes close wearily, I gave a little shriek – fearing the worst – at which his eyes fluttered open. As he drew in his breath to speak again a deep shadow appeared in the hollow of his throat as if a dark moth had landed there and spread its sinister wings. I could not keep from staring at it and the horrible idea took hold of me that something had indeed landed in Henri's throat, so much so that I almost leaned forward to try to pluck it away but as I leaned towards him, he coughed and whispered, and his eyes fluttered open.

I put my face close to his, to whisper: Henri, please – I know it is not the time, but there is something I want to say to you, something that presses my heart . . .

He acted as if he had not heard me; his reply was a mere croak: what is it about the boy – about Victor, why does he remind me so much of Joseph?

I withdrew my hand.

What?

Victor. His colouring is all wrong, he is thin and pale where our lad was plump and rosy . . . He is older than Joseph ever reached . . . and yet . . . is it the eyes? Is it only me, Marie-France? Or do you see it too . . . ?

He started up coughing again, ribs heaving, face rolling up like paper in a ball.

His words had pushed me from my purpose and I was

labouring to find my way back there. I soaked a cloth in cooling vinegar, wrung it out, placing it across Henri's waxy forehead. I spoke harshly to myself. How much better you will feel, when you unburden yourself. Perhaps he knows already. These thoughts chased themselves around my head, but they did not find deliverance on my tongue.

My poor Henri was hot as a burning log, his cheeks two dark red spots of colour, the rest of his face chalky.

Did God send him to us? Why us? Why . . . was he brought to our house? There must be a reason . . .

Well as you know, Henri, I am no longer on speaking terms with God and have no more interest in His design than –

But he did not let me finish.

He is a sweet boy, this savage. He is not as they say he is. He is not an idiot, but he is not one of us, either. In the same way that Joseph . . .

It is Joseph I want to speak of, not Victor.

I peeled the folded cloth from Henri's brow, and it seemed so hot that steam might have risen from his damp forehead. I wrung it out and refreshed it with more vinegar, replacing it for him, stroking the wet hair away from his brow.

He was racked by another great coughing fit and when he could speak again he whispered:

Our boy. Never a day goes by . . .

Oh, don't, *don't*! I sobbed.

And so he closed his eyes and closed his mouth and that was it. I had not really meant it: I had stoppered his mouth just as truly as if I had pushed a handkerchief into it. There was an icy moment where I heard my own heartbeat as if a horse were approaching – faster, faster – from a great distance away. Wind rattled the wooden shutters. And then I leapt up. I flung almost an entire bottle of English drops at him, I threw myself down on the bed, I wept into his hair, his eyes, his skin, I soaked his pillow, I screamed at him, calling him every name in God's kingdom and a few from elsewhere; I ran back and forth in the room, I begged him to come back, I told him it was not time yet, I was not done with him, there was something I needed to tell him, to *confess*, I summoned him, I cursed him for deserting me. Finally I buried my face in his neck, my mouth in the very same spot I had spied my fanciful moth, breathing in the smell of him; bouillon and lemonade and wood-shavings and grass-cuttings and soap and smoke and sweat and twenty-five years of married life and I cried and cried and whispered to him: Henri, *please*, not yet, not yet. How will I look after the wild boy without you?

With my face pressed close to his, I stared at the lines around his mouth, watching them glisten deceptively with the moisture from my tears and trying to trick myself into believing that something in him stirred, but for all that, with my cursed good sense that never leaves me, even in the most extreme situations, I knew that those were simply the last words Henri would ever say to me. *Never a day goes by . . .*

Faintly as if from hundreds of miles away, I heard knocking at the door and shouting from the doctor in his most agitated voice, calling up to us. I remembered him for a moment and the boy, and my life here with the child, but then those facts tiptoed away from me and down the stairs and I did not think of them again.

I held Henri in my arms until the sun rose in the courtyard. Then I stood by the window and stared dry-eyed at his wheelbarrow, up-turned in the yard, watching the light turn from pink to gold on the axe handle and the two piles of kindling neatly stacked beside it. Early yesterday, he had been taking Victor for rides in that barrow, the boy squealing with delight and taking hold of Henri's hand, making him wheel him again and again, and then later he had been teaching Victor to use the axe, endlessly patient as Victor waved it treacherously this way and that, my heart near stopping every time it swung near Henri's ear. Not Henri, though. You could see he had grown to trust the boy. He always believed the best of people, my husband. That was his strength and his weakness too.

If I had told him, would he even have believed me? Some things the heart doesn't want to know, the mind will never take in. He would have made excuses for me, he would have done it from love, I know, but by now, by the time a woman gets to my age, she doesn't need that kind of love, she wants to face herself squarely.

What was it that Doctor Itard said, in the beginning, when Julie was so exercised about Victor's story, calling it unimaginable? Nothing is unimaginable, he said. Perhaps. He does not strike me as a man with great knowledge of the human heart, his own least of all.

No, there is only your own sweet self in this world to call upon. No God, no doctor, no daughter can ease your suffering, share your burdens.

And now, no husband either.

It is nine p.m. the following day and Victor is setting the table for supper in Madame Guérin's kitchen. He sets three places, one for himself, one for her, and one for Monsieur Guérin. He puts three spoons next to three forks, he measures carefully with his thumb to be sure there is precisely the same distance between spoon, fork and bowl at each setting. He carries a jug of water to the centre of the table and sets down three glasses, each beside the bowls, again measured carefully to be the exact same distance from each bowl. Then he pulls out a chair and waits at his place. His stomach rumbles in anticipation of his supper. He waits and waits for her to appear. The smell of white, of her apron and bonnet. Of flour and butter and coffee, of smoke from the fire. Of the steaming plates of lentils, beans, the wheaten bread.

But here she is and instead of food, instead of warm and green and steam and garlic, there is screaming and tumbling and a plate crashing. The white, the apron and the bonnet, are crumpled on the floor and the room is full of something he cannot touch or name or reach, but he knows it, he has been in this room full of something before.

And still he is hungry, and he waits. Still the beans and the lentils, the wheaten bread, do not appear.

Frimaire 6
Year Eight

These last few weeks have been difficult. Madame Guérin has been – understandably – preoccupied since the death of her husband and, although she has continued with her duties, bringing the boy to me here in the library, she is much distracted. Each request for a glass of water for Victor, or for the blindfold or the letters, or a pen, an acorn, the bag of nuts – each time I must put my request to her at least three times before she hears.

Her daughter came to stay for a number of days: when I discovered it I had reluctantly to forbid it. The effects of the daughter on Victor are disturbing. Or rather, in the interests of accuracy, Victor is displaying disquieting signs of puberty, and the presence of a lively young woman, aiding her mother with his bath-time massages, serves to exacerbate them. I am not sure if his governess is now aggrieved that I have banned the daughter (I am only following the abbé's policy for the Institute, and it was she and the daughter who drew my attention to it, after all), or if it is my imagination, but the taciturn Madame G is now more taciturn than ever. She seems to carry some new resentment towards me. It is all very unpleasant and produces in me a most childish desire to placate her, which I am at pains to stifle.

My work with Victor is progressing slowly.

The work with the blindfold and shapes in a bag is a

limited success. Yes, it improved his sense of touch, his ability to discern from his fingers alone whether he was holding an acorn or a coin. I would hold up the same and then, blindfolding him and offering him the bag, instruct him to find one like it. But it also excited him beyond what is helpful. (It is also true that this sense in him is already well developed. I feel I should be concentrating on speech and hearing.) He was in the habit of jumping up, shrieking, screaming and running around the library, crashing into the glass cabinets, up-turning his glass of water and then laughing hysterically until the blindfold was removed. This was made more insufferable owing to the slowness of Madame Guérin's response. On one occasion, struggling on the floor with a laughing, rolling Victor, trying to remove the cloth from his eyes and dodge his kicks at the same time, I glanced up and there was Madame Guérin, staring at us, making no effort to come to my aid.

When I was a little sharp in my remonstrance with her, she only muttered: he thinks it is a game.

And even, on another occasion: why do you never let him play with the other boys? Why must he always be on his own, or with you?

He is afraid of them! I quickly told her.

As well he might be, since he has so little to do with them.

Her opinions are bordering on the insolent. Of course, I put this turn in her character down to her bereavement and am doing my best to remain patient.

For two days I worked alone with Victor, giving her leave to remain in her quarters. However, those two days proved very taxing. I did not feel confident to persist with the blindfold without the presence of another person – for emergency reasons only – and instead concentrated on our other work: letter and word recognition.

The main hindrance to progress is that I do not know

how to prevent Victor from his new and disgusting habit of touching himself how and when he pleases, with indecorous abandon. This sight fills me with the most powerful feelings of – anxiety, made worse by the thought that someone – perhaps the abbé – might come across us and believe that I have permitted, or worse, even encouraged such behaviour. Yet I do not know how to make Victor stop! Resorting to slapping his hand lightly with my cane whenever it wanders only produces squeals of laughter, seemingly persuading him that the game is worth continuing. I have noticed that Madame Guérin has more success with her firm but merely verbal rebuke. At times I find myself deeply envious of the natural authority that she holds over the boy.

Was he attached to this Guérin fellow? Virey asked, during one of our discussions about Victor's progress. We were in a café in the depths of the Faubourg St Honoré, a place we have taken to meeting in, since we are invariably surrounded by a dozen gloomy punters playing Faro, and this is an atmosphere that Virey favours.

Not especially, I replied, and then examined myself for the truthfulness of this statement. Well, I continued, it is impossible to tell with Victor, whether he is attached or not. He does not express affection in the normal way. He shuns physical contact unless he himself has initiated it; he makes so little eye contact, he shows so small an interest in the desires or feelings of another, if one is angry or serious with him, it only induces further giggles –

My answer was interrupted by a shout of Raise it seven times from one of the gamblers, followed by a small commotion when the lady of the house stepped forward to accuse him of turning down the corner of his card. Virey had told me that the fifteen-year-old girl with the pink cheeks and flattened blonde curls (his real reason for frequenting this place) who always played amongst the punters was her daughter, planted there to make a sign to the mother should any cheating take place.

Now I had lost Virey's interest, since the game had claimed it. Conversations with Virey are always thus constrained. He will throw out some question about Victor, often an extraordinarily useful one with much food for thought, and then *pff!* His attention is lost and he casually changes the subject. His own experiences amongst savage people, his observations of those creatures of the dark continents, are illuminating, although he is not without prejudices and superstition.

I offered Virey some snuff, hoping to disguise my frustration in a show of friendship: he shook his head dismissively. Once thus claimed, no efforts on my part can drag his attention back. He was even now shifting his chair towards the over-heated blonde, who clicked her fingers towards her mother. A hand of cards was brought for Virey. He loosened the bow at his neck and surveyed the cards, his heavy bottom lip jutting out in a pout of pleasure.

I picked up my hat, and left him.

So I tried talking to Victor, which, it seems to me, is what Madame Guérin would have suggested, had I dared consult her.

Victor, you understand now that Monsieur Guérin – the gardener – your putative father, I suppose in a manner of speaking – you understand now that he is – he suffered from a wretched illness of the lungs –

It is not an easy task to explain death to a mute twelve-(surely, now thirteen-) year-old boy. Victor was more interested in exploring the sensations in his breeches than in listening to me.

Victor – that is not – we do not do that in public . . .

We were walking (trotting) in the Institute grounds at the time. We passed the very spot where Guérin tended his vegetables, we stood briefly under the pear tree I had seen him prune earlier this year. Victor spied the wheelbarrow, up-turned and soaked by the rain of the last few days, and ran over to it. I followed him at a slower pace, continuing my speech.

He is not coming back, Victor. Death is final. We do not know for certain what happens to us – to our souls – after our death but for myself I have wavered in my faith; ever since the deaths of those dearest to me: first my dear mother, then Father and finally, dearest of all perhaps, my uncle. I can no longer – in all confidence of truthfulness – recommend to you a belief in the existence of an after-life, but then again –

Victor was dragging on my arm, pulling me towards the wheelbarrow. He turned it upright and climbed inside.

Now I know that Monsieur Guérin was kind to you. He tickled you and took you for walks and he has been a simple, reliable presence in your life these last few months, so it would not be unexpected if you had some – fond affection towards him –

Victor began shouting his liquid *lli* sound and when I continued speaking, leapt out from the wheelbarrow and grabbing hold of my hands, placed them on the handles. Satisfied, he then climbed back in and lay on his back, staring up at me with an air of anticipation. At last I understood what he meant. I started pushing.

I know, for example, that Monsieur Guérin probably played this kind of game with you.

I was becoming too breathless to continue my speech. Victor made it clear, from shouts and vigorous kicking at the bottom of the barrow, that he wished me to go faster, that the game was more exciting if I sprinted around the gardens. Soon I was so warm, despite the early evening frost, that I had to remove my coat and place it over an urn by the pond, an action that produced angry panic in Victor, who seemed to fear the game was over. With my shirt-sleeves rolled, I returned my hands to the handles and resumed our game with more speed. My speech was abandoned.

Victor was squealing too hard to hear a word of it. I was breathless anyway, and found his mood infectious. I even began whooping and hollering a little myself as I steered him around bends and twists in the gardens, in a figure of eight around the willow tree. The barrow was awkward to steer and wobbled perilously with his weight. Whenever I paused, or indeed, when I wanted to give up, Victor would urge me on, until my shirt clung to me in wet patches and my lungs twisted with the effort. Enough, Victor, enough – you have exhausted me!

The sun finally slipped behind the Institute walls, and a sickle moon took its place. I succeeded in returning Victor to his room by a clever trail of moonlit chestnuts laid out across the grass and up the stairs and by running ahead of him, almost crashing into three astonished boys and one master, who was about to reprimand me before being silenced by recognition. We arrived at Madame Guérin's panting noisily, our hair and clothes dishevelled, Victor's breeches caked in mud from the bottom of the wheelbarrow and my coat abandoned somewhere in the garden.

Well, look at you two, she said and for the first time in weeks, she smiled.

I stayed for supper (I believe Madame Guérin was hungry for companionship now that her husband has gone. I wished only to offer her some solace; however I was served with a succulent gigot d'agneau, an excellent Roquefort and a generous glass of brandy, so my consideration was amply repaid. In truth, consciousness of the menu on offer at Madame Richard's may well have influenced my decision to stay to supper.)

When Madame Guérin had bathed Victor and taken him to his bed (rebuking him in the manner I have indicated for his new fascination) I was alone with a glass of brandy and a spluttering candle, staring into the fire.

When she returned I voiced my thoughts.

Do you think that Victor misses your husband?

Her hand flew up to her mouth in a startled gesture and I realised that my question had been intrusive. There is something about the daily routine of visiting her family home, eating at her table, watching her bathe the child, clean the dishes, light the fire, empty the boy's chamber-pot; even myself aiding her sometimes by picking up a jug, a basket he has sent flying in one of his furies . . . it has led to a false sense of intimacy; something most confusing in a man like myself, who has had so little experience of intimacy to judge by. I apologised at once.

No, no – it is nothing, insisted Madame Guérin, struggling, it seemed, to find a reply.

He – I did mean to tell you. You know he sets the table at supper for me. Henri taught him, he takes great pride in it. Well, the evening after, after what happened. He set the table just as he always does, with a place for Henri. And I came into the kitchen and saw him waiting there and an empty place for Henri – well, I am sure you can imagine. I was upset. I think I stumbled a little. I know I dropped a plate. But the thing I wanted to tell you. Ever since, he has never made the same mistake. He only sets the two places, mine and his.

She was watching me with an expression of expectancy. I did not know how to respond. She then folded her arms in a typical gesture and her voice was impatient.

He knew that he had upset me. It is the first time I have seen it. Even a glimmer, you know, Doctor – a glimmer that he thinks about me. Perhaps you imagine it is a little thing?

Her voice had begun to sound piqued.

Well, perhaps to you it is not a great accomplishment. I suppose it is not, if you are comparing it to – making a chalk-holder!

No, I understand, Madame Guérin. I do not believe it

trifling. I agree – it is enormous progress – it is the first sign. That he thinks of others, at all.

That he has a *heart*, said Madame Guérin. Her eyes glittered dangerously.

The doctor was not in the least impressed by what I told him but the man knows nothing of children, as I have said, so what should I expect? In the time he has been with us, I have not known that child to show the slightest sign of care for the feelings of another living soul. To him I am just the food on the table, the drink in his glass, the warmth of the fire. A hand to guide a cup of milk. Not a person with a life of my own. And then that night, when I fell to weeping in the kitchen. He looked at me and something shifted.

His behaviour since. His careful setting of the table for only two people. How else can I explain it? He understood. Not just that Henri is gone, but that it upset me to be reminded of it. I have thought and thought about it. If he has a heart, he cannot be possessed by the Devil. He cannot have been sent to me in the way that I believed. What the doctor is not sensible of is that children don't always learn when we want them to, in the order we demand. They learn their own lessons, in their own time.

That first time I showed Joseph a bird. *Look at the bird, Joseph, look at the bird!* First he was looking at the tree. Then a leaf. *Cheep-cheep, the bird, Joseph, not the leaf.* Pointing, not too hard, we don't want the bird to fly. And then he sees it! Realises that there is something moving, something portly, something with two legs, something with a pointed nose, something little, not a toy, not a ball, something which makes a sound, a sound *cheep-cheep*, not a child, not a thing, but more than a thing, not a word but also a word, but not a maman either, it's a *bird*, Joseph, a little bird, not a bird-like thing, not an idea, not a dream, not a name, my darling, but a *bird*.

Watch it fly, Joseph! See the *birdiness* of it . . .

How many you will see, I told him then. How many there are in the world. Your life will be filled with them now, Joseph, you will hear them in the morning, you will know them by the flutterings in a bush, by the twitch of a branch, the rush of feathers beating, they will be a backdrop to every place you ever go, all your life, Joseph, there will be birds soaring overhead, nesting in trees, puffing their feathers out, taking their dust baths.

The Dauphin is dead, I said. The Austrian Queen is an evil bitch who feeds her darlings on cakes and wine, who drapes her throat in diamonds, while my baby is eating black bread and screaming for water, but now her head is going to roll and men will be free, as free as birds, Joseph, I told him.

How little I knew then. I was worse than Doctor Itard, I had no idea at all how matters would turn. My life was nonsense and bluster, ignorance.

Frimaire 7
Year Eight

Now I have given a lot of thought to Madame Guérin's contention that the wild boy has 'a heart', as evidenced by his consciousness of having upset her by setting a place at table for her deceased husband. I share her sense of triumph, of the importance of such a demonstration, but I find it impossible to accept her simple explanation. My obsession with this question led to an unfortunate encounter. Awkward in the extreme. But, firstly, to Victor.

Again and again this morning, throughout my other work, I thought of him. At one point I was examining the ears of Marcel, experimenting with a new instrument I have designed for exactly this purpose, but my mind was elsewhere; I accidentally pushed the instrument too far into his ear and the poor boy leapt from his chair, yelping and gesticulating. Since I am the only one here who does not speak the language of signs I was unable to reply to him; however it did not take fluency in the language to guess at his meaning.

In the early evening I found myself in the courtyard of the Val-de-Grâce, taking by habit the route I used to take before my position at the Institute and my work with Victor filled my every waking hour. Who should I come across but Julie Guérin, appearing on the columned porch flanked by nuns, still wearing her nurse's bonnet and apron. She greeted me shyly and told me she was on the way to visit her mother. Of course I noticed that the young women accompanying her were snickering behind their hands but I coughed, took my hands from my pockets and pressed on with my determination to invite her to accompany me to a cup of coffee in the Maison Guillemard on the Rue St Jacques. So delighted was I when I spied her, and when she accepted my invitation, that a part of me might have suspected I had engineered the meeting, had I not known myself incapable of such petty self-deceptions.

The other young women walked away from us, throwing those most feminine of backward glances. For a moment my nerve failed me and I would have marched back to my lodgings with my hat pulled low over my eyes but Julie was standing beside me smiling in that simple way she has and I could not do it. After all, meeting her on future occasions will be unavoidable. I did not want her to think me discourteous (although it is probably too late to prevent her from thinking me strange).

All day, musing on the significance of the incident with the dinner-setting, I have been trying to decide with whom I might discuss it. Virey is frustrating; we almost had an argument two nights ago when, in describing to him the strengths I have observed in Madame Guérin's dealings with the boy, he challenged my use of the word 'strength' in relation to a woman. His unexpected line of attack produced the dreaded stammer, which impedes all my most heartfelt arguments, and I was not able to convince him of my meaning. After Virey, I considered Lemeri. Since I have grown more comfortable being followed on walks with Victor by onlookers, I have had less need of the refuge of his hut and glad to avoid the one-sided gossip which passes for conversation within it. No, Lemeri would not listen, he would hold forth with his own opinions and deny me the possibility of winnowing out what troubles me most. If not Lemeri, could I talk to Sicard? . . . No. The instant I conceived it, I rejected it.

I quickly related all of this to Julie, ending with: so then I thought of you! And how pleased I am that we met accidentally, like that.

Julie accepted the coffee and the silver spoon and little jug of cream that the waitress placed in front of her and did not immediately reply.

I am flattered, Doctor Itard, if you consider my thoughts might be of –

You are always so frank and blunt. It is refreshing.

But an impediment to natural discourse immediately presented itself. I had never been alone with Julie Guérin. Well, that is, we were not alone, of course, in the Maison Guillemard. We sat in front of a screen, behind which four men played cards. Every so often, one or the other one would bark in triumph, slapping his cards down on the table. Each time, Mademoiselle Guérin, who sat on a leather banquette with her back to the screen, visibly jumped. I supped pastis but the sweet aniseed combined rather badly with the strong carbolic smell, the smell of the military hospital, which hung around my companion. Neither was Julie's manner the assured one of the day of our visit to Versailles. She peered over her cup at the men in the café; once she dropped her spoon, bent to pick it up herself and then exclaimed: oh, should the girl do it?

There is something I wish to ask you, I said, hurriedly and

clumsily. She was bent to pick up the spoon and I spoke to the back of her head. It is about Victor, I mumbled.

The Guérins are right to suppose I have little experience of the feminine sex. Madame Guérin has intimated several times – ha! if hints were made of lead she would have broken my toe by now – that I should be spending less time with Victor, more time in search of a wife. The first time she hinted, I was startled to discover how little consideration I have given to that proposal. Then I saw how this would appear to others and was gripped by anxiety, a terror of revealing, well, quite how timid, how far from such thoughts I am. The next time she made a similar suggestion, I was better prepared, muttering swiftly that my preference for my own company, my love of my work, have all conspired against it.

In the beginning, I believe Madame Guérin hoped I would consider her daughter in this light. It's true the girl does have qualities to recommend her. If I did feel myself pressed to look for a wife – and I do not know why I should feel so pressed, since I am only twenty-six – I suppose one matter I could be assured of: Julie Guérin would at least understand the importance of my work with Victor. She would be a useful helpmeet, as her mother has been. She would understand my shyness, my abhorrence of social occasions. Yes, she would understand Victor's immense importance, not just to me, but to the entire Republic, no, further than that, of course, to the human species. She would appreciate that there are times when it is essential that I be left alone with him.

Of course her language is immoderate: all is '*divine*' or '*terrible*'. She uses superlatives too frequently. Politically she is ignorant and sentimental. She is full of the silly vanities of girls her age, spending her money on ribbons and fripperies, on pockets full of sugar or needless gifts for Victor. I cannot help but wonder how Uncle would regard her. The question is rather dispiriting. I do not believe he would have liked her. But then Uncle envisaged a future for me rather like his own: a solitary life, perhaps with a close companion, a young protégé like myself to steer and shape. And in that, his wishes for me have been granted, after all. I have Victor.

You are someone who knows Victor. Who knows him well, I said to Julie, after several minutes of silence. What do you think of his relationship to your mother? And to . . . me? Is it simply . . . gratitude? Or is it something more?

Are you speaking of his feelings towards Maman? Or to you?

Well – either. Both.

The door to the café opened then, bringing a cold draught, a blast of the street with its smell of horse manure and chimney smoke. My real problem was that I did not quite know what it was that I sought an answer to. Perhaps it was not heart, but imagination we spoke of. Does Victor have an imagination? The ability to see things from a viewpoint other than his own? Must such an ability be taught, or is it one of the few innate qualities that a human being might possess, needing only minimal prompting to be awakened?

Her answer was not in the least what I had expected.

I do believe he has grown fond of – me, she quietly said.

You?

She pushed her hair back inside her bonnet and raised her eyes from her cup.

You find that so surprising, Doctor Itard?

I am sorry – if – if I appear rude. But, on what evidence do you make this claim?

Well, he is – it is to do with – he is a boy. You have decided he is aged thirteen but to me – to a person who has – to a girl of my – experience – in the hospital I mean, I would say he might be a little older. Fourteen. When I arrive, he wants me to tickle him. He cries if I stop. He grabs my hand, he laughs, he plays with my hair, he calls my name . . .

He seeks sensation! It is perfectly natural. And I am very

surprised to hear you question my professional judgement on the matter of his age.

Maman says he has a heart. And I agree.

She said this very plainly and did not take her gaze from mine. Suddenly, I remembered her, in the back of the room, during my speech to the Society of the Observers of Man. I had never asked her about it.

You were there, when I gave my paper, were you not? You heard my report on Victor, you heard me say that I searched in vain for evidence that his puberty had awoken in him the first sign of some higher emotion. You heard me say that no such thing had manifested, that instead Victor's drives were entirely base, directed indiscriminately at both men and women and, even then, to no one person in particular. I also explained that this unlooked-for truth cast a very unfavourable light on our beliefs about our own natures, the true nature of man, that is.

I did not hear you say that. I suppose I must have – already left.

She sipped the last of her coffee and replaced the cup neatly on its white saucer. Her mouth was a smooth straight line, with no sugar at the corners.

I do not agree with you, she said.

The boldness of the statement was a severe shock. I struggled to disguise my affront. After a moment I said: you are fond of the boy yourself, that is all. You are misguided.

I might offer the same reply to you, Doctor Itard.

My glass slipped. A great puddle of blue-white pastis spread across the wooden table. I leapt back in great speed, so that it would not reach my shirt, but was too late: a stain instantly appeared. My chair fell over, the noise making others turn and stare. Julie Guérin was sitting very still and had not taken her gaze from mine. I signalled to the girl to bring us a cloth and when that commotion was over, I stood up, replaced the chair and reached for my hat.

179

It is late. Let me walk you home, I said.

She said that she was perfectly capable of walking home herself.

I walked beside her, stepping aside to let her exit first. I did not know how to rescue the situation. I was relieved when Julie seemed to change her mind just as we stepped outside and smiled again, saying tenderly: it is foolish for us to quarrel over such a trifle. My feelings for Victor are those of a sister. Yours of a brother –

Yes, yes! I said. I was profoundly grateful.

Do you have a brother, Doctor?

No. That is, I did, have three. They all died young. I am the only surviving –

She nodded. We walked uphill along the Rue St Jacques in silence. Then a painful memory was drawn from her. She told me she too had lost a brother, Joseph, when she was only five and he just two years old. She did not properly remember him, all she did remember was this: her mother believed the child bewitched, since he did not smile, nor reach out his arms, nor seek caresses of any sort.

The boy was slow-witted? He had a disease of the brain?

Perhaps. I do not know. Maman – she did not think so. I do not remember.

I did not press her on the revelations about her brother, since she was reluctant to furnish more details and I was only glad that matters had returned to a more comfortable footing. Instead we spoke hypothetically of what it would mean to live inside the bubble of our own existence, without a desire for others, nor the ability to imagine their thoughts or feelings. Perhaps it would be appealing at first: never to care for the opinion of our peers, to pursue only our own desires, to obey all the savage instincts of the flesh with absolute abandon. But if we did, if each of us did, what barbarous chaos would ensue? This question ventured onto rather awkward territory, of course, for it was impossible to avoid the conclusion that we had many times in our recent history seen men behave exactly as if they had no ability to imagine the needs or sensibility of another human being. Thankfully, we had by then reached the Val-de-Grâce, glowing a creamy yellow in the light from the lanternes, as if its dome were made of paper lit from within by a candle flame.

We paused at the gates and meaning to bid her a hasty farewell, I instead prolonged our goodbyes by making nervous pleasantries about the building, remarking, I believe, on the artistry of Philippe de Buyster's carvings.

Yes, look at that one! Julie said, laughing. She was pointing at the naked figures adorning the dome. I saw at once what she meant. Where the other young men were artfully draped, their expressions angelic and sober, this one had allowed his robes to slip and, with raised arms, seemed to be inviting us to admire him. I knew what she would say before she opened her mouth.

That one is just like Victor, she said.

I laughed lightly to show that I did not find her remark scandalous.

We parted on the most cordial of terms. The night was cool and my wet shirt soon ceased to cling to me; but the smell of the spilled pastis lingered on my skin and my fingers. When I undressed that night I realised it had even reached the hair on my chest. Since there was so little time to bathe before falling into bed, it scented the sheets too, with its sticky aniseed sweetness. It was not altogether unpleasant. At least, after the disturbances of the evening, I passed a good, comfortable night.

I went to Saint Germain des Prés to see if I could offer a prayer for Henri but nothing was as it should be. Seeing the destruction and a place of near rubble with Our Lady of Consolation propped against a wall, her eyes closed, not in piety as I used to think, but in despair, the baby in her arms a skinny monkey of marble and gold, not the Son of God at all, I did not even dare to light a candle. I stood for a moment in the chapel of Sainte Geneviève where even the door hangs from a thread and saw every window smashed, and wondered at the fury of it all, mine as well as theirs, and tried to raise some feeling in myself that would allow me to kneel on the marble steps and ask for forgiveness or at least, if not that, for the release of Henri's soul. I glanced again at that baby Jesus in Our Lady's arms and I swear I never noticed all those years ago, how he has one little leg cocked, ready to escape, and how cold his eyes are, how unseeing.

Victor was screaming and running between the broken pieces of the fonts with no more respect for where he was than you might expect, and after a moment, a minute or two when I searched myself and found – nothing, nothing at all, I left.

Since that offered me no comfort, I have taken instead to walking, walking in the Jardin des Plantes or the Jardin du Luxembourg. I walk and Victor runs, and this way we are both appeased.

I took the boy to the Observatoire. We have passed it often enough on our walks. I have stopped to admire the building where those men with high foreheads, the sort of men who now sit in my kitchen, drinking my coffee!, sit on their leather couches, looking through their enormous lunettes – the size of cannons, Doctor Itard tells me – staring up at the night sky, learning their great lessons, making their great discoveries. That is, I have thought about that and Victor has entertained himself picking at the moss growing between the cobbles, or sniffing the crumpled leaves and crushing them in his fist, and between us we've both been satisfied.

A couple of days ago the gates were open and most of the workmen were huddling around a fire and I took a notion to walk right inside with Victor. They did not look up from their cards as I slipped past them over the pink and gold cobble-stones (the exact colours of a plate of tartes au sucre, fresh from the oven).

It was not even nightfall, but it was not the moon or stars which drew me.

Victor ran wild in the wide space; he ran up and down and round and about in one of those fits of wildness that grip him sometimes in new places, shouting and flapping his arms. I did nothing to stop him. It was the behaviour of any child who feels himself let off the leash. It was a little warmer inside, sheltered from the wind and drizzle. It smelled just as the church did, the smell of rubble, of dust from broken stones, of wet boots. But a strange sort of church, of course, full of wooden globes and maps of the skies, pointing out the Great Bear and the other stars with their fancy names, and with all the bizarre bits and pieces of equipment waiting to be assembled: in one corner an enormous circle of green glass, trapping a dozen tiny bubbles, just like insects caught in a saucer of jelly.

I directed Victor up the stairs, plodding behind him, clutching at the iron handrail whilst he sprinted ahead. He was led by the light, which shone down the stairs in a fine beam. Naturally the boy thought (I realised too late and was sorry for it) that we were headed for an open space. Freedom beckoned her hand to him. Instead we arrived in another large room, with good square arches above us and a great high ceiling, stepping through a doorway tall enough to fit three men one atop the other. Victor paused for a minute, disappointed I suppose, and then spied a further set of stairs and was off again.

Here I fretted that we should turn back. Victor was already in the narrow stairwell, sniffing at the walls, smoothing his palms over the wooden handrail. It was dark and steep, scant room to place your foot squarely on the stair. I was glad when Victor shoved at the half-open door and light streamed over us. Cold air smacked us in the cheeks, and it was a blessed relief to stand beneath that grand bowl of ice-blue sky, as pretty as any of my dishes from Sèvres.

We were on an open roof of rough stones and chimneys, gazing at the finest view I have ever seen – directly down the avenue de l'Observatoire with its rows and rows of Liberty trees. (What a wretched choice of tree for this tough Parisien soil! I have always said it. From this angle it is clear how right I was – how feebly they grow; their trunks crippled and twisted, where they should be straight and strong.) But even the failing trees did not prevent the catch in my throat, the little jump in my heart at the sight of the city spreading her arms out for me, something I have never seen before. I said to myself, imagine that: the pigeons and sparrows have more knowledge of this wonder than you have, Marie-France, working, grubbing at ground level all day long. It was a mistake to let my thoughts wander. With the word 'grubbing' I pictured the vegetable garden and Henri kneeling at it, like a man in prayer. Tears welled up. So many times he had said he wanted to come up here, to the Observatoire, to see 'what all the fuss is about'. The doctor's friend, that fellow Lalande with the great dome of a forehead and the prickly, whispering voice, who came to our house those times to see Victor, isn't he the director here? Henri thought the 'great man' would have let us in. Little did either of us know. How easy it was to walk in, any time.

And so it was that I was lost in thoughts of Henri and not paying attention to Victor.

A thumping sound pulled me up short. Victor, standing near the edge of the terrace, had fallen to his knees. For one terrible, heart-stopping moment I thought he was about to fall over the edge and a cry was rent from me, like the cry of a wolf or a cat, a squeal it was, quite horrible. But Victor did not fall over the edge. He dropped to his knees on the roof-tiles and remained tight as a ball of wool. I ran to him, knelt beside him with cajoling words but he would not move. His whole body was trembling and the back of his neck, where I laid my hand, was burning.

Oh, Dieu, Victor, I said. What is it? Not fear of heights, surely, for you can climb a tree swifter than a squirrel –

Victor only trembled violently and tightened the grip of his arms around his knees.

So it *is* the height that frightens you? You stepped too close to the edge when I was not watching you, is that it? Well, we must go down, that is all there is to it.

I held out my hand for him but he did not open his eyes, release his face from the floor, nor look up. I sat down beside him, bending my face close to his ear.

A big boy like you, Victor. For shame. All those nights in the forest alone. The padding of the paws of the Beast of Gévaudan. How brave you were then! And now you let a little height defeat you? I cannot believe it.

I hoped by this to rouse his anger, but his trembling only gave way to whimpering. I put my arms around him and fell to awkwardly rocking him. The sky was turning to black ink. I laid my body over him, thinking the warmth of my body might comfort him. He was as lifeless as a little sack of bones. So then I fell to rocking him, my face up close to his, breathing in the smell of him, that smell which so terrorised me in the beginning. It must be the time he has spent in my care, or maybe something has melted in me. In either case, it no longer terrorises me. It's just the smell of the woods, of damp mushrooms and hidden berries, of rotting tree stumps, mulched leaves. The smell of back home, of the old days. The belly of the forest floor.

Come on, child, let me take you home.

His rocking continued.

Home, Victor. With me.

Perhaps it was my tone of voice, but he was roused at last. He allowed himself to be led along the roof to the doorway, he gripped my hand as we stepped into that dark tunnel of stairs, his trembling gave way to a nervous shriek of *lait!* as we entered the main hall again.

I told the doctor later, of course. That is, I told him that Victor was afraid of heights, despite all those stories of his great feats of daring, climbing trees. Itard said that the one did not cancel out the other; the terrace of the Observatoire is far higher than any tree, after all, which is true. He asked whether Victor showed any interest in the 'marvellous science of the skies' and I hummphed and folded my arms as I often do when talking to the doctor and he coughed in embarrassment and no more was required.

But I didn't tell him that *I* had stood under that bowl of sky and seen the city as God sees it. That I saw my little baby Joseph floating in that black sky like an angel, with one leg cocked at the knee, as if ready to leap, and cold stars for his eyes.

It would only be Henri – who knew me to have both finished with God and not finished with him at all – only my poor Henri who could put up with me, understand me, when I talked like that.

At sunrise Victor smells snow. Even through the walls of his room, the walls of the Institute, he knows it is snow and he leaps to the window where the sky is a giant white bird shaking its feathers. He has learned to pull on the breeches, so he attempts this much. But in his excitement one leg won't go in the right place and he is hopping and falling and jumping to the door to bang on it, so he casts them off, frustrated. He throws himself with all his might against the door, knowing it is early and she may not hear him. He smells her arrival. Chocolate melting. The smell of the fire, of almonds, of the coffee beans she grinds, of the coffee-dust sinking under her skin. Hot chicken fat, garlic. The rustle of her skirts as she comes to open the door. Hurling himself again against the door.

So that as it opens, he bursts at her, ignoring her shriek as he pushes past. He has spied something so rare, he can't believe his luck. The door to the kitchen, the door that opens onto the stairs, the stairs that lead to the Institute gardens; that door is open. And so he is past her in an instant, a quiver of bare white flesh. She puts out her hand but he flies right through. Spores sailing on the wind.

Now he is outside, in the middle of the white, sweet-tasting ice. The woman is chasing him, the white and blue of her, held out to him. Hot kitchen smells through the sting of the snow. He opens his mouth to a taste of flowers and rain falling through leaves, biting his tongue, crunching under his teeth, pinching his nose and ears. To the familiar patterns, patterns he knows so well. The blue and silver of a winter night sky, veins on the inside of his wrists, cobwebs in his old house. Splinters on a frozen lake; the whiskers of an old man he used to know, a mirror he dropped; a cracked white plate. Fragments, scattering into the finest, tiniest threads.

Tears slipping down his cheeks. To hear that blue-white hush in both ears again. The feathers have stopped falling and the sun lights up the granules, the crystals of fine sugar, those shapes he has longed for, he has missed for so long, he thought he would never see again. Now here she comes with her hot stink of kitchen, and she is going to take them away from him.

Nivôse 10
Year Eight

This morning's tiresome proceedings ended extremely badly. In the belief that the only way to learn from this is to examine all the factors, so that in future I might be able to eliminate one or another of the antecedents to Victor's worst behaviours, I will (despite the pain it causes me) consider events in detail.

The day did not begin well. Madame Guérin greeted me to complain that the snow had seized Victor from his room; she had had the devil of a job to return him; he had rewarded her with a brutish kick to her shins for her pains (she showed me the bruises). Consequently she was late in bedecking Victor for the important visitors. I endeavoured to assist and together we dressed the sulky boy in breeches, stockings and some blue-ribboned boots belonging to Julie. (His last pair were hurled on the fire in his room, a habit he has developed to rid himself of items that displease him.) It was to be hoped that the esteemed gentlemen would be too enraptured by Sicard's speech to glance down at Victor's feet.

We arrived a little breathless in the hall, moments before the visitors. The entire school was assembled – some eighty boys squashed into the low-ceilinged hall: the smell of unwashed feet was pungent. The guests arrived; one of them, this man Dawson-Warren, the English vicar, the so-called peace envoy, was actually wearing his cleric's cap, gown, hood and bands, which must certainly have raised Napoleon's eyebrows when he met him. They were ushered in by Massieu, Sicard's star pupil, but their faces were stony: clearly they did not enjoy being wedged into a sea of blue uniforms. (Two boys, Emile and Jean-Paul, were indulging in their customary game of gossiping with their hands, shielding them from view behind Emile's opened jacket, which must have looked, to outsiders, very queer.) I took my place at the front, alongside Sicard. As I did so, I felt Victor stiffen beside me and knew that the crowd unsettled him.

Unfortunately Sicard's speech was long and boring. He required frequent demonstrations from Massieu. Victor hopped from one foot to the other; I gripped his arm. He gave little chirps and nodded his head vigorously: I gripped harder.

I must point out the distinction between those who are deaf from birth and consequently dumb from infancy and those who become deaf through accident or illness, droned Sicard.

The instruction of the former is a work of great difficulty for we have not only to teach them to express but also to conceive ideas; the latter have only to find a new mode of expressing what they already believe.

He made signs to Massieu and asked: what is electricity? Massieu wrote the sentence on the board behind him and then returned to the front to translate it into sign language for the boys. Underneath it he wrote his answer. This was corrected by Sicard, who told him it was a 'species of fire'. Of course, this error had been rehearsed. It led conveniently into a long discourse on the particular difficulty of communicating abstract ideas to the deaf, such as a word like 'species'.

Next, Sicard asked Massieu: what is galvanism? And the young man again wrote his answer on the board. (It seemed to have been translated directly from Galvani's own words.) A man near the back with the Dawson-Warren party then rose and gave us a long account of how to excite this species of electricity, which might have been interesting had I been able to hear it (his voice was very low). During this, Victor stopped chirping and hopping. Madame Guérin had joined us and now stood on the other side of him, occasionally whispering in his ear. The softness of the speaker's voice agitated Victor less than the abbé's louder one and he seemed at first to be calming himself. Then, glancing over at him, I realised how he was achieving this and my blood froze.

I could not catch Madame Guérin's eye in order to alert her. Since we faced the whole school, I could not reach over and prevent Victor from doing what he was doing. The man with the soft voice had lost the interest of the audience. After all, only a handful of people in that room could hear and, even for those, he was too softly spoken. The boys in front of me banged their feet on the floor and poked fingers up noses. Then Jean-Paul spied Victor and let out a roar of laughter. Heads turned at once. The boys, who have trouble containing their wild noises at the best of times, erupted into unintelligible shouts and screams. The whole place swarmed with laughter and mayhem.

Victor, stop at once! I hissed, pulling his arm away, and when that failed (he simply snatched it back again) I stood in front of him, my face aflame, attempting to block him from view. I could see from the disturbance at the back of the crowd that the visitors had not yet discovered the source of the laughter, but now even the abbé had noticed Victor's arm pumping up and down furiously and was signalling and hissing: for God's sake, Itard, get him out of here! Madame Guérin opened the door beside her, which would usually have sufficed, but Victor hardly noticed; so intense was his preoccupation. I had to wrench him to the door. Two streams of cold sweat were trickling down the inside of my shirt. I could still hear that wild laughter, see the children in front of me, hear the abbé's words. *For God's sake, Itard.*

I held my face in my hands; my palms were as ice against my blazing face. The mortification could not have been worse if I had been the offender.

Victor now leaned against the wall of the corridor, closing his eyes luxuriously. Madame Guérin spoke softly to him, which caused me the greatest surprise and intensified my embarrassment. Why did she not scold him? Instead she was leading him towards the garden, steering him gently, and she allowed his hand to continue its fruitless agitations. Part of Victor's problem is that, despite being tormented by the tumult of his senses, his search for fulfilment is always thwarted. He does not understand the root of his desires and can thus find no solace for them. His gestures are not purposeful, only angry and desperate. It is as if he tries to push that part of himself away: to bid it retreat, lie down. Little does he realise that his own caresses only serve to intensify his frustrations.

I followed Madame Guérin and Victor out into the garden. Wiping the snow from a bench with her hand, the governess sat gingerly upon it; gathering up her skirts. Victor began again his whooping and hollering of earlier; the snow captivating him once more. I saw how wise her decision was: the snow would distract him, appease his desire for physical sensation, and the icy snap in the air would cool his passions still further. Not for the first time, I was chastened by the superior wisdom demonstrated by this simple woman of peasant stock. I made a private vow to read Jean-Jacques Rousseau again; and this time, to be slower to dismiss him.

I pondered the antecedents to Victor's behaviour.

Crowds, and being required to stand patiently in a large group, make Victor very anxious. One might even say afraid. Fear causes his body to flood with sensation; this sensation is contained in every organ, not least the sexual organs. Victor is vaguely conscious of his desires, but they are purely physical, not provoked by any deeper sentiment. Thus, he seeks only to attend to their physical origin. Of course, he has no concern for when or where might be the proper place to do this.

I tried, with much difficulty and delicacy – for naturally, I could not simply ask! – to discover what Madame Guérin thought of the matter. I succeeded only in drawing from her a grunt and the comment that boys, they are all the same (which I resented horribly, and which caused a second deep blush, whilst I considered for a moment my own boyish self and had the sudden chilling sensation that women, mothers such as Madame Guérin, might know things about me that I cannot bear to reveal, even to myself).

But his lack of modesty? What can be done? I shall have to bleed him again. We must increase his baths –

I am to increase his baths but without the help of my daughter?

I sat down on the bench beside her, first brushing aside the snow as she had done, and removing my hat to tip a light flutter of snow from that.

191

From what you told me the presence of Julie only increases Victor's – torment.

But you denied it, Doctor. You said she had no more – what was it you said? – no more hold on him than anyone. Than you, for example.

I had no reply to this. Seeing her advantage, she continued sulkily: seems to me you are right, Doctor. He has no care for our Julie especially and that word he says, that *lli* sound, it's as meaningless as a cat mewing on the hearth . . .

Well now, I am not so sure –

Oh, you have changed your mind about my daughter?

About your daughter? Changed my mind? In what way?

My voice betrayed alarm. It was necessary to return matters to a firm scientific footing. I gave my prescription promptly.

Two cold baths a day will suffice. Julie can assist, if she is present, and you will report to me any adverse effects on him. I will come to bleed Victor this evening after his lessons –

Only *adverse* effects?

Should his violent desires increase –

What of – what is the opposite of adverse? What if she – makes him – what if she soothes him?

Soothes him?

Something in my voice seemed to offend her. Whilst we spoke Victor was contenting himself by rolling on the white lawn, then falling on his back to kick up gusts of snow. Thankfully his earlier preoccupation was forgotten. Madame Guérin stared at him without speaking. An unspoken disagreement hung between us. Perhaps my tone was more disbelieving than I had meant it to be, or more sarcastic. Perhaps it was simply the vexed subject of the daughter. In any case, she gave me an unreadable look and then returned to staring at Victor. She clamped up, her chin sinking towards her chest, and in her usual clever way made it absolutely clear that the conversation was over. My admiration of a few moments earlier turned immediately to anger. How she did that, how a subordinate, a woman with scant skills or status except as a governess, or putative mother, how such a woman managed to silence me, a man of learning, a doctor, these days a renowned doctor, I have no idea. But despite the bitterest of resentment, I could not find another word to say to her. I picked up my hat from the bench beside me: the brim was laced with snow. As I began walking towards the steps, a few light flakes began to fall.

I will be in the library! I called over my shoulder.

Walking away from her, I had the sensation that her eyes flew at my back, like darts.

So I waited for Victor in the library. I believe I was pacing a little. I was highly unsettled. Hot shame continued to flare in me; at any moment I expected the abbé to burst into the room and accuse me of ridiculing his school in public. Every kind of ugly confrontation and embarrassment loomed before me.

Humiliations, real, remembered, past or present, leapt at me. Every brown leather corner of the library groaned with some fresh spectre from the past. I felt again the pang of a leather strap across my knuckles, punishment for forgetting to lock the gate and letting the horses bolt; a fierce rebuke from Father for failing to remember my catechism; or being shown into the drawing room – as a very young child indeed – to apologise to my mother for 'stealing' an item of her clothing. Father made the most innocent of acts appear gross and obscene when he spoke of it in his insinuating whisper. The shame, the inarticulate fury I felt at not being allowed to speak up. I longed to explain that I had not stolen the chemise, only hidden it, wanting to keep it as a souvenir, knowing I was soon to be sent to Riez to live with Uncle. The chemise, what a fuss was made of it! I did not understand, but I knew how sad, how terribly sad, my actions had made her. I was frightened, my face burned, I could scarcely look into her wide green eyes. I remember my father saying: Jean-Marc, how *disappointed* we are in you, and with those words, some inexpressible further wrong was voiced, some profound way that I knew his disappointment in me was complete.

It was not merely for my own self that I was reprimanded. The loss of my brothers hovered in the room in the same way that a flicker will linger in the darkness for a moment after a candle has been snuffed. Small-pox took the three of them: I had escaped with barely a scar. I stood with my head bowed, arms behind my back. From lowered eyes I glimpsed the terrible expression on Mother's face, the trembling of her bottom lip, the drawing together of her brows, the engulfing sadness in her eyes.

She was always afraid of Father. He was on a constant vigil to drum out signs of weakness, unmanly behaviour, in me. He found much to occupy him. I am sure it was partly behind his decision to send me to live with Uncle. He knew Uncle would be unstinting and Mother would not be there to interfere; to introduce feminine sentiment into his system.

For almost twenty years I have given no thought to the wretched incident of the chemise. It is the sense of being wrongly accused which has so inflamed me. But in now dwelling upon it, a startling idea has presented itself to me. Could it be that Mother's expression, her sadness, might not have been about my supposed misdemeanour at all, but was because her eight-year-old son was being sent away? That, as a mother, she knew my real intention, knew that I would want a keepsake? She also knew herself powerless to act against a decision of Father's.

This astounding thought did nothing to calm me. If anything, it only increased my fury. If Father was disappointed in *me*, how disappointed I have been these many long years in Mother, at her cowardice, at her failure to defend me against his unjust accusations. Why is it that mothers, with their superior capacity for empathy and compassion, are fatally weak, treacherously unwilling to act upon their insights?

194

I grappled with myself. But my mood, when Victor was brought to me, was not calm.

Madame Guérin brought Victor after a half hour or so; he carried a handful of lentils and his pockets were stuffed with beans and chestnuts. I knew she did this to make him more biddable, I knew it was a gesture of solicitude to help me with my work. Nonetheless, I was intensely irritated and instructed her to empty his pockets at once. This was achieved with much shouting from Victor.

You can leave us today, I told her, turning my head away so that my eyes would not meet hers.

If you are sure you can cope, she said pointedly. She glanced at Victor, busily cramming beans into his mouth, dangling his legs from a high bench, his gaze fixed on the snow outside, before clicking down the three smooth wooden steps to the library door.

I will be just behind the door, if you need me, she said, in an infuriating way.

I addressed my words to the back of Victor's head and told him in a resolved tone, ready to repel all protestations, that today we would continue our work developing his powers of distinguishing by touch. He continued to gaze at the snow.

However, no sooner had I produced the bag and the blindfold than Victor jumped up, squealing in delight, knocking the jug of water from the table, where it smashed to the floor, bringing a triumphant Madame Guérin at once running into the room to attend to the mess.

I decided at once to abandon the work with the blindfold.

Our time will be better spent in Victor's chamber, with my new invention, I told Madame Guérin, careful to disguise the annoyance in my voice. The broken glass picked up and the water mopped, the three of us proceeded to Victor's room; Victor, of course, hopping and shouting, flinging himself from wall to window in his excitement to be in the snow again. Madame Guérin kept a very tight grip on his arm.

Whilst she set about building up the fire in the grate in Victor's room, I fetched the board and the pieces of paper; a circle of red, a triangle of blue and a black square and all the further more complex shapes that I have been adding to Victor's repertoire of recognition; a pale blue parallelogram, a grey square, an orange oval. Victor's task, which he sometimes performs impressively, is to match these shapes to the ones attached to the board, by placing them over their counterparts. By refining his ability to recognise and match shapes and colours I hope to introduce to him his own ability to judge similarity and dissimilarity, to 'discuss' with me, in effect, how a blue square is not the same as a grey one.

The first time I tried the experiment, Madame Guérin clapped excitedly whenever Victor got something right; but she soon became bored. Today I dismissed Madame Guérin from the room, and then scattered paper shapes around the bed, instructing Victor to place them in their correct positions. I said nothing about the fact that the shapes were blue, red and black and those on the board were yellow, grey and green. Victor picked up the shapes with eagerness, quickly positioning a circle on a circle, a triangle on the same and so on, with no regard for the difference in colour. When I took them off again, insisting that he do it again (from a wider selection of shapes that I produced) he looked at me in mute fury.

No, Victor, I said calmly. He easily understands the word 'no' and it rarely fails to intensify his anger. He grabbed at my hands, taking a random selection of paper shapes from them and again placed them on top of those on the board, again with no regard for the colour difference.

No, I said, again, removing the shapes.

Then his anger gave way to action and he swept at the

board with a shriek, scattering the paper on the ground. He went further; he plucked at the pieces of paper and threw them in the air, then flung himself on his bed on top of the pasteboard.

Pick them up, Victor. Pick every one up.

I pointed at the shapes with my finger. I picked up the first for him. He made no sign of moving. His frustration often erupted in this way when we worked together. Of course, one can hardly blame the child for not being able to see the purpose of his task and being thus disgusted with it. His anger is in some degree perfectly natural, but still it is necessary for me to overcome it.

I shook his shoulder and pointed again to the pieces of paper. Pick them up, Victor.

He sat up, rubbing at his eyes. Reluctantly he accepted the red circle I handed to him and with exaggerated slowness, picked up the other pieces. He now had six shapes and there were three placed on the board for him to match them with. He stared in some despair at the shapes in his hand. And then with a shout, he flung them on the floor once more and leapt on the bed, thumping the wall with his fist.

You must – learn – to – master – your – anger – I said, rather breathlessly, trying, as I spoke, to restrain Victor by grabbing hold of his fists and clamping them to his chest. I was not unconscious of the irony of my remarks. He tossed his head and rolled his eyes, like a horse trying to break free from a harness, with the same ferocious strength. Mindful of the kick he had given Madame Guérin, I was careful to hold myself at some distance from his feet, which did not make restraining him easy, and he soon escaped me, whereupon he scampered to the fire. Picking up several hot coals, with his usual astonishing imperviousness to pain, he hurled them at my feet. One skimmed past my boot in a black streak, like the mark of charcoal, a pen mark. A line drawn.

Victor! I roared. ENOUGH!

The sight of him this morning in the hall flickered in front of me. *We are very disappointed in you*. His stupid, bleary-eyed, transported expression, the disgusting vibrations travelling along the wooden floor, the look on Madame Guérin's face as she said: boys, they are all the same.

Victor threw another coal, which hit me with a smart sting above the ankle, spitting as it grazed the fabric, bouncing off across the floor. Then something swelled in me, a feeling so powerful, I hardly know how to describe it, except to say that I could no longer see the child in front of me, so swamped was I in this enormous feeling; a hardness, a coldness, a fury that hissed at my ear like a snake, and the snake was whispering, seething, saying: is the child not trouble enough, what has he done, the wretched devil, but show ingratitude, *savagery*; and the voice was telling me to pick him up, to carry him to the window, to open it, to suspend him the four storeys above the courtyard below, to shake him there, to dangle him like a flag fluttering in the wind, triumphantly. To be deaf to his screams, blind to the bleached face of Madame Guérin. And she tugging at my arm, saying Doctor Itard, Jean-Marc-Gaspard, have you gone mad the boy is scared look at him he is terrified did I not tell you he is afraid of heights what are you doing you will kill him you must let him go and Victor screaming and screaming until only, finally, at last, only when I felt his body spasm as if in an epileptic fit, felt a warm liquid seep from his legs and trickle over my arm, only when I saw that dark puddle fan out on the floor at my feet and felt the boy limp as a crumpled shirt in my arms, only then, trembling, sweat pouring down my neck, only then did the swelling in my chest subside, the voice in my head fall silent; only then did I put him down.

He folded to the floor. I left the building and I did not look back.

*   *   *

Well the doctor has gone quite mad and did I not say to Julie only three nights ago that he was showing signs of strain and that it is quite unnatural for a young man of his age to be locked up day in day out with a boy of thirteen who would tax a saint and him not even a blood relation either. I did not say to Julie (for what mother could say it to her own daughter) that a child could uncover in you a rage such as you never knew existed in God's earth, let alone in your own bosom, but I said it to the doctor as he was leaving, though he gave no sign of hearing.

It was a wicked thing to witness just the same. The thought of it makes my hands fly up to cover my eyes, as if that might block out the memory. The way Victor's little body shook, from head to toe. It made you know he has seen more terror than most. I never want to behold that much fear in a child again and yet now I have, the sight of it won't leave me. My mind comes back to that scar on Victor's throat and what the doctor said of it. 'A wound made by a cutting implement.' A hand 'more disposed than adapted' to acts of cruelty.

More disposed than adapted. Not practised. The hands in my dreams, the gloves.

Julie had an opinion, as she always does where discussions of the doctor are concerned; she can never tire of hearing his name mentioned, whether in complaint or praise, it's all the same to her. She said that the man was dedication itself. I told her she was not there and knew nothing. It was not a question of blame, only of telling the truth. The doctor had lost his mind for a moment. And in my humble opinion as the child's governess, of course not that a soul listens to the likes of me, he should leave off for a while, let Victor be.

The argument was soon afire. Without Henri's soothing voice, without his gentle: *now, now, my girls.* We are too alike to talk peaceably. It was all foolishness since we were both defending the doctor in our way; the matter was only that *she* would not accept what I had witnessed with my own eyes. Itard's intention. What the man was capable of.

So then, as so often happens, we circled and circled, with heat blazing at the centre from each of our undeclared positions. She with her heart set on the doctor, mine set on Victor. The evening ended with her flouncing out, tossing over her shoulder the news that in any case, Itard had been offered a position by the Tsar of Russia, so would no doubt soon be leaving to work in that frozen land. This had me running to the door after her to ask her what she meant, but seeing Victor leap up, ready to follow me, I changed my mind and locked it behind her.

As I gave Victor his bath that night, I told him he had been wearisome indeed and that he would have to try harder if he wanted the doctor to continue his interest and his allowance too, which after all, is keeping us all in beans and lentils.

God knows I took care of the changeling boy, the boy who was not Joseph, as best I could. I washed him, I dressed him, I fed him the softest bread I could find, I sewed him bonnets, I made dresses for him with no buttons (buttons made him angry), I poured myself into him, I did things for that boy I never did for our Julie and never knew another mother to do: I spoiled him, I petted him, I could no more say no to him than I could stop the breath moving in my lungs. Did it make him love me? Did God take pity on me and send my own child back?

When I close my eyes now, I can see myself leaning over the crib, my arms floury and my cheeks hot from the fire, holding out to him the little spice cake I had just spent an hour fashioning for him, while Julie slept with her face to the wall and the rest of us living off soup without a sniff of meat. I can hear Henri saying it won't make a whit of difference, Marie-France, that boy is possessed by a devil and no amount of cakes is going to change that.

So of course then I took him to the priest, in secret – because that was the beginning, the beginning of secrets, of not being sure any longer – and I watched while Joseph was plunged headfirst into the waters of the Tarn, held in that one bony hand like a chicken ripe for plucking, and I watched my little boy with his face scarlet with fury, felt the splashes from his angry kicks; pressed my hands over my ears to drown his screams, to drown the breathless shouts of the bald priest, his cap nudged from his head and whirling away on the rushing river waters, the priest who screamed that he was being attacked with the fiery heels of a hundred devils, not just the one, who called on God to purify this child, to drive out the evil spirit, who panted desperately as he struggled with this two-year-old boy who had the strength of four adults, a babe who nearly plunged them both into the currents, who opened his mouth until it swallowed up his whole face; who looked at me in one brief moment, who opened his eyes only to give me a look so icy, so freshly cold that I tell you, it would stop a leaping cat in mid-air: a look to say that he hated me, that nothing I could do would ever make him better and why did I not face it: my darling little blond boy was lost, *lost*, and no one on this earth would ever find him for me. And I remember a bird, a big bird, one with the wings that sound like a man running, a bird flew over the three of us and screamed stupidly and told me that God himself was laughing at me for wanting it otherwise.

But giving up, it is not in my nature. I gathered up my child, I swaddled him in my fichu and carried him the two miles home and he was limp and tired and warm against my breasts, a great watery circle spreading out from my heart where his wet head lay. I was so tired I could hardly put one foot in front of the other and all the time a voice inside me saying what have I done to deserve this, what mother in the world is so wicked that her own child does not love her? So I sat on the moon-silver ground and rocked him and still he whimpered until I took out my breast and he clamped his hungry little mouth around it. The milk rushed in me, blood hammering in my body in that old animal way to answer him and I thought and thought about the changeling and the Devil and God and his plans for us and I whispered to him that I still loved my son and I begged him to send me some sign, a sign to help me, to let me know what to do. And while I prayed Joseph sucked, although, God knows, in those days we were all so starving that there was scarce a drop in me but, even so, his body finally grew heavy and full and at last he was asleep.

Am I forgiven? I whispered to his cheek. I kissed him, and I thought for a moment that it was my old Joseph back again. I could tell you even now exactly how his skin felt: you would not find silk finer in the noblest house in Paris. I remember the taste of him, the smell of him, I remember as if it were this morning, exactly how my washed-in-the-river darling felt to me, you know we were hungry then, always hungry, and that night I was so hungry, my stomach ached like it had never ached before and my boy he felt like the most delicious loaf of warm bread, sweeter than the opal moon on a river and, if I could, I would have opened my mouth wider than the banks of the Tarn, and eaten him right up.

I have never seen a child weep the way Victor wept after the doctor left. I have never seen Victor weep at all, come to think of it, and now he lay on his bed, face down, his body shaking. Although I stroked his head and his neck and anywhere else I could reach, he was not much comforted; the sobs and gulps rippled through his body, until a sob was wrenched from my own heart, so painful was it to see him like that.

For weeks after his outburst, the doctor did not return. I heard from Julie that he had not taken up the post in Russia, so that much was a blessing, but I did not hear more. The snow melted and green shoots stuck their heads up through the frost in the urns, the pond cracked and opened and Victor was able to dip his hands in it again, but still we didn't see

Itard. Julie came every day after work to keep me company, our argument forgotten.

Her arrival with a basket of chestnuts and a jug covered with muslin and brimming with creamy milk saved the evenings. She took these gifts to Victor's bedroom, and after he had sniffed them and licked at a few of his own tears (he seemed surprised, which made me ask myself whether the child *knew* that he could weep), he would take her hand and jump off the bed, leading her to his favourite cup.

When she had poured him a drink he sat in front of the fire in the kitchen, seizing her other hand and using it to stroke his own head.

Why does he want him to match paper shapes? Julie asked one time, as if we had left off our discussion of the doctor's methods and madness just minutes ago, not weeks. She held up a blue paper circle, which had mysteriously found its way onto my kitchen tiles.

Oh, he is teaching him his letters, I answered, as if that explained everything. Julie let this pass.

Do you believe he will give up?

Who, Itard? Not likely. He has scarce begun, to hear him tell it.

She fell to stroking Victor again and the boy murmured, pressing his body against her like a cat, tilting his chin, offering his throat.

How did it heal, do you think? Perhaps it was not deep –

I knew what she was speaking of. I have often pondered it myself.

I overheard him talk of it once. With that fat one – Virey, is it? Virey said that a beast's licking would have healed it but the doctor laughed at that. He said it was united by the 'first intention', whatever that means. And healed by the 'timely succour of nature', he said.

Isn't that the same thing?

We did not like to talk of it in front of Victor, and fell

silent again. A pan of water bubbled on the fire, fetching the colour to our cheeks. You would think that a boy who did not see the inside of a bath-tub for years on end would not mind the odd evening without a dip. But these days if it is knocking ten o'clock and his water is not drawn, he will take the bucket, place it in my hand, fold the towel and hang it over my arm as if I was one of those fancy waiters in the Palais Royal, drag the bath-tub from its hook on the wall to the centre of the room, bang on the tub with a spoon . . . he is as bossy as he is fastidious, which is strange, when you consider his other bad habits and how little he cares then for hygiene.

Well Victor had been in a queer mood that evening, I should have paid more heed to it. It was the lull after a squall, but with an edge. A threat of rolling thunder, one of those low clouds that hang over Paris like a blanket of violet-grey, something that makes you think all is not as it should be, not one whit. He sat by the fire, rocking in the fashion he has not rocked in now for many weeks, and the floor creaked and murmured with his rhythm. Julie left at midnight. It is a tart sorrow to me that she seems to find little solace in talking about her father and when I turn the conversation in that direction, sifting through my memories of Henri to find one that we can share, she will leap up suddenly, see that a coal is about to spring from the fire, or that the bubbling pan needs topping up; or that the nuns at the Val-de-Grâce will be furious with her for being so tardy returning.

After she had left I melted chocolate in a pan for my supper, all the while chattering to Victor, who cried *lli! lli!* in a soft voice. Then I thought I had better go to Victor's room to put out the fire since he is given to using anything he pleases for fuel these days. This took me a minute to do, I am sure of it. Three minutes at most. I am truly sure that I had not left the kitchen for more than five minutes. But when I returned, Victor had gone.

The unlocked door blew open. In the grey moonlight melting there, I saw Victor's sooty footprint. Coal dust from the fire on my newly brushed step. A perfect little foot, but only one; as if the boy had somehow hopped, or flown, or in some other fantastical way escaped, planting just one foot down for just one moment, to show his poor old governess that she was not dreaming, to prove that he had ever been here at all.

I ran to Julie's and together we went to the doctor's lodgings in Rue St Jacques. The doctor appeared at the bottom of the stairs whilst his landlady peeped out of her own doorway, wearing a huge white bonnet, and cradling a dog, like a babe, in her arms. The doctor wore no hat or coat or collar; his face sleepy, with the mark of his bolster still pressed in one cheek. The sight of a man suffering is an affecting one for a sensitive girl like my Julie. Combine that with a man torn from sleep, his countenance dreamy, a feather caught in his hair: the effect is lethal. If ever a man wants to possess a woman, he need only appear to her like that, though few seem to realise it. Julie gave a tiny shriek. It was thanks to my quick thinking that nothing worse occurred: I planted myself firmly between them.

Julie said: Victor has run away!

I had to leap forward and anticipate him, so strange was his skin, just exactly like the lining of a mussel shell: palest blue or green, I cannot tell you exactly, in any case not a human colour at all. You might have thought he would collapse in a dead faint, or stagger a little at the least, but unpredictable, even in a crisis, the doctor did nothing of the sort. As soon as Julie's words were out, he was master of himself again. After fetching his hat and his long black coat from his room upstairs he clattered to the street in great haste. He gave us his lamp and told Julie and me to run one way, whilst he went the other. He would meet us back at the clock-tower at the Institute at first light of dawn.

The church next door has had a new bell installed these last few days, now that the First Consul has declared a cease-fire on the war against worship, and it rang out now with a tinny, empty sound, nothing like the deep, watery ring of old. I tell you, it would make the gayest heart melancholy to hear it. I trudged beside my daughter along the Rue de Feuillantines, holding our lamp before us, straining our eyes to catch the glimpse of a swift dark running boy or the flutter of a white shirt, which we hoped at every turn to see. Every scurrying rat, every trollope in white skirts disappearing into a doorway, drew fresh hope from us, only to dash it again. It was a cruel few hours.

By the time the rooster crowed in the courtyard we were exhausted. Itard was a picture of misery, his coat flapping, his chin dropped to his chest; we knew before he spoke that he had not seen a hair of Victor either. He said he had seen Lemeri and the old man reported a sighting of the boy minutes earlier, charging down the hill towards the Seine. I didn't say it to the doctor, but Lemeri is just the sort to claim to have seen him, whether he has or not. I wouldn't set too much store by it.

We parted then: Itard walking Julie back to the hospital, me mounting the stairs of the Institute. Never have I been so reluctant to go home. The gaping door, Victor's bed with his sheets turned down, the fire cold in the grate.

I lay down on the floor in front of that dead fire, too weary to make it afresh, and was soon half-asleep. I had a fearful dream. I was sitting in the doorway at my old job, sewing a pair of white kid gloves, holding an enormous pair of scissors. Then I was not in the glove-maker's home but in the tannery, and everywhere was that stench again, the smell of goat-skins, the cheesy, milky smell, the smell of babies' hair, the worse smells, the ones I told you of. And sounds too, the sound it makes being cut, the membrane, snipped. In my dream I was not cutting leather but skin and there was screaming, far away. There was a far-off tinkling of bells from the brebis in the hills, there was the finest chevreau velours stretched across my hands and across my mouth, and there was my little lamb, my baby Joseph, and somewhere else, screaming.

Despite the most assiduous efforts, I have made an appalling error of judgement. Victor has gone and I can only believe that it is my own fault, the result of over-zealous discipline, of a fit of temper and scaring the wits out of him. At least, I had feared the onset of epilepsy in the child, but had not considered that he might run away. It feels like a just punishment for my sins.

Julie and her mother assisted my search for the boy. The torments of the last few weeks were nothing compared to the anguish I felt on news of his escape. I walked the lamp-lit streets until the hour when old women emerge from doorways to begin sluicing steps. I saw no hint of Victor, nor heard any fresh account of him.

Towards the morning, when my spirits had sunk lower than I could have believed possible, I met up with the Guérins. Madame Guérin parted from us at the Institute walls and I accompanied Julie home. We paused at the gates of the Val-de-Grâce. The hour was violet, I was tired and half-mad with wretchedness, I had thought of nothing but Victor all night long. I do not know how, I can barely remember how, but it happened. Julie Guérin leant towards me. I had no presentiment of what she was about to do, although I doubt she would have believed that. I saw her face loom at me and my fear was not swift enough to prevent it. She kissed me.

My immediate impulse was to push her. To push her forcefully. She uttered a startled scream and so, I believe, did I. Then we stood in the half-light like two children after a fight and stared at one another. I could not believe what I had done. But neither could I account for the trembling in my body, the urge I felt to wipe my lips, at the spot where the ill-fated kiss had landed. Her mouth was scented with carbolic; the smell of the military hospital which clings about her person, the smell of desperation and suffering, overlaid with sweet violets or some other hopeless, suffocating perfume. I struggled to hide the violence of my emotions from her, but I knew she was not deceived.

She gave a desolate little sound, the pitiful cry a kitten makes; a half-sob, and fled from me.

Julie! Forgive me!

I knew she would not turn around. I had no idea how to snatch back my cruel impulse. My misery was complete.

It is the sun melting pink through the trees, the shade of blood mixed with water, waking him. Warm sunlight licking at the tips of his ears, pouring down his neck like spilled water. Jacques-Pierre is curled in the position he was abandoned in; head to his knees, back curved, speckled with the dots of dew. Under his wet throat a monster rages at him. Pain – he doesn't have a word for pain, he has very few words and pain is not one of them. He only knows that something presses him into the soft ground, something sucks at his throat, is trying to draw him back, draw him under. He makes no fight. He is not interested in fighting the monster he finds beneath him, but he is awake and troubled by something new, a new sensation. A new smell. The hot dank stink of something. A rough furred scratching at his throat.

Many days pass, days, nights; no one ventures into the forest. The child is not especially missed. His father drinks a pitcher of wine, standing in the kitchen with his neighbour, sobs convincingly at his own story, that the boy ran off, that he searched for him everywhere, that the wolves must surely have him by now. Times are hard. This is sure to be a bitter winter. He would not be the first to abandon an imbecile child in this way.

Félicité holds up her chemise and lifts her legs over his neck, the way she promised.

Days pass quickly, morning blurs into night; the tap of a woodpecker is replaced by the hoot of an owl. The child feels warm licking, tickling at his throat. He sees pink, nipping in and out of yellow teeth. The monster starts to dissolve, retreat. It is many days before he sits up, before he lifts his head. He feels the bark of a tree, scaly against his skin. When he rocks against the tree, his body makes the same tap as the woodpecker; they tap together, the same rhythm, though neither bird nor boy is conscious of it. Like two bodies asleep, hearts beating pointlessly in time.

Sometimes waking, he feels something warm over his back, warm and heavy and beating. Other times the licking again at his throat. One morning he lifts his aching head and he smells something he can recognise. Morilles St Georges. Pieds de mouton. Cèpes. Words he has heard, but he couldn't say them. His stomach yawns, a great aching yawn, a hollow inside him opens up, urging him towards the white and yellow flesh. He bites, but he is weak and that is all. Two small bites and he vomits the white speckles onto the stony ground. He falls back into unconsciousness.

Sometimes there is water slipping down his throat, drop by delicious drop; he is lapping by a lake, there are others, silent like him. The only sounds are lapping and supping and snuffling and there are smells; the smell of water, green and sweet, a dragonfly that flits over your face, the rank dark smell of shit, the brown furred smell of the silty river bed. These times might be dreams, they might be something he remembers. When he wakes from them the others are no longer with him. The coat his father flung over him as he turned to run from the forest is buried in leaves and sticks and shit. The smell of fur and dank; the feel of something licking, something gentle and tickling. He remembers that feeling. Someone used to tickle him like that, under the chin. A long time ago. He can still smell their fingers; butter and flour and soap. He doesn't know how much he liked it.

In time, perhaps weeks, perhaps longer, he no longer feels the tickling at his throat. With his fingers, he touches the place, but there is no itching, no scratching tongues, only a raised hot lump there, a line. If he taps his head against the tree, he can feel the scaly bark scratch a groove into his neck. If he rubs a stick in the soil he can watch ants, beetles, tiny busy insects driving their intricate maps into the earth. He can watch this until the sun goes down. He can overturn rocks, find more grubs, truffles or mushrooms. He opens his mouth sometimes, when the dank hot smell is strong, the furry heat all around him, and accepts the milky pulp with the bitter, wooden taste that he finds there. Sometimes he bites at the roots he discovers, digging in the earth with his long black nails, and sometimes he vomits up what he eats, but more and more often he doesn't. He doesn't know what drives him on, what urges at him, to eat, to seek shelter, he who thinks he does not want or need anything, but something does.

Once he found berries, red and sharp; he spent all day by the bush, picking each individually, never together, clearing a branch at a time, until the whole bush was stripped bare. He is good at this. He is methodical, methodical things please him. He doesn't take a berry randomly, he takes care to pluck them consecutively, always in the same pattern. But when he is finished he hears a monster; there is a monster crashing through the forest towards him – for eating the berries, for stealing all the berries – and he is afraid and manages to scramble clumsily up a tree, until the monster has passed.

In time he learns to fall asleep up there, feeling safer. Knowing he is less likely to meet the monster. He wedges small branches between his bare toes and doesn't notice if they are bleeding. And for many hours, perhaps days, he sleeps. Then the days grow shorter and darker. The nights are cold. He looks for the black overcoat, but he can't find it. He doesn't know if he has wandered far or if he is in the same spot. He likes to draw circles in the ground and forget about the cold. But the ground has turned hard and is now covered in a fine glass that he can splinter with his stick; he likes to break up the muddy pieces and place them on his tongue where they dissolve and transform into good, cold water.

Sometimes he runs, like he used to at home, he runs for no reason, and laughs, feeling the cones smash beneath his feet, the twigs cackling like a mad hag, the squirrels racing for the trees, birds scattering in panic. One day he hears voices, something he faintly remembers, although he could not say now how long it is, how long he has been here. The voices make him run, faster than he has run before, and he knows better than to laugh, and although he is skinny and black as a monkey, he is bigger than he was and his legs carry him further, carry him with ease.

The black ice turns to snow. This he can drink too, so cold it makes his tongue burn, the line in his throat opens up and screams at him. His favourite branch is heavy with snow and too slippery to climb on. Looking for berries he stumbles into a bush which turns into a hollow and it has the good strong smell from before, from when he was waking up in the forest in the beginning, and he knows he is safe here, in this milky grey darkness with this soft ground beneath him, strewn with old, damp, blackened leaves. Some memories fly back to him here. Those fingers under his jawline. Tears slide down his face and he rocks back and forth. He likes watching the great drops bounce from the end of his chin, onto his knees. Watching them makes them stop. He doesn't know how to make them come back.

Is it tenderness, those fingers under the chin? Is it something real, something sinister, something else? At night sometimes, flinty yellow eyes surround him, candles round a coffin. He sniffs, flares his nostrils like a horse, continues drawing with his stick. Dark wings swoop down over his head, sweep up again. Sleeping, one blackened, skinny limb hangs out from his den, the foot little more than a filthy bone, covered in snow. He starts to soak into leaves, seep under the rocks. If his father came to search for him, which he never did, if he came now, he would never be able to see him. So little time before it happens: the child's matted hair studded with clods of earth, his face a nest of mud and grass, and only his eyes remain sparks of something else; something sharp and white as memory.

Part Four

Germinal 3
Year Nine

I have been afraid to visit the Guérins and yet tortured with the possibility that they might have news of Victor. Finally, desperation for news of Victor overcame my fears and I ventured to Madame Guérin's home. To my immense relief, Julie was not there.

If Julie spoke to her mother of what happened between us, Madame Guérin gave no indication of it. Reassured, I allowed myself to be coddled with wine and a bowl of bouillon and soon fell into the habit of visiting nightly, putting aside my dread of encountering Julie. After much consideration, I decided upon a strategy. I should treat the embrace as if it had been an ugly dream. I need not raise the subject but had only to act as if nothing was amiss between us. By that means, the entire sorry occasion would soon be forgotten. This strategy soon struck me as the only one possible and I adhered to it faithfully. In only a matter of days I was persuaded that my imagination had exaggerated matters out of all proportion. My response to Julie had not been unnatural nor foolish. Only perhaps ungracious. It had been the just response of a preoccupied man, distraught with anxiety over his beloved charge. Any man would have reacted in such a way. My behaviour was not peculiar nor even to be regretted. Julie's work with the soldiers at the Val-de-Grâce has obviously sullied her, made her bold. It was surely she who should regret her rash deed. I decided not to point this out to her, but to be instead kind and discreet, so that she might infer my meaning by my exemplary manners.

I was not put to the test, however. Julie did not appear

for the next two weeks. Madame Guérin did not question me; she spoke only of Victor and only in the most dispiriting fashion. There was no news of him. Whenever Madame Guérin expressed her fears, my own anxiety flared anew. She lit a taper in me whenever she mentioned Victor's name. We were not capable of reassuring one another. And yet I could not stay away.

The man looks crazed. He has come to the house these last few weeks, his chin dark with stubble and neither hat nor cravat in place; he accepts a half bowl of cassoulet or snatches some bread and cheese, swallows some wine, and then he is off again, searching the streets for Victor. How young he looks without his hat! Now having spent these many long years tending an invalid, it is habit enough in me to offer him the same attentions I offered to Henri, and sometimes it is all I can do not to gather him in my arms and pull him to me. Something about the man, for all his cleverness, for all his stiffness, in fact, because of it – he strikes me more and more as a motherless child, as lost, in his way, as Victor is. I did ask him once, being curious naturally, but he did not venture much detail about his family. His father, a carpenter, married again, after his mother's death. He had three brothers, younger than him and I believe all three died of the small-pox. (Now that's a burden for any eldest brother.) He was sent to live with his uncle – a priest – at a young age, in the way that boys from his background so often are and I suppose that his mother died not long after. That's as much as I know. He's one of those men who would like you to believe he arrived here fully formed; hat and cane in place, flapping his great black coat and standing on a podium; that he never lay in a crib howling, was never caressed in a mother's arms.

It's two weeks since Victor left. I think of him every time I see the beans, shooting up in the garden, but with both my

Henri and now Victor gone, I barely have the heart to tend to them. Julie has been over most nights to see if there is news of Victor and to keep me company, but mostly to suffer over some little secret now between her and the doctor. She will not share it with me, she believes her mother too stout and too old to have ever been in love. Let her keep her secret in that locket around her neck: I don't need to tell you that no good can come of it.

Itard arrived in my kitchen last night in a such a bad state that I truly feared for him: he looked feverish, the green tint of his skin that I first noticed on the night that Victor ran off now more startling than ever. I think he must be dosing himself with some potion, something to calm his nerves, but I told him, I did not hold back, no, not one whit! I told him: the way he was heading he would be no use to Victor when he *was* found, and he should throw whatever he was taking in the Seine, before it finished him off.

And you a doctor! At this rate, you'll glimmer in the dark, I said, taking his coat and hanging it on the hook by the fireplace. I handed him a large glass of wine and poured myself a smaller one, adding a splash to the rabbit I was stewing on the trivet above the fire.

He slumped into Henri's old chair, sinking his chin into his shirt, running a hand through his mass of black curls, before murmuring: so you believe he will be found, you are sure of that?

A boy like Victor – known throughout all of Paris? How could he not be? And now I hear the abbé has offered a reward for his discovery, so it can only be a matter of time . . .

The doctor sank further into his chair, fell silent. I turned my back to him, again tending to my cooking, the wine giving the juices a good rich red colour, but then realised Itard was murmuring something, and came nearer to his chair to hear him.

Did you ever hear the story of the Beast of Gévaudan? he asked me.

The Beast of Gévaudan. I did of course. I heard it often, growing up. It was a wolf, an enormous beast with a reddish tinge to its coat, who slew many children. Always disobedient children, to hear the nuns tell it.

Will you not eat some rabbit, Doctor Itard, you look as thin as your own cane and ready to snap in two –

He gave me a half-smile and accepted the bowl I placed in his hands.

The story used to frighten me. My uncle had a long pointed face, he had a chin with a wisp of beard exactly like the long under-hanging beard of a goat, and he used to tell me that story, leaning forward, using his body to show exactly how the wolf used his great bulk to knock over his victims and then sink its teeth into their faces.

It's a sport with some, to torment children. When I was a girl the nuns were just the same.

But Itard did not seem to be listening. He barely touched the bowl I put in front of him – that's a whole rabbit wasted – and young Georges had brought it just this morning. It was his way of saying that the deaf boys knew of our anxiety over Victor and were thinking of us.

Itard simply stared into his dish as if the rabbit might leap up and bite him.

You were there that day, he said. I knew Victor was afraid of heights! I thought to cure him of his independence of spirit. It was a method used by Boerhaave in the hospitals in Haarlem ... It came to me then as a possible cure, but now I am not persuaded ... did I exceed the bounds of ... did I ask too much of him? Was I cruel? I have searched my heart for the answer to this question ... Did I drive the child away?

I didn't know how to answer him. What solace could a woman like me offer a learned doctor, I said. He glanced up when I said this and asked if I remembered the ending of the story of the Beast of Gévaudan.

I said that I did and wasn't a famous wolf-hunter – Philippe Donneval – dispatched by Louis XV to kill the beast.

But he failed, did he not, to kill it? Itard said.

Well, I believe, a second great hunter was called in. And this time, he had a troop to assist him and a pack of dogs. An ugly great wolf was hunted down in the woods of the Abbaye Royale and shot between the eyes.

But it was the wrong wolf, was it not? It did not have a reddish tinge and the slayings of children did not cease.

Well now you know your story, so why are you asking me?

The ending, Madame Guérin. What was the *ending*?

As I remember it, there was no end to it. Every time a wolf was caught, villagers hoped that was it. Then another child would be taken. One time they gathered round a fountain in the square and plucked a little pair of breeches from the wolf's stomach . . .

It was a red shirt!

Breeches in the story, as I heard it. What does it matter? It proved that the fearful creature had eaten human flesh.

But I believed it a true story. Uncle told me it happened in 1765, he named the village, although I have forgotten it.

Does it make it untrue to change the details? Whether breeches or shirt, the story is the same. A beast struck many times, then was caught. Each time villagers would cook up a storm and whoop with joy, sending their children out to play again, and then – pff! – another one gone. In the end, a wolf was slain, with the proper red tinge to its coat, and a bigger beast you never saw. And then one more child was taken, his poor pitiful little arm left behind on a doorstep, to make us know the truth. The beast was still at large.

The story was never at an end. It continued for as long as the speaker wished it to.

You could say that, yes . . .

Did it succeed? Were you afraid?

As a child? I was not much different to the woman you see now, Doctor Itard. I have always possessed a superstitious nature. It would make me tremble in my bed, on nights when the moon was up, or if I heard the howling of the wolves.

You did not think it might have been a man?

A man?

The Beast of Gévaudan. For myself, I always wondered. They slew one wolf, then another, but the attacks continued. And everyone knows that it is a rare wolf to wander into a village, generally it is only the sick or lame who stray from the pack. So I was persuaded it was a *man* who left that half-eaten arm, not on a doorstep, as in your version, but next to the flock of sheep, which were unmolested. A man who sank his teeth into children and left half-eaten bodies strewn for his trophy –

I was trembling. I pushed my bowl away: he had quite ruined my rabbit for me. Itard himself, in the shadows thrown on him by the candles on the wall beside him, had never looked worse: green as a frog's backside, his eyes sinking beneath that great shelf of a brow. Suddenly it came to me how hot he looked; I put a hand to his brow and the sweat which had sprung up there gave me the queerest notion: he looked like he was made of wax, and melting.

For Victor, you think he has more to fear from the streets of Paris than from the beasts in the forest of Lacaune?

I spoke very softly. He didn't answer me, so I grew bolder, and spoke as a mother would.

Your bed is what you need. For the search, for tonight – abandon it. There are others looking out for Victor, now a reward has been offered –

Finally – and the effort it took me you cannot imagine – finally, I succeeded in sending the doctor home, locking and bolting the door behind me, crossing myself as I did so. I drank three glasses of wine and lay down on my bed. I left a candle burning, for it wasn't a night for darkness. Even so, I knew I would have no peace and I was right: the instant I lay down, the memories came crowding at me, one atop the other.

First it was only a piece of fabric, a snip of yellow silk, sprigged with blue forget-me-nots. Then the fabric became a dress, the sodden fragments of a dress, a dress that was bloody and clinging to a headless body. And then it was 92 and Joseph dead and the bitterness fresh in my heart, and that dress, that body was atop a pike, carried in the arms of a great crowd and I was swept along, until I saw the second pike; on that they carried her head. I held it too, I placed my hands around another's hands and held the pike aloft, jeering and shouting as the head of the Princesse de Lamballe bobbed above us, her neck a bloody mass of lace and blue-sprigged fabric and flesh. Her expression was such as you would never wish to see, not in all your life, and now I can never stop seeing it, prevent her from staring at me: her eyes wide open, her mouth pulled at the sides by invisible fingers. My Joseph was dead, you see, and the whole of Paris had gone mad. There was a man who took a snippet of the blooded hair from her most private parts and twirled it on his own mouth for a moustache, there was no end to our mockery, for the next thing I remember someone called out that they would present her to Marie-Antoinette and then we were on our way to the Temple, and I snatched up the bonnet I was wearing, a bonnet rouge of course and flung it in the air where it landed on the Princesse's yellow curls and I laughed, amazed, and screamed: look, look, now she is one of us – a *tricoteuse!*

And I danced along with them, I was caught in a fever, the crowd was my body, the ground a river of feet beneath me. I had one hand on the pike, holding aloft the Princesse de Lamballe with her torn-at-the-sides mouth. Her head wobbling, turning this way and that, for all the world as if she were graciously nodding and bowing to the crowd, all the while splattering blood onto me, onto my dress. Suddenly I must be asleep and not remembering at all but dreaming, or perhaps it is the wine I drank making my head spin, because Joseph is there, alive again and clinging to me and Julie as a baby too, the children are in my arms.

My babies cry out in fright and Henri is there too but with a look you could not fathom: he is moving away from me, melting into the crowd. The bonnet on the Princesse's head is a bedraggled cap of blood, floating above us. In the old days this dream would end before they reached the walls of the Temple but now it carries on, right up to the moment when the Queen appears at the window of the Tower, takes one look at her dear friend then falls in a dead faint. I wake with sheets tangled around my legs and the smell of my little boy in my arms.

The wild boy is gone and those days are gone but that fury, that wicked hatred, I can taste it still. I held her to blame, the Austrian Bitch, I hated her with every ounce of my strength, but now that hate has poisoned me, given me these fearful dreams and poisoned my waking too. I want to be rid of it, I want to forget, I tell you there are many like me in Paris who want the same thing: our souls laundered of memory; we long to be washed clean.

Sitting in the gardens the following evening as the boys took their exercise, I planted myself on a bench by the weeping willow, so that they would believe their governess to be supervising them whereas, naturally, I was merely staring into the pond, thinking of Victor. The straggle of boys snaked past, nodding, waving; uttering their queer, meaningless shrieks, led by Jean-Pierre, a poor wretch with a neck so feeble that his head bobs constantly to one side, like some manner of dipping bird.

As I said, the garden grows unruly without my Henri's

tender care. Everything in that garden was wrong, it struck me then; boys ran, jumped and chased a ball in silence; a bird sat as one paralysed, one child gave a sudden appalling scream which none responded to; that great beast of a dog, Marat, had managed against all possibility to balance himself along the narrow ledge of the library window, no wider than a blade of grass, and there he slept, snoring like an old man. A bitter memory came to me, of Victor, leaping in the air and shrieking when Marat sniffed around him. The child would fling himself at me, his skinny arms clenched around my skirts. Surprising, I thought, than an idle beast such as Marat is able to inspire him with fear, since that dog bears little resemblance to the vicious hounds that chased Victor the day he was caught. How much poor Victor will suffer then, alone with the dogs of Paris, the armies of limbless beggars whose bodies rise from the paving stones like monsters rising from beneath the earth; the crowds; the great thundering wheels of the carriages, splashing through the mud. We have made him soft with warm baths, with as many beans, as many chestnuts as a boy can eat; with a soft bed to lie on. How will he fare when the boys of Paris nod their terrible heads at him, swing their terrible arms?

Well, as you know, I am not a sentimental woman and God knows that child has caused me trouble enough since his arrival but my tired old heart has begun to melt towards him these last few days. Soon enough I felt tears spill down my cheeks, when I pictured my poor Victor, running hither and thither in the streets of Paris. That must be how I did not see the woman enter the garden; did not see if a master showed her in, or unlocked the door for her, but only realised finally that a young woman with hair the colour of copper in an old-fashioned blue dimity dress, who had the look of a peasant, was standing near the vegetable garden, staring at the string of boys in the distance. She cupped her hands around her eyes to shield them against the slipping sun, which shone straight at her; she seemed to be searching the boy's faces for someone she knew.

I stood up, clapping my hands. I waved a few more times and Jean-Pierre finally saw me and stopped short, making the others stumble right into him like a row of nine-pins. I jumped up and down from my position near the pond, clapping my hands and shooing the boys towards the doors of the dining hall, while Georges and his rascally friends pretended not to understand me. When I looked back, meaning at once to ask the young woman what business she had here at the National Institute of Deaf Mutes, she was gone.

I thought no more about her but the nightmares did not stop. In one of them I was cooking a rabbit which turned into a little white boy; sprang from the pot and ran away from me, obliging me to chase it. *Run, run as fast as you can*, he taunted me. Even in sleep, I was exhausted. I could hear myself panting as the little white boy slipped around dark corners into shadowy streets, where I had no desire to follow; but I knew I must, I must keep chasing. My ribs ached and my feet groaned but I longed for that child with every inch of my being. There were wolves too, softly howling in the distance, or in the corners of my eyes; whenever I turned my head, the yellow teeth and dripping jaws would slip out of view. Once, the rabbit-child turned around, and he too had the jaws of a wolf. I opened my mouth to scream and his face slipped back to the face of Victor, with his dark, sad eyes and his upturned nose.

But the worst part, the part I am coming to, is that the young woman with the copper hair was in the dream which, as you know, to dream of someone the first time you meet them, is a very bad omen indeed. She had the pointed face of a little fox and a great red tail beneath her skirts. One moment she was standing in the garden as I saw her, here at the Institute; the next, she had taken off her sabots and left them at the river's edge and was swimming across the

224

Seine; her hair caked with mud, her dress floating around her like one of those exotic blue flowers, the colours unnatural and foreign. On her back she carried an object small and white, which from my position on the bank, I could not rightly see.

When I woke, the next morning, that was what troubled me most: what was it, lying on her back, what was it that I couldn't properly see?

These dreams are my punishment, they are growing worse. Without Henri to shake me awake, to wrap his arms around me and press his hot face into my hair and call me his silly girl, there seems to be no end to them.

Germinal 8
Year Nine

Victor has been found. He had apparently reached Senlis. A note was brought to me at home (by a highly suspicious Madame Richard, who grumbled heartily at being forced to bring it herself up the flight of stairs to my room), asking me to collect him in the Rue d'Enfers. I made all speed. When I arrived there, with Madame Guérin, but thankfully without Julie, a crowd had gathered and I feared the worst.

A most touching scene ensued. Madame Guérin, with her usual staunch nature, pushed her way through the throng of young men, calling them ill-licked cubs and worse. I saw Victor, in the midst of them, crouched on the floor – in a craven position, very similar to that first occasion I spied him – my heart contracted painfully at the sight. But on seeing his governess he began squealing and rolled his eyes up to the heavens, leaping up to sniff her all over. He then fell on the floor in a faint, whereon Madame Guérin picked him up and carried him high above the heads of the men who crowded her, pushing and elbowing her way towards our carriage. I could only follow with my cane raised, repeating her threats, albeit in a quieter voice – in my case, the ruffians might actually have taken me up on them; she, after all, has the protection of her sex.

Once the driver had snapped the reins and our horse had moved off, Madame Guérin succeeded in reviving Victor and, big as he is, held him on her knee like a baby, whilst examining him for new injuries and signs of illness. The boy is very thin. His hair and skin and general appearance is ragged and unkempt and he was caked in thick dirt, with a smell of the Parisian streets: urine, horse-dung, coal dust. His teeth, always yellow, seemed more so than ever. But his eyes – often a good indicator of general health – were bright, and his disposition on being reunited with his governess was good. He was lively, excited; he repeatedly ran his hands over her arms and buried his face in her bosom to sniff at her (Madame Guérin did not reproach him), thereafter bursting into peals of laughter.

Naturally I did not give Victor a full examination inside the carriage, but I judged him to have survived his sojourn alone relatively unscathed. One might even describe it as a flair he has, for surviving, as Julie Guérin once proposed.

We may never know quite where Victor has spent these missing weeks. The jailer who sent word to the Institute claimed that he had believed him a vagrant and had locked him up for 'the public protection', but that was only in the last few days. Lemeri suggested that prior to that someone must have taken him in, perhaps hoping to make money from him as an adept pickpocket, then tired of him when they realised that he would leave the gold coins and choose keys every time. Or perhaps, having reached the woods of Senlis, poor Victor discovered that his former skills had deserted him and his desire for human company overcame his desire for freedom and he allowed himself to be 'caught' by La Charbonnière, who has arms as thick as any man's from mornings spent unloading coal and could easily overwhelm him with her strength, if not her wit. It was La Charbonnière who turned him over to the jailer at Senlis, after he had bitten her viciously. She now claims a share of the reward; a problem that is thankfully Sicard's duty to resolve, not mine.

We hastened to Madame Guérin's home. She busied herself in preparing a hasty meal for us and building up the fire, whilst I removed my boots and took some snuff, settling into my favourite seat in a humour as different from yesterday's as it is possible to imagine. We enjoyed a grand but simple meal of onion soup, rye bread and a half pint of red wine while Victor ate copious amounts of lentils and chestnuts. It was just as Madame Guérin was taking the plates to wash them that the front door opened and, to my dismay, Julie appeared.

She looked as startled as I felt on discovering me there.

Good evening, Mademoiselle Guérin, I said, in what I hoped was a gay voice. It came out rather loudly.

Doctor Itard, she replied, a little stiffly, I thought. Then: oh, *Victor!*

Julie flew towards Victor with her arms outstretched. He was sitting on the floor, half under the table, searching for fallen lentils, and squealed in surprise as she flung herself upon him, kissing his hair and his ears and his neck and all the parts of him she could reach. Watching her, my embarrassment of the last few weeks began to melt. The girl is immoderate in everything. I am sure she can hardly have given the occasion a second thought. It is only I who have accorded it more significance than it merited; I with my anxiety and my shyness, my awkwardness in the simplest of social situations. I have exaggerated matters quite out of proportion.

Victor flapped his hand at Julie, evidently rather over-whelmed by her unseemly show of affection. I smiled.

She withdrew at last, sitting back on her heels and gazing

up at me in unabashed joy. Her dark hair had come undone from beneath her bonnet and her fichu was smeared with traces of the onion soup.

I ran here when I heard! He is well then? He looks thin, Maman. Was he *extraordinarily* delighted to see you?

Once he had sniffed me all over to assure himself it was truly me, he fell in a dead faint! replied Madame Guérin. Her voice, I thought, contained a hint of pride.

There was a silence. Both women were looking at me. I could not imagine what they expected me to say, so endeavoured to smile again, to convey an attitude of ease. When they continued to stare at me, I nodded benignly and directed another easy smile at Victor.

Finally, Julie spoke. Her question seemed rather pointed. If I were not of a generous disposition I might suspect she is still . . . displeased with me.

Was he pleased to see *you*, Doctor Itard?

Me? Why – yes, yes of course he was. Delighted. Yes. He did not – well, he is not demonstrative especially, are you Victor? He shares that aspect of his nature with me . . .

Perhaps this comment was too close to the truth. I hastily continued.

But naturally, Madame Guérin is the one he has the fondest feelings for. After all, she is his food and his drink, his warm bed and his plate of lentils!

I beamed at both women. Madame Guérin was scowling. My remark had not pleased her either, in the way I had intended.

He has forgiven you then? Julie continued. Her voice, I thought, was sly. I was careful to keep my own tone light and indifferent.

Forgiven me? What on earth can you mean? What has he to forgive me for?

It is all forgotten, is that not true, Victor? We are all the best of friends, interrupted Madame Guérin firmly. She was frowning at her daughter. Julie returned her look with a harsher one of her own. I pretended to observe nothing.

And so the evening continued, and a most unpleasant occasion it became: simmering with hints and hidden accusations filling the atmosphere with snips and sparks like spitting embers from a fire. Yet since nothing was voiced aloud, I could not defend myself. I was at a great disadvantage in the company of a young woman whose skill at the unspoken slight was far greater than mine. I heartily wished I had found a more graceful way to refuse Julie Guérin. Had I had more experiences with young women, I should have known that one as pretty and impetuous as she would not take such a clumsy refusal lightly. But in truth, I knew that my rejection of her had been utterly spontaneous. I had been powerless to stop myself. Now it could not be undone and it seemed impossible to make amends. After all, she had kissed me without warning. I had not offered her encouragements. Why should it be I who now suffered such shame?

When eventually Julie announced that it was time she left, I made no offer to accompany her. I only stood briefly and held out her fichu for her.

Her insinuations had finally succeeded in wounding me. I was remembering that yes, it was true, on seeing me for the first time, Victor did not immediately acknowledge me. My first sight of him in the Rue d'Enfers was blocked by the crowd. When he awakened from his faint in the carriage I ventured to give his back a reassuring pat, and twice picked up his hand to squeeze it, but he was preoccupied in weeping and laughing and fondling Madame Guérin. I do not remember a single sign that he noticed my presence in the carriage with them.

These thoughts weighed heavily on me. After Julie had left and Madame Guérin had taken Victor to his bed, I went to say goodnight to him. As soon as he saw me in his room he sat up and held out his arms. The gesture was astounding. But when he saw that instead of going to him I stood where I was with a cold demeanour and an angry face he dived back beneath the covers and began to cry. I increased his emotion by my reproaches, uttered in a loud and threatening voice; his tears increased and he sobbed long and hard. When I had taken him to the utmost degree of emotion, I sat down on the poor penitent's bed. This was always my signal for forgiveness. Victor understood, made the first move of reconciliation and everything was forgiven and forgotten.

I sat on the crib and held Victor in my arms. He put his face against my chest, his sobbing made my own body shake; his tears soaked my shirt. We must have remained like that, locked together without moving, the boy sobbing, I holding him, in that little darkened room, for a good ten minutes. Then I came to myself again.

I am vindicated. Victor is mine once more.

Well I was so glad to have the boy back and the house filled again with his own appalling smell, which I have grown so used to, foolish woman that I am, that I might even admit to missing it when he was gone! Victor spent his first day at home in a restless spirit, turfing out cupboards and drawers, until the floor was scattered with my pots and pans, wooden spoons, scissors, knives, plates, napkins – all manner of things. When he had covered the kitchen floor and the room looked like rooms used to, in the old days, when one of the sans-culottes had just up-ended it, flushing out a refractory priest (and you will be surprised to learn that I indulged him, I was in no hurry to clear it up again; I was curious to see what he was searching for), he rummaged through it, casting aside with a great flourish everything his hand descended upon and shrieking in dismay at not finding what he wanted.

What is it, Victor? I asked him, though of course he could

not tell me. I do not think he knew himself but a great tension seemed to glow in him; I could tell he was troubled.

Did you miss me? I said cosily, trying to take him in my arms. Of course he struggled to free himself. I soon realised that his brief adventure has not changed him that much. That burst of affection when we were first reunited – perhaps that will be the only sign he gives me that my hard work in taking care of him is not in vain. With a sigh I fell to picking up the mess that spilled over the floor. I handed Victor a plate of dried beans and an empty bowl to throw the bad ones into and instantly felt the crackle of his wild energy ebb from him, as he sat himself at the table, intent on his task.

You might not think it is very much: a dead faint, a burst of weeping, and an up-turned kitchen, as a reward for a year's care and affection. Six months ago, I would have said the same. But with my Henri gone, and my nights here as lonely as the cry of the owl, it is suddenly enough. I saw what happened to Doctor Itard without the child to pin his dreams upon. And I saw Victor's big black eyes swim with tears when he upset me, setting the place for Henri after Henri had no need of it. He has never made the same mistake again. Last night that child held his thin white arms wide for me and, although he never said it, has never said *Maman*, I know now that the word is in his heart and no one will ever tell me otherwise.

So you understand now why it was such a shock when the abbé told me. He came to me today, in the kitchens, just as I was dipping a ladle into the last of the cabbage soup, he spoke so sharply that I splashed a hot spoonful over Marcel's hand, the poor boy being next in the line. Marcel squealed and I mopped at him with my apron while the abbé said roughly: Madame Guérin, come to my office at once. There is someone there I want you to meet.

And he led me to a room above the library, a room that sits at the top of the winding staircase, a room I have often looked up at, thinking to myself that the light in the stairwell seems to fold somehow, like the layers in a millefeuille pastry, and it is a room I have never yet been invited into, so I knew it must be something terrible. And I did not bring Victor with me, preferring to leave him in the kitchen with the door locked, as I often did during my dinner-time duties: some instinct told me that if bad news was about to befall us, better I be the one to break it to Victor.

The abbé opened the door, and there she was. The copper-haired vixen from my dream. She stood with her back to the window so that her hair glowed an unnatural colour, she wore a woollen fichu and the same blue dress as the first time I saw her, in the gardens of the Institute. Her arms were folded across her chest. Something in her stance was familiar. I would warrant her no more than twenty years old, so that what the abbé said next made no sense at all.

This young woman is from Aveyron. She claims she is Victor's mother.

Victor's mother! I repeated, stupidly.

Where is he? broke in the girl, without further explanations.

He is . . . he is in the kitchen. The doctor – Itard – will be here soon for his lesson. You are his . . . mother . . .

My name is Félicité Colombe. And now, can I see the boy?

A wicked bitterness rose in me. The abbé did not give me my chance to batter her with questions: if he was her son, why had she not come forward sooner? Was hers the hand that slit his throat and left him for dead? How could she now claim a mother's fondness for him, a child she had not seen nor sought in seven or eight years?

Perhaps the reward the abbé had offered for Victor's capture when he was at large in Paris had attracted her attention? Where was the proof that she was related to Victor, and where was his father?

She volunteered that his father was dead and that they had long believed the same of the child, 'Jacques-Pierre' as she called him. As she said it, the strange name, something shifted. I pictured Victor, as I had left him, sitting at my kitchen table, lining up his keys. I stared at her, forcing myself to listen to the rest of her story. Jacques-Pierre had been captured by soldiers descending on her village during the unrest of 94 and it must have been they who tried to kill him and left the boy for dead.

When she spoke furrows appeared in her brow and her eyes narrowed and I saw that she was not twenty but perhaps nearer to thirty years old, easily old enough to be his mother. She had a weary voice, rough as a husk of corn. I know her type. I know she has had a hard life, and I should have more pity.

It was, she said, only the notice his case had attracted recently through the child's escaping towards Senlis, which someone had told her of, that made her think he might be her long-lost son. Being wild with grief over the death of her husband, she now longed to see again their only son, whom they had both believed for all these years to have been left for dead in the woods near Rodez. The abbé was moved by her story. He told her he remembered vividly the turmoil and confusion of those years, offered her his handkerchief and insisted we hasten to Victor's 'home'.

Outside the door, we collided with Itard's arrival. I hardly dared tell him the news. I was glad when the abbé blurted it out, stumbling through the introductions. Itard's mouth dropped open and he stood there gaping. I have never seen a man look more stupefied. In his expression I could read all the anguish of my own thoughts and knew that if Victor were to return to Aveyron with this woman, it would be hard to say who would suffer most.

Of course we waited to see what Victor would do when reconciled with his long-lost mother. On unlocking the door to the kitchen I heard him leap up. We shuffled into the room, with the nervous young woman a step or two behind Itard. The fire had gone out and Victor had paid no heed. His keys were on the table, about twenty of them, lined up in order of size.

My kitchen had never felt smaller. Someone had sucked all the air from it: there was barely enough to breathe. The door was firmly locked behind us, and Victor sniffed each of us in turn. She was the last to enter the room. I watched her edge forward, I watched her eyes. But Victor, he merely sniffed at her with the same idle attention a dog gives to a mouse running across the floor. Then he ran back to the table and pulled out his chair. He put his face very close to his keys and then picked one up, the way he does, and examined it as if he had never seen it before, holding it up, twirling it, like one of those savants, those visitors in my kitchen, examining their specimens.

Keys! The girl blurted.

She said something else that I couldn't understand, or hear, and then threw herself on him, smothering him with kisses, her arms around his neck, weeping and calling on the saints and Our Lady and all manner of folk besides, and trembling from head to foot. I did not dare to search Itard's face, nor even to let out a breath. The only sound in the room was the stranger's sobbing and the chink and thud of Victor's keys on wood.

I don't need to tell you that 'wood' might just as easily have described Victor right then.

He has been injured by his loneliness and his life of silence, Itard said, simply. You cannot expect him to be the same child as the one you lost.

No – of course, said the young woman, untangling herself from around Victor's neck. In her great *suffering* and *weeping* she had not burdened herself with care for my kitchen and had knocked over a glass jar of peonies that I'd set in the middle of the table. This is what I concentrated on, picking up the scattered purple petals, mopping at the water.

And does he speak? the girl asked. This question seemed important to her. She had already asked the abbé the same thing twice and been told that Victor had only uttered the word *lait* and regrettably showed few signs of learning – or recovering – any others.

Did he speak? asked Itard. The way he asked it, barked it at her, made me realise this was the all important question to him. This was everything. The young woman turned to look at the doctor when he spoke to her like that. Her little mouth twitched at the corners.

Oh, yes, our little Jacques-Pierre! How he loved to chatter . . .

Jacques-Pierre, said Itard, stupidly.

Itard had not sat down. He was at the opposite side of the table, his eyes fixed on Victor's dark head.

And will – will you be taking him ho-home with you? asked Itard. I noticed he had great difficulty pronouncing the word 'home'. His face had turned the colour of milk: all the blood had drained from him. His back was to my dresser, my rows of plates. How many times has he arrived in my kitchen, standing in that exact spot, looking at Victor with hungry eyes, while he removes his hat and coat and hangs them on a peg, dropping his cane in the pot by the door, eager to begin. Despair clutched me. Surely Itard would prevent it? He could not let her take Victor.

I suppose you have no – evidence? The abbé said kindly. Nothing to prove the child is – who you say he is?

I have a letter from our priest, answered the young woman, quickly, as if she was expecting this question. He last saw the boy three nights before the soldiers came. He can tell you that our son was dark with the blackest eyes you ever saw and a sweet little chin and a mouth like a strawberry . . .

She handed the abbé a tightly folded letter which she had been squeezing in her hand all this time, but he did not think to let me read it. When she spoke so tenderly of her little boy, Jacques-Pierre, the bitter taste in my mouth sweetened a little, thinking of Victor being at last with his family, but still there was nothing to compensate me for the cloud that had passed over my eyes the moment I saw her standing in the abbé's office and knew that for me, as for Itard, the arrival of this copper-haired citoyenne could only mean sorrow. *Just when I found you again.* I had the strangest feeling: I always have it. If you have lost a child, you will understand it. That child is always there somewhere, not frozen in babyhood, but a boy growing up beside you, sometimes an infant in his crib, sometimes a baby dandling on my knee; then the boy of six he should have been, floating a wooden boat on a lake, playing loto on a table; sometimes a man. All the things he never was, never will be. A beautiful tall man of twenty with glorious hands, hands that can wield an axe and slice wood like butter and build homes and break hearts, a man you know like the back of your hand, the blue-eyed man you brought into this world, you brought here, the man you dreamed when you carried him in your belly, the man you knew your boy would become, God willing. Only for some reason, for some reason you have never yet understood, God was not.

The abbé folded the letter away. I thought for a minute he was struggling with himself, but no, not one whit. The words came out with ease. The decision was final.

You must take him with you, back to where he belongs. I imagine the doctor will be relieved to see that his charge has a real home. And his governess here. The boy is not punctilious in his habits, you know, he still prefers his old savage life to the rules and regulations of a civilised society . . .

Both myself and the doctor broke in with a great clatter of words. It was as if a signal had been given for the plates and cups to topple from their shelves: I felt as if the room itself was tumbling in on me. You know I am not always orderly and I am a woman who speaks her mind, but my voice came out as if some fellow was squeezing his hands around my throat, I could hardly make myself understood. The abbé nodded but his position did not shift. It was for the best, he said. My loyalty and affection for the savage were splendid, laudable, but Nature dictates. *Nature!* That man dares to speak of Nature to me! A cold fury settled in me then. It set like wax in my veins. It set my tongue in my mouth and I couldn't utter another sound.

Our squabble disturbed Victor. He leapt up, picked up an empty glass, banged it on the kitchen table, seemed disappointed to find that it did not smash to a million pieces, then with a sweep of his hand, sent the keys he had lined up smashing across the table and jingling towards the fire. It was a fine noise, I was glad of it. He then sat down on the floor again and laughed. I glanced at the girl, in triumph, I suppose. I hoped to see her shaken or in dread. That witch only stared right back. I know she saw that I despised her.

And Jacques-Pierre, Victor, I mean, he does not speak? was all she said. It was the fourth time she asked it. The abbé assured her that he does not.

At first, when Félicité fulfils her promise and lies with him, night after night, it is possible for Jacques Colombe to forget. Her long hair falls over his face, tickling him. She has tricks up her sleeve, pleasures he had not known existed, never dreamed of tasting. Wanting her, working all day at his bench with his plane or his saw, back and forth, thinking of her, makes the moment when she comes to him, blowing out her candle, climbing upon him with her heat and her softness and her smell of corn and grass, unbearably sweet.

In the field one day, he watches her walking towards him. She is unhurried, she walks as if she owns time; tugging at grasses, plucking at poppies. As she comes closer she cups her hand up to her mouth and blows, scattering seeds. He sees them on the wind and knows he is like them, he is spent, he is scattered, her mouth, her soft breath can undo him in an instant.

He marries her and the deal is sealed. He does not think of Dominique, he does not think of the boy. He surprises himself with how little he thinks of him. He and Félicité have never spoken of the child. One time he returns home and the few remaining clothes, the boy's blanket, a tan leather pouch that Dominique had made him to hold his keys, a pair of tiny sabots that the boy refused to wear, have been cleared away. He did not know they were there until he returns that day and sees them gone. And for some reason this disappearance angers him.

Félicité makes him supper: an omelette of mushrooms she gathered herself, from the woods, only an hour ago.

The chestnut woods? he asks her in disbelief. You went to the chestnut woods?

He pushes the omelette away and to punish him she tells him she has a child in her belly. She wants a bigger house. She wants tiny white linen and tiny white kid boots for the baby, with blue silk ribbons to lace them. She wants bonnets and a lace coverlet for the crib. She is like a child herself with her wants, he cannot believe how many there are. How could he not have seen this before; how simple, how much of a child she is?

They fight then and he shouts at her that she had *promised* him, he thought that she had promised *everything*; he will not share her! Did I not do this terrible thing for you, and was that not the bargain?

He is told he is ridiculous, since the child is his own doing, what is he blaming her for?

Her pupils darken and blacken and, when she is angry, he sees her teeth. He thinks of her walking towards him, tearing at the poppies, the red folding skins fluttering like butterflies behind her, her hair full of sunlight, her skin tasting of the river. He thinks he is afraid of her. That she drove him to lose his mind, to commit a wicked, wicked act, that she mesmerised him. She says nothing to this. She stares dreamily into the fire, she pats her belly. She has even taken up knitting. The needles click and duck and her elbows move up and out, flapping wings.

Now he grows sick. He cannot lie with her. The child in her belly frightens him. He dreams of it and it has big black eyes like Jacques-Pierre, like his own little boy. It is white and wriggling and slides out of her then springs up on four legs, bleating like the Devil. He knows this child will be like the first. He watches her breasts grow big, the veins steal over them. He cannot touch her. Desire leaves him as surely as it came and when she puts her arms around his neck, when she kisses him, he only wafts slightly towards her, like a breeze that flutters a piece of paper and then lets it drop. After that, he is limp as a fish.

The sickness creeps across his chest. A rash of red blisters splits, crusts with blood and pus. His nights are feverish. The baby is born in the kitchen with the help of the tanner's wife and Félicité's evil screaming rends the walls, threatens to splinter the glass beside his bed. In his fever, he smells a witch's brew of wormwood and juniper smouldering on the fire. He knows before he is told that the baby was born dead.

He struggles out of bed too late to see the child for himself; the tanner's wife has carried it outside to bury it and Félicité does not venture to tell him whether the boy was natural or not, whether he had all his limbs, whether his head was misshapen or his eyes wide open or whatever other terrible freakishness he imagines.

She begins to taunt him. What kind of a man kills one child, stills the other in her belly? A man who only fathers freaks or monsters. He cannot believe how freely she can speak of it. She seems unafraid that others will hear. You are so wrong about me, she tells him, over and over, but he has no idea what she means, which part he is wrong about. Pots fly, plates crash. Provoked, finally he hauls her by her red hair over towards the fire. He threatens to smash her face into logs if she speaks again. Does she think he wouldn't do it? For days an oily silence holds. But then she is off again and spitting.

Monster! Bastard!

Each blames the other. The truth is twisted, mangled. He has no idea whose idea it was, who persuaded the other, only that he was the one who said yes. He had thought he was a good man. He believed she was Nature herself, personified. But his was the hand that held the knife.

In his sickness he cooks up a mania to go back to the woods to look for his son. He pictures the shape that he left there, the little hunched figure. He could not say, in his feverishness, how many years have passed. He never told Félicité that he had run back and thrown his coat over the boy, knowing how angry she would have been. Your coat, you fool, why not leave a note, write it down for all the world to see: it was I, Jacques Colombe, who killed my son?

His dreams are peopled by children with faces as blank as the moon, their mouths open, ready to accuse him. I did it for you, Dominique, he cries, in his delirium. He calls Félicité, he wants to tell her: you made me do it. Then later, I did it for the child. What kind of life is it, ensnared by silence, unreachable, unlovable, trapped behind a wall of glass? I did it for him and us and it was not evil, it was a blessing.

Félicité knows he is dying. She tries to soothe him, she tells him to sleep, she wants a truce. *Many have done worse. The whole country was possessed. It is done: let us think no more about it.* Closing his eyes and letting himself drift, thinking again of those spores on the wind. He feels her breath on his face as she leans over him. He feels himself scatter into a thousand tiny pieces and in one of them, the last, he knows he is a speck of nothing and that he is floating away.

Germinal 15
Year Nine

Astonishing information: the young woman who claims him assures me that as an infant of five Victor spoke. 'Chattered' was the word she used. I ought to be elated. It confirms that Victor, or rather, Jacques-Pierre, as she refers to him, was not the idiot that Pinel proposed. Having the gift of language once, the burden of re-introducing it should be made lighter. But I am not elated. Everything has altered and my marvellous opportunity to tutor Victor must come to an end. Furthermore, her reply provokes more questions than it answers. Why, if he was so fluent, has he remained mute for longer than I anticipated? Why has he made so little progress? Was the damage caused by his isolated life or by the deprivation of human care, more lasting than I first imagined? Are my methods to be blamed? Her information does not contradict my theories about the impact of environment on our developing faculties. But it does nothing to explain why Victor still does not speak.

So it has been arranged for Madame Guérin to accompany the young woman and Victor on their journey back to his home. It is with bitter disappointment that I contemplate this. And yet I also know I am entirely selfish and must struggle with myself.

Surely it is best for poor Victor to be returned to the bosom of his family? I am told he has a living grandfather and this poor gentle peasant woman, with her voice husky with suffering and her eyes clouded with pain, has surely suffered enough, since suffering is visible on every inch of her face, and our hearts, if they were fairer, ought to gladden at the thought that she has been reunited with her child. I do not understand why I cannot feel more compassion towards this young woman. I know that Madame Guérin does not like her, but that is only to be expected. As for me, as a doctor who wants only what is best for his charge, I should be more dispassionate, I should be grateful to fate or circumstance which has returned the boy to his rightful place, to the arms of his true mother.

It is a fiendish failure on my part that I can only feel wretched, that I cannot feel more generous.

And so, struggling to think only of the needs of Victor and not to consider my own needs or the future of my career, I admitted a distraught Madame Guérin to the library and stood firm while she begged me to keep Victor with us, implored me to intervene with Sicard and somehow prevent Victor's return to Aveyron. I do not like the girl, this is the wrong thing for Victor, he cannot go backwards now, it will not make him happy! His home is here with us, she stormed, with great irrationality, entreating me to 'look in my heart' and admit that surely I too had misgivings.

If I do, I answered gravely, their source is a terrible selfishness. We must only think of Victor, of his future, of the life he has lost.

I tried to speak more gently, for I long ago realised that this kindly woman has formed an attachment to the boy and since this is to her credit, and has been Victor's gain, I have not up until now wished to undo it. Now I see that I must. So I spoke more candidly.

How many of us are given a second chance in life, an opportunity to mend some terrible wrench that has long hurt our hearts? I know how much you care for Victor, and he in his way for you. But would not each and every one of us, given the opportunity, not long to step back into our past, and mend some rift, alter the course of events, bridge some chasm that seems unbridgeable? How can we deny Victor this second chance that we so long for our-selves?

My words had an alarming effect on her. Her round face, which recently I cannot look at without thinking of a baked apple, the skin slightly puckering around her eyes, seemed to melt in front of me and, for the first time, Madame Guérin wept openly. Even after the death of her husband she was at pains to hurry away from me whenever such torrents threatened; as much as the tears themselves, it was her abandonment to them that I found most disturbing.

By waving from the window of the library I was able to gain the attention of one of the young masters, Massieu, hurrying across the garden below, his arms full of books, who thankfully arrived promptly. Appearing only a little bewildered, he read my written instructions. (Since I have never learned the language of signs, and Massieu has recently become the first master at the Institute to share the affliction of those he teaches, spoken words were pointless.) He then obeyed, escorting Madame Guérin back to her quarters. I had also instructed him to open the windows as far as the safety bolt would allow and to administer brandy and English drops.

Victor's journey is planned for the morning and the carriage will be here at ten.

I cannot intervene with this rightful turn of events, no matter how much I might desire it.

Madame Guérin reeled at my words about second chances. I was shocked to see how much they affected her. And yet, uttering them, I was thinking of myself. Of the memory Victor has often brought forth, the scent of that grassy tree hollow, the snap of bark, flaking beneath my fingernails; the sight of an ant creeping its purposeful route over a stone and inside a crevice; the taste of gooseberries, dotted with earth, fierce as salt on my tongue. Until now, I have always assumed that this childhood picture is at my uncle's, playing in a tree hollow; hiding, waiting, avoiding something. But as I spoke to Madame Guérin of 'rifts' and 'chasms' and 'second chances' the most astounding picture floated to me. I was not in Uncle's garden at all. It was long before that. It was a time so lost to memory that I can scarcely pinpoint it but from my position belly down in the tree hollow, I can suddenly see Mother's skirts, the sun bouncing from a cross that dangles at her throat and hear her calling playfully: *Jean-Marc-Gaspard, Jean-Marc-Gaspard, where are you?*

Words formed in my mind and yet never reached my tongue: *here I am, Maman!* I was eight years old. Her playful tone was treacherous and I knew it. Sorrow – the deaths of my brothers – billowed around her like folds of a dress, like a smell, a taste, something I could touch, swallow. She was sending me away. An uncle I had never met was to raise me. They said it would be safer, the small-pox had not swept Riez in the same fashion that it had swept our village, and Uncle would educate me, make something of me. They spoke as if I was candle-wax. Blank paper.

I did not utter a word of protest and I did not call to her: *here I am!* That was the beginning, I know it now. Of my tongue's cleaving to the roof of my mouth. I burrowed further into my refuge, belly down in my tree hollow, and I closed my eyes and pressed my nose and mouth against the moss, against the green taste, and it was as if I sealed it then, sealed my child's mouth shut.

They were wrong, my parents, in all that they promised. It was not *nothing* to cry about. It is a lie, a lie continuously visited on small boys, which I no longer wish to defend. I did not, as Father predicted, *soon forget*. I have tried, I have tried for nearly twenty years, and have so far not accomplished it.

After her death, when the letter came, I remember that as Uncle read it in his study, I stood beneath the shelf with that terrifying tableau of La Fontaine's tale; the Fox and the Crow with its one bad eye staring down at me, holding on to that round of cheese, and I listened to Uncle's words and struggled to remember the message of the story of the Fox and the Crow but in my confusion all I could understand was this: it is unsafe. That is the lesson. It is unsafe – when words press at my tongue, when my heart threatens to leap there, I must keep my mouth closed or, like the Crow, lose everything.

Perhaps it was the shock of his abandonment that silenced Victor. I do not believe now that I will ever know. But I cannot continue the deceit that for a boy this abandonment is nothing, this love for a mother a shameful thing; that he will soon forget, that she does not *matter*.

Well I could not take Victor on his long journey today, having woken with the most appalling pains in both my hips. Near crippled by them I was. I sent a note at once via young Marcel to the abbé, telling him that the rheumatism which afflicts me more and more these days made my legs so stiff I could never fold them into the carriage. The driver arrived, whistling up to my rooms, but was sent away without us. The young woman came to beg me at first to let Victor accompany her without me, but I stood firm, convincing her that she could not possibly manage him alone. As I spoke I was emptying the pot from beneath Victor's bed and I reminded her that in most of his habits he was scarce more than an enormous baby. Neither could she stay in Paris: she says she now has another child, left with the grandfather, or was it a cousin, and cannot bear to be apart from him a day longer. You can imagine how loudly I snorted at this: a mother who has been parted from one child for approaching nine years, claims such devotion to another that nine days is too many! And did she not describe Victor as her 'only child'? The young Félicité Colombe, however, showed no concern for my loud sighs, nor the eyes I rolled to heaven. She has already grown accustomed to me. She left at half past ten, to 'talk at once to the abbé' and I have not seen her since.

I have not achieved much with this performance, perhaps a week's grace for Victor. At least it gives me time to bake bread for the journey. And it means that I can be alone with Victor in the carriage. I do not think I could stand seven days in close quarters with that redhead: she smells like the countryside she comes from, the smell of sheep's milk and sheep's turds. She would surely choke me. I have told Doctor Itard all of this, and you would think the man would be pleased, but no: he said only that I am 'trying to postpone the inevitable'. And then he spoke of the arrangements to be made with *Citoyenne* Colombe (I can scarce believe it, he must be the only man in Paris still to be using the word, and for her, of all people!), arrangements for Victor's future, which he and the abbé and his Society have hastily resolved, the details of which he did not trouble to share with me. You can be sure, money was involved.

When my hips permitted me to leave my bed, I made Victor an enormous plate of lentils with garlic and spring onions from Henri's garden, but of course he picked out the onions and scattered them and the garlic over the floor in a great mush and since my knees screamed out when I tried to kneel to mop it up, the mess has remained there, half-kicked under the table.

I made gimbelettes too – you might say it was a grudging acknowledgement towards my home region, since I will soon be back there – flavouring them with aniseed and orange flower water, sprinkling them with sugar, while they were still warm from the oven. Since Julie promised a visit later, I fashioned one in the shape of a child, a little fat dough-boy with arms and legs and raisins for eyes, the way I used to when she was very young. But when it was baked, the toasted gimbelette boy troubled me. I remembered the story, an old story, of the old woman who waited twenty years to bear a child, and baked herself instead a boy from gingerbread. But what was the outcome? Over and over again the boy ran away from her: her desire was never satisfied. My little cake-boy lay on his plate, plump and golden, but how on earth could I eat him, or watch another swallow him up? It would have pleased me most to give him to Victor, but Victor of course would not touch him. He cares no more for cakes than he did the day he arrived here.

I explained to him what was to happen at the end of a week, that he was to travel back to his mother's village of St Sernin-sur-Rance – she says she has moved there recently, after his father's death, to live with a relative, I think she said, and it is not the same place that Victor grew up, but I cannot remember her telling us where exactly that was. It seems curious to me that these are the very villages where he was found, and yet at that time, he did not come to her attention. But Aveyron – your region – Doctor Itard asked, is it not very remote, cut off? Villages dotted between long mountain ranges? *Rouergue*, I corrected him, for of course, back then, I mean when I was a child, that was what we called it, and I reminded him that I am originally from the mountains in the north of the region, so I do not know exactly the village where Victor lived. But gossip passes through such places quicker than streams, and still I find it hard to believe a boy could be found within twenty miles of his home and not be claimed.

Though I spoke aloud as I always do, Victor pretended not to understand me. He was in lively spirits, hurtling round the kitchen table, round and round, a hundred times, springing at flies that buzzed above his head; restless since my bad hips had prevented me from taking him out for a walk. When Julie came he spent most of the evening flinging himself into her lap and leaping out again, bursting into peals of laughter. A new game. I think borne of his happiness at being home again. It twists my heart to see it. Julie and I drank four glasses of wine, dipping our gimbelettes into them and discussing the mysteries of Victor's story.

She gave me a hint or two about Doctor Itard without disclosing to Maman the full story, her eyes growing wide and brimming with tears when she spoke of him. She was angry but she also called him an idéaliste. Victor sat between us as we spoke and the silly girl lowered her voice, speaking of the doctor as if Victor could hear, as if he cared one whit what she thought of Itard. When she said passionately: I will not make the same mistake again! she pulled Victor to her suddenly, kissing his head in such a fashion to make the child shriek and then scream with laughter, putting the flat of his hand to her mouth, to beg her to do it again. She obliged him and the kissing and squealing were repeated, over and over until I had to cover my ears with my hands and beseech them to stop. There's not a thing can interrupt that rascal, once his heart's stuck on a path. Truly I think that's his greatest pleasure of all, not the kissing or the tickling, but the repetition, the sameness. Still, foreboding probably made me indulgent. I do not like to remember how quiet and still a kitchen is apt to be, once a boy like Victor has left.

At midnight, the foolish pair had finally exhausted themselves; she snored in the chair by the fire and Victor slept on the floor at her feet, face down, arms tangling her legs, his shaggy head warming her bare toes like a rug.

Before I blew out the candle, I ate the very last of the gimbelettes, which by chance was the boy-shaped one, and struggled to bed on legs that might have been carved of wood: they were stiff as nine-pins. Of course I prayed heartily that they might remain so, for longer than the agreed seven days.

I heard in the morning that Félicité Colombe had left for St Sernin in a carriage, that same night. She left word with the abbé of her address and how to join her, and he told me that she 'wisely' preferred not to come upstairs to wish Victor goodbye as it would only disturb him and, after all this time, an extra week apart was a further torture to her.

The abbé stood in my kitchen to tell me this. Drifts of white powder floated from his hair to my table as he shook his head solemnly, pressed his hands together.

A sad tale all round, he said.

The man could not take his leave of my kitchen soon enough, near tripping up, in his haste to be rid of us. Do I believe her sorry tale? It is certainly muddy round the edges, there are some parts that cast no light. I suppose there are some things we can never know for sure. They are too far in the past, the birds ate the trail. As a story, it is creeping up on me. I can tell you this: I believe it is as likely as any other.

Six days flew by with no respect at all for the state of my heart, and on the seventh the stiffness had left my bones as mysteriously as it had arrived. No further excuses were possible: the carriage arrived in the early hours of the morning. Plumes of cold air snorted from the horse's nostrils whilst I bundled a sleepy Victor into his seat, and pushed our bags on after him. The coachman, standing beside the berline smoking, did not lift one finger to help me, which will tell you right away the fine kind of journey we were likely to have. Marat, the black great dane, raced beside our coach, barking passionately as we pulled out onto the Rue St Jacques. He was our sole farewell.

Itard took his leave of Victor last night, and a sorrier way of doing it you never saw.

He neither gathered him in his arms, nor touched him at all. He had brought Victor a present, turning it awkwardly in his hand as he spoke. It finally fell to me to remind him of it, practically plucking it from his palm in my curiosity to see what it was and give it to Victor. And then – such an extravagant gift! The gold and sapphire pin that the Emperor of Russia had offered Itard to entice him to come work for him. What a gift to give a child! Victor of course merely sniffed at it and would have dropped it carelessly amongst his keys, had I not rescued it and wrapped it carefully in a lace handkerchief, placing it in the round leather purse I had already packed.

The doctor wished his charge well and hoped that he would not forget the things he had learned in the city. Victor hung his head, singing softly *lait, lait* and playing with his pizzle. I smacked his hand.

Then the doctor left, without remembering to wish me well.

A long trip stretches ahead of us. I am glad that Victor is still sleeping. Itard, thank God, did at least remember last night to bring me a draught, something to make Victor sleep long and hard, as the thought of spending so much time with him under the leather canopy of the berline was more than a woman my age could bear. When you consider, you have to marvel at the confidence – or stupidity – of those who brought him from Aveyron to Paris over a year ago. I settled into my seat with my bag held on my lap, as Victor's head fell against my shoulder. The long wall enclosing the Institute – that overgrowing lichen is one dark mass now and I don't know who will tend to it! – slipped away from us. I wondered if Victor would ever set eyes on it again.

We reached St Sernin by Sunday and I was glad indeed to be greeted by the sound of a tuneless old bell, banging out the hour. You know my thoughts on God but, all the same, after what we have been through these last ten years, I still find it a comfort to find that in some places, nothing much has changed. Victor was awake and dipping his hand into a bottle of pickled walnuts I bought him yesterday in the market square at St Affrique. A bag of orange raisins glistened on the floor of the berline. Every time I glanced at them I was reminded of a sack of sticky wasps, which gave me a little start and made me throw my bonnet on top to cover them.

I have watched that boy for the last few hours the way an

owl watches for a mouse, seeking the tiniest twitch to betray its whereabouts, but so far Victor has given me no sign of knowing where he is. That is, he sniffs the air the way he does, his chin lifts and his ears prick at the sharp cries of the birds, which naturally are a much greater nuisance here than they ever were in Paris, but he gives me no hint that he has been here before.

Yesterday we rested at supper-time by the side of the road so that the great lazy oaf of a driver could let his horse – which matches him ear for ear for ignorance and ugliness – drink from a stream of water bubbling out of the rocky mountain terrain. Seeing as the pair of them were in no great haste, and poor Victor cramped and restless from his journey, I spread a blanket on the ground beneath us, for Victor and me, so that we could watch the swifts skating above us, swirling and gliding in a display to make you giddy. For a long while we watched them, catching the uplifting winds, giving their odd little screams. I put my head back on my arms and stretched out my legs, glad to feel earth and twigs and stones beneath them for the first time in years. I was not thinking of anything much, or at least anything I can remember, or that is I might have been remembering when Henri and I were first courting and we used to lie like this in the chestnut woods not so very far from here; or maybe I was thinking that it was just as if I was lying under water, birds skating on the blue ice above me. It was for all of that, for the thinking and not thinking, that at first I did not notice. The sounds Victor was making. High notes, chirrups, squeals. Sounds he used to make when he first came to live with me. *Mon Dieu.* The child speaks a perfect imitation of the birds.

A picture entered my head before I could stop it of Victor as a small boy, his hair wild and matted, just as it was before we took our scissors to him, his skin scratched and marked, bleeding in places. He is crouching naked to sip water, bubbling over a rock. And around him is the silence of the woods and the mountains, which everyone knows is a silence teeming with sounds if you are a soul all alone and listening hard enough. Birds twitter, twigs snap, bees buzz, a rabbit flees over crackling leaves and rustling grass. Five years old, waking alone, he tosses his notes up to the sky, with only the birds to hear him. Cries as sweet, clean as water. But asking, or telling, what?

I put my fingers in my ears. I closed my eyes against the picture. The driver had to nudge me with his foot to make me open them. He said that he wanted to reach the next village before nightfall and if I could move that 'great mule of a boy' we could continue our journey. Victor's chirruping stopped. He sat up. He stared about him with an expression, well an expression of someone waking from a dream. It took me a long time to persuade him back into the berline. The coachman threatened to abandon us both if we wasted any more time but, apart from threats, made no effort to help me. Victor sat at the roadside rocking slightly, staring blankly at the horse, then lifting his dull gaze along the road and up to the mountains. The sun was beginning to slide. Since entreaties had failed and scolding was worse, I tried pulling him by the arms. He began to whimper, his body turning limp, crumpling to the ground.

Come on, Victor, not so far now. For your mother and your grandfather, your cousins. Think! Soon we will see them again, I told him. The coachman gave a violent snap on his whip. He jumped down from his seat and, without a word, threaded his arms through Victor's and bundled him, kicking, shrieking, into the berline. I gathered up the damp blanket, without even time to shake off the twigs, told the man he was an ignorant bastard with a pustule for a face and a turnip for a heart, and took my place beside Victor.

And so it was by the time we reached St Sernin on Sunday morning, having spent the night in an 'establishment' that no woman who knew how to lift a bucket and swish a cloth would consider a fit place for strangers, that the coachman could not wait to turn back. (He was well paid from Itard's purse, so there is no need to waste sympathy on him.) He dropped us at the bridge crossing the Rance river, where the village first appears. We finished our journey on foot. I looked up at the village toppling out of the rocks above the water, dangling its washing from its windows, its flowers and children from the balconies. The rough stone rooftops, the one wobbly church spire with that tuneless bell. I could so easily have been back home in Millau, which did nothing to soothe my mood.

The whole place hung with the reek of brebis, the hides stretched like so many white cut-out patterns along the walls of the bridge, drying in the spring sunshine. A smell of milk turning sour, of pared animal hide exposed to the air and rain, that same smell which clung to the girl Félicité. Once, I must have smelled like that myself. I have not smelled it in all the years I have been in Paris. The sheep with their pink skin were grazing on the grass at the other side of the river, bells jingling as they moved. Victor sniffed and cocked his head and again I wondered: did he recognise the smell? We did not pass a soul. Victor picked up a piece of quartz, a pine cone, a twig, a dried sheep turd; this way we dawdled up the hill, passing all the hides on the wall beside us, then taking a narrow grass-lined path between two houses, which Félicité Colombe had described to the abbé and which he had related to me. Where it ends, she said: there is my house.

The alley smelled worse than the village. Sheep, shit, dogs, chickens: years of pissing and throwing the slops there. I threw my fichu over my face and hurried, startled to be greeted at the other end by two dogs as big as wolves, baring their teeth and barking at Victor. He hid behind my skirts. I took a step back and nearly stood on him. The dogs did not advance, as cowardly as those stupid beasts often are, but making a great noise about it to try to persuade us otherwise. I picked up a stone and threw it at them, but, stout-hearted as I am, I did not dare take a step further.

There was no house. Behind the beasts, an empty road and a backdrop of mountains, a wall of green, capped in snow. No buildings at all. I backed into Victor and showed him with my hand that we must go back. This must be the wrong alley. Either that, or I had missed something vital in Félicité's instructions.

It took me a long time to fathom things out. All of that day, all of the next, maybe even into the third day of staying at the inn with the Carayons, I was still asking everyone I met about Félicité and the Colombe family and Victor's father Jacques and his grandfather, and the priest, a man named Batides, and I was still desperate for it not to be true. I know I never liked the girl. I know my dream should have warned me. Even so, I could not take it in.

Had no one heard of the boy?

This is where he was found, the Carayon wife told me. Down by the bridge. He wandered into the house of a dyer, a man named Vidal. If villagers had known this family you speak of, do you not think we would have tried to return him to them?

Had no one heard of the girl?

See how small we are. More sheep than villagers. There is no one here named Colombe. No young women with red hair!

Monsieur Carayon chuckled and offered Victor another olive. His black moustache was powdered with flour from the fouace he was eating, and his blue eyes flickered over me and yes, a woman knows what kind of man would never fail to notice the Félicité Colombes of this world, and he was certainly one of them.

Still, I cannot understand why; you would think I would be glad, *relieved*, but Victor was beside me, happily eating and

254

strumming at his pizzle (I had thrown the blanket over him, although I am not sure that deceived anyone) and I knew I had to do my best for him: I could not easily give up.

This girl, the redhead with the crack in her voice. She said she moved here, from another village. Recently I think she said. After the father died. She claimed she had another child and, I believe, a father still alive. The name of the village – what was it? Belmont-sur-Rance?

Belmont-sur-Rance. It is about twenty-three miles from St Affrique. Perhaps you should ask there?

Perhaps. But, no. I do not think so.

By now, finally, wearily, I was ready to understand. That dream, the vixen, the little white shape on her back. Someone had been trying to warn me. All my protestations to the doctor, all that weeping and dreading. My instincts, that twist in my heart whenever the girl spoke: it was because nothing she said was true. She was no relation to Victor. She was no more a mother to him than – than . . . But I could not think of someone who was as much not a mother to Victor as that ice-hearted bitch, Félicité Colombe.

The name of the village – there was no mistake. This was the name written on the paper she gave to Abbé Sicard and on the letter from the priest, this man Batides. What could it mean, other than this? That Félicité Colombe had never meant us to return to her village. That she had never wanted Victor back. That if I had travelled with her, as we had originally planned, she would have had some other trickery, some other way to carry Victor off, to take the money – a year's income! – for Victor's upkeep and then escape me. I did not shrink from considering exactly what she may have had in mind for myself or Victor. A girl like that. Her soul is full of maggots.

We slept that night in a wooden crib pushed into an empty stone buron: being spring now, they no longer shelter the sheep here. Victor lay on his back beside me, snoring lightly but I was choked with the overpowering sour sheep smell; the grass I could feel in the darkness, growing from the walls beside my face to tickle me. How many times, I whispered to God in the darkness, too angry to remember that I have abandoned him, how many times are you going to make Victor motherless?

Moonlight wrapped us in its grey blanket and I turned on my side to stare at Victor's shape beside me, able to make out the lift of his chin, the trembling of his bottom lip as he snored. It is, of course, a very long time since I slept beside a boy, a young man. And outdoors like this, with the smell of the animals, the hay. The strong smells of the tannery. How could it not bring it all back, to be surrounded by sheep out here?

I have given them a good deal of thought, the doctor's words. His speech had a fearful effect on me, for when he spoke of second chances, I remembered something. That the only moment that my Joseph looked like himself again, the moment he looked like God had replaced him with his own sweet self, was when I carried him dead in my arms and ran screaming round the tannery.

The soldiers had left, the danger was over, we came out from our hiding places behind the vats, Henri, his brother, Julie and me. I was carrying Joseph and screaming. It was as if – call me fanciful if you like, but a grieving mother is surely indulged her fancies – as if, then, the room exploded with my screams, the vats of dye burst their seams, spilling their black ink everywhere. We had been so silent, we had held our breath, we were afraid to let our own hearts beat for fear of being heard, and now I could not stop with my noise, so that Henri had to hold me and that's all I can remember, the wooden beams on the roof of the tannery and my screams hitting it. I would not let him prise the baby from me, I screamed that God had taken him, those bastards, those murderers, he had died from the fright. Henri took his thumbs and went to close the baby's eyes but as he did I saw him. I saw my own boy again. I never understood that look. How dead eyes could have more love in them than living ones. How any child could love a mother who did what I did.

For of course it wasn't God who took my baby Joseph, but then you must know that by now. I did.

Victor sits up and stretches: his fingers stroke his chin without any consciousness that he is doing this. His hand travels down the rough material of his loose shirt with the same absentness; he pushes at the heat, at the troubling feeling he finds there, but does not succeed in bidding it lie down. Blinking until the door to the buron, a black square outlined in silver moonlight, makes itself visible to him. He gives it a shove; another piece of the moss encasing the roof in its dark green skin breaks off, two soft thuds, as clumps falls to the ground.

The smell of shadowy bats flickers around him, their soft wings brushing the air about his face. Behind him, in that room, still sleeping, is something he does not have a word for. He leaves his shoes, coat, the knapsack he has clutched to him for the last seven days. Sharp stones, sticks, stab at his feet, grown soft now. He bends to rub them and the word swims back to him. So strongly that he glances behind him at the stone shelter. The door is slightly ajar.

Frogs call across the blue night to one another. The river can be heard even from here: he follows the water's voice, heads towards the mosquitoes that swarm in clouds above his head, follows the stones until they soften to earth and then wet mulch. The frog's song leaps at him, louder now, bouncing from one stone to another.

Victor lies on his stomach at the water's edge, puts his mouth to the water, which flows in front of him like a great sauce of liquorice, like the inky water of the tannery. He laps at it, his tongue darting out, a baby at the breast, or a lover, eyes closed. Then he sits back on his heels. Earth, blood, milk. Something else. He does not know the word. But he knows there is one, there is a word and there is not just this: smooth, cold, wet. *Eau. Lait.* These are all words. He knows that he knows this. It is all over and also, only just beginning.

He moves away from the water's edge. He puts his face next to the earth, breathes in, rests his cheek on a small smooth stone. His fingers fold over something hard, warm. He has no word for it but he knows that he wants it, it calls to him, it asks him to stay here, it is stronger than anything else he knows, he will never have a word for it: he curls himself around it. Tears slip over his cheeks, snaking their way into the whirls of his ears. In Paris a doctor like Itard, a philosopher like Virey, may always dream of him; in her sleep Madame Guérin may well fling an arm across the pillow, reaching for him. But here in the woods of Aveyron the moon simply turns him a milky blue, exactly the same colour as the grass he lies on, as the houses with their wooden shutters melting into the stone, just as it did through seven long years, on nights far colder than this one.

Of course I feared Victor had gone. I woke to blades of grass stabbing at my ear, a fly buzzing at my face, my head full of memories, half-dreams of being a girl again, of the glove-shop in Millau. All night long I had been in that darkened room again, stretching and smoothing and stretching and smoothing at the hides until that smell of sour milk and flesh seeped into my fingers.

We were afraid for our lives, that much was true.

If they had found us, they would have run us through with their pikes, their pitch-forks. They torched the houses in our path. They burned down the glove-maker's house, his wife and children in it. There was such confusion, none remembered that I was just an orphan taken in by a grand lady, that I was loyal to the same cause as them. It did not matter any more, from one village to the next. Some were loyal to the King, some to the Revolution. I've seen brother set against brother, son against father. None were spared.

And they came for us one night, so we hid in the tannery.

It was not only my own life at stake. There was Henri, his brother, my Julie. Can you weigh the life of one baby against four others? I make no excuses. I crouched behind one great wooden vat with Julie and Joseph. My fear bled from me to her. With my daughter there was no need of words. With a natural child, a mother's heartbeat is the only language. Julie crouched beside me, she buried her face in her knees, she did not look up, or move, or breathe. But not that rascal Joseph. I could not make him understand. He wriggled, he twisted to be free. He opened his mouth to shout. Light from a burning torch wavered over the vats, landed on the stone floor at my feet. Henri and his brother were to the left of me, behind another vat. In the darkness I could neither see nor hear them. So good was their disappearing that I did not even have a sense of them, smell their fear. It fell to me to perform the same trick for myself and the children: turn us all to a waft of smoke.

My insides had turned to liquid, I could hear my heart pounding. The light skimmed over the basket of gloves beside me, lighting them the colours of the fire. The sound of footsteps. Joseph's head moved and my hand came out. I felt for Joseph's face. Found the hollow of an eye, the heat of a mouth. I pressed one hand and then both hands around his mouth, his nose. He was wriggling and struggling and I knew that if I freed him he would shout and we would all be skewered right through the middle and as the Lord God is my witness I hated that child in that moment for he had refused all his short life to understand me and so I pressed tighter, tighter than you would believe possible and I squeezed with fingers with the Devil's strength in them until the child turned limp. His skin in the growling, stinking dark was blue as liver and even after every protest had been squeezed from his tiny body by my terrible hands, I went on, squeezing, wringing every last drop.

I have longed to spill the beans, let the cat out of the bag, *vider mon sac*, as we say, for so long. May God forgive me: I will never forgive myself.

Beside me in the tannery was that basket of gloves, of empty, bloodless hands. That phrase the doctor used, writing his reports, describing the attempt on Victor's life. A hand 'more disposed than adapted' to acts of cruelty used a 'cutting implement'. Those are his exact words. Julie told me. She heard him read it out at some important meeting she attended. But I wanted to tell him, tell Itard. It was not a hand. Not the severed glove of my dreams. That hand belonged to someone.

Just as the hands that squeezed the life from little Joseph belonged to me.

The sun was up and Victor's side of the cot was empty. I hurried to pull my bodice and skirt on over my chemise and some shoes and ran onto the dew-covered grass and I knew he would have sought out the river, I do not know how I knew that, but when I arrived there, an eagle was circling way overhead, and there, on his back on the grass, was Victor.

I fell on my knees in the wet grass beside him, an old woman with her stiff legs bending like a girl of six and he was pink as a bud in the early morning light and his eyes tight closed and I saw that he was sleeping. I whispered all kinds of nonsense to him, I have no idea what possessed me to tell him then the things I told him; it was something in his closed face and his sleeping and in my grateful self, that he had not left me. I spoke for hours, days to him, who knows? I told him that I loved my Joseph and my Henri and my Julie and I was not at heart an evil woman, although I had done wicked, unnatural things, that I had been given a second chance, a chance to atone, and for that, I loved my Victor best of all. I told him if he wanted to stay here in Aveyron, he could do it. I would go back to Paris, I would tell the doctor a story, any story he liked, my mind was set, I would free him back to his old beloved life, I would take whatever path it took.

Let us shed not a single tear over Félicité Colombe, I told him, nor her fantastic story. We will turn our faces to the future, both of us. Besides, we have no means of knowing whether it was true.

A tiny lizard, no bigger than a finger, came to join us, creeping its way over the rock beside Victor's hand, raising its head like a pen, poised above paper. I saw the yellow neckerchief at its chin and the beady eyes and its fine-toed feet. I saw a beetle then finer than any creature I have ever seen, its head the colour of a bead of honey, its wings a dazzling cape of gold and green.

The child opened his eyes and looked up at the sky and then at me, and then away again. He sat up, spied the beetle beside us.

In a movement swifter than a thought, he snatched the insect in one hand. It vanished into his mouth faster than a woman can blink.

Victor is walking in the forests again. He is moving through light, moving through green, the green of his dreams. No objects, just green. The green passes through him and he passes through it. This makes him laugh. For how long now has he sought this green, tried to face this light again, to taste it. Rocking, staring, humming, balling his fists into his eyes: all these things sometimes bring it back, the green.

The air is full of moving spots. He stares into them and is ecstatic, lost. No people to obscure his view. No one grabbing at him, no hands grasping at him, no mumbling jumble of words clamouring at him, no sounds. No feathers dipping into ink, chalk scraping across a board.

As he walks, everything comes back to him. Brambles tear at his feet. He laughs. A green yellow blue lattice of shapes is the sky above him. He stretches up, reaches out hands. Bark and earth and mud and sap, sweet, brown smells. He bends down, sniffs and laughs again. Everything here is moving, twitching, fluttering. No words or hands clamour at him. This is how it used to be.

He holds out his hands and a hundred spots of white and green pour into it. He tips his face up; the light licks his face. An old tongue, the light. His first love.

Well, I tried to make that child understand. No one could say I didn't. For a boy who so hates to be confined, to ride in a coach, there was no sense to it. He climbed in the fiacre beside me, carrying the leather pouch I'd carefully packed with a little round circle of cheese and the rest of the pickled walnuts. Food I intended to leave with him. At the bottom of the pouch was the gold and sapphire pin Itard gave him, still wrapped in my good handkerchief. (I knew Victor didn't care for it but it would have been a sin to keep it.)

You stay here, Victor, I said.

The Carayons had agreed that he could stay with them, at first. I gave them a hundred francs. Victor could chop wood, gather kindling and mushrooms and help them with the chestnut harvest. If he took off for the forests, they would see to it that he was not disturbed. We none of us had any doubt – having seen him these last few days, rooting out the tiny red strawberries beneath the green that no other soul can spot, sniffing out truffles better than any hog – that he would not starve. It wrung my heart of course, but I was determined. It was a penance, of sorts.

He sat beside me, stiff and still. I tried to shove him back towards the door and the steps. There was an old man in the fiacre with us, with a great pink pate for a head and a nose blackened with snuff, who eyed us suspiciously. I had to whisper: go, Victor. You stay here. I am returning to Paris, to the Institute. You know, the boys. The doctor.

He looked at me so clearly then, it made me shudder. You know it is rare. In all the time I have known him, that child has scarce once brushed me with his eyes. I could not but believe that he understood me. Understood me perfectly, the chance I gave him to remain in the forests.

Then again, with Victor, how could I be sure? The boy is so stubborn, stubborn for no reason. It might just as easily be mischief, wilfulness.

I heaved a sigh, fit to scatter the birds from the trees, but made room for him on the seat just the same. If I've learned one truth, it is this: I am no match for that child in strength nor will. The coachman closed the fiacre door.

Vendémiaire 17
Year Nine

I have vowed to put the events of the last few months behind me and renew work with Victor. Confusion over the disappearance of Félicité Colombe leads me to doubt her story. It remains just that: a story. I am no nearer to knowing Victor's origins. Whether he spoke once, or not. Progress is slow, a resurgence of his explosive puberty interferes with our efforts, but today there was a development of such significance that it has strewn my thoughts in all directions.

It happened like this. Victor and I were taking our customary walk to the Jardin du Luxembourg. The day was fine and the gardens were busy; a group of young women and children stared but did not follow us; a student with a heavy bag over one shoulder only nodded a greeting as we passed. (From this I deduce that the name of the Savage of Aveyron no longer elicits the same interest of a year and a half ago.)

Victor ran in front of me, pausing at each tree to sniff happily at their leaves and touch their trunks with his hand. Before we reached Lemeri's hut we spied the gardener, pushing a wheelbarrow with a heap of red and gold leaves in it. I greeted him and he indicated with a wave of his hand that the door was open, we should go on ahead of him, which we did.

We reached the cabin and I pushed open the door. Victor followed, pushing past me, twitching his nose and laughing at the fusty old smell of wet grass, brandy, tobacco and damp papers which signifies Lemeri's habitat for him. Victor then reached into the pockets of the breeches he was wearing. I was astonished to see that he had secreted there some metal letters from the morning's lessons. I think I was more astonished than I have ever been to see what he did next. He laid out the letters on Lemeri's table.

I ran outside and shouted and waved so that Lemeri, for all his years, dropped the handles of his wheelbarrow and came running.

The letters lay on his table. Lemeri, throwing open the door to his cabin so that a splash of light danced from the metal letters, made a soft whistling sound, which turned quickly to a chuckle.

Well I never, he said. We both stared at the table.

LAIT, we read. Victor had pocketed only the four letters he needed and had intended, obviously, to use them exactly thus. Lemeri laughed louder. He ruffled Victor's head and went to fetch the milk he kept covered with muslin in a jug in the coolest corner of the hut.

Well I never, Lemeri said again. So your boy can write now, can he?

I had no idea, I said.

This morning had been as frustrating as any other, with my deep disappointment and constant bewilderment that Victor is not learning anything at all. I had asked in exasperation at one point: should we give up? Do I expect too much of you? What use will reading and writing be to you, in any case?

Now Victor had demonstrated exactly what use reading and writing might have in his life. The evidence could not be starker.

Lemeri poured the milk into a bowl and handed it to Victor, who stood by the window of the hut and stared out, sipping slowly and luxuriously, a faint moustache of milk clinging to his upper lip. I could not see his eyes, his face being slightly turned away from me. But from his profile the strongest impression came to me. His stance, something in his satisfied half smile. I swear that Victor, in the friendliest possible way, was enjoying a joke at my expense. Fancy even led me to believe for a moment something which is probably quite preposterous, but just then did not seem so. I wondered if Victor had been saving this demonstration for just such an occasion. That he had planned it thus.

Had he been able to read all along?

The 'teaching' of Victor that I have been striving towards for some considerable time is becoming less satisfying to me. My interest in teaching has been replaced by an interest in the mysteries of learning. Victor's willingness or reluctance, capacity or incapacity to learn – it is that which astonishes me. And that which dictates whether we make any advancement at all.

Were it not for the constant tumult of his emotions, and his restless attempts to assuage the assault on his senses, I believe he would be in a state to receive learning more often. Since his return from Aveyron, Victor's passions have seemed more troubling than ever. I suppose he might be said, now we are entering winter again, to have passed another birthday – who knows? – and at a guess, judging by his height and greater bulk, I might conclude that he is closer to fourteen than twelve. Or even fifteen, if our earlier guess was incorrect. On a daily basis now, I notice how Victor is consumed by desires of the most savage nature without once realising their purpose or source.

Against my better judgement, I sought Virey's advice. Or rather, I made the mistake of responding candidly to Virey, one evening in the Café de Chartres, when he enquired about progress with Victor. I gave a vague mention of our work being impeded by the 'intervention of nature', to which Virey laughed so much he nearly burst a button on his waistcoat.

Why in the world haven't you shown our ignorant lad what to do with his poor stiff pizzle?

This was an unfortunate remark, considering that Virey had squeezed his corpulent self onto a banquette between two young women, who were now attempting to continue their conversation by leaning in front of him. The girl to his left tugged at his curls, calling him a vulgar devil. (I have always hated those flaxen curls around Virey's ears and was obliged that someone had finally succumbed to the temptation to yank them.) I was searching for a way to change the subject when Virey leaned forward, splashing the cuffs of my shirt with the last of his red wine, as he aimed for the table with his glass and missed.

You know I share a little girl with a friend and we pay for her rooms in the Rue d'Enfers. Since your boy Victor cannot possibly have the pox, I will make you a gift of her!

I must have appeared stupefied.

Virey pressed me further.

Then take him to one of the bitches who hang about the Café de Madrid. Give him a demonstration if necessary, eh, or let him watch another at work. Cruelty to keep him in such woeful ignorance. Nothing blissful or innocent about it. Downright cruel.

I was alarmed that he should speak so freely in front of the two young women. Thankfully, the dark-haired one was now standing up, trying to attract the attention of the waiter to order more drinks. I studied Virey's face over the candle on our table, weighing my reply. His heavy eyelids droop at the corners, giving him a humourless expression, even when he is joking. I decided, after a few moments, that on this occasion, he was serious.

I gave a half-smile, waved my hand dismissively. At all costs, I did not wish my ignorance of such matters to be revealed.

A fine suggestion, Virey, but have you considered the perils? He has no – no care for public decency or decorum. Once revealed to him, the lures of the flesh may forever hail him with an ever-increasing power. He might indulge in the beastly behaviour only worthy of a satyr! What decent woman would be safe?

Virey refilled his glass from the jug on the table, then swayed towards me, so that I caught a whiff of strong cologne. Beastly behaviour . . . worthy of a satyr. He laughed uproariously. Itard, what a delightful prude you are! There are plenty of decent women, and men too, for that matter, who would welcome a good strong attack from a boy of his rope . . .

I took my leave of him. But I believe his words had more impact than I have allowed. I found myself, several nights later, wandering amongst the crowds in the Palais-Royal. (This place has had so many name changes of late that one can hardly keep up; I referred to it to Virey as the Palais d'Egalité, only to be corrected and told it was now the Palais du Tribunat. I suspect that many Parisiens do as I do, and revert to old habits.) Men and women – dressed like Greek goddesses in the flimsiest of dresses, courting ill health, offering as they did no protection at all against the nip in the evening air, and especially exposing of the chest – bustled noisily against us, myself and Victor. I kept a firm hold of Victor's arm. He was in agitated spirits, troubled by the shouts, the barking of small dogs, the shrieking laughter of women, the choking smell of hair-powder, beer, snuff and pipe-smoke, the cloying sweetness of aniseed, bewildering our senses.

With an eye far from practised, I tried to pick out a suitable woman. A scraggy redhead with a freckled, wrinkled bosom – as if she had spread a pencilled map of villages and rivers over her chest – pressed close to us, pinching Victor's cheek and taking a step back when he bent his head to sniff her neck. Sniffing's extra, she said, without humour. I hurried on. Two urchins with huge black eyes and bare feet tugged at my pockets, offering the two of us an hour with the pair of them, for the cost of a bowl of bouillon: I shook their hands vigorously from my pockets, feeling as I did as if I was shaking loose the tentacles of an octopus, and strode further into the crowd.

Of course, I had no idea what might be Victor's preference, if he could be shown to have one. I once saw him march around and around a young sister from the hospital, a friend of Julie Guérin's. The girl was portly and brown-haired, with a nose which turned upwards. One would not have described her as pretty. When he had tired of marching, Victor threw his arms around her shoulders and hugged her tightly. Of course she yelped and pushed him away, which only added to his vexation and disappointment. Bearing this in mind, I found myself searching for a woman of advanced years, with an experienced air, so that she would not spurn his caresses. Also stout legs and a motherly nature. It occurred to me, as I shook my head to the flimsy blonde and the tulip-necked brunette, that I had used the same criteria to choose a governess. This led inescapably to a picture of Madame Guérin, in a context I have no desire to consider her in. Working to stamp it out, using my uncle's method of picturing a bowl of fruit in place of beastly thoughts, was not easy, distracted as I was by the tumult of the crowd and by my consciousness of Victor fidgeting under my fingers, wrenching to be free. Peaches, with their obscene seams, loomed in a dish beside two firm plums, smeared with a blue sheen. I gave up.

Just as I did, a sturdy blonde with a face as round as a china dish and a clean appearance smiled at us from the edge of the crowd, beckoning me. She was sitting on the steps of what used to be a grand house, wearing peasant's sabots and eating from a bag of burnt almonds. Beside her was a box, with two rabbits sleeping in a nest of shredded paper. Although young, and with several teeth missing, now that I was up close, she was certainly willing, with an openness to her offer which I found disconcerting. She told me her name was Satin. I shuddered at the terms she offered us, the parts of her person she happily suggested for penetration. After a few moments of conversation and the information that her 'papa' would manage everything, I found my eyes drawn to a row of bruises, which resembled inky thumb-prints along her upper arms. I was overwhelmed by shame and disgust at the prospect of using a child – or any young person – in such a fashion. A picture of Victor, the bowl of fruit scattered and pulped, shrieking in his characteristic way, flashed before me. It would be as if a great dog, a dog whose mouth drooled foam, whose eyes glittered, whose feet pawed at the earth, his entire body straining at the leash, was set free. I could not do it. To her, or to Victor. How could such unleashing truly improve matters? It might merely inflame him, whilst inadvertently teaching him that desires are always to be met, at all costs and at all times, with no regard for the person in question, for their desires or sensibilities, for their tender years, for questions of power or virtue or propriety.

I gave the girl some coins for her trouble and she smiled and offered me a burnt almond, or her sister, who was prettier. She said she would fetch her from upstairs. I refused. At this, the child returned to her box of rabbits, stroking their ears and petting them. Victor took a great handful of the almonds. I steered him wearily back in the direction of the Faubourg St Jacques, my tread slow. I could never raise the subject with Virey again. Victor was doomed, let down by my cursed imagination, compassion for a girl I hardly knew. After all, the girl made good money from her profession, and was cheerful, and seemed to care nothing for her intimate person and only to please her 'papa'; and if the number of places she was willing to be penetrated had surprised me, if the pansy-like row of bruises along her arms had shocked me, well, why should she be denied, or Victor cheated, on account of my sensitivities, my terrible tender-heartedness?

I am sorry Victor, I muttered, walking beside him.

He hopped lightly from foot to foot, crunching on his almonds. His head craned forward in his usual eager fashion, so that the nape of his neck beneath his dark hair was presented to me. I have always considered necks to be the most vulnerable part of the human body. There is something excruciatingly tender about them.

The sight of Victor's neck. I had to pause for a second, close my eyes. My body was trembling violently.

How can I teach Victor what it is to be a man? I do not know myself. Or rather, I know perfectly well what others believe a man to be, and I know without a doubt that I, Jean-Marc-Gaspard Itard, can never be it.

Avoiding Julie Guérin has proved impossible. Yesterday, having neglected my breakfast, I discovered I was ravenously hungry and made a detour to the Petit Pont to buy a tisane and some rolls from a crippled boy who customarily sets up a stall there. The morning sun was so dazzling and so low that the whole of Paris was latticed with shadows from the balustrades on the bridges and the wrought iron fences, and we all stood with our hands shading our eyes. Even the Seine that morning was not brown and oily as usual but instead glittered in green dots; a river of sizzling autumnal light. That was why I did not see her. Julie Guérin. I was squinting and she was walking towards me, with the sun a white ball of light behind her. Her walk is unmistakable; her stride rather wider and swifter than one expects in a woman. I think I have noted before that she is a nimble runner. She was upon me before I had the opportunity to lose myself by burying my nose in a philosophy book on one of the trader's stalls.

I was forced to nod, remove my hat and greet her politely. I continued to squint, shading my eyes with one hand.

Mademoiselle Guérin. A beautiful morning, although a little chilled, is it not . . .

We have all dispensed with *Citoyenne*. It seems I have been the last man in Paris to maintain it, but even to my ears, it sounds pretentious now. Pretentious, or hopeless, I cannot decide which.

Doctor.

You are on your way to the hospital?

I am late –

Oh! Let me not detain you –

She paused then and gave me a most searching look.

You appeared to be walking in that direction yourself?

No! Walking? I mean, I was standing quite still. I was – I *am* breakfasting.

As if to prove my point I stared in some confusion at the cup I held. The tisane was drunk and the crippled boy held out his hand for the empty cup. Likewise, my roll was all but finished. Julie smiled suddenly. I could not tell if she found my suffering droll or whether she wished to make amends. At any rate, she said in a low voice: shall we walk together, Doctor Itard? It would have required a particular species of insolence for me to have refused. I did not possess it.

Conversation began awkwardly with talk of Victor. Julie remarked that I must be very glad to have him back and apologised for not visiting as often as she used to, but claimed she had been busy etc. I did not know how to reply. She prattled a little about the malice of Félicité Colombe and the narrow escape that Victor had had. She then asked plainly if the incident had confused my opinion of Victor and was I still persuaded in my original diagnosis?

To this I replied, truthfully, that I must give a new paper soon to the Society of the Observers of Man and that I did not yet know what I would say to them.

She chattered on, confessing herself 'charmed' by the story her mother told her of Victor's new reading skill and suggested that I must be very proud of him.

Proud? The word made me stop. We were alongside the Collège de France, casting its great block of shadow over us and onto the sunlit wall opposite. Julie walked on a step before turning back to stare at me.

Proud? I said again. I do not believe it is pride I feel. Once, yes, you are right, once it might have been pride.

She did not press me for an explanation but remained where she was and nodded, as if she understood. Then a carriage thundered past and we continued walking in silence. Suddenly, the most peculiar emotion welled in me. I believe it was gratitude. That gesture from her, that simple nod, seemed to convey so much. A silent acceptance of all that had changed for me in regard to Victor. It was such extraordinary kindness on her part. My relief was to feel understood, without words, without explanation.

Nothing altered in our walk. Not our pace nor our conversation. But I felt at last that our awkwardness was put to rest, that the ice between us had melted. I do not know what had been explained. It was as if Julie Guérin knew better than I did myself what Victor meant to me. Or rather, that she knew and so did I but the knowledge need never be spoken, need not, as it were, break the surface.

Proud is what a father feels for a child. Proud is what Uncle felt of me and it was not in the end what I longed for. I longed to be seen, known. I did not wish to be his prize.

I was quite, quite wrong about Victor. He is not mine. He is the forest's child, or else he is nobody's. I will never possess him.

I turned into the Institute gates and Julie continued down the Rue St Jacques. My tread was slow. I did not run up the marble staircase as I used to do. I did not look up at the light tumbling down the spiral staircase and think of ears, of my marvellous career, of mysteries. I thought of myself as a young man, green and stiff as a blade of grass, a new surgeon at the Val-de-Grâce. I remembered Uncle and the letter from his housekeeper that followed me to Paris, telling me a week after I had arrived here that he died peacefully on a rain-swept night, the night I left his home.

Now Victor knows that everything has a home, a name. A book is not paper, a razor is not a knife, a glass is not a paperweight. He can spell, he rarely gets these names wrong. A boy is not a rat, who can live in the coal-sacks on the banks of the river Seine. Nor is he a handful of stones, to be tumbled down the cellar steps, to lie in darkness beside the wine and the dogs and the bones, the scraps of food.

He can write some words now. Verbs. To kiss. To chop. He knows *to chop* is not the same as *to kiss*. A boy is not the spots in light, although he can lose himself in them, he might wish to, sometimes. Wish and be are not the same.

In his sleep he calls her name: *lli, lli*, and wonders where her tickling, her scent of chocolate and violets and the cold soapy stone walls, her ribbons, her rustling, has gone. He knows that *lli* is not the same as home or maman but no one has offered him a word for what it is. She sits beside him when he lines up his keys. She examines the keys with him, turns them in her hands as he does, makes the same noises and faces as him. She shares his keys with him, loves them

273

as he does. Her face is close to his, her hand is in his hair, tickling his skin, her hand moves softly against his neck.

He has no other name for this. She whispers one. Victor tries to repeat it but the sound which comes out is only *lli, lli*.

Victor seemed to have been infected by my melancholia. After his third refusal to sit and write his name, I opened the kitchen door and allowed him to sprint towards the gardens. He ran down the steps yelping. I followed at a slower pace, preoccupied by my own thoughts, by my recollections of Uncle.

Uncle and I had quarrelled before I left Riez to come to Paris. It was not our first quarrel but it was our most heated. In it I denounced his beloved Rousseau. I told him to look around him, to see that it was education and civilisation which led to the best in man, not botanising and walking alone in the mountains, idealising the savage life. You are in flight from your own nature, Uncle had countered, from the life of solitude and study that you know to be your rightful path. What do you know of my nature? I had asked bitterly; what if all that we believed to be most vile and *unnatural* was in fact Nature, where are Rousseau's theories then? Uncle counselled me for the millionth time against arrogance and I replied angrily that if I had become arrogant it was because I had had a fine example. He shook his head then, and pulled at the beard beneath his chin, as if endeavouring to wring his misery from it.

Of course, it had been my intention to make amends. I do not count myself as the only man in the world who procrastinated, when faced with the irksome duty of offering an apology.

As I dwelled upon these sorrowful thoughts, I heard a bell striking noon. The church of St Jacques has opened its doors again. The Revolutionary calendar is about to be abandoned, just as it was beginning to come more readily to the pen. So

274

great was our confidence, for a moment, did we not believe that we might alter Time itself? I reflected bitterly, that in every respect, the glorious experiment of Uncle's dreams is over. Of course, Uncle died at the height of the Terror, already disillusioned. But what would he have made, not of the Republic, but of me? What would he have made of my efforts with Victor?

I stood behind Victor, staring down at the top of his head. He did not acknowledge me, but only sighed from time to time. Sitting in his favourite place, beside an urn spilling dying flowers towards the keyhole-shaped pond, he plucked a fallen leaf from the ground, then tossed it into the water, so that he might watch it float there.

I was remembering that occasion when I first began work with Victor, when Professor Pinel and I had crossed paths, here at the Institute. My image of him, standing by the giant Dutch elm, how it had converged with a memory of Father, then of Uncle. I had been afraid to disagree with Pinel and yet I had felt strongly that I must, that my career, my own beliefs, my very existence, demanded it.

Could it be that I was wrong, after all?

The Society has requested a second report from me and, as I confessed to Julie, I am in turmoil. I feel at the very edge of what I can possibly understand. Everything Uncle taught me, everything deep inside me, has persuaded me that man is pliable, perfectible; that the most extraordinary quality he possesses is the ability to change. What of Locke's remark that the little and almost insensible impressions of our tender infancies have important and lasting consequences, how then could Victor's silent, queer, isolated life not have a most significant impact upon his behaviour?

And yet. Could it really be true, that after all, he is only some kind of mental defective, an idiot? But if so, how to explain those fleeting moments when he feels so truly present, how to explain his ability to suddenly learn, just when the tutor is about to give up, skills such as reading, or distinguishing between objects on the basis of their written sign alone? How to explain those times – rare though they may be – when Victor rests his eyes on me, eyes so intense, so lively that none could doubt the perception of the person trapped within?

Oh, Victor, I suddenly said, dropping to my knees beside him and speaking as if he could hear me: unhappy creature, since my labours are wasted and your efforts are fruitless, go back to your forests, or go die of poverty and boredom at Bicêtre!

I could have believed myself fully understood; for barely had I said these words than I saw an expression of great sorrow on his face, his chest heaved with sobs, his eyes closed and tears streamed down his cheeks.

The temptation to put my face close to his, to wrap my arms around him and kiss his tears was so powerful that I closed my eyes in giddiness. Immediately I could taste the salt of his skin, feel his lashes sweep my cheek like the softest of grass. A dog barked wildly. I felt my blood rise, spiralling upwards. There was the sound of a door banging and the jangle of keys. I opened my eyes.

Victor calmly turned his face away from me, back towards the water. A master had appeared in one of the doorways opening onto the gardens. I stood up quickly. My knees shook so violently that I feared I might fall. I pulled my heavy coat about me and succeeded in walking steadily past the master, with Victor trailing behind, still uttering his intermittent sighs.

*   *   *

Draft of the Second Report on the Progress of
Victor of Aveyron 1806, printed 1807
Addressed to his Excellency, the Minister of the Interior

That burst of enthusiasm which urges one sex towards the

other, which one might have expected at this point in the boy's development, is lacking. Victor has shown only a sort of blind instinct. He has a rather indistinct preference, which makes the society of women tolerably more agreeable to him than the company of men. He does not seem to experience any true emotion in this connection.

The society of women tolerably more agreeable than the company of men. I have long waited for the same burst of enthusiasm in myself and since the incident with Julie Guérin I have understood, with great finality, that it will not be forthcoming.

I have seen him sometimes in the company of a young woman, trying to find some solace for his feelings by sitting next to her and gently squeezing her arms, hands and knees, carrying on thus until his restless desires were increased rather than calmed by these strange caresses; and then, unable to see an end to these painful emotions, suddenly change and angrily thrust aside she whom he had so eagerly sought, only to turn to yet another in his search for fulfilment.

Unable to see an end to these painful emotions. It is as I always suspected: man's lot on earth is simply this: to suffer and to die. Julie claims that Victor is in love with her. I myself cannot see it. It is true that his stubborn heart has opened somewhat, especially these last few months, to unmistakable feelings of friendship and gratitude. If we have succeeded in creating needs in him, then he 'loves' the provider of these needs. That is not the same as human pity. I for one do not intend to be seduced by these illusions. Let Julie deceive herself if she so wishes.

Eager and happy to help when the services demanded of him are not in opposition to his needs, he is a stranger to that selfless helpfulness which considers neither deprivations nor sacrifices. In order to sympathise with the sorrows of others, one must have experienced them oneself or at least have the power to imagine them.

I do not believe Victor possesses this power. For example, I do not believe for one moment that he imagines my privations. That he gives them a second's consideration. That I enter his thoughts at all.

There is something in the emotional system of this young man which is even more astonishing and which defies all explanation: it is his indifference to women, in spite of the signs or symptoms of a well-developed puberty.

Now I contradict myself. Did I not write in my first draft that he showed an indistinct preference for women? Which is it to be? Does he show indifference or not? I cannot decide. I cannot decide what to write for the wretched report. I know for certain that whatever it should be, Cuvier will seize it, tear me to shreds.

When his tumult of the senses burst upon us, it serves no purpose to have cold baths, a soothing diet or violent exercise; his naturally sweet temper is transformed and passes swiftly from sadness to anxiety and then to fury; he turns against the things he most likes; sighs, weeps, utters shrill cries, tears his clothes and sometimes even goes so far as to scratch and bite his governess. But even when he is prey to a blind and uncontrollable fury, he still demonstrates a genuine remorse and wants to kiss the hand or arm he has bitten.

I must present a fair picture. I must show my triumphs and my failures, with equal impartiality.

My observations draw me to the following belief: if there exists in man a relationship between the needs of the body and the emotions of the heart, then that sympathetic harmony is, like most great and noble passions, the fortunate fruit of man's education.

Do I dare to write that? Is it not the same suggestion that so incensed Cuvier on the last occasion? And yet I must. I have not laboured these five years to deliver a report which is a lie.

I present to you, my Lords, less a story of a pupil's progress, than an account of a teacher's failure.

Let the devils make of it what they will.

Victor, Victor, why do you not speak to me?
He does not look up. Here we are in the library together. His shoulders are broad now in his laundered shirt. The hair on his face, his throat, shows dark and new, a shiny black. I write a word. He copies it in his unsteady hand. He matches the word *book* to the leather-bound volume I put on the desk in front of him; places a pair of scissors next to the metal letters spelling *scissors*. He rocks a little, taps his fingers on the desk.

I place two nails of different sizes on the table. I write the word big and small, on pieces of paper, as I did yesterday with the big and small books. Victor slowly picks up the nails and places them without hesitation, in the right positions, alongside the word describing them. Big nail and small nail. I marvel anew that such a difficult abstract concept such as size should be so easily grasped.

Victor, why will you not speak to me?
Do you know it is over five years now, Victor, that we have worked together like this? A long time, is it not?

Hours upon hours, alone with you. More time than I have ever spent with another human being.
You have made *some* progress, Victor. Look at you! You cannot be blamed if the ideals I had for you – if the dreams

I fixed upon – were, what shall we say, unrealistic. Why, Madame Guérin told me that most people from your village – if indeed it is your village – still speak the old language, langue d'Oc, and French may not even have been your native tongue . . .

You will no more speak, divulge your secrets, than a tree or a leaf will speak. I can dream of you, but never know if you dream of me. Of what you dream, or if you dream at all. Your face will only greet me as a mirror.

The Society was impressed with my report. I was, Victor, as you might imagine, rather surprised. Pinel even chided me for unnecessary pessimism. To properly assess you, he said, you should only be compared with yourself, the boy you were when first you came to me. In that respect, it is true, yes, you are unrecognisable. Of course, sad though I am to say it, they are now confirmed in their belief that they were right all along. You are, in their esteemed opinion, an idiot. I have proved that idiots may be educated, indeed should be educated. When I offered the suggestion that you had missed an important stage in the infant's life for learning language and that perhaps the power of imitation in you was now weak and beyond repair, there were only the faintest of murmurs, only a hint of assent. I should be chastened, divested of my foolish belief that man's environment is of any importance in shaping him, compared to his natural endowments. And yet. I have not quite accepted it. I believe there is something else. Something I cannot possibly know.

I am standing at an enormous door, holding your beloved bunch of keys. Like you, I cannot use them. They are perhaps the wrong keys, the wrong doors. I do not know how to fit them, how to turn them. I only know that we have keys, you and I, and words, and locks.

I will endeavour to bow out gracefully, Victor. Now, for the future, be assured: I feel confident that the formidable Madame Guérin will take very good care of you. You know that you and she will be moving together to your new home in the Impasse des Feuillantines. You know, I hope, that all will be paid for by the Society. You need have no care of that. You can be assured of comfort and stability there. You can be assured that you – well, it is my wish for you, indeed for both of us, but I feel I may be more optimistic on your part – that you will never be lonely again.

My heart creaks like a branch. You have weighted it heavily. Over and over I felt it bend to the point of breaking; bend or break, Victor, and sometimes both.

It is four o'clock on a winter afternoon and the library is growing dark.

Too late, I know, to return you to your forest home. Let us close the leather books and drink a glass of water together one last time.

I will never be able to use my warm hands to soften and shape you, never watch you raise your wooden arms and your silent wooden tongue become flesh. It is finished.

For all that you have taught me, I thank you.

You have little care for this observation, but I will confess it anyway. Taxing though they were, these were the happiest days I have known.

He only came once, in all these years, the doctor, to visit us in the Impasse des Feuillantines. Victor answered the door to him. I heard the door open in the hallway and a cry of '*Mon Dieu!*' from Victor and a gasp and shriek – almost a scream – from whoever stood there, and then I heard that familiar voice, and knew it was the doctor. His voice was little changed, although he must be nearing fifty now. Victor himself is probably thirty-seven. A big man now, Victor, although still handsome enough and it is not just me who believes so. Still with that striking, dark stare that merely grazes you in its path, never settling.

Victor brought the doctor into our kitchen – well, our only

room – and the two of them stood there. Victor put his hand out for the doctor's hat and cane and he did it so suddenly that there was a moment's confusion in which Itard appeared startled and even took a step back and then he realised what Victor was asking, and handed them over. The boy towered over the doctor; that was the first surprise for the poor man; and the second, that I am an old mab now with grey hair, hair that I have scarcely even troubled to catch up with a few pins. His eyes travelled around the cold, worn tiles of the room, the threadbare carpet, the old-fashioned cot of painted wood in the corner. Well, if we had expected visitors I might have drawn the calico curtains around it, I would of course have stuffed the crack in the window with my Ternaux shawl. As it was, the wind ruffled the newspapers by the fire, flapped a tear in the wallpaper. I saw the doctor's eyes take it all in, landing at last on the basket of potatoes. Glad I was that a clean gauze bonnet rested on top, along with my best pair of kid gloves. I offered the man a drink and Victor fetched the glasses.

The doctor seemed astonished to see us thus, although what surprised him about our home, I cannot imagine. At any time, this last – what, nearly twenty years – he could have visited us and found us very much as we are now. I said this to him and won a rare smile.

I am glad to see that time has not blunted your tongue, Madame Guérin!

I have no idea what you mean.

In truth, I knew very well why he had never visited us. I am not blind, nor deaf, nor dumb, though some might prefer to believe it. I could not have worked beside him for those five years – nearly six! – without seeing the anguish he suffered, how he wrestled with himself.

And Victor, can it be true that you are now able to speak? You have found it in yourself to make conversation, now you are alone with your beloved governess?

Mon Dieu, said Victor.

The doctor's gay manner faltered.

I handed him the wine and nodded at him to sit down. There was a plate on the only free chair, with the remains of a meal on it. I gave Victor a nod, and he removed it.

He says three things, one more than he ever did, I told Doctor Itard. *Mon Dieu, lait* and that *lli* sound. You remember, I always said it was his name for my Julie? Although you never agreed.

The doctor murmured something here. I remembered that he always had a blind spot where Victor's feelings for Julie were concerned and so hurried on, saying: he has all the words he needs. A curse, or a faith; food, love. Or is it women? It is still not easy to fathom you out, is it my boy?

Well I saw the disappointment plain enough on Itard's face. The way his eyes followed Victor hungrily. Victor remained standing, sipping his glass of water, his back to the window. Queer to remember now how all those important men were forever talking about Victor, how he held the answers to their marvellous questions. It's clear to any halfwit, as my Julie said recently, that Victor's just Victor. He doesn't represent anyone but his own sweet self.

And how *is* Julie? asked Itard, as if I'd spoken aloud.

Now this, you must agree, was stout-hearted. He didn't even stutter, which perhaps means he has been cured of that particular affliction. Or perhaps only cured of his embarrassment. Julie never did have any place in his heart. She always had a rival, poor girl.

Oh, Julie. She visits us every week. Victor still likes his tickling. He's as fond of her as he always was.

I paused but the doctor did not take the bait.

She's big as a house! Her fourth, you know. Due any day.

I held up the knitting I had almost finished. A tiny white bonnet of the softest wool. Itard smiled and nodded, clapped his hands together. Victor jumped at the clap. Clapped his own hands, his glass still held between them. Thought it was some kind of game. It was a miracle the glass did not shatter.

Stop that, I warned him.

Good, good! Send her my best regards, Itard said.

She often talks of you, I could not resist saying.

Oh, yes? The creases at the side of his smile remained, although his smile faded. That great shelf over his brow has sunk over the years. His face is very tired. I do not think many would think him handsome now, the way they used to. But for me, I prefer it. He has grown into his face. It carries an expression more fitting to his character, these days. Yes, that's it. Like Victor. The face and person are no longer at odds. Victor has lost his – his fleet quality, these twenty years. He does not run the way he used to and his movements are stiffer, slower. Only his eyes are black as ever, like two dark stones, that reflect nothing, like chestnuts if you find them in winter, when they are sucked dry and hard.

Did you never marry, Doctor?

No, in fact, I never have, I –

She keeps me up to date, our Julie. She tells me you are a very great man.

He said nothing to this, only smiling and nodding and so I searched myself for something more to say.

You have made all kinds of inventions, have you not, things to help those poor deaf souls to hear and published papers and such like?

Well, I never was a talkative woman but there was a hole so gaping in that room, I felt obliged to fill it.

I am not sure of the details but she assures me, yes, indeed, you are a great man now. A savant. She says the others believed you were wrong but still they marvelled at all you achieved. She says that mental medicine and the education of idiots and deaf mutes has advanced – oh! an enormous amount –

The doctor interrupted me here, rather disrespectfully, I thought, and sipped his wine in great gulps and told me that sadly, he could not stay long, but was so glad to hear of Julie, and to hear that she was happy with a husband and all, and I said well no, I did not mention any husband, and then he quickly patted Victor on the shoulder and told him how glad he was to see *him* so happy and Victor jumped back, startled by the pat. He has never grown used to being touched unexpectedly, but these days he is better at hiding his dislike of it, so he began humming, tapping his glass on the window-sill, watching the water jump in it. I said well we have not even begun to speak of my rheumatism and the pawnshop tickets, well sorry to mention it but some of us have found that a pension of 500 francs does not go very far at all when there is a young man to feed, and you remember how Victor could eat, Doctor, making up for all those years of hunger and who can blame him, but expensive, just the same . . . and how wretched it makes Victor when I am too ill to go out walking with him. But he did not let me complete that sentence either, finishing his wine with an unseemly gulp, and he did not let me show him our latest collection, Victor's that is, the keys.

No, he did not stay long, the doctor, and considering how little he has seen of Victor and how much affection he had for Victor, you might have thought he would have lingered a little. I cannot help but conclude that he had expected something more from us than a wild old woman and a silent young man living amongst a pile of broken clogs, in a one-room house where a kitchen serves for a bedroom and the walls are speckled with flowers too greasy and blackened with age for any but an idiot to give them that name.

Still, Victor did not mind, not one whit, as it irks him to have his routine interrupted. He showed Itard to the door, took his leave of him in the English style, pushing the hat and coat into Itard's arms and nodding, saying: *Mon Dieu!* in a spirited fashion, several times, whilst I stood behind him to encourage good manners. I saw Itard's eyes, not on my face, but travel to my bare feet, no doubt shocked to see that, yes, I too have toes just like any other human being, and ones which are as able to grow a curling nail of good length, if left to their own devices, as the next woman's. I know he never spied my bare feet in the five years I worked for him. I used to wonder if he believed it was natural to me, all that cleaning and wiping and slopping a bucket around. Did he never know that I had to be taught it, that I was by nature a slovenly girl, that the nuns and then my glove-maker's wife had to scrape cleanliness into me with a wire-brush, the exact same way that the priests in his life – his uncle, was it? – hammered his catechism, his great knowledge about this Condillac fellow, into him?

The doctor's expression, as Victor firmly closed the door on him, told me more than words could, that we would not see him again.

Then Victor came back into the kitchen to begin his task for the evening: sorting the black lentils from the yellow. I cooked us saucisson en brioche and a fine rich soup of onions, lentils and bacon. Afterwards, whilst I dozed by the fire, I could hear the regular thud and crack, the panting and sighing that Victor does as he takes the logs from the corner of the room and splits them, piling them neatly: that useful way that he so enjoys and which my Henri showed him, all those years ago, when he first came here, to be our son.

Here's Victor as a grown man, chopping logs. The doctor has left and with him all those old words and smells, the leather books, the chalky light. He raises his arms as he was taught, to make a fine good arc, without slippage. He never misses his mark. Axe meets wood with a satisfying bite and each time he yells *Mon Dieu!* He rubs his hands on his thighs in delight.

There are other children like Victor, wild boys. They have different names now but still they have names, new words. Still dogs bark under the wrong trees. The forest beckons and the children are always escaping. Let me come with you, their mothers call to them. Come back.

Afterword

Victor died in 1828, at the age of forty, in the home of Madame Guérin. This remarkable woman cared for the wild boy for twenty-eight years and yet little is known about her. She makes an appearance in François Truffaut's 1971 film of the same story, *L'Enfant Sauvage*, as a shadowy figure in a bonnet, who took on the care of the boy without a murmur. When I visited the Deaf Mute Institute in Paris (now renamed the National Institute for Deaf Children, but still in the Rue St Jacques) to enquire about her, I was told that, although interest in Victor and Itard has continued in the thirty years since Truffaut's film, I was the first person to ask about Madame Guérin.

Itard died ten years later than Victor, at the age of sixty-four, justly recognised as a pioneer of special education who influenced, amongst others, the famous educationalist Maria Montessori. Itard does seem to have been a solitary figure: he never married. He wrote in his will that he wished his body to be returned to the earth intact and unmutilated by the 'ballooning research with cadavers', which he believed to be of little use for the art of healing, being convinced that 'nothing can protect man from that sad condition of his life which is to suffer and to die'.

I have taken many liberties with Victor's story. Itard's preface and report *Of the First Developments of the Young Savage of Aveyron* is taken from an English translation entitled *An historical account of the discovery and education of A SAVAGE MAN, caught in the woods near Aveyron in the year 1798*, which was published in 1802 and is reprinted verbatim on pp. 276-279 by kind permission of the Trustees of the British Museum. This and a further report by Itard published in 1806 are mingled with imagined reports and an imagined account of their relationship. The events of Victor's early life, before he came to the Deaf Mute Institute, are also imaginary, since the trail quickly went cold and those interested in Victor's case seem not to have been particularly curious about his origins.

The recorded facts are these: a child was found, in the region of France described; Itard did try to civilise him, more or less as described; he did employ a Madame Guérin; she did have a daughter named Julie (or Julia) who did not live at home with her; Itard did give up his work after five years, and Victor only ever spoke the three or four words I mention.

Itard's reports were translated into English in 1802 and are republished in *Wolf Children and the Problem of Human Nature* by Lucien Malson (New Left Books). There is also an excellent book by Harlan Lane, *The Wild Boy of Aveyron* (Harvard University Press), that discusses in great detail the significance of the case for psychologists, educationalists, philosophers and language therapists, amongst others. *The Forbidden Experiment* by Roger Shattuck (Secker and Warburg) was also useful. I read a brief but first-hand account of Victor in *My Paris Journal*, a book published in 1802 by the Vicar of Edmonton, the Reverend Dawson-Warren. Dawson-Warren also supplies descriptions of Versailles and Paris that informed mine.

Interest in Victor has waned in the region of Aveyron where he was found, but there is a museum in Lacaune that contains some supplementary information and a curious room depicting L'Enfant Sauvage in which he is modelled by a giant doll in a wig; also the evidence that those who captured him originally named him Joseph. St Sernin-sur-Rance boasts a small statue of Victor and a chestnut liqueur named after him.

I first came across Victor in Uta Frith's book, *Autism: Explaining the Enigma* (Blackwell Publishers Inc). A more recent book, which was both painful and inspiring, was *Growing Up Severely Autistic* by Kate Rankin (Jessica Kingsley Publishers). In it, the author's own son, Gabriel, is described as a modern-day wild boy.

My heartfelt thanks are due to the Royal Literary Fund for the fellowship grant that provided me with the time and place to work on this book. I am also grateful to both my sisters, Debra Dawson and Dr Beth Dawson-Goumy, for their help with research and translations; to my editor Carole Welch and her assistant Amber Burlinson for sensitive, invaluable advice; to my wonderful agent, Caroline Dawnay, for her enthusiasm and boundless energy. Meredith Bowles is exceptional in every way and I can never thank him enough. He has so many gorgeous qualities and on top of that he is the kind of reader of which all novelists dream.

Lastly I would like to thank Madame Balle-Stinckwich, archivist at the National Institute for Deaf Children in Paris, for all her help, and for allowing me to sit in the library where Itard worked, or walk in the Institute gardens by the pond, where Itard, Julie, Victor and Madame Guérin must often have walked, and imagine.